DOG DIRT DORIS

DOG DIRT DORIS

H. O. WARD

TATE PUBLISHING & Enterprises

Published by Tate Publishing & Enterprises, LLC
127 E. Trade Center Terrace | Mustang, Oklahoma 73064 USA
1.888.361.9473 | www.tatepublishing.com

Tate Publishing is committed to excellence in the publishing industry. The company reflects the philosophy established by the founders, based on Psalm 68:11,
"The Lord gave the word and great was the company of those who published it."

Book design copyright © 2008 by Tate Publishing, LLC. All rights reserved.
Cover & Interior design by Kellie Southerland

Published in the United States of America
ISBN: 978-1-60604-677-7
1. Fiction: Historical/War & Military
08.07.23

DISCLAIMER

While this story is fictitious, it is woven among the tapestry of places and events of the periods described. Therefore, any reflection or similarity to any real living or deceased person is purely coincidental to the portrayal of the books characters. Likewise, the use of author's licence in describing and portraying the places, organisations, and events contained within the story line may not be entirely factual. Therefore, the author disclaims all and any recognition to persons, place, organisation, or event described within the fictitious story lines of this book.

TABLE OF CONTENTS

INTRODUCTION

The story of Dog Dirt Doris is a fictitious representation of a life, which, as with all lives, should not be judged on the merits of circumstance or the surroundings in which the person is first encountered, but by the complete understanding and quality of that person, if it should then be "judged" at all!

The character, Doris, is introduced as a lost and tragic vagabond on the streets of London, where her misfortune is to become ill and taken to hospital by her newfound friend, who then tells the story of her life that brought her to that point.

Dorothy's story, as she is better known throughout the book, encompasses the trauma of World War II, as a caring Queen Alexandra Military Nurse, her romance amongst the glamour of Renaissance Florence, Italy, and the tragedy of becoming a homeless vagabond on the streets of London, all new and alien environments for a doctor's daughter brought up in a comfortable home in Bath, England.

The story begins…

LONDON, ENGLAND
1966

Doris sat looking at the weather-beaten face lying in her lap; her hand gently closed his eyes, brushed down his bushy white beard, and wiped a tear from her cheek. A tear, partly for Joe, but one also for her friend Mary and the men she had cared for. All night Doris had remained comforting her patient, hoping he would make it for another day, as rays of sunlight began warming the air and lifting the morning mist.

Doris looked at Joe's rolled bundle of newspaper. It had been his only possession, constantly under his arm or inside his long black overcoat. Carefully Doris pulled the bundle, releasing it from its protector and owner, put the paper by her side, and slumped against the red brick of the archway wall. A blank stare on her face, she unconsciously stroked the forehead of her patient, her eyes becoming heavy from her sleepless night. Minutes passed. Her head fell forward and instantly jerked upright, bringing her back to consciousness. Her eyes, now wide open, observing every object, person, and movement, her shoulders tense, consciously questioning her location. Then, with the recognition of the familiar surroundings, her shoulders drooped, and with a tired sigh she relaxed.

Pushing her hand under Joe's neck, she lifted the weight of the tramp's head from her thighs, shuffled sideways, and gently lowered it to the pavement. The fading mist swirled round them like a grey ghost as it lifted to the sunlight. Her patient had gone, like hundreds before, in the drifting battle smoke that claimed their souls.

Slowly Doris gathered her thoughts and looked down at Joe's rolled paper bundle, lifting it to her lap, her eyes inspecting the outer tightly rolled layers of worn and weathered pages of "The Times" newspaper. The inner parcel was tied with twine and gave no clue to its contents. Doris removed the double layers of neatly folded wrapping, each layer a quarter turn of the parcel from its preceding layer. Her eyes glanced to the now pale face of the parcel's protector. She stopped. Doris looked at the prostrate body wrapped in a buttoned-up black city coat, black turn-up trousers frayed against worn out, leather-soled brogues. His white beard and long, wild white hair covered a matured and weathered face. She thought of Father Christmas as she looked back at the paper parcel. She knew nothing about her lost patient other than his name but began to wonder why this apparent down-and-out man wore fine tailored clothes and constantly protected his neat paper package. Her fingers tore at the final layers of paper. The smell of leather filled her nostrils as the gleam of white cricket boots emerged into the sunlight. Polished studs protruded from the stained green leather soles, the whitened laces tied and tucked inside each boot.

"They're worth a bob or two," the voice echoed, distracting Doris from her thoughts.

"Yes, they probably are," Doris replied, looking up at the young man standing before her.

Doris struggled to her feet, leaning on the wall for support. The weight of Joe's head resting on her legs for the last few hours had reduced her blood circulation, and now pins and needles rushed from her feet and up her legs, causing her to remain lent against the wall.

"We need to report his death," Doris commanded as she bent down to rub her tingling legs.

"What's this 'we' bit?" replied the now familiar young man.

"You're the witness," said Doris, looking firmly into the blue eyes of a surprised face. "So let's go."

Doris bent down, rubbed her legs, and picked up her new cricket boots. She looked at the boots and decided to collect some of the paper wrapping for their protection. The previous owner had looked after them so well that it was the least she could do.

Doris and her young witness left Joe's stiffening body on the pavement and went to report his death.

Harry sat watching over his mug of tea as Doris chatted and tended to her patients, passing along the drunks, druggies, and dropouts like a bizarre line in a doctor's waiting room. She had a comforting word for each case as she tended the results of the latest falls and brawls. Comments of banter and thanks passed between patient and nurse as each casualty would seek her attention. Their respect was obvious and genuine. It was almost their only comfort.

The day had started a little differently with the passing away of Joe and the complications at the police station reporting the fact. It had taken most of the morning, and by early afternoon they had managed to pawn Joe's precious cricket boots.

The autumn sun was setting low behind the grey stone buildings of the busy London streets, and the promise of a damp night was already in the darkening clouds. Young Harry pulled Joe's liberated city coat round his shoulders and cupped his warm tea in his hands. Thankfully Joe's boots had raised sufficient funds for the hot tea and some warm food to look forward to before the night set in. Doris came and sat on the bench, picked up her lukewarm tea, and smiled at Harry.

"Where would madam like to eat this evening?" Harry quipped with a grin. "The Ritz?"

"Champagne at the Ritz will be fine, kind sir," Doris replied with a large smile in return.

Despite the age difference, their friendship had grown over the past few months of their meeting. Harry now provided a background protection for Doris as she went among her patients. Although there had not been a problem, she was pleased he was around, a reassuring support, just in case.

In many ways Doris wondered just how she would have managed if she had not met Harry. He knew the street life and how to survive in it. He was a carefree, laid back, only interested in painting-type artist, who, despite having had some success, had run out of luck and now found himself on the street. Harry was charming, cheeky, always with a smile, and Doris enjoyed his cheery presence, as he would distract her from her current hardship with his colourful cockney chat. His ability to think ahead and provide for their situation was also supportive to Doris, who had almost no experience of a street life-survival existence.

The evening drizzle turned into rain as Doris and Harry finished their soup and burger from the Ritz Burger Bar, a mobile caravan trader that tempted the night owls with the smell of greasy fried onions and hot dogs as they flew from the cinema and pubs to the fleet of passing busses and taxis. Hurrying along they turned into the side street and headed for the quieter shop doorways, hoping they were not too late to occupy one of the few dry spots for the night. Harry spotted a vacant door and rushed across the road to secure their retreat. Doris quickly followed, knowing it was just large enough for two, and they would not have to tolerate the antics of other drunken tenants.

Together they turned and looked out into the black sky and watched the falling rain dance on the dark pavement tiles, wash across its smooth foot-worn surface to cascade over the curb, and run back toward the neon glow of the high street. The distant traffic passed randomly from left and right; their reflections, in the rippled waterlogged road, hissed at their wheels as each vehicle passed. Now only the occasional pedestrian scurried by, shadowed under the glossy glow of their illuminated umbrella.

Back in the side street the rain patted onto the cardboard-roof canopies protecting over the growing homeless village that could be seen farther along the road by the railway arches. Doris squatted on her ankles, her chin resting on her knees and arms wrapped round her legs. Harry, with one protective arm round

Doris's shoulders, held the warming city coat over the heads of the two friends.

"I hope this doesn't last all night." Doris sighed. "I don't mind the cold, but cold and wet is too much."

"Try to sleep," Harry replied in a concerned tone. "You hardly slept at all last night. You need to rest and save some strength for when it gets really cold."

"Okay, I'll try." After a short pause, Doris continued. "Who do you think he was?"

"Who?" replied Harry.

"What did he do, where was he from?" Doris continued, ignoring Harry's ignorance of her comments.

"Who?" quizzed Harry.

"And what about those cricket boots? They were special," Doris stated.

"Who, Joe you mean...who knows?" Harry now replied, catching up with the conversation. "Maybe he was a banker who played cricket?"

"He could have been," said Doris out loud. "His clothes were well tailored, not what everyone wears round this part of town."

"Maybe he nicked them," quipped Harry.

"Nicked them," said Doris, wondering what Harry meant. "Nicked what?"

"The boots," Harry continued. "Maybe he just stole them off someone, or found them."

"No, the rest of his clothes suggested he was a man of position. I mean, look at this coat. It's a Crombie. Something must have happened for him to finish up on the street. Look at me, for example," pondered Doris.

Harry didn't reply; his gaze was down on the pavement, watching the rain pattern the puddle as he thought about the stories Doris had told him of her previous life.

The rain had stopped in the early hours of the morning. Harry woke as the warm rays of morning sunshine lit his face. He was alone, covered by the warm coat his friend had caringly placed round his shoulders. The day was already alive with traffic and people busying to work. Harry kicked his legs out from his squatting position and sat on the doorway floor. He watched the morning activity from his lowly position, looking up at the blank and sleepy faces as they passed.

"Spare a tanner for breakfast?" he called to likely prospects.

"Excuse me, young man," came a stern voice standing in the doorway. "I wish to enter, and you have no right to be here."

"Sorry, missus, just keeping out the wet," Harry replied as he stood up. "Any chance of a cuppa?"

"Get out of the way and don't let me find you here again, or I shall have to call the police, you lazy layabout," commanded the well-dressed woman as she started to unlock the shop door.

"Yes, ma'am, no, ma'am, three bags full, ma'am," Harry sarcastically replied as he walked away from his night lodgings toward the sleepy cardboard village to look for Doris.

He found her, as usual, amongst her homeless vagabonds, tending their needs.

"Doris, come on...leave them today. Let's go and get a coffee," Harry called.

Standing by the side of the railway station coffee bar, they shared a large hot mug of strong black coffee and a cheese roll. Harry was aware of the sideways stares and glances as customers bought their morning papers and cigarettes or stood to drink their coffee while distancing themselves from the two undesirables.

"Why do they always do that?" Harry murmured into the coffee mug. "Why do they always look at you as if you're some piece of dog dirt? Aloof and smarmy, 'I'm all right, Jack' attitude. I bet most of them are worse off than we are."

"Harry, be quiet," said Doris, giving him a stern glare.

"Well, it makes you—"

"Harry," interrupted Doris, and continued after a pause. "They are only people, just the same as you."

"Yea, but—"

"Harry..." Doris smiled. "What are you planning for today?"

"What?" replied Harry, half paying attention to the chastising.

"You always have something planned when you want me to leave my patients," Doris stated.

"You need a break, Doris, and we need some cash. Three days

you spent with Joe and you're knackered. No sleep, hardly eating, you're not doing yourself any favours, Doris," Harry replied.

"I'm all right," said Doris.

"That's why you were coughing all night then," continued Harry.

"So what do you have planned?" asked Doris, avoiding Harry's comment.

"Let's just go and rest, away from all this for the day. I'll sketch and you collect the cash. It's a good day. Don't look like rain and the drawings will last a while. Maybe make a bob or two," Harry suggested. "What do you think?"

"Mm, I'd like that, Harry," Doris sighed; her thoughts drifted back to hot Italian summers wandering the art galleries. "I hope it stays sunny."

Doris sat watching as Harry quickly sketched, transferring the hard grey paving slabs into earthy rocks and boulders and cascading water you could almost feel splashing onto your face. Harry was lost in his creation, his pastel-coated hands constantly arcing, stroking, smoothing, blending colour into colour, oblivious to the marvelled expressions of the gathering onlookers and the growing copper collection on Joe's laid-out coat. This was his world; nothing else existed as his thoughts materialised in a blaze of colour before him. Doris coughed. Harry stood and looked at his waterfall, his head cocked to one side, and with an approving, tight-lipped smile, he squatted at fresh paving stones. Within an hour it was almost as if the sun were shining out from a hole in the pavement and illuminating the faces of his audience. Harry's natural ability to create light to shine from his paintings matched the warmth that shone from his face when he smiled. He signed his name under the pictures, shuffled over to Doris, and leaned back against the wall.

"*Wild thing, you make my heart sing,*" Harry sang as he leaned on Doris, showing approval and satisfaction with his artwork.

"Do you always sing when you work?" Doris asked with a cough.

"Sometimes the mood of music creates the painting," Harry replied. "Sometimes I have an idea for a picture, and music brings it to life. Rock, Blues, Jazz, all have different moods that create the picture, and if I play or sing or feel the music, it helps me paint," Harry explained.

"That's one way to approach it, I suppose," said Doris, slowly nodding her head in approval. "All I need now is my bathing costume and I could go swimming under your waterfall."

"You like it? asked Harry.

"You have talent," replied Doris, breaking off to cough. "You just need someone to back you. Oh, look, now the water really is wet."

Raindrops began falling as if to bring the waterfall to life while washing away Harry's work and returning the pavement to match the grey overhead skies. Quickly Harry collected the coins from Joe's coat, put them in a pocket, and pulled the coat over his and Doris's head as they rushed back toward the railway station.

They wandered the station hallway, sat on the platform bench, and stood under the archway of the station entrance, watching the rain and trying not to associate themselves with the drunken homeless who are regularly moved out into the street.

The rain was falling heavily with torrents of water gushing from rusty iron drainpipes to wash the pavements. Taxis pulling into the station swished through the growing puddles, their passengers' faces lowered and wincing at the rain as they alighted and rushed toward the dry welcome of the station entrance hall. It looked like a long, wet night, and Harry knew they would not be able to remain in the shelter of the station. He guided Doris toward the display of timetables and pretended to be passengers looking for their destination and departure time, aware that a porter had now been watching them for some time. The porter headed their way. Harry took Doris by the hand and walked toward the platform, stopping at the gate. He turned to face Doris but looked past her to check the porter's movements. Harry put his hand into Joe's coat pocket and pulled out some of the coins collected from his art exhibition and gave Doris a penny piece.

"Here, go to the loo," Harry said anxiously. "The porter knows were not going anywhere, and we'll have to move when he catches us. Just sit in there for half hour; maybe it will stop raining by then. I'll meet you at the coffee stall in half hour."

Doris took the penny and headed to the ladies. Harry walked

back to the notice boards to watch the porter before heading to the safety of the gents.

Harry was just collecting two hot mugs of vegetable soup as he saw Doris approaching.

"This will give us some warmth and buy us time until the porter throws us out of here." Harry smiled as he handed Doris her soup. "He's watching us all the time now."

Doris took her soup and offered an empty smile to Harry. They stood in silence, drinking slowly, cupping their hands round the mug to gain all the warmth they could. Doris coughed. Their mugs had been empty for ten minutes when Harry put them back on the counter. Turning to survey the station and find the all-attentive porter, Harry was not surprised to find him between the coffee bar and the route back to a dry night's shelter.

"It looks like a night in cardboard village tonight." Harry grunted. "Maybe we can get by the fire if we hurry."

The rain continued to fall heavily. Doris and Harry were soaked through by the time they reached the makeshift village. The customary fire in the old oil drum was nothing more than smoke rising from the sodden embers and ash. The hours of rain had returned the vagrants early, and they had been settled for some time, taking all the best-sheltered positions.

"It's no good staying here, Doris," said Harry, wiping his wet face. "We'll just be sat in the rain all night. We'll have to find somewhere else."

Harry lifted Joe's coat back over their heads and headed back along the side street. All the doorways in side streets in the area would now be occupied, and the main streets would only lead to eviction and trouble. Trying to muscle in in a new area would be difficult. Harry thought hard, trying to think of some nearby shelter, and headed toward the park. He cut down a residential side street, guiding Doris with one arm round her shoulders while holding Joe's coat aloft with the other. His jeans, now wet up to his knees, stuck to his legs and flapped rhythmically at his ankles and waterlogged desert boots as he walked. He could feel the inside of Joe's Crombie wet against Doris's back and her woollen overcoat and knew he had to find shelter soon. Between the row of regimented doorways of the houses, he spotted a shop window that broke rank and accommodated a set-back doorway. They approached, stopped, and Harry looked up and down the road. The doorway was empty. It would be risky if they got caught in a residential area. They could stay until the rain stopped or until the morning alarm clocks roused the regiment sleeping behind the doors, he thought to himself. He looked once more up and down the road. Nothing moved other than the rainwater flooding along the curb of the roadside and gurgling down the drain. Quickly he pushed Doris into the doorway, back into the shadow against the door. They stood huddled together, catching their breaths, the once protective Crombie now a sodden cloth hanging heavily over their heads.

"Take your coat off," ordered Harry.

"Take my coat off?" quipped Doris, surprised. "It's pouring with rain, Harry."

"Take your coat off and put mine on. It's dryer than yours," explained Harry.

Doris followed Harry's request, dropping Joe's wet Crombie sponge to the floor in a squelch of water and removing her own water-logged blue woollen overcoat in exchange for Harry's much dryer anorak. Feeling better, Doris sat on the floor against the glass door, drawing her feet up to her bottom and out of the rain blowing into the doorway. Harry assumed the same position next to her and pulled Joe's coat over their knees. Doris coughed as Harry put his arm round her shoulders to keep her warm.

"Try and sleep," Harry suggested as they snuggled together.

"I'm cold," Doris replied, coughing again.

"Me too." Harry chuckled. "Wet as well."

"No, I feel cold," said Doris in a short tone.

Harry could feel Doris shivering and tried to snuggle closer.

"How's that?" replied Harry.

"Thank you," coughed Doris, "but I'm still cold."

The rain continued all night, blowing into the doorway, dancing and splashing in the road and puddles. Harry sat and watched most of the night, woken from his occasional naps by Doris's worsening coughing and shivering body. With no reply to his questions, Harry was not sure if Doris was sleeping or just not answering, but was distracted as lights slowly turned into the side street from the main road and silently progressed, splashing through the growing puddles along the glistening tarmac. Harry watched, stopped breathing and pressed back against the door. The vehicle stopped; the peaked caped driver in a black rainproof coat emerged and turned toward the back of the vehicle. Harry squinted through the rain and faint morning light, trying to see what the driver was doing. A long sigh blew from Harry's lips as he saw the driver lift two white milk bottles from their crate and proceed to the first of the regimented doorways.

"Phew…the milkman." Harry sighed, guessing that it must be about six or seven o'clock.

Harry waited until the milkman was almost at their shop doorway before waking Doris. He wanted the milkman to see there was nothing sinister in their presence, only that they were sheltering. The clinking of milk bottles ceased as the silent milk float halted at their doorway.

"Doris…Doris, come on. We have to go," Harry whispered as he gently shook Doris by the shoulder. "Doris," he repeated louder.

"I'm not well," Doris replied in a faint voice without moving.

"What's wrong?" questioned Harry, squatting down to look closer at his friend.

Doris was shaking. Harry put his hand on her wet face and felt her hot cheeks.

"Oh, blast," Harry whispered to himself.

"Come on, you two. You don't want to be seen here," the milkman said as he stood looking into the doorway, holding two white bottles between his fingers. "You're asking for trouble if someone sees you."

Harry remained squatting, his hands cupping Doris's cheeks, feeling their heat, just as he had done hours before with his hot soup.

"She's sick!" Harry shouted over his shoulder in reply.

"What's wrong?" asked the milkman, who was now coming into the shop doorway.

"I don't know. She has a fever, her cheeks are burning," continued Harry, his whole attention focused on Doris.

"You can't stay here," replied the milkman, looking up and down the rain-soaked road. "This street will be waking soon and won't care for the likes of you littering their doorways," he continued, trying to be considerate.

"She's sick, can't you see?" Harry grunted, thinking of all the care she gave to her homeless patients and desperately wanting someone here to care for Doris.

"Bring her to the float," said the milkman, stepping back into the street.

"What?" replied Harry, turning to look at the milkman.

"Put her in the milk float. It's not too warm, but it's out of the rain and out of trouble," the milkman said, gesturing toward the blue and white vehicle at the roadside.

Harry helped Doris to her feet and supported her while she climbed onto the bench seat of the electric milk float. Harry jumped in alongside Doris and sat holding her hand as he watched the milkman scurry from doorway to doorway, depositing white bottles of liquid like a prowling ally cat marking his territory. The milkman slipped into his vehicle, sandwiching Doris, pushed the long-levered handbrake forward, and at the same time jammed his foot on to the peddle below the triangular handlebar that he pulled to his left. The milk float silently glided forward, turning right and across the road.

"There's a hospital on my route," began the milkman, as the electric milk float hummed along to the sound of chinking bottles and splashing water.

It was eight o'clock as the blue and white float swished up to the Accident and Emergency entrance of the hospital. Doris sat holding Harry's hand; her wet chestnut hair, flattened and stuck to her face, looked black against her now grey complexion and blue lips. The usual constant sparkle of her hazel green eyes was flat as she stared straight ahead, watching the rain beat on the windscreen. She was wet, hot, and shivering from the heightening fever gripping her body. Harry helped her from the milk float, almost having to carry her weight, and headed toward the hospital entrance.

"Okay, mate," called the milkman, watching them shuffle toward the doorway.

"Yea, cheers, mate," replied Harry, turning and looking over his shoulder toward the direction of the voice.

"Good luck. See ya," said the milkman as he pushed his foot down on the accelerator and silently glided away.

The warmth of the hospital bathed their faces and seeped through their soaked clothes as they squelched through the entrance door. Harry called for help while looking for someone to assist. He wasn't sure where to go. Their wet clothing left a watery trail on the polished hallway floor as they wandered first one direction and then another.

"Can I help you?" came a soft voice from behind a glass window.

"Yea, she's sick," replied Harry, turning toward the window while helping Doris in the same direction. "She has a fever. She's blue. She needs some help. She's really sick," Harry repeated stressfully. "And she's a nurse," he added hopefully.

"Just one moment, sir. I'll call a nurse," came a polite reply. "Would you take a seat?"

Harry looked round and saw the row of seats.

"Please, she needs some help quickly," Harry called back to the polite voice from behind the window.

The critical glares from the occupied seats of the reception room cut into Harry, as he knew what was going through their thoughts while they waited patiently to be attended. He stood dripping into a growing pool of water while he looked for a seat for Doris. A wheelchair was parked by the wall. Harry squelched forward and sat Doris on the end seat of the row while he went for the wheelchair. He could feel the glaring faces follow his every move. As he pushed the chair back toward Doris, a nurse appeared at his side and helped him lift her into the wheelchair.

"She doesn't look very well at all," commented the nurse. "I'll take her for a checkup right away. What's her name?" asked the nurse as she began to disappear down the corridor.

"Doris," replied Harry as he slumped onto Doris's vacant chair, "I mean Dorothy," he called, correcting himself as he remembered where he was.

Harry remained slumped on the chair as the warmth of the

hospital began to make his clothes feel uncomfortable, and the pool of water round his feet grew larger drip by drip. He watched the glares as people came and went, their heads turning in unison toward Harry as they passed by or came to sit on the row of seats. Each glare had the same disapproving expression he wanted to answer but remained quiet, restrained by Doris's displeasure of his sly comments when in such a situation. He wasn't sure how long had passed when a doctor appeared, looked in Harry's direction, and with a realizing gesture walked toward Harry.

"I guess you're the young man who has brought in the wet lady with the fever, Dorothy, I believe?" the doctor questioned.

"Yea, sure," replied Harry, sitting up and getting to his feet. "How is she? She's going to be okay, yea?"

"We're going to keep her on a ward for a while. She has pneumonia and is rather poorly at the moment but nothing to worry about," the doctor informed Harry. "How has she become so wet? Where did you find her? And look at yourself, you're drenched."

"Yea, it's a long story," Harry replied uncomfortably, not wanting to volunteer too much information. "Can I see her?"

"Tomorrow," said the doctor. "At the moment she's sleeping. Go home and get yourself dry and warm. Tomorrow you can see her. In the meantime, if you would give some details to the nurse at the reception window, it would be appreciated," the doctor concluded and headed back down the corridor.

Harry watched him disappear and gathered his thoughts. "Go home and get warm, yeah, sure, Doc. Chance would be a fine thing," he mumbled loudly.

Ignoring the doctor's last request, Harry left the hospital and wandered the streets, sheltering in shop doorways and the railway station away from the persistent rain. Dusk began to fall, and he headed through the rain back to the cardboard village, hoping there would be some shelter while he waited for tomorrow to visit his sick friend.

The rain had almost stopped by the time he reached the makeshift village. Harry stood by the fire in the old oil drum, steaming like a waiting train at a station platform as the heat dried out his sodden clothes. His thoughts were far away with Doris. Only when the heat of the fire reached through to his body and burned his skin would he turn and present a new wet section of clothing to the fire. It was the first night without Doris since meeting her some six months previously. He remembered chatting and laughing for hours their first night together huddled in a doorway, not sleeping until the glow of dawn appeared in the morning sky. Her stories filled his head, and he became angry that she should have to be carried to the hospital like the casualties she had spent so much time caring for. Harry yawned and began to look around for somewhere to spend the night. He squatted between two unconscious drunks, pulled their cardboard blankets over his head, and, leaning against the archway wall, settled down to sleep.

The morning arrived with a bright, clear sky and the first hint of the frosty winter to come. Harry pushed the cardboard blankets back over his two sleeping partners and exhaled his hot breath into the cold morning air.

At least she's in a warm bed, Harry thought to himself as he climbed to his feet and stretched his legs.

Making his way toward the smoking fire drum, he picked up some cardboard blankets from the sleeping vagrants. He tore one into pieces and pushed it down into the ashes of the oil drum. With another board he fanned the bottom of the drum, driving air through the breather holes until a flame began to grow from the refuelled fire. Harry quickly put the remaining cardboard into the fire. He stood as close as possible to the raging flames, holding Joe's coat wide open like a cape surrounding the fire and capturing its warmth. He was almost scorching as the flames began to die back into the smoking ashes. Pulling the coat across his chest, to trap in the warmth, Harry headed for the railway station buffet stall and a hot mug of coffee.

He searched deep into the corners of Joe's coat pockets, collecting every coin they contained. Looking first at the coins and then up at the menu board, he was pleased to be able to afford a hot sausage roll, as it was almost two days since he last ate. Cupping his hands round the mug of coffee, he stamped his feet and blew his hot breath into the air as he watched the commuters scurrying around the station.

Doris entered his thoughts, and he wondered what time he would be allowed to see her.

I'll walk slowly and get there for eleven, he thought to himself as he headed out of the station and into the bustling street.

"I've come to see Dorothy. I brought her in yesterday," Harry said through the window of the hospital reception.

"Oh, yes! Take a seat please. The doctor will see you in a moment," replied the nurse, startled by Harry's voice and sudden appearance of his figure looking through her window.

Harry returned to his seat of the previous day and sat on the end of the row. He applied the same discipline to the disapproving looks of his new audience as he waited for the doctor to arrive.

"The doctor will see you now," said the nurse, appearing at Harry's shoulder, and she led him down the same corridor that Doris had travelled the previous day.

The doctor's office was small; there were two chairs for visitors between grey filing cabinets and a large wooden desk, behind which was the doctor's chair. Harry sat down, uncomfortable about the situation, wondering why a doctor wanted to see him. He looked round the room and waited again for the doctor.

"Good morning," began the doctor as he entered his office. "I would like you to provide some detail, Mr..." he exclaimed as his words petered out and he looked directly at Harry.

"Harry," replied Harry, tensely.

"I would like you to give me some detail about the woman you brought in yesterday, Mr. Harry," resumed the doctor.

"How's Dorothy? Is she okay?" began Harry. "That's her name, Dorothy," he continued, feeling anxious about news on his friend and what to tell the doctor.

"Dorothy is still poorly and resting at the moment," replied the doctor, using her name to reassure Harry that she was being taken care of.

Harry warmed to the doctor's calming voice and began to tell how Dorothy had become ill.

"You mean to say you're homeless and live on the streets?" questioned the Doctor, interrupting. "Who is Dorothy? Where is she from? You said yesterday she is a nurse."

"Like I said yesterday, it's a long story. Her name is Dorothy Wainwright," Harry said anxiously, "and she was an army nurse, a Queen Alexander Nurse. She uses her old lanyard to keeps her pants up. Have a look if you don't believe me," he continued, desperately wanting the doctor to understand and keep Dorothy in the hospital until she had recovered strong enough to face the winter.

"I have no reason to doubt you, Mr. Harry," replied the doctor, "but how has she become to be homeless?"

"Dorothy left home in nineteen forty-three," began Harry.

SCOTLAND

1943

Dorothy watched the smoke curl across from the green locomotive racing round the bend, pulling the train along the inclined track ahead. Beyond rose the Cumbria Mountains of the Lake District, their peaks hidden in heavy rain clouds that cast a bland shadow over the landscape. She held her breath as the black smoke wafted through the open window filling the compartment with a taste of soot and steam.

"Shall I close the window, hen?" said the soldier sitting opposite.

"It's fine, really," Dorothy replied, glancing at the partially standing figure and returning her gaze out of the window. "The train is just rounding a bend. The smoke will be gone in a moment, unless you find it cool."

"Nay bother, hen. Glasgie will be just as breezy this time o' year." The soldier smiled and returned to his seat.

Dorothy smiled in return, her face in view of the soldier's attentive gaze while her eyes watched the grey stone-walled fields and countryside roll by.

Hen…does he think I'm some sort of chicken? she thought to herself.

Her smile grew larger, and she turned her head to watch the scenery falling behind the train while she hid the amused thought showing on her face.

Conscious of being the only female in the compartment, Dorothy had spent most of the journey from London looking out of the window and listening to her fellow travellers: two young soldiers sitting opposite each other by the door; a sailor sitting next to her; and two older soldiers, in red tartan kilts, sitting facing her and travelling in a backward direction.

The window had been opened earlier to let out the cigarette smoke that accompanied the conversations of who had been where and stories of warfare action. The young soldiers had listened intently to the action stories and glared at each other, directly in the eyes, in horror at the atrocities described by the Scots-accented soldier sitting opposite Dorothy.

The compartment fell quiet, and Dorothy looked around at her companions. The young soldier sitting opposite by the door, the middle of the older kilted soldiers, and the sailor were sleeping, while the remaining young and older Scottish soldier smoked and looked out of their windows. The kilt of the sleeping soldier opposite had ridden up his leg, and Dorothy looked at the hairy knees protruding from underneath. Yellow and blue colouring of scar tissue was just visible on the inside of the soldier's right leg, and Dorothy curiously leaned and angled her head to see if she could see more of the scar.

"It's true what they say," echoed the Scots accent.

Dorothy jumped and looked at the soldier sitting opposite. His grin disappeared as he inhaled on his cigarette and blew smoke up and out of the open window.

"Is it really how you have described it…the war?" asked Dorothy, distracting the soldier from expanding upon his mistaken observation.

"Aye, lass, and more ya cannot speak about," replied the soldier, forgetting his previous comment and drawing again on his cigarette.

Dorothy gave a tight-lipped smile and returned her gaze out the window.

Lass…well that's better than being referred to a chicken, I suppose, she pondered as her thoughts drifted by with the passing fields. *I wonder what will become of me. I hope I can cope when the time comes.*

She listened to the distant puffing of the steam engine at the head of the train and the clacking rhythm of the carriage wheels on the rail track as she closed her eyes and joined her sleeping companions.

The train slowed and clattered over the rail junctions as it began its approach into Glasgow Central Station, waking Dorothy from her sleep. The coach corridor and smoky compartment was now busy with people stretching, standing, and lifting kit bags from the overhead racks above the seats.

Dorothy rubbed her eyes and looked at the grey rainy overtone through her wet window. She noticed the Scots soldier opposite remained sitting, smoking his cigarette and looking out of the window as the sailor handed her kit bag. Dorothy stood and put the bag on her seat while she looked in the mirror on the compartment wall, attended her hair, and straightened her uniform. A rush of hot steam hissed into the compartment through the open window as another train passed. Rowdy soldiers in the corridor could be heard above the young soldiers chatting in the compartment as the train stopped with a sudden jolt alongside the platform. Dorothy fell against the Scots soldier opposite; his firm hands held her waist while she gained her balance.

"Thank you," said Dorothy, turning to face the soldier.

"You be careful, hen. Keep ya head down and Godspeed ya home, lass," said the soldier, looking straight at Dorothy as he winked his eye.

She wanted to reply, but the soldier turned and joined his comrades pushing down the carriage corridor and spilling out of the train onto the platform. Dorothy followed and joined the line of khaki soldiers, like ants marching along the platform toward the station hallway.

The scarlet tippet and white veiled headdress of the senior sister assigned to collect Dorothy was easily visible amongst the brown throng of soldier ants surrounding a small group of blue uniformed sailors gathering at the station entrance.

"Wainwright," said the senior sister as Dorothy approached.

"Yes, ma'am," answered Dorothy.

"Follow me!" barked the senior sister.

"Yes, ma'am," Dorothy replied, taken back by the crisp, efficient greeting and falling into quick march behind the departing senior sister.

A wake of parted soldiers watched as the two nurses marched out of the station to a waiting staff car parked by the main entrance. Files of soldiers lined up behind a fleet of trucks as they waited their turn to climb aboard and disappear behind the green canvas covers over the rear of the trucks. Military police stood in pairs watching the organised chaos, occasionally directing civilian cars and vehicles away from the congested area.

An MP standing by the waiting staff car opened the front and rear passenger doors for the two approaching nurses and took Dorothy's kit bag. Dorothy bowed her head to enter the rear of the car and was surprised to see two more nurses already occupying the seat.

"Oh, hello," said Dorothy, squeezing into the corner of the seat.

The boot of the car closed, and the MP at the front of the car stood to one side and waved for the driver to proceed forward and away from the busy station.

"Sorry about the short, sharp reception, Wainwright. I just had to get away from all that commotion and staring faces, and it's better we're ahead of the trucks. The roads are not the best," said the senior sister in an apologetic tone.

"I know what you mean, ma'am. I had one soldier who stared almost the whole journey," replied Dorothy.

"This is Nurse Lawrence and Nurse Campbell. They're local

Voluntary Aid Nurses just assigned to the hospital," continued the sister, introducing the two young women sharing the backseat. "I am Senior Sister Waldron, assigned to HMS Quebec Hospital at Inveraray. I'll introduce you to Matron when we arrive."

Less-formal introductions and topical conversation continued as the brown army staff car journeyed out of Glasgow, northwards toward Loch Lomond. The rain had cleared and the clouds lifted, promoting a warm, sunlit view of the loch as the car wound its way along the shoreline road. Dorothy watched out of the window as the hills and peaks passed by and compared the open highlands to the tree-covered hills and valleys that surrounded Bath, her hometown.

"This is Loch Fyne. Over on the other bank you can see the castle and the small cluster of white buildings, that's Inveraray," commented Senior Sister Waldron. "You can see it better in a moment," she continued as the staff car approached its destination. "HMS Quebec is farther down the Loch, where all the ships are."

In parade fashion the three nurses turned their heads to face the distant shoreline and glimpse the described buildings through the blur of passing trees.

"You are all billeted in the Maltland building in the castle grounds just by the hospital in Jubilee Hall," concluded Waldron as way of introduction to their new home. "We'll meet Matron first, and then I'll show you to your quarters and you can meet the other nurses at your leisure."

The staff car crossed an old twin-arched road bridge over the Aray River. Ahead could be seen the silhouette of the small town of Inveraray reflecting in the loch as the red September sun sank into the gathering clouds. Before the view could be appreciated, a right turn into the castle grounds swept the car to the guardhouse and halted at the closed barrier.

A duty MP stepped forward and looked through the driver's opened window at the three uniformed nurses occupying the backseat.

"New recruits for the hospital, Sergeant," Senior Sister Waldron explained, looking at the MP and smiling.

"Thank you, Sister. Proceed," replied the MP, standing upright and signalling to the soldier operating the red cantilevered barrier.

The barrier raised, and the car crawled forward into the military base. The road climbed away from the shore of Loch Fyne as it wound its way through the castle grounds. The huts of Dukes Camp were visible among the trees to the left, a barricaded right turn lead to the Cinderella-like castle, seat of the Campbell Clan, at the end of the short, guarded road. The car approached a large square building with a gateway leading to an inner courtyard as the road wound right and up the long raise of grassed parkland.

"That's the Sergeant's Mess and Quartermaster's Store, Cherry Park," Senior Sister Waldron explained. "Jubilee Hall and Maltland is just across the river, over the hill."

A further spread of wooden huts of Dukes Camp was visible, stretching down the slope back toward the castle. The car crossed the Aray River again and climbed the hill as it passed still more camouflaged huts and military vehicles nesting among the trees.

"This is now Castle Camp," continued Waldron. "The base is quite extensive; there are further camps behind Inveraray and along the shore of the loch. Oh! Look, there's the hospital just ahead."

The uniformed driver parked alongside an ambulance outside Jubilee Hall, got out of the car, and opened the doors for his passengers to alight as he unloaded their kit bags from the car boot.

"I'll take you to meet Matron and then show you your quarters. Follow me, please," ordered Senior Sister Waldron.

Together the three nurses followed Waldron into the hospital building.

"Ah, Waldron," said the matron, walking into the reception hall through a swing door, as if knowing the precise time of their arrival. "These must be our new recruits?"

"Yes, ma'am, Sister Wainwright, Nurses Lawrence and Campbell, ma'am," replied Senior Sister Waldron. "May I introduce Matron Murdock," she concluded, looking at the three new recruits.

Matron directed the small congregation into her office and stood behind her tidy, polished desk.

"The hospital here at Inveraray supports the military's amphibious landing training activities and exercises of 'Number

One Combined Training Centre.' There are fifty beds, mainly occupied by casualties returning from the front, and occasionally we accommodate poorly local civilians. The activities here at the hospital vary according to the centre's training demands required to support military operations. There are hundreds, if not thousands of soldiers who pass through this centre during these exercises, and their numbers vary according to the scale of the operation at that time. Unfortunately we see some of these soldiers here on our wards. I operate an efficient, orderly, and disciplined hospital and expect you to accomplish your responsibilities in a similar manner," Matron explained, efficiently and orderly. "Well, you must be tired from your journey," she concluded, passing a glance at each of the nurses. "Waldron will show you to your quarters, and I will see you on the wards tomorrow, six o'clock sharp. Thank you, Waldron."

Introductions complete, Waldron escorted the newly recruited nurses out of Matron's office and to their assigned quarters.

Despite the late evening, meeting new faces, and chat about hospital routine, Dorothy was up early to press her uniform and be present on the ward before six o'clock sharp. Dorothy crossed over from her dormitory block and stood for a while at the main entrance door and looked out over the castle grounds at the spread of wooden huts and tents, the movement of trucks and marching soldiers preparing for their day, and the tree-lined hills that surrounded the camp, their tops flattened by the grey mist rolling across the peak. With a shivery shrug of her shoulders, she turned and walked into the hospital hallway.

"Good morning, Sister Wainwright," Nurse Campbell greeted on her way to the wards. "It's not always overcast and rainy, Sister. We also have some lovely sunshine when the countryside looks even more beautiful."

"Have you been on a military base before?" Dorothy enquired.

"No, but it's exciting, don't you think? All those soldiers," replied Nurse Campbell with a smile and a sparkle in her eyes that replaced the missing sunshine.

Sister Penrose, of plump, rosy-face character, was working in the ward office as Sister Wainwright and Nurse Campbell entered.

"Good morning, Sister," greeted the two nurses.

"Sister Wainwright, ma'am."

"Nurse Campbell, ma'am."

"Good morning," replied the sister, looking up from her paperwork and sitting back in her chair. "I'm Sister Penrose, welcome. Well, you seem to have chosen a good day to start on the ward. There will be exercises today using live ammunition. And this being the casualty ward, we must be prepared for any eventuality, as there is usually someone who comes away injured from these necessary exercises. Casualties will go straight to theatre, if required, and until that's not possible, then we will have to do what is needed here on the ward and prepare them while they wait. Injuries that don't require surgery will also be treated on the ward," she said cheerily, concluding her brief summary of introduction to the ward under her control.

"Yes, ma'am," replied Dorothy and Nurse Campbell.

"Nurse Monroe," Sister Penrose called to a nurse passing the office doorway, "will you take Nurse Campbell and introduce her to the morning routine. Thank you, Nurse." The sister smiled looking at Nurse Campbell.

"Oh my, exercises with live ammunition on my first day!" exclaimed the departing Nurse Campbell under her breath as she retreated from the sister's office.

"Pray no one is injured," retorted Sister Penrose while turning to address Sister Wainwright. "I will brief you on our current patients later. Oh! Matron will be here at six fifteen, so we must have everything ready for her morning inspection. She is very particular about clean beds, Sister Wainwright, so make sure dressings have not been leaking during the night. I'm sure you know what is what, but matrons do have their own special peculiarity, and it's much easier to know what they are rather than have to find them out."

"Yes, thank you, I'll remember that," replied Dorothy.

The ward was clean and tidy. Beds, particularly, were made with their occupying patient, wherever possible, sat propped against puffed pillows and were covered neatly to their waist by the smoothed and folded blankets. Sisters Penrose and Wainwright stood outside the door of the tidied office, while Nurses Monroe and

Campbell stood by the first bed on either side of the ward. It was six fifteen by the large clock above the double swing doors of the ward. Dorothy was just brushing down and straightening her grey uniform dress as the doors opened and Matron Murdock entered.

"Good morning, Sister," said the matron as she proceeded into the ward.

Sister Penrose and Dorothy replied and followed the matron. Progress and statistics about patients were discussed at each bedside as they moved steadily from bed to bed, a formality that hardly ever included participation from the patient. The distant roar of engines from the trucks and jeeps on exercise and the rhythmic sound of nail-soled boots marching on tarmac drifting in through the open windows distracted Dorothy from the matron's murmured discussion and the stillness of the ward. A louder, more sudden, and fading rumble burst the silence, followed by another and another. Repeated cracking of gunfire erupted. Dorothy thought of similar explosions from the air raids over Bath and felt her palms begin to sweat and was conscious of her increased heartbeat.

"Do you have a supply of morphine available?" commented Matron, casually, as she continued with the murmur of statistics.

The stillness of the ward was again broken as the swing doors opened and Nurse Lawrence quickly marched in to take up her position alongside Nurse Campbell.

"Sorry I'm late, ma'am," she said breathlessly, facing forward, but looking sideways from the corners of her eyes at the collection of nurses gathered at a bedside.

Matron continued her inspection as Nurse Lawrence discreetly made herself more presentable, and the explosive roar of battle echoed from the exercise fields hidden among the tree-covered slopes that ran along the shore of Loch Fyne.

"Thank you, Sister," said the matron, completing her inspection. Then she turned to face the newly arrived nurse and, with a polite but more authoritarian voice, quietly commented, "Please don't let that happen again, Nurse Lawrence," before marching from the ward.

Matron's departing and disapproving comment to Nurse Lawrence's late arrival proved to have a lasting effect upon the ward.

Patients remained quiet, reading, sleeping, distant to the sounds of battle practice that raged beyond the confines of their beds. Sister Penrose delegated responsibility of ward routine, and the attending to patients' needs continued throughout the morning. It was not until after midday and the anticipated arrival of a casualty from the exercise field that the mood in the ward changed.

The soldier arrived on the ward directly from theatre; he was bandaged almost from head to toe with only his left arm and leg visible. It turned out a shell had exploded close by him, and he was hit down his right side with flying dirt and shrapnel. The bandaging made things look worse than his injuries, when they eventually became apparent, but his arrival provided a real, first experience of nursing in a military hospital ward. Fortunately, he was the only casualty of the day's exercise, which was a relief for Nurse Lawrence, who, while coping very professionally, was quite emotional about the soldier's misfortune.

Dorothy, being the only other Queen Alexandra nurse and sister on the ward, remained attentive during her morning's briefing, as she was to share the responsibility of ward routine with Sister Penrose.

Covering both day and night duties, Dorothy quickly adjusted to the busy daytimes, attending patients and ensuring the smooth operation of the ward was to the acceptance of Matron, while the nights were long and quiet.

Following a long and rather unusually busy night, due to the arrival of new casualties from a recently docked naval ship, Dorothy returned to her room in the Maltland, tired and in need of sleep, but also excited by the prospect of her first allotment of free time. She kicked off her shoes and lay on her bed, her head spinning and wondering what she would do, then she remembered that she had agreed to meet Nurse Campbell for lunch. Visions of the arriving casualties on stretchers carried by the orderlies and ambulance drivers flashed through her mind while the ceiling shadows reflected the arrival of dawn breaking through the curtained window as she fell into a deep sleep.

The busy sound of trucks grunting through the camp woke Dorothy to the bright sunlight streaming onto her bed. A moment of anxiety passed over her as she looked out of the window at the commotion of vehicles while fumbling for her wristwatch in an effort to determine the time and what was happening.

"Gosh, twenty to eleven!"

She removed her creased grey uniform and headed for the shower, trying to be considerate for the other nurses still able to sleep through the noise.

Having quickly dressed and not wanting to be late, she marched hurriedly through the camp, downhill toward the guard-house. From the entrance of the military base Dorothy could see Inveraray's small wooden pier reaching into the calm waters of Loch Fyne. A paddle steamer was moored along the far side of the pier, and a crowd of spectators was also assembled by a collection of army vehicles. A fleet of landing craft was manoeuvring out on the loch. Two Jeeps scampered past the front of a long line of whitewashed buildings stretching from the pier; they passed under an archway extending from the Argyll Hotel and disappeared along the road at the west boundary of the base.

"Morning, ma'am," said the duty MP standing outside the guardhouse. "There are exercises taking place in the town at the moment, ma'am. Go careful."

Dorothy strolled by the hotel and the row of buildings she had witnessed the Jeeps passing. She turned into Main Street and enjoyed the warmth of the October sun as it reflected off the whitewashed walls of the small shops and houses that lined either side of the wide, almost deserted street. She had arranged to meet Nurse Campbell in the "George," a hotel and bar frequented by private soldiers, on the corner at the far end of Main Street. Dorothy saw the hotel on the opposite, shaded side of the street and began crossing the road.

The roar of engines and rattle of nail-soled boots echoed from the square that surrounded the parish church visible at the end of the street. Dorothy quickly crossed the road and stood in a shaded doorway as a scout car and armed soldiers entered Main Street. Crouched behind the steady-moving scout car and scurrying from doorway to doorway, the military procession passed along both lines of buildings. Local residents, now accustomed to the armed activities, went about their daily shopping, ignoring the melee of soldiers, while Dorothy stood straight and tensed, apprehensive in her doorway as the soldiers engulfed her.

The military spectacle passed, and more engines could be heard from the direction of the square. The short distance of pavement from the shelter of her doorway to the George's entrance was free from soldiers, and Dorothy rushed quickly toward the door as more armed forces rounded the corner.

"Oh my God," breathed Dorothy heavily. Her heart raced and beat against her chest as she faced the new procession of soldiers on the opposite side of the hotel doorway.

The advancing soldiers stopped.

"After you, ma'am," said the corporal standing upright in front of his forward crouching, rifle-pointing platoon and politely gestured for her to enter with his outstretched hand.

Dorothy quickly entered the George, thanking the corporal as he resumed his crouching position, and strode off along the side of the whitewashed wall, ahead of his men.

Inside the hotel was quite dark by comparison to the sunlit street, and Dorothy stood for a moment while she recomposed herself and caught her breath. Nurse Campbell had observed Dorothy in the doorway and went to greet her.

"Dorothy, over here," came Nurse Campbell's voice through the darkness.

"Oh, you're here, Mary," replied Dorothy as she began to make out figures and objects through the dimness of the room. "Have you seen all the soldiers exercising in the street? Gosh, it's quite frightening."

"They have captured the town three times already… apparently," Mary commented in her cheerful Scots accent. "They send different units at a time to gain experience, something to do with landing assaults. Come, sit down, pet."

Dorothy entered the hotel lounge and sat with Mary by the window. Shafts of light cut through the dim stone-walled interior and reflected from the flag-paved floor against a large fireplace that became more visible as her eyes accustomed to the natural light of the room. She could hear the chatter of conversation from silhouettes at the bar and tables farther back in the shadow.

"Do you mind if we go for a walk?" Dorothy asked. "There's a little pier round the corner, and we can see the water while the weather is nice."

"You just want to see those soldiers again," Mary replied, smiling while standing and picking her handbag from the table. "We shall have to wait for Jean though, so long as she's not too late."

"We could walk to the corner and meet her on our way," Dorothy suggested.

Mary agreed, and the two nurses ventured on to Main Street and joined the bustle of military manoeuvres as they made their way back toward the loch and Front Street corner.

As the two nurses stood waiting for Jean to arrive, a group of soldiers rushed to the corner and formed a line, leaning against the wall of the Temperance Hotel, a popular establishment run by the "Mother of the Fleet," who provided more homely comforts for the soldiers during their free time. Holding their rifles against their chests, leaning and pressing back against the wall, their chests lifting and lowering in unison with their panting breaths, they waited for their lieutenant's order. Dorothy stood by the iron railings at the edge of the road and watched as the lieutenant peered round the corner toward the direction of the wooden pier before grunting a command and gesturing his line of men to file round the corner. He leaned back against the smooth whitewashed wall and looked back along Main Street as his platoon collected in the hotel doorway protruding out from the building and providing another corner for them to gather.

"Hello, miss," said one of the soldiers stepping forward away from the wall. "Remember me? We were on the train together."

"Oh, yes, hello," replied Dorothy, surprised at seeing the young soldier again.

"You don't want to be seen—"

"Stand back, be quiet," growled the lieutenant as he passed the young soldier and resumed his position at the head of his platoon.

Another gesture from the scowling lieutenant signalled a brisk dash forward, and the soldiers headed off toward the pier.

"Here's Jean coming," said Nurse Campbell as she waved at Nurse Lawrence walking briskly along the road away from the camp and heading toward the corner.

"Sorry I'm late," Jean said, slightly out of breath as she arrived and joined her friends.

"Well, you're a dark one, Dorothy. You kept him quiet," exclaimed Mary as the three nurses strolled toward the pier.

"Not really," Dorothy replied. "He was on the train when I travelled here."

The pier was busy with people boarding the paddle steamer that was getting ready to ferry them across the loch. Groups of relaxed soldiers were gathered smoking and talking along the edge of the quayside, their training exercise through the town's streets now complete.

"Look, he's over there by the quayside," said Mary excitedly. "Let's go and talk with him."

"Who...What's going on? Who are you talking about?" Jean eagerly enquired.

"Dorothy has a secret admirer," said Mary.

"Really?" Jean asked.

"He's not secret and he's not an admirer," explained Dorothy.

"Well, he obviously remembers you, Dorothy, and it will be nice to meet someone new," Mary continued.

Dorothy was nervous about approaching her travelling companion with so many other soldiers about and tried to avoid Mary's suggestion, especially as he was standing with his army comrades. Mary was very persuasive, walking slightly behind and giving little pushes in the small of Dorothy's back.

"Just say hello," Mary whispered loudly and encouragingly.

Dorothy was relieved when the young soldier saw them approaching and stepped forward away from his platoon friends.

"Hello," greeted the young soldier, securing his rifle over one shoulder while tugging his uniform jacket to a more presentable order.

"Hello. Where's your friend?" replied Dorothy, not knowing quite what to say.

"He's in another platoon," said the young soldier, pausing. "It's good to see you again. What's your name?"

"Oh, I'm Dorothy. This is Mary and Jean. We all work together," Dorothy said, feeling more relaxed about the meeting.

"Hello," echoed Jean and Mary.

"Hello, I'm Barry. I'm from London. I've just joined up and have been sent up here to continue my training," he said confidently, looking and smiling at Dorothy.

"Are you going to the front?" asked Jean, in her soft voice.

"After my training, but I'm not sure when," Barry replied, his eyes fixed on Dorothy as if his conversation was only with her.

"Do you want to go?" Dorothy enquired.

"I don't know really. I want to do something for the war. This training is supposed to give us some experience of what to do in the real situation, but from the stories I hear, I think it's a lot different than this," said Barry. "What will you do?"

"I've just been posted here. I'm not sure," replied Dorothy.

"What were you trying to say at the corner?" asked Mary.

"Oh, nothing really," said Barry, smiling.

"Something about not being seen, you said," Mary stated, eagerly.

"It's just not somewhere you should stand, that's all," Barry replied, looking and directing his answer at Dorothy.

"Well, I didn't see anything wrong." Dorothy shrugged.

"Your lieutenant wasn't too pleased at you talking either," quipped Mary.

A whistle blow suddenly pierced the air and interrupted their conversation.

"*Fall in!*" came a load shout from the sergeant major standing by the roadside.

"Look, I've got to go. Can I see you in the George tonight, seven o'clock?" Barry asked as he prepared to respond to the sergeant major's order.

"Yes, if you like," replied Dorothy as a feeling of excitement washed over her.

"Bring your friend," called Mary as the young soldier returned to the ranks.

Barry stood to attention in line with his platoon. The slimness of his rifle paralleled his youthful figure buried in his khaki uniform. He was not alone; the platoon consisted of young recruits all contributing their bit for the war. Dorothy stood and watched them march away and realised what her posting to the military base was all about.

"Oh, look, the ferry is leaving," said Jean, distracting Dorothy from her thoughts.

Together the nurses watched the ferry steam out across the loch, its paddles churning the dark water into a flurry of white spray and sending ripples across the calm glass surface. A convoy of canvas-covered trucks could be seen through the trees on the opposite shore, heading toward Inveraray along the contoured road at the edge of Loch Fyne.

Dorothy continued to watch the convoy as the three nurses walked back along the row of whitewash buildings facing the loch that provided the picturesque image to the approaching trucks that she remembered on her arrival at Inveraray. The nurses stood at the road junction outside the Argyll Hotel, their route obstructed by the convoy as the trucks passed under the wide archway that spanned the road between the hotel and the opposite whitewashed house. The flow of trucks under the archway stopped while the parted remainder of the procession continued steadily along Inveraray's picturesque Front Street before turning into Main Street and heading out along the loch on the other side of the town.

Dorothy and her two friends passed under the archway and continued along Oban Road, at the western limit of the military camp, making their way toward the NAAFI canteen. The trucks that had obstructed their way could still be seen heading toward Town and Avenue Camps located on the field slopes behind the new town and All Saints Church.

"Soldiers have been arriving for two days now," said Jean as the nurses queued for their food in the canteen.

"There are lots of ships collecting too. I noticed them today out on the loch as we talked with Barry," Dorothy added, carrying the tray with their mugs of tea.

"One of the casualties that arrived on the ward last night said that Mussolini had been rescued by the Germans and sent back to Italy to lead the Fascists and support the Germans," continued Mary, "and the allies fighting in Italy are beginning to win."

"Well, I don't understand it," said Dorothy. "The Italians surrendered last month while Mussolini was captured and have now declared war against Germany. So if he has been rescued and sent back to Italy to help the Germans, that must mean the Italians are fighting both the Allies and the Germans at the same time."

"That does sound strange, don't you think?" queried Jean.

"Maybe that's why all these soldiers are here," concluded Dorothy.

"To go to Italy, you mean," stated Jean, stirring her tea.

"We could find out tonight. There will be lots of soldiers out, and there is always someone who has an idea of what's happening," suggested Mary. "What's Barry's friend like, Dorothy? Is he tall?" she continued, changing the conversation and thinking of their arranged meeting for later that evening. "I hope they come."

The nurses finished their meal and returned to Maltland to get ready for their evening. Mary and Jean converged on Dorothy's room for the privacy that was not possible in their dormitory. Sister Penrose, who also shared the room with Dorothy, returned from her day shift on the ward to further congest the small bedroom. Continuous and excited conversation rallied between the buildup of activity at the training centre, anticipation of the night ahead, and news of what was happening in the hospital.

"Why don't you come with us for the evening?" Dorothy asked Sister Penrose.

"Thank you, Dorothy, but I have arranged to go to the cinema this evening," replied Sister Penrose.

"Do you mind if I came to the cinema with you, Ruth?" asked Jean.

"Not at all," replied Ruth. "I am only going with a sister from theatre."

"Jean, we have arranged to go to the George and meet those two soldiers," exclaimed Mary.

"Yes! Two soldiers and you and Dorothy," Jean replied. "I would sooner go to the cinema, if that's all right."

"There will be other soldiers there," Mary answered, trying to encourage Jean to stay with their arrangement. "It won't be the same without you coming—"

"Jean, you go to the cinema if you wish, Mary and I can go and meet Barry and his friend, as we have said we would go," Dorothy interrupted, trying to resolve the situation. "We can all meet later in the NAAFI after the cinema has finished."

"We could all walk together back through the camp. It will be dark then, and I don't like to walk alone in the dark," Ruth added in the hope of gaining more support and company for her return from the cinema.

Together the nurses departed for their evening. Dorothy and Mary continued on past the NAAFI after leaving Jean, Ruth, and her friend from theatre in the growing queue of soldiers and sailors outside the small cinema. They cut through the back of town toward the George and the square round the parish church. Pockets of soldiers and sailors littered the square, talking, smoking, as if waiting for something to happen but not knowing what or when.

A mass of boisterous uniforms engulfed the pavement outside the hotel.

"Gosh, Mary, all these people, how will we find them?" Dorothy asked, surprised by the amount of soldiers congregating.

"Hello, Miss. You're Dorothy, aren't you?" asked a young soldier standing at the hotel doorway as the two nurses arrived at the George.

Dorothy stopped and looked at the young soldier, surprised at him calling her by name.

"I'm Barry's friend, Norman. We travelled together on the train from London," continued the soldier, trying to introduce himself.

"Oh, hello," replied Dorothy, still struggling to recognise the young soldier. "Where's Barry?"

"He can't make it, and he asked me to come and apologise," said Norman apologetically.

"Why can't he come?" Mary quickly enquired.

"He told me not to say other than he's sorry and hopes he can see you on another occasion," the young soldier replied uncomfortably, looking at Dorothy. "He really fancies you, miss, and is disappointed that he can't come."

"Well, I find it strange," said Dorothy, "especially as he asked only a few hours ago if we could meet."

Mary could see Dorothy was disappointed and could not quite comprehend the situation. "Is there something you're not telling us?" she asked.

Norman paused thoughtfully for a moment before beginning to explain.

"He's in jankers, miss, but don't let him know I told you," said Norman.

"In prison!" exclaimed Mary. "What for?"

"What has happened?" enquired Dorothy. "What has he done?"

"He said he met you this afternoon when he was on exercise—" began the soldier.

"Yes, he spoke with us and asked to meet tonight. That's why we're here," interrupted Dorothy.

"I know, but he first spoke to you when he was on exercise with his platoon and his lieutenant caught him," Norman continued.

"I said his lieutenant wasn't very happy," Mary commented.

"He has been charged for putting the platoon in danger and has got two days in jankers for it," Norman stated.

"But that's silly," replied Mary. "What danger was there saying hello?"

"That's not how the lieutenant saw it," sighed the young soldier as he completed his explanation.

"Where is he? Where is the prison?" Dorothy enquired.

"It's just round the corner. Here, come and look," Norman answered, beginning to walk toward the corner of the square, beckoning Dorothy and Mary to follow.

The prison, a large and imposing red-and-grey-stoned building, nestled amongst the whitewashed town at the end of the square facing the parish church, its high, surrounding wall backing onto the shore of Loch Fyne. Dorothy looked at the prison; its dark shadow outlined against the dusk sky of evening. She felt sorry for Barry, locked away for wanting to be remembered.

"Do you think we could see him?" Dorothy enquired, still staring at the prison.

"I don't think so," replied Norman. "It's not allowed."

"Under the circumstances, Norman, I have to accept Barry's apology this time. Tell him, but he had better not do this again. He must be more careful," Dorothy commented while beginning to smile.

"Dorothy!" exclaimed Mary. "It's not his fault, he—"

"The crazy boy, I hope he's all right," concluded Dorothy, not listening to Mary's comment and looking back at the daunting prison. "Tell him I will see him when he comes out please Norman."

"He'll like that, miss. He was very angry. About not being able to come tonight, I mean," replied Norman.

"Well, it can't be helped now," said Dorothy.

"Can I buy you both a drink?" Norman asked.

"Oh, that will be nice, thank you," said Mary, smiling wide-eyed at Dorothy. She held onto Norman's arm as if making a claim and pulling him back toward the hotel.

Returning to the George, Norman pushed his way through the rowdy soldiers and sailors packed at the bar while Dorothy and Mary waited by the doorway. The landlord apologised for not having a glass in which to serve their drinks, and Norman returned empty-handed to explain.

"You need to bring your own jar if you want to drink here," interrupted a soldier standing close by, listening to Norman's explanation.

"What do you mean, 'your own jar'?" quizzed Mary thoughtfully.

"There are so many men here that the bar hasn't enough glasses to serve us, so you need to bring your own glass or a jam jar or go thirsty," replied the soldier, smiling and taking a sip of beer from his own jar. "You might try round the corner at the Argyll. The officers drink there and they never go short of anything."

"Aye, thank you," replied Norman, looking at the two nurses and shrugging his shoulders as if to say he was sorry.

"Never mind. You can walk us to the NAAFI, Norman, and we'll all have a cup of tea," Mary offered, trying to salvage something from the evening.

The following morning the three nurses returned to duty.

Matron's early inspection spurred their sleepy momentum onto the ward and focused their attention to the new arrivals brought in from the front on the last night before their free time. The casualty ward became busy as the day progressed. Three soldiers were admitted from the exercise fields with broken limbs, two of the arrivals from the front had to be prepared for further surgery, and Dorothy had to take over patients' reports left by Sister Penrose, who was now enjoying her day of free time.

Mary chatted all morning as she assisted Nurse Lawrence, informing her of Barry's misfortune, how nice his friend Norman was, and that she had arranged to meet him again when Barry was out of prison.

Dorothy worked in the ward office trying to concentrate on the patient reports but was interrupted with niggling routine questions and casual visits by sisters from other less busy wards. She put her pen down and sighed as she thought about Barry locked away in his prison cell. She hadn't paid too much attention to him during the train journey but was aware he had been looking at her during conversations in the compartment. She smiled as she thought how nice it was of him to say hello, even though it got him into trouble.

Leaving the office for a break from paperwork, Dorothy went onto the ward to check that all was well. She found Jean and Mary chatting with a patient as they made his bed more comfortable and removed his bedpan.

"No problems, Nurse Lawrence?" asked Dorothy, half smiling at the threesome.

"No, ma'am," replied Jean, maintaining the formal etiquette Matron expected on the wards as she positioned the puffed pillows back behind the patient.

"We need some laundry returning, ma'am," Nurse Campbell informed. "We are getting low on bedsheets."

"I'll see to it, thank you," said Sister Wainwright as she turned and headed back toward her office.

"I could do with some medicinal whiskey, Sister," called the patient as he laughed with his two attending nurses.

"That medicine is kept out of reach. You have to be well enough to go for that type of medicine yourself," Dorothy replied over her shoulder.

Before Dorothy could return to the office, Matron entered the ward and waited for Dorothy to approach.

"Could I have a word, Sister?" Matron requested quietly.

"Yes, ma'am," replied Sister Wainwright as they entered the small office.

Dorothy stood by her desk as Matron pushed the door to.

"We have a small annex at HMS Quebec that requires another sister, and Senior Sister Waldron, who is in command there, has asked for you, Sister Wainwright," Matron began as she turned to face Dorothy. "You have some naval understanding, I believe. You nursed in Bath naval headquarters, and as it is mainly the navy over there, Waldron believes you would be suitable."

"Yes, thank you, ma'am," replied Dorothy, realising she had no alternative and was purely being informed.

"I'll arrange for transfer tomorrow, Wainwright. You'll like it there. It's a small hospital annex by the loch. You'll also billet there. They have a small hut accommodation. The Hen House, I believe the sailors call it," said Matron with a bemused expression appearing as she finished speaking.

"Thank you, ma'am," repeated Dorothy. "Will I remain there, ma'am?"

"Who can tell under these circumstances? We all have to do what is required. There is no allowance for preferences, Sister Wainwright," the matron answered thoughtfully.

"It's not a preference, ma'am. I would just like to know if it is temporary," Dorothy asked.

Matron stretched out her arm and arced her open palm round the office to indicate the whole of the hospital. "I hope all this is temporary, Sister. Nursing is a wonderful commitment, but the consequences of war are unnecessary and sometimes unfortunately become permanent for those who we must care for during these times."

"Yes, ma'am," replied Dorothy, realising she was witnessing a softer side of Matron. "I'll pack my things and be ready in the morning, ma'am."

"Soldiers or sailors, Sister, they are still our boys and need to be cared for," concluded the matron, returning to her normal authoritarian composure. "Report to my office o-seven-hundred, and I'll have you transported to Quebec first thing."

"Yes, ma'am," answered Dorothy as the matron turned and marched out of the office.

Dorothy sat behind her desk, leaning back into the chair, staring blankly into the room. She was just becoming familiar and settled at the hospital and now had to transfer to another ward away from her friends. The matron was right; how could anything be permanent during a war? She thought long and hard about what was going on around her and what she should do to learn to be accommodating. Her life was not hers for the moment; it belonged to the Queen Alexandra Nursing Regiment for her to contribute her bit to the war.

The evening was spent in her room chatting with Sister Penrose, Mary, and Jean, while she packed her few belongings and uniforms. They promised to keep in touch with each other as best they could, realising that they may not know where any of them may go or how much longer the war would last. Dorothy asked Mary to take her apology to Barry and the hope that maybe they would meet again somewhere. She was not comfortable and excused herself, wanting to go for a walk and some fresh air.

The night was still as Dorothy strolled round the military base lost in her thoughts.

The next morning Dorothy knocked on the matron's office door; it was o-seven-hundred.

"Come," called Matron Murdock, already busy with her day. "Ah, Sister Wainwright," she continued as Dorothy entered the very orderly office.

"Good morning, ma'am. Reporting for transfer, ma'am," Dorothy said in a confident manor.

"Yes, transport should arrive any moment, Sister. I have your papers here," replied Matron, looking up at Sister Wainwright, surprised by the tone in her voice.

"May I speak, ma'am?" continued Dorothy.

"Yes, of course," said Matron, sitting upright, clasping her hands together on the desk in front of her and looking directly at Dorothy.

"I have been observing all the activity here on the base and in the hospital, ma'am. There are also many more ships now out in the loch and all the men who have been arriving these last few days. This is a training centre for assault landings, ma'am, and I wish to volunteer to be included and support this next mission, as I believe that is what is happening, ma'am," said Dorothy.

"You're very observant, Sister Wainwright," began the matron. "Activities are building for an invasion, you are correct there. However, you are required at HMS Quebec for the moment. I shall have to consider your gallant request. In the meantime, I would ask that you keep your observations to yourself, as there is to be no loose gossip," Matron concluded.

"Thank you, ma'am," said Dorothy, relieved.

The past few days listening to topical conversations and watching her surroundings had become irritating, as she felt she had no commitment to the war, unlike the influx of gathering troops and ships already destined for action.

The same staff car in which she arrived at the hospital collected her from almost the same spot she had alighted some two months previous. This time she was alone as the car passed through Inveraray and out along the shore of Loch Fyne. The morning twilight and typical Scottish mist combined in a murky grey drizzle over the loch. Nothing was visible apart from the road and shoreline immediately ahead, fading into the grey fog. The driver drove steadily as the road was busy with military vehicles looming out of the mist ahead, grunting past them and disappearing back into the mist.

Dorothy stared out of the window at the grey blanket over the loch. She observed a denser outline emerging from the mist, stretching out across the dark water of the loch.

"Can you see that, driver, out in the loch, in the mist?" Dorothy asked.

"It's probably the fleet, ma'am," the driver replied, not looking, concentrating on the road ahead.

"The fleet," gasped Dorothy. "You mean they are all ships?"

"They will be more visible in a moment. We are almost at HMS Quebec," said the driver, still concentrating.

The shore disappeared as the car turned away and climbed a long rise in the road and passed through the wooded countryside that lined the edge of the loch. A few minutes into the woods and the driver turned down a narrow road and stopped at a guardhouse.

"HMS Quebec, ma'am," said the driver.

The guardhouse was on higher ground, and Dorothy could see over the camp toward the assembled fleet skulking in the mist.

Dorothy spoke in amazement. "I have never seen so many ships in one place. They must stretch to the other side of the loch."

"Papers, ma'am," said the military policeman, poking his head in the window.

"Oh yes! There you are," replied Dorothy, still looking at the fleet anchored out in the mist that stretched beyond the wooden huts of the camp.

The MP disappeared into the guardhouse and returned a few moments later, handing Dorothy's papers back through the window. He didn't speak, just waved for the barrier to be lifted and for her car to proceed so that he could attend to the large truck that had pulled up behind them.

To the right of the guardhouse, in front of an open square, was a large brick cinema. The staff car followed the one-way system of the narrow roads turning left through the Nissen huts and heading down toward the loch. Blue Grey landing craft moored along a large jetty stretched out into the loch and disappeared among the merging congestion of trucks, boats, and mist. Still more landing craft could be seen on slipways running in front of workshops that followed the beachline. Trucks and boats, tanks and field guns, soldiers and sailors seemed to be everywhere in comparison to Jubilee Hall. Turning left away from the shipyard and along the line of trees that hugged the shoreline, the driver followed a quieter road through the rows of wooden huts, halting outside the hospital annex.

Dorothy collected her kit bag from the driver, said good-bye, and walked up the few steps to the entrance. As she reached the top step, Senior Sister Waldron and another nurse rushed out of the annex entrance door. An ambulance had already replaced Dorothy's departing staff car.

"Sister, quickly, come with me," Senior Sister Waldron ordered as she climbed into the ambulance.

Dorothy put her kit bag down on the steps and jumped in the ambulance alongside Waldron.

"I will have to stop meeting you and dashing you off in a vehicle," Waldron commented. "Only we have an emergency down on the jetty. A sailor loading one of the ships has been crushed and fallen into the water out in the loch; they are brining him ashore now."

"Gosh!" said Dorothy, stunned by the thought of what had happened and the suddenness of being involved.

"We can sort out formalities later, Sister Wainwright. First we have to get this sailor to the hospital at Jubilee Hall. I think he is hurt quite seriously," continued Senior Sister Waldron.

The ambulance drove along the congested jetty, blowing its horn and weaving through the obstacles of cargo crates waiting to be loaded on board the boats. Platoons of infantry soldiers were boarding landing craft, preparing for their training in assault landing on one of the beaches along the loch. A congregation of uniforms could be seen securing ropes and mooring a motor launch farther along the jetty. A khaki-uniformed corporal standing by the boat was blowing a whistle, waving for the ambulance and clearing a way for it to approach. The ambulance stopped alongside the grey navy launch now moored at the jetty.

Dorothy and Senior Sister Waldron jumped down from the ambulance and proceeded toward the boat. In their grey and scarlet uniforms and white veiled headdresses, the two nurses stood out amongst blue and khaki of the sailors and soldiers. Waldron took control of the situation, organizing the stretcher to be lowered from the boat.

The sailor had been correctly secured to the stretcher, and there was nothing more that could be done. The sailor's face was grey, his eyes glazed and dilated. Waldron asked for him to be put into the ambulance straight away. Dorothy noticed that the nurse who emerged from the hospital annex with Waldron had prepared the ambulance ready to receive the sailor. Dorothy had forgotten her in the excitement and assumed she must have travelled in the back of the ambulance but was immediately attentive when the sailor began coughing blood as he was carried toward the ambulance.

Waldron's attention was drawn to a second stretcher being lowered from the boat.

"Who is this? I was told there was only one casualty," Waldron asked, slightly surprised by the situation. "What is wrong with him?"

"He slipped and injured his ankle helping to transfer the other sailor," replied the corporal. "We're not sure if it is broken or not."

"We have to get that other sailor to hospital quickly," said Senior Sister Waldron, looking over at the ambulance. "You can bring this one to our annex and we can take a look at him there," she concluded, looking at the second casualty.

"Sister Wainwright, stay and arrange for this sailor to be transferred to our annex. I will take the ambulance to Jubilee Hall," Waldron called as the ambulance doors closed and raced away along the jetty.

Looking around, Dorothy tried to think of what she should do. Now she was in control, and the corporal looked to her for instruction for what he was to do with the injured sailor. These were new circumstances that confronted her, and she was briefly confused. It was the first hour at her new posting, and she was unfamiliar with the suddenness of being left to attend to a casualty in the field.

Dorothy instructed the corporal to commandeer the jeep parked just along the jetty, load the stretcher and the injured sailor onto the rear of the jeep, and drive them to the hospital annex. The corporal followed her order, dashing off and calling for the driver of the jeep. The jeep pulled alongside the stretcher as four soldiers lifted the injured sailor. Two soldiers climbed into the rear seats and held the stretcher in place as it rested across the jeep's side and rear rails. Dorothy got into the passenger seat, and the driver proceeded along the jetty toward the hospital annex.

A feeling of accomplishment washed over Dorothy as they drove along the busy jetty. A small smile lifted the corners of her lips and she relaxed a little. She began thinking that this must be what it would be like at the front, supporting the boys as they fought their battle. The feeling grew and fuelled her desire to be part of the preparing assault operation as the jeep stopped outside the wooden annex.

Dorothy passed her kit bag on the steps as she went to open the double doors of the hospital entrance. Her two assistants and jeep driver lifted the heavy stretcher and injured sailor off the jeep and carried him into the hospital. She had not been inside the annex before and was not sure where to direct the stretcher-bearers when a nurse opened a second set of double doors leading onto the ward.

"This way please," she requested. "We can manage from here, ma'am," she said, looking at Dorothy as the soldiers disappeared into the ward with the injured sailor.

"It's his ankle. It may be broken," replied Dorothy as she returned to the steps to collect her kit bag before entering the hospital and closing the annex doors.

The hospital was small and cosy compared to Jubilee Hall. An office and a storeroom ran across the end of the hut to the left of the entrance doors. The entrance hall separated the ward that occupied the rest of the hut to the right of the hall; toilets and a washroom were opposite the entrance.

Dorothy put her kit bag in Senior Sister Waldron's large, spacious office before entering the ward to check on the progress of the injured sailor and introduce herself to the nurses. Five beds ran down each side of the ward. The new arrival occupied the middle bed on the left of the ward where two nurses and the doctor were attending to his ankle. The jeep's driver and the two stretcher-bearers were talking to a third nurse just inside the doorway.

"They are just waiting for the casualty to have his ankle dressed, ma'am, and then they can return him to his own quarters," said the nurse, standing with the three soldiers. "His ankle is badly sprained, ma'am."

"Thank you, Nurse," replied Dorothy as she went over to check the sailor.

"How are you? Is your dressing comfortable?" Dorothy asked the sailor.

"Yes, fine, thank you, ma'am. At least it's not broken, ma'am," replied the sailor.

Dorothy joined the doctor and continued round the ward, checking on six other patients who had returned from operations at the front with bullet and shrapnel injuries. She chatted with the patients as she made adjustment to their beds or read their notes. One soldier had had his leg amputated in the field hospital before being shipped home, and another had lost his arm.

"The battlefields of war must be a lot different from this morning's incident," thought Dorothy aloud.

"Sorry, ma'am," said the patient as Dorothy tidied his bed covers.

"Oh, nothing," replied Dorothy, realising she had spoken. "Just thinking."

"You girls do a wonderful job out there," continued the patient. "The lads respect your presence and commitment. You don't have to go."

Dorothy looked at the patient with a serious expression on her face, then gave him a warm smile and replied, "We do!"

The nurses completed the ankle dressing for the injured sailor and helped him off the bed. One of the soldiers who had carried him in on the stretcher came forward and supported the sailor as he hobbled out of the ward. Dorothy followed the group of soldiers and nurses into the annex entrance hall to offer her good-bye.

"You must be Sister Wainwright," said one of the nurses as the annex doors closed behind the departing soldiers. "I'm Nurse Lindsey, this is Nurse Cooper and Nurse McGowan."

"Hello, good morning," replied Dorothy. "Is it always like this here?"

"We do have our moments," said Nurse McGowan, smiling, "but not quite like that, not when you're just arriving for the first time."

"I thought you had arranged a special welcome exercise at first, until I realised it was real," continued Dorothy.

"Senior Sister Waldron has gone to Jubilee Hall with the other casualty?" stated Nurse Lindsey.

"Yes, he was quite serious, poor chap. He started coughing blood as he was put in the ambulance," Dorothy informed the group. "Perhaps a rib has punctured his lung. He has been crushed quite badly, I believe."

"Shall I make us all a cup of tea?" enquired Nurse Cooper.

"That would be lovely, thank you," said Dorothy.

The nurses sat together in Senior Sister Waldron's office getting to know each other and enjoying their morning tea. Nurse McGowan popped to the ward to check that there were no problems with the patients and returned to the office to continue the conversation. The morning remained quiet and relaxed after the initial flurry of activity. Nurse Cooper informed Dorothy that she would be sharing the office with Senior Sister Waldron and Sister Duff, a stern disciplinarian who was currently on night duty and would share the small corner desk with Dorothy.

The welcome reception had gone on long enough, and Dorothy encouraged the nurses to return to work in order to instil that, while she may not be as formal as Sister Duff had been described, she did expect duties to be accomplished before any relaxation could be permitted. The three nurses left Dorothy alone, seated at the small desk. Everything was neat and tidy, similar to Matron's example. Patients' files were together in the tray at the top left corner of the desk, which Dorothy began to read and was still reading when Senior Sister Waldron returned.

"Welcome to HMS Quebec, Sister Wainwright," said Waldron as she entered the office.

Dorothy had heard her arrive and was already standing behind her desk anticipating her entry. "Thank you, ma'am," she replied.

"Not quite the way I anticipated your arrival sister but you performed admirably under the circumstances this morning, thank you, well done," Senior Sister Waldron commended.

"Thank you, ma'am. I was a little taken back and nervous at the time, ma'am. I was not sure if it was really happening to begin with," replied Dorothy.

"Not to worry, Sister. The sailor has broken ribs that punctured one of his lungs, a cracked pelvis, and a broken arm, but he will survive, I am pleased to say," Waldron informed Dorothy. "What was wrong with the other sailor's ankle, is he on the ward?"

"No, ma'am. The doctor inspected him. It was just a bad sprain.

Nurse Cooper attended to him, and he has gone back to his barracks, ma'am," Dorothy said, still standing behind her desk.

"Dorothy, I believe that's your Christian name, isn't it?" enquired Waldron.

"Yes, ma'am," answered Dorothy.

"Dorothy," Waldron began again, "I like to be a little less formal when we're away from other's ears, so you don't have to keep addressing me as ma'am. My name is Elizabeth. and friends call me Beth. On the surface, as you may have noticed, I am very formal in the right places and at the right times. but I am not Matron and this is not Jubilee Hall."

"No, ma'am," replied Dorothy.

"We all work together here. and I ask that you remember your position when situations require it. Especially as we have Sister Duff to tolerate and everything has to be by the book. It is so lovely when she is on night duty and we can relax a little. The patients enjoy the less-formal atmosphere also and give Sister Duff quite a hard time in return for her military manner." Elizabeth smiled.

"The other nurses have commented on her, ma'am," replied Dorothy, feeling more relaxed and comfortable with Senior Sister Waldron.

"Just be warned though, Dorothy, her desk, as you can see, is as precise as she is prim. Although I must admit my job is much easier in some ways with her here, she is very efficient," Elizabeth added.

"Thank you. I am sure we will get along," said Dorothy, trying to form a picture of Sister Duff.

"Well, let's get to work, Dorothy. Your duties while you are here…" began Senior Sister Waldron. "Oh yes, Matron informs me that you have volunteered and want to be part of this next operation."

"Yes, ma'am. I have been observing and listening to what is happening here and feel that my place is at the front," Dorothy answered. "I don't know why, maybe because that is where the war is and where I feel I'm needed, where I can be of most help. When I look at all these men doing their bit, I want to do mine too."

"Your performance this morning showed you have the right aptitude to be at the front line, Dorothy. I have said so to Matron when she spoke of you earlier," Elizabeth replied. "First you would need some training though—"

"Training!" interrupted Dorothy.

"Yes, Dorothy, landing and assault training. The operation training here is for assault landings from the sea, and you will need to be trained before you can be expected to be part of a landing operation. Establishing a beachhead is not an easy task. Look at the men on our wards; some of them are from the Sicily landings in Italy. They were met with fierce resistance there, and without the training it may not have succeeded," explained Elizabeth. "God knows what they must have gone through. Some of our nurses from here went too and are still in Italy. Being a nurse is only a part of the requirement, Dorothy."

"How silly of me! I haven't thought far enough to realise I would be involved in assault landing. I have just thought that at the front is where I want to be, but then how else would I get there?" asked Dorothy, realising what Elizabeth had just explained. "Watching the activities from Jubilee Hall, you feel separated from it all. You can see and hear it happening, but you're not really part of it," Dorothy continued. "But here, already I feel as though I am involved, if you know what I mean."

"Yes, here we are close enough to get a real taste of the preparations," replied Elizabeth, "and I know what you mean about Jubilee Hall. I thought the same when I transferred here, although my being here came about a little different to yours. How old are you, Dorothy?"

"I'm just twenty, ma'am," answered Dorothy.

"And already a sister," proclaimed Elizabeth.

"My father is a doctor and Mother is a matron in Bath's Royal Hospital, ma'am," Dorothy informed Elizabeth.

"You must have had a very influenced childhood," stated Elizabeth.

"I was a nurse from leaving school before I joined the regiment. My father wanted me to study, to go to university, but I just wanted to nurse," said Dorothy, shrugging her shoulders and smiling. "I do enjoy nursing, ma'am, and have no regrets about university."

"Do you have brothers and sisters?" Elizabeth enquired.

"Just a younger brother, Christopher. He's still at school. He'll be thirteen in January," replied Dorothy.

"Right, Dorothy, duties. I need to explain to you something of how we operate here before Sister Duff arrives. I will talk again about your request to volunteer next time I see Matron," said Elizabeth, changing the conversation.

Senior Sister Waldron showed Dorothy round while explaining her duties and the routine operation of the small annex.

The afternoon passed quietly, although Dorothy was aware of the increased activity and noise that surrounded the busy hospital.

Daylight faded into darkness, and the bustle of HMS Quebec slowed to a halt. Dorothy sat at Senior Sister Waldron's desk, finishing off a patient's report with only the desk lamp illuminating her work. She had previously tidied the small desk she was to share in the hope that it would please Sister Duff to see that her new assistant was not untidy.

Senior Sister Waldron was busy on the ward with the other nurses.

Unexpectedly, Sister Duff entered the dimly lit office. The desk lamp, tilted in such a manner, illuminated a short, stocky middle-aged woman whose square, flushed face and black, tied-back hair looked to be haloed by the white-veiled headdress of her uniform.

"Sister Duff reporting for duty, ma'am," said the stern voice standing to attention in front of Senior Sister Waldron's desk.

By contrast, the desk lamp shone down onto the desk, and only a body in a nurse's grey dress uniform was visible to Sister Duff.

Dorothy was surprised and looked up at Sister Duff, whose haloed figure was not quite in keeping with the image that had been portrayed earlier. Realising her face was not visible to Sister Duff, she permitted a small smile in response to the contrasting image before her and also at being mistaken for Senior Sister Waldron.

"I'm sorry, Sister Duff. Would you put the office light on, please?" Dorothy replied as she removed her smile and stood up behind the desk.

Sister Duff, confused by the unfamiliar voice, turned and flicked the light switch by the door.

"Hello, I'm Sister Wainwright. Sorry for the confusion, Sister," said Dorothy, now clearly visible in the brighter light.

"Yes," replied Sister Duff, her face a little more flushed. "I was expecting—"

"I'm sorry. I didn't realise the time. I should have prepared a better reception," Dorothy said, trying to ease Sister Duff's embarrassment.

"That won't be necessary, Sister, thank you," replied Sister Duff, recomposing herself and moving behind her desk. "Pleased to meet you, Sister."

"I have completed the patients' reports for today," Dorothy offered as she placed her last finished item on top of the report pile in the tray at the corner of the desk.

Sister Duff sat down, picked up the report files, placed them in front of her on the desk, and proceeded to shuffle them into order.

"I like to keep the reports in bed number order, if you don't mind, Sister," said Sister Duff.

"I'll try to remember," replied Dorothy, realising that her tidying of the desk had been over looked and accounted for nothing.

"You can find things much easier if they are orderly, Sister Wainwright," continued Sister Duff.

The office door opened, and Senior Sister Waldron entered. "Ah, Sister Duff, you have arrived. You have met Sister Wainwright," said Elizabeth, stating the obvious.

"Yes, ma'am. A little confusing to begin, but we have introduced ourselves, ma'am," replied Sister Duff, standing up behind her desk. "Will there be anything to attend to this evening, ma'am?"

"No, Sister Duff. A quiet day really, just the normal duties this evening," answered Waldron. "Sister Wainwright, you have not yet been shown your accommodation, I believe," she continued.

"No, not yet, ma'am," replied Dorothy.

"Very well. Come with me and we'll get you settled into your quarters," said Senior Sister Waldron, turning to leave the office.

"Will that be all, ma'am?" asked Sister Duff.

"Yes, Sister Duff, that will be all," Waldron replied.

"Good night. Nice to have met you," said Dorothy as she followed Waldron out of the office.

"Good night, Sister," replied Sister Duff.

Dorothy followed Elizabeth out of the hospital annex and down the steps. They crossed the small annex parking bay and over the narrow road, then up another set of steps and through the entrance door of the "Hen House," a long wooden hut located among a row of similar huts and directly opposite the annex that accommodated the quarters of the nurses attached to the small hospital of HMS Quebec.

Dorothy was shown into the end one of three bedrooms on the left of the entrance hall. Shower rooms and toilets were to the right, and opposite the entrance another door led through to the dormitory that contained beds for the nurses.

"I think you will find everything here, Dorothy. I'll leave you to settle in and see you in the morning, six o'clock," said Elizabeth, leaving the room and closing the door.

"Yes, thank you, Beth. Good night," Dorothy replied, putting her kit bag on the brown and cream striped mattress of the bed, then sat down beside it and looked round her new room.

The squeaky steel-framed bed was pushed in the corner facing the door. A small curtained window separated the bed and a tall wooden cupboard that stood in the opposite corner. There was a bare wooden table and chair pushed against the wall adjacent to the cupboard and a small red rug, left by a previous occupant, covered the plain, creaky floorboards by the bed. Brown woollen blankets, two white sheets, and a pillow lay in a neatly folded pile at the foot of the mattress.

Dorothy pulled herself together, made her squeaky bed, put her uniforms and belongings in the tall cupboard, and visited the shower room. She returned to her room and lay on her bed. Her blue-striped pyjamas, plain blue dressing gown, and long black socks were not so warm, and she climbed into the bed, pulling her blankets up under her chin. She lay looking at the dim light bulb and brown-panelled ceiling while reflecting on her day.

Assault training, all that shouting, explosions and guns firing, the noise must be deafening if I can hear it on the hospital ward. And sail-

ing in a landing craft, I wonder what that would be like? I've never been to sea. Mmm, Sister Duff! I will have to try and not upset her. Oh, that poor sailor. I wonder what happened to squash him, and Elizabeth, she is not like I imagined her to be. I wonder what Jean and Mary have been doing. Barry! He should be out of prison now. I hope he is none the worse for his ordeal. He seems to be a nice boy. Gosh, I'm hungry; I've only had breakfast today. Assault landing, I need to have my training if I am to go to the front. Maybe Elizabeth will talk with Matron. Being a nurse is only part of what is required to be involved at the front, Dorothy. The noise, the gunfire. Being a nurse is only a part, Dorothy…Dorothy.

There was knocking on her door. "Dorothy, it's gone six o'clock!" called the voice.

"Yes, coming," replied Dorothy, waking and taking a few seconds to gather her thoughts and comprehend her surroundings. "Oh bother, I'm late."

The door to Senior Sister Waldron's office was open as Dorothy approached, and Sister Duff, with a clear view through the door and into the entrance hall, watched Dorothy all the way. She gave a small knock as she entered the quiet office.

"Sorry I'm late, ma'am. My apologies," said Dorothy as she turned and faced Senior Sister Waldron.

"Thank you, Sister Wainwright," Waldron replied. "Please try to remember that you must be here on time in order to relieve Sister Duff and allow her to hand over any important information that you may need for your day's duties."

"Yes, ma'am. My apologies, Sister Duff," Dorothy repeated as she looked at Sister Duff scorning from behind her very tidy desk.

"That will be all, Sister," concluded Waldron.

"Thank you, ma'am," said Dorothy. "It won't happen again, ma'am," she added for the benefit of Sister Duff.

"Do you have anything to report, Sister?" Dorothy very politely asked Sister Duff.

"I checked the medicines cupboard. I have prepared a report and requisition here. You should replenish the stock as indicated, Sister," said Sister Duff, handing Dorothy the report.

"Yes, thank you, Sister. I will see it is attended to today," Dorothy answered as she took the folded sheet of paper.

Sister Duff stood up, put the chair back under the desk, and walked round to stand in front of Senior Sister Waldron's desk.

"Will that be all, ma'am?" said Sister Duff.

"Thank you, Sister, that will be all," replied Waldron, looking up at Sister Duff and offering a smile.

"Good morning, Sister, ma'am," said Sister Duff with a small nod of her head as she departed the office.

Dorothy walked behind Sister Duff's desk, pulled out the chair, and sat down. "I am so sorry, Elizabeth. I have never been late before for anything," she said exasperatedly.

"I understand, Dorothy, but you have made it difficult for yourself with Sister Duff," Elizabeth replied.

"Yes, I am aware of that, and that is not what I wanted," Dorothy despaired.

"It will work out, Dorothy. Sister Duff is difficult for all of us, and I cannot imagine that she prioritises whom she is difficult with. It's her nature, and we have to get along with it, myself included," said Elizabeth, trying to console Dorothy.

"Yes, ma'am. Thank you. Where do I get the medicines and dressings that Sister Duff has listed?" Dorothy asked, putting behind her the morning's misfortune and holding up the folded list given to her by Sister Duff.

"You will need to go to Jubilee Hall. See Nurse Cooper or Nurse McGowan. They are familiar with the routine. They may need to arrange laundry also," Elizabeth suggested. "Make sure I sign the requisition before you go," she concluded.

Dorothy left the office and went to the ward. She found Nurse Cooper making beds and discussed the arrangements for them to go to Jubilee Hall and collect the medical supplies.

Nurse Cooper and Dorothy sat squashed together in the front of the ambulance as it journeyed to Jubilee Hall. The low morning sun was reflecting off the water of the loch and shining directly through the windscreen, making it difficult to look out over the water as the road skirted the shoreline of the loch. While the driver watched the road, Dorothy tried to make out the dark reflections on the water farther ahead. The road cut back into the woods, away from the loch, and as the ambulance rounded a corner, the driver slowed down in preparation to stop for the armoured car blocking the long open stretch of road that lay ahead.

A loud explosion of cannon fire and flurry of smoke erupted from the tree line down by the loch as two tanks came growling out of the wood, making Dorothy and Nurse Cooper jump. The second tank fired, its shock wave ringing in the ears of the two nurses. Together they ducked their heads and shrugged their shoulders to their ears as their bodies tensed. Anticipating the tanks to fire again and through squinting eyes, they watched the charge of soldiers rush out of the trees and through the drifting smoke emitting from the two tanks. The continuous rattle and cracking of firing Tommy guns from the advancing soldiers was suddenly drowned as the ambulance shook to the deafening explosion of a third tank firing from the trees just ahead of the roadblock. The burst of smoke from the spent cartridge bellowed from the muzzle of the tank, drifted across the raising ground toward the road, and engulfed the waiting ambulance.

The white breathless smoke cleared the cab of the ambulance, and the long stretch of open road was filled with hundreds of soldiers running, shouting, guns firing as they advanced toward the woods high on the sloping field that climbed away from Loch Fyne. The tanks roared ahead over the dew-moistened grass to provide cover for the advancing infantry following in their tracks. The ambulance shook again as the passing tank thundered another shell into the trees on the higher ground above the road Dorothy and her colleagues were waiting to pass along.

Noise of aircraft engines was suddenly heard as two planes flew out of the morning sun, over the loch, and dropped a flurry of bombs into the woods where the tanks were continually firing. The long, thin brown line of advancing soldiers crossed the road and followed the tanks into the smoke and trees of the bombarded high ground.

The last soldier disappeared into the woods, leaving the road and field deserted, except for the armoured car that still blocked the way, flying a red flag from its high aerial. Morning sun glistened on the water reflecting through the trees lining the loch. Nothing moved. Dorothy could see the grey shape of landing craft resting along the beach as the gunfire erupting from the trees on the high ground fell silent and time stopped for a few moments' recovery.

Another red flag fluttering high above a second armoured car could be seen coming along the open stretch of road followed by a procession of brown canvas-covered trucks. The armoured car blocking the road against Dorothy and her colleagues reversed into the field then drove back onto the road ahead of the advancing convoy to lead it past the stationary ambulance.

A soldier appeared, protruding from the turret of the armoured car, waved to the ambulance driver, and signalled it was all clear to proceed.

Dorothy and Nurse Cooper, numb from the experience of what they had just witnessed, remained silent as the ambulance continued its journey to Jubilee Hall.

"I can attend to the supplies, Dorothy, if you want to visit friends," said Nurse Cooper as she entered through the hospital door and marched off down the corridor.

"Thank you," replied Dorothy, leaving Nurse Cooper, and headed to the casualty ward to visit Mary and Jean, only to find they were on night duty and had returned to their quarters to sleep. She entered the ward office and sat chatting with Sister Penrose about the mock exercise she had just witnessed and her encounter with Sister Duff earlier. Sister Penrose expressed her admiration toward Dorothy volunteering to commit to the war effort, that everyone thought she was very brave, and that Jean and Mary would be disappointed to know that Dorothy had visited and not to have seen her.

Dorothy returned to the entrance hall, anticipating that Nurse Cooper had collected the supplies and would be waiting. Matron saw Dorothy waiting and called her into her office.

"Sister Wainwright, I'm pleased I've caught you," said Matron as Dorothy entered. "I have your papers here for you to be transferred to the field unit accompanying the campaign that is currently undergoing exercise training. You are to report for training tomorrow. I would like you to hand these papers to Senior Sister Waldron, and she will explain in more detail."

"Oh! Thank you, ma'am," replied Dorothy, surprised, her heart suddenly drumming against her ribs. "I wasn't expecting things to be so quick, ma'am."

"The war waits for no one, Sister. You're a brave young woman, and I wish you well in your duties and a safe return home," Matron continued. "I just have to find a replacement for you at the annex now, but I'm sure Waldron can manage for a while."

"Thank you, ma'am. I'll do my best," said Dorothy as she began to comprehend the extent of Matron's instruction and the contents of the envelope.

Matron stood and walked round to Dorothy's side of the desk. She stretched out her arm and warmly shook Dorothy's hand as she handed over a brown paper envelope.

"You are one of many nurses who have left from this hospital to serve on different campaigns, and many are still there doing so. I am very proud of you, as I am of all my staff. Good luck, Sister," said Matron, walking with Dorothy back into the entrance hall, and then watched from the main doorway as Dorothy departed in the waiting ambulance.

Arriving back at the annex, Dorothy handed the brown envelope containing her transfer papers to Senior Sister Waldron, sitting behind her desk, pondering over her paperwork.

"It looks like you'll be leaving us, Dorothy," said Elizabeth, recognising the envelope being handed to her.

"I'm sorry, Elizabeth. I had no idea things would be so quick. I have only just arrived here, and you have made me feel so welcome," Dorothy replied. "I was so surprised when Matron told me."

Elizabeth remained quiet while she began to read the transfer papers.

"Well, officially, you transfer to the field unit to receive your training, which begins tomorrow. When you're not on training exercises, you're to remain here with us. You will also remain here in your quarters until you depart," Elizabeth said aloud while still reading. "So I still have my compliment of staff for a while longer," she concluded as an afterthought while looking up and forcing a smile.

"What training do I start tomorrow?" Dorothy asked.

"You should report to the field unit on the parade square in front of the cinema at o-seven-hundred. It doesn't say what exercises you will be doing," answered Elizabeth.

"Gosh, we watched them charging across a field on the way to Jubilee Hall. It was so noisy. The tanks are really frightening when they fire; not at all like the air raids and bombs I remember from the shelters in Bath. Even the ambulance shook from the blast as they fired," Dorothy said as she went and sat at her desk. "Do you think I will have to be part of that?"

"You will need to know what it is like. Dorothy. If you are posted to the support units out in the field, then what you saw today was only part of what to expect. Remember, at the real front, Gerry will also be firing back," said Elizabeth. "Would you like a cup of tea?"

"Yes, I'll make it," replied Dorothy. getting up from her desk and going to the small utility room.

"Have you been to the front, Elizabeth?" asked Dorothy as she returned with the cups of tea.

"Yes, at the beginning of the war I was in France. I was wounded while trying to recover casualties from the field; now I'm here," Elizabeth replied, taking the offered cup of tea.

"Oh, I'm sorry. I didn't know," said Dorothy, surprised.

"I am sure you will do wonderfully well, Dorothy," Elizabeth said, trying to direct the conversation away from its current topic. "What do your parents think to you being here and volunteering?"

"I've not had chance to tell them, it's all happened so quickly," Dorothy said thoughtfully. "They were sorry to see me leave when I left the hospital to join the regiment, but I'm afraid they know nothing of me going to the front. Perhaps I should write them."

"I think they would like that, and the sooner you write, the better," Elizabeth suggested. "The speed at which your transfer has come through may suggest you could not be here for much longer."

"Yes, ma'am, I will begin tonight after supper," said Dorothy as she finished her cup of tea and began tidying her desk. "First I will check the ward and see that everything is ready for Sister Duff, and I am sorry about transferring so quickly, Elizabeth. Matron did say she would find a replacement for me."

"You are my fourth replacement in as many months, Dorothy, thank you. I am sure I will have many more before the war ends at this rate," remarked Elizabeth.

Dorothy left Senior Sister Waldron to continue her paperwork in the office and went to check round the ward. The morning sunshine had long since disappeared behind grey rolling thunderclouds, and the remaining light was now fading into darkness as the first of the heavy rain began beating on the ash-felt roof of the annex. Dorothy checked the collected supply of medicines against the requisition written by Sister Duff and locked them in the store cupboard before returning to the office.

Elizabeth and Sister Duff were chatting as Dorothy entered.

"Senior Sister Waldron informs me you are transferring to the field unit, Sister," stated Sister Duff.

"Yes, Sister. I begin my training tomorrow apparently," Dorothy replied, a little perturbed at Sister Duff's lack of greeting.

"Have you managed to collect the medicine supplies I requested?" asked Sister Duff, changing the subject as if disinterested in the reply, looking directly at Dorothy with an authoritative stance before turning to sit at her desk.

"I have just checked them against your requisition and locked them in the medicine cupboard, Sister," Dorothy replied politely, placing the requisition on Sister Duff's desk. "There is fresh laundry in the store room also."

"Will that be all, Sister?" answered Sister Duff rudely.

"Other than to wish you a pleasant evening, Sister Duff, that is all," said Dorothy, offering a warm smile as she turned to leave the office. "It will all work out, ma'am," she added, glancing at Elizabeth as she departed.

Dorothy dashed through the heavy rain toward the mess hall to get her supper. The rain had stopped when she had finished her meal, and she decided to stroll along the water's edge and slipways in front of the engineering buildings that lined the shore of the loch. Compared to the tremulous shimmer of the morning, the water was black and menacing as it lapped against the hulls of the landing craft moored along the quayside.

Banging and hammering and grinding metal made by the sailors and soldiers still working in the flood-lit workshops and on the slipways as she passed among them were unheard. Her thoughts were far away in Bath with her parents and what she should tell them of her new commitment to do her bit for the war.

Rain began to fall, bringing Dorothy back to the noise and commotion of HMS Quebec's dockyard, and she walked quickly back to her room opposite the hospital annex. Removing her wet grey uniform and pulling on her dressing gown, she sat at the bare wooden table, laid out her writing pad, and began her letter to her parents as the heavy rain drummed on the roof of the wooden hut. She wrote thoughtfully long into the night before she retired to her bed.

It was just before o-six-hundred as Dorothy entered the annex office. There was no light on, and Sister Duff was also not present. Dorothy flicked the light switch as she went and sat at her shared desk. Paperwork was scattered across its worn surface, and a cold, half-empty teacup stood in the middle. Dorothy tidied the paperwork and returned the teacup to the utility room. A bemused and startled Sister Duff was sat at the desk adjusting her hair and veil when Dorothy returned.

"Sister Wainwright," croaked Sister Duff, surprised by Dorothy's appearance. "I thought you were on training exercises today."

"Not until o-seven-hundred. My duties continue here in the meantime, Sister, and I am here to relieve you from your night duty," Dorothy replied politely while observing Sister Duff's uneasy posture. "Is there anything to report, Sister?" she continued.

"No, nothing, Sister Wainwright. Everything is just fine," replied Sister Duff, still feeling ruffled by the situation and preparing to leave the office.

"I just returned the teacup to the utility room. I'm sorry if you were not expecting me today," said Dorothy as a reminder for Sister Duff.

"Yes, thank you, Sister. Have a pleasant day. Good morning, ma'am," Sister Duff flustered as she left the office, almost bumping into Senior Sister Waldron in the doorway.

"Good morning, Sister," said Elizabeth with a startled expression on her face. "What was all that?" she enquired, looking at Dorothy.

"I think it's all working out, ma'am," replied Dorothy. "Would you like a cup of tea before I leave for my training?"

✤ ✤ ✤ ✤ ✤

When Dorothy arrived at the parade square, there were already colourful groups of grey and scarlet nurses congregating with khaki-dressed ambulance orderlies and soldiers along with blue-uniformed sailors. A staff car pulled up at the edge of the square from which a sergeant and two smartly dressed lieutenants emerged and called the assembly to order and to "fall in."

One of the lieutenants explained loudly, in Pidgin English-styled commands, that the day's training would be on landing craft techniques and that while the Queen Alexandra Nurses where to be issued with and change into their new battle dress uniforms, the rest of the men were to proceed with loading ambulances and field cars onto the two landing craft being used for the exercise.

Curiously, Dorothy proceeded into the cinema entrance hall to collect her new uniform and was presented with a pair of khaki trousers, a short khaki jacket, a light khaki cotton shirt, a white armband with an emblazoned red cross, a pair of black boots, and a steel helmet. She became very disheartened when issued a grey and scarlet cord lanyard that she regarded as discrimination and degrading of her as a Queen Alexandra Nurse.

Dorothy had heard that nurses assigned on campaigns had been reissued with more convenient and practical khaki uniforms, but she was not quite prepared for the sudden loss of her distinguishing and traditional grey and scarlet uniform. Sadness passed over her as she left the cinema to return to her quarters and change her uniform.

Rain began falling, and Dorothy ran up the inclined road leading to the hospital annex and her room in the "Hen House." Her breathing was puffed as she burst into her room, put her new collection of khaki uniform on the wooden table, and sat dejected on her bed. She looked at the new uniform on the table, then round her bare wooden room and back to her khaki uniform.

She remembered her own bedroom at home in her parents'

house, the fine mahogany wardrobe and dressing table with its cushioned stool; her large brass head-framed bed with soft pillows and quilted eiderdown; the full-length curtains and drapes round her window; the warm, lush carpet against her bare feet when she kicked off her slippers.

Dorothy sighed and looked again at the pile of khaki uniform on the bare wooden table. It wasn't the Hen House bedroom that was annoying her; she was happy to accept whatever her accommodation might be. It was the new uniform that was hard to bear. She went to the washroom across the hallway and looked at herself proudly in the mirror in her grey and scarlet uniform.

"This is my uniform. I am a nurse, not a soldier," Dorothy spoke, frustrated, out loud to herself as tears filled her eyes. "How will they know who I am? How will they know I am a nurse if I'm dressed in some silly khaki trousers? I will just look like another soldier!"

Dorothy wiped her eyes and began to take off her Queen Alexandra's Nurse uniform. She carefully folded her grey dress and placed it on a shelf in the tall wooden cupboard standing in the corner. She folded her white-veiled headdress and placed it on top of her folded scarlet tippet and put them on top of her grey uniform dress already lying on the shelf. Dorothy stood and looked at her uniform for a few moments before closing the cupboard door and began dressing in her new khaki outfit.

The trousers were rough against her legs, and she pushed her large man-sized cotton shirt down each leg for protection against the course material. Dorothy found a pair of long socks and pulled them up to her knees before pulling on her black boots. She put her arm through the loop of the new grey and scarlet lanyard and pulled it up to her shoulder, fastened her tunic epaulet over the lanyard, and secured the free end to her tunic button.

"Hmm, just another soldier nurse," she said out loud.

Dorothy smiled and sniffed as she thought about Barry and remembered how lost he looked inside his oversized uniform. It was sufficient to lift her spirit. She wiped her nose and eyes, slid the white and red cross emblazoned armband up her arm, picked up her steel helmet, and headed back to the parade square to be taken to the landing craft and to commence her training.

The gathering nurses at the parade square all chorused their feelings with regards to their new uniforms, parading like fashion models or performing military marching routines and laughing at each others' comment or action.

"I actually like my new man-sized clothes. The arms can wrap round me and protect me when I'm in danger." Mary laughed, parading with her arms wrapped round herself. "Don't you think, Dorothy?"

"Mary!" exclaimed Dorothy, turning round to see her friend. "What are you doing here, and Jean too? Oh, it's lovely to see you both, but why are you here? We're all here for assault landing training," she continued as she hugged each friend excitedly.

"We heard you had spoken to Matron, so we decided to volunteer and come with you," replied Mary.

"But you shouldn't come because I have," answered Dorothy in a concerned tone.

"Sister Penrose told us after that night you went for a walk," said Jean, "and we talked about it ourselves—"

"Matron asked us if it was really what we wanted to do," Mary interrupted.

"We told her we had discussed it and that it is what we want," continued Jean.

"But it doesn't mean we will all be together," said Dorothy.

"Dorothy, I talked to Norman and Barry, and they said everyone here will be leaving soon to support the campaign in Italy, and we don't want to be left behind," Mary added.

"How do they know?" asked Dorothy.

"They don't know exactly, but everyone is talking about the Italian campaign and how important it is," replied Mary.

"Everything happening here is building up to something happening soon, and then everyone will go," Jean stated reassuringly. "Just watch!"

"But you cannot be sure we will remain together," argued Dorothy.

"We thought about that too, and we're prepared to take that chance," said Jean.

"Well, it's still lovely to see you," Dorothy said warmly.

A canvas-covered truck pulled to a squeaky stop at the parade square.

"Attention!" bellowed the sergeant as he jumped down from the stationary truck.

"What will be will be," concluded Mary.

The sergeant ordered everyone inside the rear of the truck before it headed off to the jetty and the waiting landing craft loaded with the jeeps and ambulances that would be taking part in the training exercise.

The initial excitement of sailing in the landing craft with Jean and Mary soon gave way to the physical rush of racing the ambulance ashore through the shallow waters of Loch Fyne, joining the mayhem of activity on the beach and following the thin line of advancing soldiers as they forged forward and upwards, through the shallow gradient of trees and undergrowth that lined the beach and the steeper inclines of the forest beyond. The grunting of vehicle engines, shouts and screams from charging soldiers, and smoke and explosions from cannon fire added to the mud and dirt that covered the strategically placed casualties awaiting attention from the supporting medics.

Dorothy's lungs were bursting, and her heart pounded as she rushed to attend a fallen soldier. She fumbled through her medical bag, dropping the dressing to the floor as she was distracted by soldiers running by shouting. Calling two stretcher-bearers, she gave orders for her casualty to be returned to the beach as she headed upward into the forest in search of further casualties. The confusion of the battlefield began to fade as she learned to focus her attention toward the needs of the patient she was attending. Returning to the beach with a retrieved stretcher casualty, she was suddenly aware of the silence in the forest. The assault landing exercise had concluded for the day. Her retrieved soldier reached for his cigarettes, raised himself from the stretcher, and strolled off along the beach, smoking.

Dorothy sat down exhausted.

A covered truck returned Dorothy to the parade square at HMS Quebec, and she trudged drearily along the dark roadway toward the Hen House. She was tired, hungry, and dirty and wanted to sleep more than eat or shower.

As she approached the hospital annex, she was startled by Sister Duff emerging from between the annex building and the adjacent hut, adjusting her attire and followed by a soldier fastening his tunic buttons.

"Oh! Good evening, Sister Wainwright," gasped Sister Duff as she quickly stepped backwards in an attempt to stop her companion from emerging from between the huts.

"Hello," Dorothy quietly replied as she continued her weary way home, desperate to reach her bed, paying no attention to the incident.

The following morning Dorothy woke and dressed in her familiar grey and scarlet uniform as she prepared for her normal daily duties in the annex. Looking in the mirror, she paid particular attention to putting on her white headdress and scarlet tippet, wondering how much longer she would be able to wear her distinct uniform. When she was satisfied she looked her best, she closed her bedroom door and marched across the narrow road and up the steps leading to the annex. The long night's sleep had put her in a good mood, despite her lingering aches from the previous day's strenuous exercise.

"Good morning, Sister Duff. Would you care for a cup of tea?" said Dorothy as she entered the annex office.

"Good morning, Sister. No, thank you," replied Sister Duff uncomfortably. "I need to be going."

"Is there anything to report?" continued Dorothy as she turned to leave the office and make herself a cup of tea.

"No, nothing," said Sister Duff.

Dorothy went to the utility room to make her tea and was surprised to find Sister Duff still sitting in her chair when she returned to the office.

"Are you sure you wouldn't like a cup of tea?" Dorothy enquired.

"No … no, thank you, Sister," replied Sister Duff, still sitting in her chair.

Dorothy took a sip of her tea and looked round the office for something to make comment about, unsure about Sister Duff, as this was not her normal abrupt manor.

"About last night, Sister," continued Sister Duff awkwardly. "I want to explain about last night."

"There's nothing to explain," Dorothy replied politely.

"Yes, there is," said Sister Duff, her voice softening from its normal harsh military tone.

"Perhaps a glass of water would help?" Dorothy asked warmly. "It sometimes helps, and really, there is nothing you have to explain."

"No, I'm all right, thank you." Sister Duff sighed.

Dorothy sat at Elizabeth's desk and sipped her tea. She said nothing in reply to Sister Duff, allowing her to talk when she was ready.

"I'm not normally like this," began Sister Duff in her stern military voice. "I used to be happy and enjoy life."

Sister Duff paused, sighed, and sat back in her chair.

"Last night, it's not what you think...Oh look, I'm sorry, you're right, I don't have to do this," said Sister Duff, getting out of her chair and standing behind her desk. "It's no concern of yours or anyone else," she stammered, unsure and uncomfortable with the situation and with herself.

"We all have our difficulties, Sister," said Dorothy softly.

Sister Duff sat back down.

"I don't know how to begin...and I'm afraid I won't be able to hold myself together if I start," began Sister Duff.

Dorothy smiled warmly at Sister Duff.

"I'm not normally as sharp with people as I am these days, but I don't know how to cope. My son is missing. He was reported missing in action nearly a year ago now...and my husband, if you can call him that! He's just a drunkard. I pray every day that Stewart will one day come home. We were a happy family before this war started."

"I'm sorry," said Dorothy. "Your husband, where is he? You live here on the camp."

"He's in Glasgow. He lives with his sister. He lost his leg and was discharged just before we heard about Stewart. He has shell shock, and I think the news about Stewart sent him over the top. He started drinking, and now he's just an angry drunkard," Sister Duff continued. "Before the war he worked in the shipyards on the Clyde. I nursed up until Stewart was born, and we didn't have much but we were happy."

"When you have home leave, don't you see him?" asked Dorothy.

"That's just the problem. He doesn't work; he spends all his time in the pub or on the street. We couldn't afford to keep paying the rent, so we had to move in with his sister. She's sick of him drinking away all the money. She has to work, and I send her my money to keep her house. We argue all the time when I go home and he just goes and gets drunk," said Sister Duff.

"You argue with his sister?" questioned Dorothy.

"No, with Jack, that's his name, Jack. It's not too comfortable with Rose sometimes, having to put up with him all the time. She has a go at me about him," replied Sister Duff. "I know it's not his fault he lost his leg and he doesn't cope with it. Well, listen at me going on, I've said far too much already."

"It's sometimes better to let it out, Sister," Dorothy said sympathetically.

"I keep it all to myself, bottle it all up, and I think that's what has made me like this, angry and short-tempered with people. I can't share things like other people," Sister Duff exasperated.

"It helps to share things at times like this. How are we going to get through this war if we don't all pull together and help each other?" replied Dorothy. "You're talking to me now, perhaps because of last night and you feel you should explain, but that's not important. We all need to talk sometimes."

"I know, and you're right, but it's not always easy. The man last night, he's no one important, but he's the first man to show me any affection for a long time and perhaps I've over stepped the mark," said Sister Duff, sitting back in her chair.

"You don't have to explain that to me, Sister," answered Dorothy.

"I've made such a mess of things here," said Sister Duff as her eyes began to fill with tears, "and everyone was so nice to me, really."

The outside door to the annex opened as Senior Sister Waldron arrived on duty.

"I have to go," said Sister Duff, standing and quickly marching out of the office before Elizabeth could enter.

"Are you two having difficulties again, Dorothy?" Elizabeth enquired as she entered the office.

"Far from it, actually," replied Dorothy, taking her empty tea-cup back to the utility room to defuse any further discussion about Sister Duff.

Senior Sister Waldron made no further enquiries to Dorothy's conversation with Sister Duff upon her return to the office, and routine in the annex passed quietly for the remainder of the day.

The following day Dorothy assembled early on the parade square for further training. First she embarked on a large troop ship that sailed to a rendezvous with smaller landing craft out in the loch where she practised transferring from the troop ship and onto the landing craft before repeating the beach landing and supporting the offensive attack in the forest.

The second day began in the landing craft waiting for dawn to appear in the damp, overcast sky. She was cold and tired; her day had commenced at four o'clock down on the jetty embarking back onto the landing craft. This time there was a hive of activity along the whole of the jetty; it seemed as if HMS Quebec was preparing to move out onto the waters of the loch. Landing craft lined the beach and slipways in front of the engineering sheds as soldiers and vehicles embarked over the lowered ramp at the bow of the vessels. One by one their mooring lines were cast, and with a roar of engine and swirling of dark, murky water, the landing craft edged away from the jetty and motored out into the dark morning.

Dorothy watched as the landing craft gathered in the cold morning darkness. The hum of their engines drowned the silence onboard the vessels as the soldiers waited for the allotted time.

"At least we don't have to prepare the beds for Matron's inspection," whispered Mary, leaning against the ambulance door, her arms wrapped round her waist trying to keep warm.

The dark slopes of the Scottish highland could be seen rising into the lightening sky. Suddenly the roar of engines echoed across the loch as each vessel surged forward and raced toward the shoreline before beaching on a long stretch of barren coastline.

Arriving on the beach with the second wave of vessels, Dorothy and her medical unit's task was to erect and prepare a tented field hospital among the trees lining the shore while soldiers engaged in camouflaging tanks and support vehicle located in strategic positions along the coastline, digging foxholes and other longer trenches that would establish, and support the defence of the beachhead.

A complete offensive campsite was to be established, with an operational command centre, mess, and canteen facilities for an evening meal.

Trench digging, camouflage dressing, and tent erecting continued into the cool, sunny afternoon, and as daylight gave way to evening darkness, the beachhead was finally established.

Oil lamps illuminated the field hospital; soldiers acting as casualties, one with an actual eye injury brought in during the day, occupied some of the beds. The operating theatre was set out at one end of the tent with access both from the ward area and directly from the camp.

"Gosh, I'm worn out. I didn't think we would do all that in one day," sighed Mary.

"Do you still want to volunteer and go to front?" replied Dorothy, sitting on the end of one of the beds, wiping her brow.

"It's more exciting than just being on the ward," said Mary. "At least I feel as though I'm part of the war effort."

"I should think the next time we do this we really will be," exclaimed Dorothy, "and it will probably be a lot different to today!"

"Come on, you two. They're serving super in the mess tent and I'm starving," said Jean, popping her head through the closed flap of the ward's tent entrance.

Following their supper, Dorothy, Jean, and Mary retired to their tent and crawled into their sleeping bags.

"This is my first time camping," said Jean, lying on her bed and watching the roof of the tent flap in the wind.

"Mine too." Dorothy laughed. "I nearly went once with the Guides, but I don't think it would have been like this."

"Camping, you two are crackers. For one thing, I like a comfortable bed, and this is not camping," Mary retorted, sitting up in her sleeping bag.

"Well, what is it if sleeping outside in a tent is not camping?" replied Jean.

"Oh, go to sleep," said Mary, lying down and trying to get comfortable.

Dorothy woke early and kicked her way out of her sleeping bag; it was still dark as she opened the tent entrance flap.

"Where are you going?" asked Mary.

"Sorry, did I wake you?" replied Dorothy.

"No, not really. What are you doing?" Mary asked again.

"I can't sleep. I'm going to see if I can get a cup of tea," said Dorothy hopefully.

"I'll come with you," said Mary, quickly opening her sleeping bag and following Dorothy out of the tent.

The two friends sat together in the mess tent quietly sipping their hot mugs of tea, watching the soldiers wearily arrive, only occasionally speaking as the mess tent gradually filled with chatter and breakfast aroma.

"I thought I might see Barry," Dorothy said casually, staring into the mess tent, her elbow on the table and resting her chin in the palm of her hand.

"He could be anywhere," replied Mary after a rather long pause while playing with her spoon, slowly stirring her tea round the edge of the mug.

"It was worth a try," answered Dorothy after an equally long pause while gazing at the movement of the hungry soldiers queuing at the food counter.

"Do you like him?" enquired Mary.

"I hardly know him. He sat in the same compartment coming here on the train, and apart from that brief chat at the pier the other day that's the only time I've seen him," Dorothy replied.

"He likes you," informed Mary.

"Yes, his friend Norman said so. I would like to have seen him again, to know him a little better. He seems quite nice really," said Dorothy casually, "and I've not had a real boyfriend. I suppose he's the nearest I have come to one."

"You do like him then?" said Mary, looking at Dorothy.

"It's flattering to know someone is interested in you, and yes, I do feel excited about wanting to see him," Dorothy replied, sitting up and taking a drink of her tea. "But if we leave for the front soon, it doesn't look likely I will see him," she continued before taking another sip of her tea.

"I tried to see Norman again before we started our training, but everything happened so quick I wasn't able to meet him," said Mary sadly. "I hope he doesn't think badly of me."

"Have you had other boyfriends?" Dorothy asked.

"Only one. I've had lots of dates. Just one boyfriend from school really. He was the same age as me, and then I dated an older boy…well, he seamed like a man actually. He was only twenty-one, but he was very mature, sure of himself. I lost interest in Peter after that," replied Mary, putting her spoon down on the table, sitting up on her chair and looking round the canteen at the growing numbers of soldiers.

"Gosh, Mary, and here I am not having been on a date!" said Dorothy, standing up and changing the subject. "Come on, I think we should go and get Jean or she will be late again."

The following day Dorothy returned to her duties in the annex and was surprised during the routine handover with Sister Duff to be handed a letter bearing her name, Dorothy Wainwright, scrawled across the front of the envelope. She assumed it to be further explanation from Sister Duff and became more intrigued when Sister Duff explained it had arrived the first day Dorothy was on training exercise.

"Thank you, Sister," said Dorothy, looking at the handwriting and sitting down at her desk.

She opened the envelope, removed the single sheet of folded paper, and looked immediately at the signature under the few written lines to read Barry's name.

"Good morning, Sister Wainwright," said Sister Duff as she departed from the office.

"Oh, sorry, good-bye, thank you," replied Dorothy without looking up from her letter.

Her heart raced as a wave of excitement pulsed through her glowing body.

Barry explained that he had two days of training to complete and would like to meet her on the evening after at the George in Inveraray.

Dorothy sat and pondered the letter. She tingled at the prospect of seeing Barry again and reflected on her conversation with Mary only the previous morning. She quickly realised that the letter had arrived two days previous and that Barry had written he was on two-days training and would meet her on the following evening.

"That's tonight," Dorothy alarmingly said. "Oh…gosh!"

The day passed slowly. Dorothy spent her time busying herself round the ward, completing her paperwork and trying to arrange transport to get her to the George Hotel that evening. Her activities were constantly distracted by her thoughts and excited anticipation of her date, her first proper date.

She wondered what her father might have said. Although she had boys as friends through school and working at the hospital, her father had been strict about her seeing them in any other regard, and consequently, because of her respect for him, she had never pursued an interest beyond their friendship.

However, Barry was different and one of the few men to have approached Dorothy as a stranger. He had awakened a more womanly interest toward men; after all, she was now twenty years old, and it was this new feeling that spurred her interest.

The train journey, when she first met Barry, and the fact that apart from looking at each other on regular occasions they hadn't really spoken until Mary persuaded her to approach him at the pier, passed through her mind, stirring her excitement with regard to her physical attraction toward him.

The large munitions truck, in which Dorothy had managed to gain a lift at HMS Quebec's guardhouse, pulled to a stop outside the George. Whistles erupted from the collection of soldiers drinking at the hotel doorway as they watched Dorothy climb down from the cab, high above the front wheel.

"Allow me, ma'am," said the soldier, stepping forward and holding her waist to help Dorothy down from the truck.

"Thank you, I can manage," said Dorothy as her feet touched the ground.

"No problem, ma'am," replied the soldier as Dorothy turned to face him.

"Barry!" exclaimed Dorothy.

"Hello," said Barry. "I wondered if you would come. I've been here some time already."

"I had trouble getting a ride and managed to persuade the driver as he stopped with his papers," Dorothy explained. "Though I'm not sure how I will get back."

"We can sort that later," replied Barry. "Would you like to go inside? It's warmer than out here."

They pushed their way through the soldiers and sailors drinking and chatting in the entrance hallway before finding more comfortable standing room by the large fire opposite the bar.

"I'm sorry about the last time I asked to meet you," began Barry.

"There's no need to explain. Under the circumstances, well… I felt sorry for you actually. Did you enjoy prison?" asked Dorothy through a tight smile, her forehead slightly frowning at her risky comment.

"I don't ever want to see the inside of a prison again," replied Barry, smiling. "I was so cold."

Dorothy enjoyed Barry's relaxed mood and felt as though she had known him far longer than their two previous meetings. They swapped family relationships and hometown small talk, laughed and chatted with passing acquaintances as they moved around the bar, discussed the war and their meeting on the train journey to Glasgow, each moment feeling more comfortable together.

Barry stood calmly, listening, which made Dorothy relaxed, despite him never taking his eyes from her face as she talked.

The evening passed quickly; homeland songs of frontline action and fallen comrades gave way to seasonal carols concluded by a resounding rendition of "Old Acquaintances Being Forgot" accompanied by a lone piper as the bar patronage began thinning.

"What time is it?" asked Dorothy as she noticed the growing space and few remaining people.

"Nearly nine," Barry replied.

"I must be getting back. The time has gone so quickly," Dorothy commented.

"I'm pleased you came. I have enjoyed seeing you, and it's been a smashing night," said Barry. "I wish there was more time to meet again."

"I hope so," replied Dorothy. "I would like that, but you know you're leaving, don't you?"

"Men are already leaving. There is only a day or two left now before I get my orders," said Barry.

"Where will you go, do you know?" asked Dorothy.

"I'm not sure, but everyone thinks it's Italy," Barry replied.

"Look. I have to go. Maybe there's time to meet again before you leave," Dorothy said hopefully.

"Come outside and I'll get you a ride back to your camp. We can talk outside," suggested Barry.

Together they stepped out into the cold night air. The sky was clear and full of stars, and there was an icy breeze that penetrated through their uniforms. Barry looked along Main Street toward the loch in the hope of stopping a passing vehicle for Dorothy. The street was empty.

"Oh crikey, Barry, how am I going to get back?" Dorothy exclaimed, looking along the deserted street.

"Be patient, someone will come along," said Barry confidently.

"Was it this cold in prison?" asked Dorothy.

"Colder," retorted Barry.

"I hope we can meet again," Dorothy replied.

"I'll send you a message, the same as last time," said Barry, trying to reassure Dorothy. "As soon as I know when I will be going, I'll meet you."

"What if you can't?" asked Dorothy.

"Then I'll meet you on Piccadilly Circus." Barry laughed.

"Don't be silly," said Dorothy.

"Promise," replied Barry.

"What, to meet me at Piccadilly Circus?" asked Dorothy.

"Sure! If we can't meet again here, we'll meet at Piccadilly after the war. What do you say?" suggested Barry.

Dorothy was distracted by the sound of a vehicle coming onto Main Street. She looked toward the loch to see a staff car rounding the corner before looking back at Barry.

"I promise," said Dorothy.

Barry stood in the road and flagged the car to stop. He asked the officer if he would take Dorothy back to HMS Quebec. The rear passenger door opened as Barry turned toward Dorothy.

"I'll see you in Piccadilly, for sure," said Barry with a smile.

Dorothy stepped forward and kissed Barry on the cheek then proceeded toward the open door of the waiting staff car. Before entering she returned to face Barry, threw her arms round his neck, and kissed him passionately on the lips.

"In Piccadilly then." Dorothy smiled.

ANZIO, ITALY

1944

Dorothy was unable to sleep. The confines of her small bunk hugging her slim body, the roll of the St. David as it cut its way through the gentle swell of the Mediterranean Sea, and the drone of the hospital ship's engine had become nauseating. She went on deck for the breeze of sea air, hoping she would feel better.

Hundreds of allied ships undetected on their northward course from Naples stretched out in a thin line from horizon to horizon. Barrage balloons flown from the tank landing ships drifted in the strong breeze, and allied aircraft flew high across the cloudless sky, providing air support to the convoy below. Dorothy leaned against the ship's rail; she let the wind blow her hair and the afternoon sun warm her face as she inhaled the fresh sea air and watched the blue open water glistening in the afternoon sun.

She half-smiled and sighed as she reflected over the past few days while watching the ship's white frothy bow wave roll away like beach surf breaking over the calm, passing water.

Dorothy had received her orders to join the invasion force the morning after her date with Barry and was to board the waiting troop ship the following morning in readiness for the afternoon tide. There had hardly been time to pack her things and say farewell to Elizabeth, let alone arrange one last meeting with Barry. Sister Duff surprised everyone, giving Dorothy an emotional hug as the nurses gathered on the annex ward to say good-bye.

The sudden departure for Italy gave Dorothy no time for sending Christmas greetings or wishes for her brother's birthday. She had intended to send cards, separate from her letter to her parents. This would be her brother's first birthday she had missed, and he had turned thirteen during her journey to Naples.

Matron's right, the war waits for no one, thought Dorothy as the breeze blew a tear across her cheek.

Dorothy remained in thought, leaning against the rail, watching the warm sun slowly descend toward the sea.

"Here you are," said Mary as she stood against the rail alongside Dorothy. "I've been looking everywhere. I don't feel too well with the ship rolling side to side like this."

"I felt ill lying in my bunk, that's why I came up here," Dorothy replied.

"Are you all right, Dorothy?" asked Mary. "You don't look too bright, pet."

"I'm all right, really. Just a bit homesick, I think," answered Dorothy.

"I felt the same as soon as we left Scotland, but I was fine when we arrived in Naples," said Mary, putting a comforting arm round Dorothy's waist. "I've not been this far from home before."

"I think it's because everything has happened so quickly, and I'm upset about missing Christmas and Christopher's birthday." Dorothy sighed.

"I'm afraid, Dorothy," said Mary. "I'm getting frightened."

Dorothy placed her arm round Mary's shoulder and the two friends comforted each other as they talked.

"I think we all are," replied Dorothy.

"All the preparations and talk in Inveraray, the war seemed a long way away, but there was urgency there. I wanted to be a part of it, and I wasn't afraid to come," said Mary thoughtfully. "Now that I'm here though, it doesn't seem real. Warm sunshine, nice, calm blue sea, all these ships just sailing along, we can watch the sun setting and I've never done that before. It's not how I imagined the war to be, and now I'm getting scared something's going to happen."

"What about all those wounded soldiers in Naples and the damaged buildings, Mary? That was real?" Dorothy questioned.

"I know, the buildings, they were different. We didn't have the destruction in Inveraray, but the rest, the wounded, we had the wounded. They were always coming on the wards. The ships though, loading all the tanks and trucks and soldiers everywhere, that was just the same. I wasn't scared either," Mary replied, "and this is where the war is."

"Have you seen anything of war, Mary?" asked Dorothy. "I mean air raids and the wounded after the all-clear. Have you been in an air raid?"

"No, not really," Mary replied.

"That's when you're frightened, Mary, when you can hear the bombs. All the time you wonder if one is going to hit you. Then, when the all-clear sounds and you come out of your shelter, you're not afraid anymore, but the dead and bits of body in the street, it's horrible," explained Dorothy.

"I've never been in anything like that. I see the wounded on the wards but they have been in surgery first," said Mary. "Maybe that's why it doesn't seem real."

"Perhaps you are right. We've come all this way to Italy, and nothing's happened. We haven't seen any Germans, there's been no fighting," Dorothy stated, "and here we are on this nice blue water watching the sunset."

"But I'm scared, really scared," said Mary, her eyes flooding with tears. "It's not real."

"Mary, we are heading for the war this time. I'm afraid, everyone is afraid. We will soon be at the front line. Operation Shingle will be the front line, that's what the commanding officer explained this morning," said Dorothy. "Every sailor on every one of these ships is watching for the Germans. They could see us and attack at any time. When I was at home in Bath, it was like this. Everyone went about their business. There was still the war, but we went to work and did our shopping. Then when the sirens went off for the air raids, everyone ran to the shelters. Sometimes if I was in the town, in a public shelter, you could see…everyone was afraid. No one spoke; everyone just listened to the bombs falling."

"I know what you're saying, and I can understand that, but I listened to the guns firing at Jubilee Hall when the exercises were taking place. At first it bothered me, and I tried to imagine what it must be like for real, to be there. Then I never really noticed the shooting. I just got on with my work and it never bothered me anymore," Mary explained, tears running down her cheek, her voice shaking. "Now I keep expecting something to happen and nothing is and it's scaring me. Maybe I'm going to die."

"Mary, don't think like that, you're not going to die," replied Dorothy, turning and hugging Mary close to her body. "We're here together, you, me, Jean, we're all here together and we'll stay together, whatever happens, but you're not going to die, Mary."

"Perhaps if something happens, I'll be better if there is something to distract me from this waiting," said Mary quietly into Dorothy's ear as they stood and hugged each other.

"Come on, let's go find Jean and have a cup of tea." Dorothy smiled. "It will make us feel better."

Slowly, the falling sun turned orange and red as it lowered into the sea. The coloured sky quickly gave way to dusk and darkness engulfed the ships as they continued northward.

It was after midnight, 22 January 1944, as the convoy reached its rendezvous and anchored off Cape Anzio. Davits swung out from the large troop ships and lowered assault craft into the calm Mediterranean water. Patrol boats speedily wove amongst the milling landing craft and began to assemble them into formation for their offensive on the small port of Anzio and its surrounding beaches. At precisely two o'clock, under the cover of darkness, Operation Shingle commenced with a volley of missile fire that bombarded the sleeping port and coastline.

The thin wafer of Italy divided the orange reflections in the smooth, dark water from the brilliant flashes of yellow appearing in the black Mediterranean sky. Dorothy watched, her hands covering her ears against the noise of rocket fire. The intermittent blasts from the tanks on the exercise fields in Inveraray, nor the twenty- or thirty-minute rumbling of bombs falling on Bath were comparable to the continuous barrage of fire power directed toward Anzio and the Italian coastline.

The calm ink blue water of the night lapped against the hull of the stationary hospital ship; silhouettes of navy Cruisers and Destroyers appeared in the bright flashing of launching rockets and against the burning horizon.

After ten intense minutes, the firing of thousands of rocket missiles stopped, and the sea was full of ships almost blocking her view of the distant glow of coastline as a fleet of landing craft surged toward the shore. Dorothy watched the flotilla disappear into the darkness of the sea. She listened to the silence; only the distant drone of engines echoed from the coast as the invading horde beached their craft.

"Those poor people," whispered Dorothy as she realised the full extent of what she was witnessing and felt very different from her previous training experience in assault landing on the shores of Loch Fyne.

Daybreak appeared in the sky as the second wave of assault craft prepared. The gentle swell of the sea buffeted the ships as Dorothy scrambled down the netting, draped over the side of the St. David, to board the waiting craft loaded with ambulance and field cars, their red cross emblazoned on a white circle clearly visible on the roof of the vehicles below.

Dorothy heard nothing, only the beat of her heart ringing in her ears and the roar of her breath burning in her chest as she descended the rope netting. The sea surged through the opening gap as the lift of a wave slowly separated the two boats and suspended the netting over the water like a giant spider's web. Dorothy gripped the coarse rope and tensed herself as the nurse beside her lost balance and rolled onto her outstretched arm. She watched the dark water rise and fall, waiting for the yawning gap between the boats to close. The two vessels clanged together and drifted farther apart before Dorothy could continue her descent. Her forearms tightened and ached from her iron grip on the taut net; her legs shook and trembled as the surge of water swelled into the dark opening between the two ships. Slowly the gap closed and, encouraged by the movement of others, Dorothy quickly descended to the waiting boat below.

Dorothy leaned against the wheel of an ambulance, her body shaking, her breath deep and long. She watched the flow of bodies rippling down the web of netting and scurrying amongst the array of vehicles on the craft's deck. Jean was helping Mary remove her foot from the tangle of netting, and Dorothy went to assist.

"Come on, we have to find our ambulance," panted Dorothy as she held the rough rope away from Mary's foot.

"That was scary," said Mary as she removed her foot from the web of netting.

"The boats never moved about like that on the loch," replied Jean. "I thought I was going to fall at one point."

"Thank goodness the sea was calm is all I can say," said Mary.

"Come on, this way," interrupted Dorothy as she marched off down the line of vehicles, staggering from side to side with the roll of the boat.

The landing craft motored away from the white hull of the hospital ship and bulldozed through the calm, dark water stretching out toward the pale blue of the morning sky and the black billowing smoke rising from the shell-shocked port of Anzio. Dorothy watched as the coast came closer. Harsh dunes rose from the gentle slope of the beach littered with tanks, trucks, and soldiers. Landing craft lay beached along the shoreline, visions she remembered of her Loch Fyne exercises, but there was something she thought was missing.

As the landing craft rounded the headland and entered the small port of Anzio, the projected point of the navy's missile and rocket fire became evident. Partial walls of ruined buildings stood amongst the smoking timbers, and rubble of stone and concrete strewn the roads and pathways. Houses without roofs and windows smouldered as their charred ash lifted in the morning breeze and blew across the open sea.

"We're lucky Gerry wasn't at home this time," said the driver as he climbed into the ambulance and prepared to disembark from the docked landing craft. Mary and Jean sat on the front seat squashed beside Dorothy as the ambulance rumbled over the landing ramp, onto the quayside, and drove alongside the rubble of buildings that once lined the harbour of the small shell-shocked port.

"That's what's missing," said Dorothy.

"Pardon?" queried Jean.

"There's no one fighting back," replied Dorothy. "Elizabeth said, 'The next time it will be different, Gerry will be firing back,' and that's what's missing."

Mary and Jean looked at each other and shrugged their shoulders, not grasping what Dorothy was talking about.

They drove up the hill, skirting the edge of the small Italian port, and toward the British First Division landing on Peter Beach northwest of the harbour. Soldiers scurried between the buildings as small groups of children stood with their parents, watching, comforting each other outside their wrecked homes.

The ambulance continued up the hill.

"Oh, look, look, prisoners," said Jean, pointing to a line of soldiers marching at the side of the road heading back toward the harbour, their hands on their heads. "They're the first Germans I've ever seen."

"What will they do with them?" asked Mary.

"They'll put them in a compound and then ship them away to a prison camp," said the driver. "I don't think Gerry was expecting us. Maybe we'll see more. There has been almost no resistance; there can't be many Germans here. They must all be at Monte Cassino. That's where the fierce fighting is."

"That's why we're here, isn't it, to get behind Gerry's defence?" Jean asked.

"Yes, ma'am. Now we have done that, I am sure someone will have sent word we are here," answered the driver, smiling at the achievement and then frowning at the consequence. "We had better get this field hospital set up, as they are sure to pay us a visit soon enough."

"Do you think so?" asked Mary.

"For sure. They will know we are here now, behind their defence line, and they won't want us able to attack their supply line," replied the driver, concentrating as he manoeuvred past two stationary tanks almost blocking the road.

Shells began exploding ahead of them, over the rise on the open grassland and down on the beach.

"Keep down," said the driver, guiding the field ambulance between the two tanks. "Gerry must have heard me. He's woken up to the fact we have landed."

A soldier at the side of the tanks waved the ambulance through the narrow gap. The road was badly cratered from the rockets fired earlier from the ships lying out at sea. Soldiers shovelled dirt back into the holes to keep the traffic moving. The driver threaded his way between the craters, soldiers, and heavy traffic as the ambulance bumped and rocked its way up the inclined road, winding out of the small harbour.

As they reached the top of the hill, above the headland that protected the harbour, the whole offensive of Operation Shingle lay before them. Hundreds of ships spread across the blue water of the Mediterranean Sea. Large blue grey naval Destroyers, Cruisers, and troop ships lay at anchor along with two prominent white hospital ships, their red crosses visible even from the coast. Grey barrage balloons glinting silver reflections as they caught the morning sunlight drifted above the brown sandy beaches strewn with lines of barbed wire and concrete defences. Support aircraft circled overhead in the pale morning sky, keeping enemy Luftwaffe at bay. Landing craft lined the shore, their ramps lowered to the sand as they discharged trucks, jeeps, supplies, tanks, and soldiers, while others motored between the shore and the ships, the ships and the shore, back and forth, unloading their cargo onto the beachhead and at the quayside of the captured port. Tanks and trucks, loaded with soldiers, ground their way over the grassland and through the congested streets of Anzio and Nettuno, a small town farther along the bay, as they moved to strategic defence locations. Soldiers, thousands of soldiers marched, dug, built, carried, and guarded their effort to establish the beachhead.

Dorothy's attention and that of her companions was drawn toward the sea as a mine sweeper hit a mine and exploded, sending a plume of water and thick black smoke high into the pale blue of the morning sky.

The ambulance continued and arrived at its location, west of the main road leading from Anzio toward the Alban Hills and the German supply line. Other ambulance and field cars, already assembled, made their location easy to find, and erecting of the field hospital had already begun. Dorothy, Mary, and Jean climbed from their ambulance and blended into the busy activity.

The morning sun climbed high into the cloudless sky and warmed Dorothy's back as she pulled the tent line tight against its anchor peg, securing one of the corner poles of the field hospital. Mary and Jean were busy hammering home another anchor peg, their faces flushed from the physical exertion and the warm sun.

"Phew! The last time I did this it helped keep me warm," said Jean, taking a rest from swinging the large wooden mallet.

"Undo your tunic, Jean. Look there's not a cloud in the sky. This is Italy, you know," replied Mary, already in just her shirtsleeves.

"But I can't swing this blooming hammer with my tunic flapping about," Jean answered seriously, wiping her brow with her forearm.

"Well, take it off then. You won't catch cold here. I've got mine off, and I'm just comfortable," said Mary, standing with her hands on her hips.

"Yes, you're just holding the anchor peg. I'm doing all the work swinging this great thing." Jean sighed, gesturing toward the large mallet.

"Come on, you two. My side's finished," called Dorothy.

"Here, you hammer for a while," said Jean, handing Mary the wooden mallet.

A flurry of explosions toward Anzio and Nettuno, fired from distant long-range German artillery, drew the attention of nurses and orderlies erecting the field hospital as they watched the rising black smoke lift into the sky and drift out to sea.

The heat of the day began to cool as the afternoon sun lowered toward the blue shimmering sea, emphasizing the large white circle and bold red cross as the light reflected on the top of the camouflaged field hospital. Beds, operating theatre, and medical supplies stood waiting for the arrival of casualty patients. The tents of the nurses sleeping accommodation, erected adjacent to the main ward, formed an inner courtyard.

Nurses, medical orderlies, stretcher-bearers, and corpsmen, their work complete, gathered round the canteen under the camouflage netting above the courtyard, leaning against the field cars and sitting on supply boxes or laying on the ground, relaxing and talking, making new acquaintances.

"Anyone for more tea?" called the chef above the clatter of pans as he gave orders to begin preparing an evening meal.

"You'll have to get used to camping now, Mary," said Jean jokingly. "Your comfy bed and Maltland are a long way away now."

"I will definitely have no problem sleeping tonight," Mary replied. "I am so tired. That was harder than the training exercise, especially in the sun."

"You're quiet, Dorothy," Jean commented.

"I was just thinking. I was rather upset when I was issued this khaki battle dress, but now I don't think I would have wanted to climb down the side of that ship and do all this tent building in my frock. I suppose trousers have their uses," said Dorothy. "What about you, Mary, are you feeling better now?" she continued.

"Why, what's wrong, Mary?" quizzed Jean.

"Nothing's wrong. I just felt ill on the ship, that's all," Mary answered Jean, not wanting to expand her explanation. "I'm fine, thank you, Dorothy. Now we are busy," continued Mary, smiling at her concerned friend.

Jean looked questioningly at her two friends, wondering what had been wrong and was just about to enquire further when they were interrupted by a nurse and asked to attend Matron's briefing. Jean thought to continue their conversation as they entered the tented ward of the field hospital and joined other sisters and nurses gathered amongst the two rows of beds, and she then let her curiosity subside as Matron entered the ward and stood between four doctors just inside the open entrance. A senior sister stood at the left side of the doctors, their shadowed faces difficult to see in the sunlight flooding through the tent's opening behind them.

"Well, Sisters, here we are prepared and waiting," Matron began. "I think we should count ourselves lucky to be in this position and not with our wards full already. However, I am sure we shall soon see Gerry again, so we should be prepared. Oh, I'm sorry, forgive me, for those who do not know me, I am Matron Parker. This is Major Parker. Please no assumptions; there is no relationship. Then we have Major Taylor. They are our two surgeons. Next we have Captain Sparrow and Captain Higgins, our doctors assigned to this unit. At the end we have Senior Sister Robinson. Now, where was I? Cover, we shall have twenty-four-hour cover on our wards throughout the whole of the operation, commencing right away. Senior Sister Robinson will run the field hospital and report to me. I will be down at the Marina Hospital in Anzio, which shall be used as the main evacuation center. Sister Wainwright, you will take control of the receiving ward with Sister Jones, please. Sister Tombs and Sister Nolan, the surgeons will greatly appreciate your experience in running the theatre. Senior Sister Robinson will deploy other sisters and nurses as she requires. Nurses, please give your usual support to the areas you're assigned. Your work is very important to the recovery, comfort, and welfare of our patients. There will be the normal field support by our orderlies and ambulance crews; they will assist with transportation to the evacuation center and, of course, deliver casualties from the field of battle. Now, those of you who are here for your first time, this is the real thing. You've done your training, so please remember what you have learned. Senior Sister Robinson is experienced; she has joined us from Sicily operations, as have some of our other nurses. I am sure she will be of great support to all of you. That just leaves me to wish you all good luck and thank you for your attention. Briefing dismissed."

Matron turned to address one of the doctors and Dorothy quickly seized the moment to capture Senior Sister Robinson's attention.

"Sister Robinson," Dorothy interrupted, "excuse me. I am Sister Wainwright, and I would like to make a request, ma'am. I know it's not normal, but Nurse Campbell and Nurse Lawrence, do you think they could work with me on the receiving ward? Only they volunteered to be here with me, and I would like to think that it could be possible, with your permission, ma'am."

"Do you think that wise, Sister Wainwright?" asked Senior Sister Robinson.

"I have explained that it may not be possible to remain together, ma'am, and they are prepared for that, but I thought perhaps if I asked, ma'am," said Dorothy. "They know nothing of my request, ma'am."

"Very well, Sister, on this occasion, but only while it remains possible," replied Senior Sister Robinson after a small pause for thought. "Should the need arise, there cannot be further preferences, Sister, and they may have to transfer to other areas. I would like you to attend a meeting, here in thirty minutes, to confirm assignments for the other nurses."

"Yes, ma'am, I understand. Thank you, ma'am," said Dorothy, happy with her accomplishment and dashed off to inform Mary and Jean of the news.

Dorothy found her friends lying on their beds in their tented sleeping quarters.

"Getting used to the accommodation, I see," said Dorothy as she put her head inside the tent. "Well, I have some good news from Senior Sister Robinson. She has assigned you to work on the receiving ward with me, so we shall remain together, at least for now."

"Oh, that's wonderful news," replied Jean. "Don't you think so, Mary? I knew things would work out for us."

"I don't suppose you're little discussion with a certain senior sister had anything to do with her making this decision then, Dorothy?" Mary smiled.

"I don't know what you're talking about, Mary," Dorothy answered, trying to retain composure and hide her disappointment of Mary's observation. "I was discussing the meeting I have to attend shortly."

"I think its lovely we're together. Having friends is going to help us get through all this," replied Mary. "Thank you, Dorothy. You don't have to pretend, not to us."

"I'll see you both in the morning. I do have a meeting to attend, and then I want to get some sleep while it's possible." Dorothy smiled in return as she started to leave the tent.

"Listen, listen!" said Jean.

Instantly the wail of the air raid siren drowned the drone of plane engines that Jean had heard.

"Quickly," commanded Dorothy, "this way...Find a truck or hollow ground to hide under or lie in."

"Oh gosh, we're in the war now," said Jean as she followed Dorothy out of the tent.

Mary followed her two friends out of the tent and ran to hide under a close-by ambulance. Jean turned to run back into the tent and collided into Mary.

"My helmet, I've left my helmet," said Jean.

Mary followed Dorothy and crawled under the ambulance. They lay flat on their stomachs, chins resting in the dirt, their hands holding the rims of their helmets to keep them in place. They watched other nurses and orderlies rushing and scurrying for cover as Jean emerged from the tent.

"Jean, over here! Come on, quickly," called Mary.

Jean joined Mary and Dorothy under the ambulance.

"Remember to keep your helmet with you, Jean," said Dorothy, spitting dirt from her mouth as she returned her face to the ground.

Despite Dorothy's instruction, each of the nurses watched curiously from the cover of the ambulance, waiting to hear, to see something. Thumping of distant gunfire and muffled rumbles of exploding bombs could be heard out at sea as the German aircraft began bombing the ships that were directing their anti-aircraft guns at the approaching enemy planes. Louder, closer, more thunderous explosions erupted on the beaches, followed by the roar of aircraft engine as the planes flew over the camouflaged field hospital and the protective ambulance. Bombs fell continuously along the beachhead, and planes screamed intermittently over the hiding nurses.

"Was it like this in Bath?" shouted Mary.

"We never saw the planes this close!" Dorothy shouted in return.

Suddenly three bombs landed almost simultaneously in the

grassland along the Albano Road adjacent to the field hospital. The ground shook as Dorothy pushed her chin in the dust and pulled her helmet hard down on her head. Her heart beat harder against her chest, and dust filled her nostrils as she breathed heavily into the ground.

Dorothy lay still, her face in the dirt. She breathed more shallow and slowly, not to disturb the dust, and listened. The guns had stopped firing. Only the drone of the planes' engines could be heard fading into the distance.

The siren wailed once more.

"Have they gone?" asked Jean.

"Yes, they've gone," replied Dorothy. "We can get out from under here now."

"Do you think they'll come back again?" asked Mary, crawling from under the ambulance.

"I don't know," Dorothy answered. "I've no experience of this. At home they were usually gone for some time, sometimes days, even weeks, but we're at the front line here, and I don't know what will happen. I think we should report to the ward just in case there are casualties arriving."

The all-clear siren brought a flurry of activity to the field hospital as nurses and orderlies emerged from their protective bolt-hole and returned to their previous activities. The electric generator started with a belch of black smoke from its exhaust and lit the theatre lights in readiness for the arrival of any needy casualty. Activity returned to the kitchen as the cooks continued with the evening meal.

Senior Sister Robinson was already on the ward when Dorothy, Jean, and Mary arrived. She asked Jean and Mary to check that everything was in order while the other duty nurses arrived and would then relieve them. Dorothy was asked to remain until the other sisters arrived before commencing with the planned meeting.

Early the following morning Dorothy rushed to the canteen tent for a cup of tea and toast before reporting to the receiving ward. The night had been free of any further German attack, but her sleep had been constantly disturbed by the sound of trucks maneuvering into defensive positions along the Albano Road and repeated skirmishes of gunfire from over the grassland to the west of the road. She felt tense and nervous, anticipating the siren to warn of another air raid, a nauseating feeling in her stomach that she hoped the tea and toast would relieve.

"Oh, I feel terrible," said Dorothy as she greeted Sister Jones. "My stomach is turning and I've hardly slept at all."

"I don't feel much better myself, if that's any help," replied Sister Jones. "We kept hearing fighting and shooting, anticipating the arrival of casualties, but no one came. Everything is in order for you, Sister. I have had the girls check and recheck while we have waited for something to happen. I feel worse than if I had been busy all night."

"Have you been at the front before?" Dorothy enquired.

"I was in Sicily with Senior Sister Robinson. We had lots of action there, but it was not as tense as this. I think because we were busy we never had time to think about things," replied Sister Jones.

"What's Senior Sister Robinson like? She seemed a little uncomfortable at yesterday's briefing," asked Dorothy.

"She was a sister the same as you and me. She's good to work with though. She got made up when they transferred her here," said Sister Jones. "So what she will be like as a senior sister I don't know."

"Well, you go and get yourself some well-earned breakfast, and the toast is lovely," suggested Dorothy. "I'll take over here and maybe it will take my mind off thinking the siren is going to sound."

Mary arrived just as Senior Sister Jones was leaving. They greeted each other as they passed through the ward's open flap doorway, tied back to allow air to circulate the ward. The morning was still cool. The sun rising behind the distant Alban Hills lit the sky, leaving the coastal flatland remaining in shadow.

Dorothy buttoned up the tunic of her khaki battle dress uniform against the morning chill as shells began exploding along the Albano Road and toward the field hospital.

"Quick, behind the field car," said Mary, rushing out of the receiving ward and lying down alongside the car. Dorothy followed right behind and lay down next to Mary.

The shell blasts moved away toward Anzio. Dorothy sat up and leaned back against car door.

"Where's Jean?" Dorothy asked.

"She was just finishing her breakfast. She said she would be here in a moment," replied Mary, still lying down, almost under the car.

"She will have to do better than this. I know she's always late for everything, but other nurses are arriving and I don't want Senior Sister Robinson to think Jean is treated differently," Dorothy said exasperatedly. "Perhaps you would talk quietly to her? I've put myself out on a limb requesting we remain together."

"So you did talk to Sister," replied Mary with a grin.

"You know I did. How else were we to remain working together?" Dorothy answered. "As soon as she arrives I will call everyone together and assign responsibilities, and then we can get familiar with the ward for when we are busy."

The morning passed slowly, Dorothy introduced herself to the new nurses under her command in the receiving ward and gave instruction on the triage procedure and routine, just to ensure everyone understood their roles when the time came. Nurses checked and rechecked everything was in order the same as the nurses throughout the night had done. Tea was brought over from the canteen, and a small social gathering amongst the nurses ensued.

Dorothy watched the infantry soldiers through the camouflage netting of the hospital, digging trenches and laying defensive barbed-wire barricades, their support trucks toing and froing over the grassland, providing sandbags and fence posts. The barrage balloons along the coast and flying from the ships still out at sea glinted in the cool morning sunlight. Mary brought Dorothy a cup of tea.

"Here you are, ma'am. We're just enjoying a cup of tea," said Mary as she handed Dorothy a large enameled mug. "Careful, it's quite hot."

"It's nice to see some of the nurses wearing their grey QA dresses," said Dorothy. "I feel like I should be out there digging a trench wearing these pants. I don't quite feel like a nurse at the moment."

"Did you bring your uniform with you?" Mary enquired.

"Yes, of course, it's my proper uniform," alarmed Dorothy, looking at Mary in surprise. "You don't think I would leave without it, do you?"

"I didn't mean that, Dorothy. Why don't you wear it? There are some strange uniforms put together here, if you ask me," Mary commented. "It looks like you can wear almost what you want when you look at some of the Americans. You might feel like a nurse again if you change your uniform, and it's probably cooler than these trousers."

"I think I will. I'll just check with Senior Sister Robinson first though, so that it's all right," Dorothy replied with a smile.

"Well, you look happier just at the thought of that," said Mary, taking a sip of her tea before continuing. "Gosh, I didn't think there would be this much waiting, not after yesterday."

"No, it's hard to believe there aren't any Germans here," replied Dorothy.

"Some of the nurses who have been transferred from the Sicily landings said they were busy right from landing on the beach," said Mary.

The two nurses stood quietly, watching the busy soldiers and drinking their tea.

"This is where Nero the Roman Emperor was born," said Mary quietly.

"Here, in Anzio?" retorted Dorothy.

"Yes, it was called Antium in those days, and it's also believed Nero came here when Rome was burning," Mary continued, still looking through the camouflage at the busy soldiers.

"Sometimes you surprise me, Mary," stated Dorothy, turning to look at her friend.

"Why? I thought you would know that, coming from Bath. That's a Roman city too, you know." Mary smiled.

"Oh, really? I never knew that. Actually, I thought about that when I found out we were coming to Italy. Coming from a Roman city and we are so close to Rome. Although it's a shame it is the war that has brought me here. I have so wanted to see Rome and

Florence and Venice," Dorothy replied, first laughingly and then more thoughtfully.

"You should feel quite at home here, Dorothy," said Mary.

"Yes, the destroyed houses of Anzio do remind me of Bath…in the destroyed parts," grinned Dorothy sarcastically.

"Do you think we will get to see Rome?" questioned Mary.

"It would be very nice, even under these circumstances, but I think we should be returning to our duties rather than stand gossiping all day," Dorothy replied encouragingly.

"Yes, sir, straight away, sir. I think you should put your QA uniform on, sir. You're beginning to look like a proper soldier in those trousers, sir." Mary laughed as she took Dorothy's empty mug and returned to the receiving ward.

Just before lunch the air raid siren sounded the red alert and the approach of the German Luftwaffe. Dorothy quickly ordered her staff in the receiving ward to take cover. She observed the experienced nurses were less panicked, putting on their battle bowlers, as they referred to their tin helmets, and choosing to lay prostrate between or under the beds of the ward. Dorothy got down between two beds, alongside one of the experienced transfer nurses.

"What are you doing? This is only a tent, and the beds won't give you much protection," Dorothy enquired.

"Where do you go?" replied the nurse. "The bombs and shells land everywhere, and besides, when you have patients to care for it's not always possible to get them to shelter. Sometimes they're too sick to be moved. It would probably kill them, and we can't just leave them."

"I never thought about that. This is my first experience, and it seems there is so much more to learn," replied Dorothy.

"With respect, ma'am, in two days you'll be as experienced as the rest," answered the nurse.

"I'm sorry, what's your name again?" asked Dorothy, lifting the rim of her helmet to look at the face of the nurse lying by her side.

Guns from the naval ships at anchor off the beach began to fire as the planes could be heard more distinctly.

"Nurse Williams, ma'am," replied the nurse as she lowered her face to the ground.

Dorothy followed suit, holding her battle bowler at the rim and pulling it onto her head. She listened to the noise of the air raid developing beyond the tent of the receiving ward. The concentration of gunfire was more intent than the previous raid, and the aircraft could be heard in greater force. Newly positioned guns returned fire at the planes as they flew in from the sea and over the grassland or along the beach, dispatching their bomb load and spitting bursts of cannon shells at chosen targets. Dorothy breathed more calmly as she listened, deciphering the noises of gunfire and bombs that landed and exploded all around the receiving ward. She pressed her thumbs to her ears to muffle the intensity of the blasts while retaining a grip on the rim of her helmet. Suddenly she tensed her body and held her breath as she felt the ground tremor from a bomb detonating close by. Unlike previously, the crescendo of bombs outside her retreat did not bring an end to the raid, and Dorothy found it difficult to regain her relaxed composure.

She thought about how Nurse Williams had described the ward with patients unable to move from their beds and Elizabeth's words, *"There's so much more than just being a nurse; that is just the beginning."* Her stiff body began to ache; her chin became sore from resting on the ground as the planes relentlessly attacked the beachhead.

Dorothy became aware of the sound of her breathing, realizing the silence, and slowly released her thumbs from her ears. The planes could be heard fading into the distant as the wail from the all-clear siren finally eliminated their drone. Dorothy released the tense position she'd been holding herself and relaxed into the ground with a relieved sigh.

Nurse Williams lifted her head and began to get up from between the beds. Dorothy followed and brushed the dust and dirt from her khaki uniform. She was surprised to see Senior Sister Robinson enter the receiving ward; the siren had barely stopped sounding.

"I think we should get prepared for our first casualties, Sister," said Senior Sister Robinson.

"Yes, ma'am. I think we are ready. We have prepared and checked all morning, ma'am," Dorothy replied.

"I believe this is your first campaign, Sister Wainwright?" enquired Senior Sister Robinson.

"Yes, ma'am," answered Dorothy, still brushing dirt from her tunic.

"I am surprised to see you shelter on the ward so soon, especially as we have no patients," Senior Sister Robinson commented.

"I was curious at Nurse Williams just lying between the beds and not going for shelter, ma'am. I lay down to question her action and then stayed there, ma'am," said Dorothy.

"She is a good nurse, Sister. I have never seen her afraid to put others' needs before her own. Her experience will help with the new girls," explained Senior Sister Robinson.

Major Taylor and Doctor Sparrow entered the receiving ward as the sound of the engine for the electric generator could be heard bursting into life outside the tent of the field hospital.

"Good afternoon, everyone," said Major Taylor as he passed along the ward to the theatre. "Let's hope this is not too serious an attack and I can return to my lunch."

"Good afternoon," responded Dorothy, stopping her pruning, her gaze drawn by the passing surgeon and his selfish comment.

"Hello, I'm Captain Sparrow. I believe we shall be seeing rather a lot of each other over the coming days," said the well-spoken doctor standing before Dorothy. "I don't believe we have met."

The doctor's tall, slim stature draped in an open white doctor's coat covering his buttoned khaki uniform; he wore brown-rimmed spectacles and greased, combed back hair that took Dorothy by surprise as she turned from observing the passing major and looked at Doctor Sparrow.

"Excuse me, please. Carry on, Sister," interrupted Senior Sister Robinson as she followed Major Taylor to the theatre.

"Hello, Dorothy," said Dorothy. "Sorry, Sister Wainwright, Doctor."

"Pleased to meet you, Sister Dorothy Wainwright," replied Doctor Sparrow, pausing and then continuing. "You have a little dirt on your chin, Sister."

"Oh, thank you," replied Dorothy, startled by the doctor's comment under such circumstance and feeling unsure where or how to wipe her chin.

"Allow me," said Doctor Sparrow, stretching out his arm and gently wiping particles of dust from Dorothy's chin with the back of his fingers.

A field ambulance pulled up outside the open entrance of the receiving ward; two orderlies quickly exited as the rear doors flew open; they pulled a stretcher and blood-covered soldier from inside the ambulance, rescuing Dorothy from her embarrassed introduction with Doctor Sparrow.

"Excuse me, Doctor," said Dorothy, using the ambulances arrival to escape the moment, brushing past Doctor Sparrow toward the ward entrance and the stretcher casualty. "Nurse Williams, Nurse Campbell, get this man to surgery as quickly as possible."

A second stretcher was being drawn from the ambulance as another field ambulance stopped alongside the first. Its rear doors opened, two soldiers climbed down from the ambulance floor, one helping the other, whose face was wrapped in white, bloodstained bandage and was unable to see.

"Get him to the doctor!" called Dorothy to the able soldier. "Jean, quickly help this man to the doctor."

Dorothy looked at the second soldier as he passed by, taken from the first ambulance, agonizing on the stretcher as the two bearers rushed him into the field hospital. Part of his thigh looked to be missing; holes across the chest and abdomen of his tunic smoldered from the hot shrapnel still embedded in his body.

A third ambulance arrived just as the first departed toward the ravaged beachhead to recover other casualties. Two further stretcher cases were removed from the back of the second field ambulance and taken straight to theatre. Soldiers arrived on foot, assisting, almost carrying their fallen comrades. Nurses accepted the wounded, injured, and dying into the receiving ward, assessing their injuries and allocating them to a treatment area. Dorothy lost count of the casualties as she blended into the busy hospital activities. Nurses attended patients lying in their beds; clean white bandages replaced blood-covered tunics as cries of pain and words of comfort passed round the receiving ward.

A resemblance of order began to appear. Patients lay occupying the rows of beds, their wounds dressed, some more serious with suspended plasma bottles connected by a thin, dangling transparent tube attached to needles inserted into their arm. Nurses comforted the patients as they attended their needs, and corpse men removed a less-fortunate body.

Dorothy saw Mary replacing a dressing to the stomach of a young soldier, his wound continually bleeding despite surgery and stitching.

"How are you coping, Sister Campbell? Everything all right?" enquired Dorothy.

"I can't get the bleeding to stop, Sister," replied Mary nervously. "Would you send the doctor over to take a look?"

"Yes, right away, Nurse," said Dorothy as she looked along the ward for the doctor.

Doctor Sparrow was attending the wreathing motions of a similarly wounded patient as Dorothy approached.

"If you could attend a patient in the same condition, when you're able, Doctor," Dorothy interrupted.

"Just as soon as I can, Nurse," answered Doctor Sparrow calmly, not looking up from the needs of his patient.

Despite the amount of blood oozing from the soldier's stomach and the number of blood-covered patients Doctor Sparrow had been attending, Dorothy noticed but a smattering of blood across the front and sleeves of his white coat.

"Thank you, Doctor," replied Dorothy as she returned to help Mary.

Doctor Sparrow appeared almost instantly at Mary's young patient's bedside.

"I so dislike losing a patient, Sister," said Doctor Sparrow. "Now, let me see what can be done for this young man," he continued, eagerly peering at the young soldier's stomach without much care for any reply from Dorothy.

Surprised by Doctor Sparrow's comment, Dorothy returned to the doctor's last patient. Jean and Nurse Williams were removing the plasma needle from the arm of the motionless body, covering it over with a clean white blanket.

"What happened?" asked Dorothy.

"He passed away, ma'am," answered Nurse Williams.

"But Doctor Sparrow, he was attending to him," Dorothy replied.

"He just died," repeated Nurse Lawrence, her voice in tremor and her eyes filled with tears as she unconsciously went through the motions of assisting Nurse Williams.

"The doctor did everything he could, ma'am. The soldier had lost a lot of blood," said Nurse Williams sympathetically. "I'm sorry, ma'am. I'll have the corpse men remove the body and prepare the bed again, ma'am."

"I've never seen anyone die before," spoke Nurse Lawrence, gazing at the soldier's motionless figure as the white blanket covered his calm, relaxed face.

Dorothy looked down the busy receiving ward at Doctor Sparrow bowed over the young soldier; how different it was in comparison to arriving earlier that morning. She wiped her forehead, removing perspiration with her forearm as she sighed and walked back down the ward to Mary and Doctor Sparrow, who were still attending the young soldier.

"There, that will see him through until we can get him to better facilities, Nurse," said Doctor Sparrow confidently to Nurse Campbell as he stood up from his patient. "Ah! Sister Wainwright," he continued with a warm smile as he turned to leave the soldier's bedside. "That seems to have taken care of things, for the time being, unless there is something more?"

"No, Doctor. We look to have coped with most things for now, thank you," replied Dorothy.

"Nonsense, Sister. You have performed wonderfully well," Doctor Sparrow commented. "Now if you will excuse me. It's nice to have met you, Sister Wainwright. You too, Nurse Campbell. I shall see you both shortly," he continued as he left the receiving ward.

"I need a drink," said Dorothy, watching the departing doctor. "Would you see if there is some tea or water you can bring from the canteen, please, Mary? Arrange what you can for someone to bring refreshment for everyone."

"Yes, ma'am, I'll see what I can do," replied Mary as she departed for the canteen.

Dorothy busied herself on the ward, organizing nurses to replenish dressings and medical supplies, checking patients and preparing for the next wave of casualties.

Long-range artillery shells began landing randomly along the beach and inland toward the field hospital and the Albano Road, causing disruption to the landing operations and ward preparations more than injury to military or medical personnel. The air raid alert primed the field hospital for further patients, as allied field artillery and naval firepower directed their attention toward the approaching fighter-bombers of the German Luftwaffe. British and American fighters supporting the invasion from air bases in southern Italy attacked the German squadrons, breaking up their attack formations and dispersing their effectiveness against the allied defence.

Mary returned to the receiving ward carrying canteens of hot tea.

"Jean, help me pass these out to everyone," Mary called out. "It looks like we're going to need them."

"Nurse Campbell, at least take some cover," insisted Dorothy, looking up from between the row of beds.

"That's the spirit, gal. We could do with a cup of tea," called one of the more-able patients propping himself up in his bed.

Jean took some of the canteens and helped pass them round the ward.

Outside the battle continued. Smoke from exploding bombs and cannon shells drifted across the grassland. A loud blast out at sea sent black smoke billowing skyward as a field ambulance stopped at the open flap entrance of the receiving ward. Stretcher-bearers rushed two more casualties into the hospital, transferred them to vacant beds, returned to their ambulance, and drove off into the drifting smoke.

"Nurse Lawrence, quickly fetch the Doc—"

"This is sooner than I anticipated. Good afternoon, every-one," greeted Doctor Sparrow, interrupting Dorothy. "There appears to be rather a lot of black smoke out at sea. I do hope everyone is all right. We meet again, Sister. How are you?"

"Thank you, Doctor, fine," replied Dorothy, bewildered by the doctor's gesticulation.

"Now, where are the new arrivals?" Doctor Sparrow asked politely.

"This way, Doctor," said Dorothy, leading the doctor to the first new patient.

"Nurse Williams, would you assist the doctor, please?" instructed Dorothy, assessing the doctor's mannerism, concluding that it may be wise to provide a nurse more familiar with the current confused surroundings.

Doctor Sparrow focused his attention to the soldier lying on the bed, dispelling the background activity with the exception of his awareness of the nurse assisting him, whom he politely provided instructions.

Suddenly the tent walls of the receiving ward bulged inwardly, and the tough canvas roof flapped and cracked. The deafening growl of an exploding bomb violently shook the plasma bottles hanging from their guideline supports running in the rippling tent roof. Dorothy's pulse rate quickened as she observed the rapid fluid movement of the receiving ward.

"Gosh, that was a close one." Mary sighed uneasily, her eyes looking at Dorothy as her tense poise relaxed.

"Get this man to surgery, please, Nurse," said Doctor Sparrow calmly before moving to the next patient.

Field ambulances began arriving at the entrance of the receiving ward, screeching planes roared low across the beachhead, blasts of cannon shell erupting fire flashes with skyward plumes of dense smoke covered the grassland surrounding Anzio, and wounded soldiers littered the field hospital. Dorothy became lost in the flurried melee of the carnage.

"The St. David, it's been hit," alarmed Mary, rushing over amidst the busy ward to inform Dorothy.

"That's a hospital ship, it can't be hit. How do you know?" Dorothy asked, startled.

"A stretcher-bearer on one of the field ambulances has seen it," replied Mary. "He said it's burning badly. That's what the black smoke is out at sea."

"He must be mistaken; they don't attack hospital ships. It is probably another ship close by," answered Dorothy anxiously. "We were on the St. David, Mary. It can't be hit."

"There's another ship helping and lots of smaller boats round it apparently," continued Mary.

"Just pray he is wrong, Mary, and see if you can find out anything more," Dorothy requested worriedly.

Dusk was setting as Sister Jones came onto the receiving ward to relieve Dorothy.

"Sister Wainwright, there you are," began Sister Jones.

"Have you heard any news about the St. David?" asked Dorothy apprehensively before Sister Jones could continue.

"Oh gosh, that's awful, Sister. It's sinking," answered Sister Jones hesitantly. "I believe the people onboard are being rescued. There are other ships helping get them off apparently."

"Oh God, how could something like that happen?" Dorothy sighed, sitting distraught on the end of one of the patient beds. "You could see it was a hospital ship, even from the shore. I saw it yesterday."

"Try to get some rest, Sister. You look exhausted," suggested Sister Jones thoughtfully. "Sometimes these things happen."

Dorothy retired to her bed thinking about the St. David, drifting in and out of sleep. Heavy rain began beating on her canvas roof, and she lay listening to the infantry advancing along the Albano Road supported by tank artillery blasting shells toward the small township of Aprillia, their new perimeter objective.

German guns rushed to defend against the allied invasion returned fire, slowing and stalling the allied offensive. The rain-soaked night was filled with blasts and flashes of gunfire, the roar of tanks forging to new offensive and support positions while field ambulance could be heard scurrying across the wet grassland, retrieving fallen infantry, and transporting them to the field hospital.

Fastening her tunic buttons and turning her collar against the rain,

Dorothy returned to the receiving ward; unable to sleep and looking to distract her thoughts, absorbing herself in the busy hospital.

Strong winds strained the guide ropes against the anchor pegs as the receiving ward flapped and bellowed under the camouflage netting. High sea and surf pounded the beach, preventing landing craft from unloading supplies and equipment. Dorothy watched soldiers sheltering in their foxholes from the pouring rain as daylight broke over the beachhead and the building German defences began shelling the allied positions.

Raiding sorties of the Luftwaffe attacked the ships and strategic land targets throughout the day while Panzer Tanks and field artillery pounded the beachhead through the night. Casualties brought to the receiving ward told stories of continuous Allied offensive thrusts and Gerry counterattacks that became the routine as steadily mounting German defence forces contained the Allied surprise and unopposed landing operation.

Reinforcements swelled, and seventy thousand allied infantry forced the enemy to retreat and extended the beachhead inland to Aprillia and Cisterna. A German army of greater strength massed its aggression along the twenty miles of occupied coastline and battled back to recover the lost ground. Days became weeks as occupied offensive and protected defensive positions yo-yoed before stagnating in ferocious bombardment of opposing and defending territories.

Supply ships carrying medic replacements returned fatigued nurses and orderlies to Naples, along with the mounting casualties. The receiving ward, relocated alongside a munitions supply dump, became more vulnerable to enemy air raids, and soldiers with minor wounds preferred their dug-out foxhole than to risk medical attention in the field hospital on what became known as hell's half acre.

Dorothy worked continuously, day and night, catnapping during quiet periods between the shelling and air raids, attending to ward supply replacements and assisting nurses with the needs of the endless flow of casualties that passed through the receiving ward.

"Nurse Campbell, would you see if there are spare plasma bottles in theatre?" asked Dorothy. "We need a replacement for this young man urgently."

"Yes, ma'am," replied Mary, disappearing to the theatre.

"Nurse, nurse!" called one of the patients. "I'm still bleeding, Nurse."

"Nurse Lawrence, this man's dressing needs to be changed when you have finished what you're doing," said Dorothy, checking the soldier's bandaging.

"Nurse Williams, would you help me with this patient, please?" requested Dorothy, moving to the soldier in the next bed.

"Nurse Goodwin will bring some plasma bottles in a moment," said Nurse Campbell, returning from theatre. "I'll prepare the patient now, Sister."

"Thank you," replied Sister Wainwright, looking up from her patient, noticing the orderlies bringing in another wounded soldier. "Nurse Williams, have the orderlies put him in the end bed, please, and would you attend to him? I can finish here now," she continued, returning to her work.

"Where would you like the plasma, Sister?" asked Nurse Goodwin.

"It's for Nurse Campbell," replied Dorothy, distracted from her patient to face Nurse Goodwin. "She is...Jenny Goodwin! How long have you been here?"

"Dorothy, well, I never expected to see you here. I arrived yesterday," said Nurse Goodwin, giving Dorothy a quick hug.

"Oh, it's so nice to see you." Dorothy smiled.

"Excuse me, Nurse," said the soldier, who lay holding the end of his bandage.

"You'll have to tell me what you have been doing," said Dorothy, returning to her patient and his bandage.

"I'm assigned to theatre. I'll come and find you when I have time and we can catch up with all the gossip," replied Jenny.

"You'll find me here most of the time," Dorothy answered, looking up from dressing the soldier's arm.

"I'm so sorry to hear about your family, Dorothy," said Nurse Goodwin sympathetically.

"Sorry?" replied Dorothy, looking directly at Nurse Goodwin. "What do you mean?"

"Your home, it was... Oh gosh, you don't know," startled Nurse Goodwin.

"What don't I know? What has happened?" asked Dorothy, her pulse racing, her chest tight, as if a steel band had been drawn tightly around her.

"Oh, I'm so sorry, Dorothy. I thought you knew," said Jenny, distraught at making her comment, stepping closer toward her old school and nursing friend.

"Jenny, what has happened? I want to know," requested Dorothy quietly, her voice crisp and firm, observing the panic on her friend's face, her eyes pooled with tears.

"Your parents' house... it took a direct hit," said Jenny, crying as she put her arms round Dorothy and hugged her close. "They told everyone at the hospital about your parents I'm sorry, Dorothy. I thought you knew. I never wanted you to find out like this."

Dorothy's eyes could not hold her tears any longer, and they streamed down her face. She sucked saliva forming in her mouth and swallowed hard as she returned Jenny's embrace.

"It was a big night raid—"

"What about Christopher?" interrupted Dorothy, closing her eyes, pushing tears down her cheeks as she anticipated Jenny's reply.

"They said they were all killed," said Jenny awkwardly. "Dorothy, I'm so sorry."

Dorothy stood motionless, embracing her friend. She stared blindly into the receiving ward. Flashes of Christmases past, her father carving turkey at the head of the large dining table, Christopher playing with his soldier round his dinner plate, her mother helping the maid place tureens of vegetables amongst the elaborately decorated crackers strewed across the table filled her thoughts.

"It's all right, Jenny. You weren't to know," said Dorothy, giving her friend a tight squeeze. "Thank you for telling me. It was nicer to hear it from a friend. You'd better take that plasma to Nurse Campbell; we have a ward full of patients to attend, Jenny."

"Are you all right, Sister Wainwright? You look troubled," enquired Doctor Sparrow.

"Yes...thank you, Doctor. I'm fine, thank you. Just greeting my old school friend," replied Dorothy, wiping her cheeks with her fingers. "This is Nurse Goodwin, Doctor. Jenny, Doctor Sparrow."

"Pleased to meet you, Nurse Goodwin, and welcome to our busy little hospital," greeted Doctor Sparrow.

"Thank you, Doctor. I'll take the plasma, Sister," said Nurse Goodwin, squeezing Dorothy's hand as she departed, "and I'll come and find you later."

"I'll be here," replied Dorothy, recomposing herself.

"Are you sure you're all right, Sister?" Doctor Sparrow repeated. "You look awfully tired."

"Yes I'm fine, really. Nurse just gave me some disturbing news. I'm fine now, thank you, Doctor," said Dorothy.

"Perhaps you should take some rest. You spend more time on the ward than I do," suggested Doctor Sparrow.

"Come now, Doctor Sparrow, we have a new patient just arrived. I think we should assist Nurse Williams with his needs before thoughts of resting, don't you agree?" replied Dorothy.

"Very well, Sister, as you wish," said Doctor Sparrow, extending his arm toward Nurse Williams, gesturing for Dorothy to proceed. "Please lead on."

The Italian sun beat down upon the brown canvas tent. Inside the air was hot and still, the light subdued. Dorothy lay on her bed, her body shaking, her face buried in her pillow, muffling her sobs. Sunlight forked through the entrance as Mary entered and sat on the edge of her friend's camp bed. She put her hand gently on Dorothy's head and softly stroked her friend's hair.

"I'm sorry about your parents," said Mary quietly. "Why didn't you say something? We're here together, Dorothy, to help each other."

"It's all right, Mary." Dorothy cried into her pillow. "I'm tired, that's all."

"We're your friends, Dorothy. It's been over a week. Nurse Goodwin has just told me what's happened...I came straight away," replied Mary caringly.

"They've all gone, Mary," said Dorothy, turning to face her friend. "Christopher, Papa, Mother, they're gone."

"I'm so sorry for you, Dorothy," whispered Mary. "You shouldn't bottle it up; it's not like you to keep it all to yourself."

"Really, I'm all right," replied Dorothy. "I've got over the worst now. It's not something I can talk about. How's Jenny? I've not seen her since she told me. She must feel awful."

"That's why I'm here. She came looking for you to see if you were all right," said Mary. "When she couldn't find you, she asked me and then told me what had happened. She's concerned for you, Dorothy. We all are."

"I know, and thank you. It's nice to know that, but I have to handle things in my own way," answered Dorothy, wiping her eyes and nose with her handkerchief. "Let's go find Jenny while it's quiet. I can tell her I'm all right and not to worry. You'll like her. We went to school together."

"Are you sure you're all right?" asked Mary.

"Yes, you said yourself it's been over a week. I've said my prayers and sent my love. They're with the Lord now, Mary," said Dorothy reassuringly.

Dorothy returned to the receiving ward, absorbing herself day and night in the busy activities. She watched the procession of field ambulance arriving and departing; the stress and tension on the faces of the nurses, doctors, and orderlies; the struggle for life against death for the stream of soldiers who passed through the ward. She listened to the stories of advance and retreat; the concerned questions from the shell-shocked and fatigued soldiers of their comrades whereabouts; the murmur of agonizing cries and words of reassuring comfort.

✦ ✦ ✦ ✦ ✦

Weeks passed. Dorothy observed the field hospital become stretched to capacity as the relentless bombing and German artillery pounded the beachhead, increasing the number of casualties. Holes appeared in the canvas walls as shrapnel ripped into the ward, causing further injury to the helpless patients and unsuspecting nurses.

"Sister Wainwright, would you assist here, please?" called Doctor Sparrow.

"Yes, Doctor. What would you like me to do?" asked Dorothy, standing beside Doctor Sparrow alongside a young soldier's bed.

"When I remove this dressing, I would like you to hold this young man's wound together. Perhaps if I apply more stitches it should stop the bleeding," requested Doctor Sparrow.

"Yes, Doctor," replied Dorothy. "Is there a replacement dressing ready?"

"Can we first apply the stitching, Sister? This young man cannot have too much blood left," insisted Doctor Sparrow. "He is almost blue now."

"When you're ready, Doctor," said Dorothy.

"Thank you, Sister," replied Doctor Sparrow.

Quickly and skillfully, Doctor Sparrow guided his scissors through the blood-soaked dressing applied to the soldier's thigh, baring his ragged, burned wound where hot shrapnel had ripped into his flesh.

"Just as I thought, Sister. Apply pressure either side of this bleeding," said Doctor Sparrow. "Carefully, there is hardly sufficient skin to hold the stitching there is."

"Yes, Doctor," answered Dorothy, staring at the boy's torn and tender thigh.

The young soldier groaned and winced as Dorothy carefully nipped his flesh together.

"Yes, beautifully done, Sister," praised Doctor Sparrow. "Now just hold steady while I get a quick stitch in ... and another. There, you'll soon be as good as new, young man."

"Nurse Lawrence, would you finish off here? Clean his leg and apply a new dressing, please. Oh, and have some plasma ready. He will soon need a replacement," requested Dorothy as she washed her hands together with Doctor Sparrow in a large bowl of red water.

"Yes, right away, Sister," answered Jean.

Dorothy paused from washing her hands as she noticed Doctor Sparrow had stopped washing and his hands were trembling in the blood-coloured water, his complexion pale and forehead beaded with perspiration.

"You don't look too well, Doctor. Are you all right, sir?" said Dorothy, becoming concerned.

"Would you get me out of here?" said Doctor Sparrow nervously. "Please, take my arm, walk me outside."

Dorothy dabbed her hands on her uniform and reached for a towel to dry Doctor Sparrow's hands.

"Quickly please, Sister," croaked Doctor Sparrow.

"Yes, of course, Doctor," answered Dorothy, holding Doctor Sparrow's tense and trembling arm as she walked him into the fresh air of the camouflaged courtyard outside the receiving ward.

Doctor Sparrow breathed slowly and deeply as he loosened his collar with his free hand. "Would you mind walking with me to my quarters, Sister? I'm not sure I could make it alone."

"Should I get an orderly to help you, sir?" suggested Dorothy.

"I just need to sit down…away from that awful ward for ten minutes," replied Doctor Sparrow, his arm now shaking more severely and his steps becoming unsteady.

Dorothy helped him to his large camouflaged tent and sat him on the edge of his bed.

"Can I get you some water?" enquired Dorothy.

"Thank you, that would be nice," replied Doctor Sparrow, breathing heavily. "Sometimes…I just have to get away…I hope I haven't distressed you, Sister."

"You always look so composed, Doctor. You have startled me a little," said Dorothy, handing Doctor Sparrow a cup of water, watching as he first took the cup with one hand and then transferred it to his lips with both trembling hands.

"It's all show, my dear," replied, Doctor Sparrow finishing the water.

"I'm not sure what you mean. Are you sure you're all right, sir?" asked Dorothy, remaining anxious.

"Thank you…I will be fine in a moment," said Doctor Sparrow.

"But you are always on the ward and you are a very good doctor," informed Dorothy. "Many of the nurses are very encouraged by your meticulous and very professional presence, sir."

"That's kind of you to say so, Sister...I enjoy being a doctor. However...the endless chain...of mutilated young men needing patching up...is beginning to make me ill. I feel more like a butcher than a doctor. If I don't hide behind this charade and force myself on to the ward...I would be sent home along with all these other poor wrecked heroes," said Doctor Sparrow slowly, regaining composure as he relaxed. "And then who would there be to put their pieces back together?"

"You once suggested that perhaps I should rest as I looked tired," replied Dorothy. "Perhaps we all need to rest, Doctor?"

"I have a duty to perform, Dorothy. Excuse me, it is all right to call you by your Christian name?" enquired Doctor Sparrow, regaining what Dorothy imagined to be more himself.

"Of course, Doctor," replied Dorothy. "I'm surprised you have remembered."

"We all have duties to perform, Dorothy. Mine is to put the pieces back together after these young boys have done theirs," continued Doctor Sparrow with a long sigh. "To forgo some short rest is but a mere sacrifice in comparison to the eternal rest of some."

"That's why I volunteered to come here, Doctor," informed Dorothy.

"You volunteered to be here?" quizzed Doctor Sparrow.

"I thought this was the place I could be of most use, the front line," replied Dorothy.

"A very chivalric gesture for such a young woman," said Doctor Sparrow.

"Not really, Doctor. There are lots of young nurses here who have chosen to be here," answered Dorothy. "It's for our country, to do our bit and help our boys."

"To do our bit...hmm...I suppose you are right, Dorothy," sighed Doctor Sparrow slowly, looking down at the floor, still trembling slightly. "Is there some more water?"

The wail of the air raid siren interrupted Dorothy as she poured water into the enameled cup.

"Here you are, sir," said Dorothy, handing Doctor Sparrow his water. "I had better get back to the ward. Will you be all right, sir?"

"Yes, run along, Sister. I will be there in a moment," replied Doctor Sparrow.

German artillery guns followed the afternoon bombing raid by the Luftwaffe and continued to shell the retaliating allied positions along the beachhead through the night and into the early hours of the morning. Dorothy watched the nurses tend the growing flow of casualties, disregarding the continuous distant rumble of blasting shells, occasionally interrupting their concentration to duck their heads as particularly close explosions reverberated through the receiving ward.

Sunlight struck the top of the canvas field hospital; groans of pain and discomfort replaced the thunder of field guns; fatigued nurses comforted their new arrivals. Dorothy smiled at Doctor Sparrow busy in the morning light, hiding his anguish behind his courageous charade.

"Nurse Williams, would you see if Chef could provide some canteens of tea? It's been a long night for everyone," said Dorothy.

"Good morning, Sister," said Sister Jones as she entered the receiving ward. "How is everything? You all look exhausted."

"Morning, Sister. We're coping," replied Dorothy, "but I'm afraid your young man who lost his legs passed away, and we lost the two bad stomach patients."

"Oh dear." Sister Jones sighed. "I thought he would make it. He seemed to be over the worst and was so determined when I left. Have there been any more new cases?"

"Thankfully, no. It's been quiet for a few hours now. I have sent for fresh supplies, they should arrive soon," said Dorothy, "and I have just sent for tea, so let's hope Gerry will be kind enough to give us time to enjoy it. Have you managed to get some sleep, Sister?"

"I've had a few hours, thankfully, while the guns have been quiet," replied Sister Jones, "but I think we lost a lot of ground last night. Our defence line looks awfully close this morning, and there's lots of movement repositioning."

"I've been listening to all the noise. I thought maybe we were advancing and sending supplies forward," said Dorothy.

"Not this time, Sister. Gerry seems to have the upper hand at the moment," answered Sister Jones.

"I hope we can beat them into retreat soon. We've been here nearly three months now," Dorothy commented.

"Perhaps you should get some rest while it's quiet, Sister," replied Sister Jones. "Who knows how long we could be here?"

"You're right; I'll just enjoy a cup of tea first. Oh, and keep an eye on this poor man. He seems to be in a lot of pain, and Doctor is concerned, as his internal injuries are close to his heart," said Dorothy, indicating to a soldier with his chest heavily bandaged and missing his left arm.

Dorothy left Sister Jones to manage the receiving ward and walked wearily with Jean and Mary back to their beds. The early morning sun disappeared behind drifting, darkening clouds. Conversation was almost nonexistent, and Jean carried her cold cup of tea, slurping occasional mouthfuls.

"Try and get some sleep. I'll see you both later," said Dorothy as she left her two friends and trudged slowly toward her tent.

"Good night, or is it good morning? Never mind, see you later," replied Mary.

"Sweet dreams," added Jean, following Mary through the line of green canvas tents.

Dorothy lay listening to the heavy rain beating on her flapping canvas tent, blowing in the showery wind, while faint rumbles of distant thunder mimicked echoes of blasting shells. The morning shower would at least stall the arrival of the Luftwaffe and provide some time for rest thought Dorothy as she fell into a deep sleep.

Exploding bombs falling on the beachhead roused Dorothy from her sleep. She instantly grabbed her battle bowler and ran to the receiving ward, her eyes squinting against the bright afternoon sunlight. Bomb smoke engulfed tanks and sheltering infantry men as it drifted over the grassland, and the field hospital generator was growling away, providing electricity for the surgeons still busy operating on desperate soldiers. Sister Jones had sent patients that could be transported to the evacuation hospital in Anzio, creating available beds for new arrivals.

A field ambulance pulled alongside Dorothy at the ward

entrance. The rear doors opened and two stretcher-bearers pulled out a badly maimed soldier.

"Put him here on this bed," said Dorothy, taking control.

The soldier screamed in pain as the stretcher-bearers transferred him to the bed and returned to their ambulance. Dorothy looked at the young soldier as she approached his bed. His blood-covered face winced and his eyes were squeezed tightly shut; his tattered ear, torn neck, and loosely connected arm oozed blood into the crisp white pillow. Still more blood soaked into the chest of his khaki uniform.

"Oh God," said Dorothy as Mary entered the ward and passed the end of the soldier's bed. "Nurse Campbell, see if theatre can take an urgent case, would you, and then give me some help here, please?"

"Yes, Sister," replied Mary, continuing along the ward toward the theatre.

Dorothy began to cut away the field dressing applied to the young soldier's shoulder. His eyes opened and he grabbed at Dorothy's arm with his free hand, knocking her scissors to the floor.

"Please, Nurse...I don't want to die...I don't want to die," cried out the soldier.

"It's all right, you're not going to die," comforted Dorothy as she bent down to retrieve her scissors.

Dorothy swallowed hard as tears began to form in her eyes. She remained kneeling on the floor as she tried to regain her composure, clutching her scissors.

Into her thoughts came the words, *"Keep your head down, pet,"* in the voice of the older kilted soldier from the train compartment on her journey to Glasgow.

A blast ripped through the receiving ward, tipping the young soldier onto Dorothy, pushing her prone on the floor as his bed flew against the bulging wall of the tent. Black smoke billowed into the ward from successive explosions as the munitions dump erupted. Dorothy coughed as she inhaled the thick smoke and pushed her face into the floor, hoping to find oxygen. An explosion blew away the center of the receiving ward, clearing the smoke, giving Dorothy a chance to cough, breathe, and spit the dirt from her mouth as beds, blankets, and plasma bottles flew through the open entrance of the receiving ward.

Dorothy lay coughing, gasping for air beneath the hospital debris as the last of the munitions detonated. The young soldier's legs lay motionless across the small of her back. Dorothy lay still, unsure of what had happened. Shouts and calls filled the open space of the ward as soldiers began to search the wreckage of the field hospital. Dorothy felt hands lifting, helping her to her feet.

"Are you all right, ma'am?" questioned the black, smoky-faced soldier holding her steady, peering into her eyes.

"Yes...I'm fine," replied Dorothy, wiping the dirt from her face. "See to the others, I'm fine."

"I think this guy's bought it," said the soldier in his American accent, looking to the soldier lying at Dorothy's feet.

"The poor boy had no chance, unfortunately," answered Dorothy quietly. "He died a few moments ago."

The American soldier left Dorothy to regain her composure and continued searching through the remains of the receiving ward. Flames from the burning munitions dump were visible through the torn, singed canvas left from the missing tent. Nurses scrambled to their feet, shocked and dazed. Dorothy looked through the silent smoke and dust, searching for Mary's face.

Panic gripped her body as she clambered through the debris toward the theatre, as she remembered asking Mary to talk to the surgeons. Losing balance, she supported herself against a soldier as he lifted a bed from the confusion strewed across the floor, revealing a white nurse's apron. Dorothy dropped to her knees, clearing away the rubble and blankets that covered the motionless body.

"Oh no...no...no," cried Dorothy as she recognized her friend. "No, not Mary...please no...no."

Dorothy hugged her lifeless friend to her chest and wiped away the dirt from her face as she cradled Mary on her lap.

"Get a doctor over here!" called the soldier standing over Dorothy and Mary.

"We're too late for that," whispered Dorothy, fighting back her tears.

Nurse Goodwin came through from theatre and took Dorothy

away from the carnage of the receiving ward. Soldiers and nurses were assembling the wounded and injured on retrieved beds and blankets in the courtyard outside the remains of the field hospital. Senior Sister Robinson was directing support vehicles and field ambulance arriving to transfer patients and medics to the evacuation hospital. Corpses lined the front of what was left of the receiving ward.

Jean, bleeding from cuts on her arms and legs, came running toward Dorothy and Nurse Goodwin.

"I'm sorry I'm late. I had to change my apron, it was so grubby. Are you all right, Dorothy?" said Jean hastily.

"Your arm, it's bleeding," commented Dorothy.

"I'm all right. The tent blew down, and I got covered with debris from the explosions," continued Jean, observing the sights before her. "Gosh, this is awful, the ward, it's nearly destroyed. Where's Mary?"

"She's with the corpses," answered Dorothy, angry and distraught.

"Where?" asked Jean.

"Nurse Campbell has been killed," said Nurse Goodwin.

"Is that true, Dorothy?" questioned Jean alarmingly.

"Come here," said Dorothy, extending her arms toward Jean, offering a gesture of refuge before explaining. "I found her…"

Jean walked briskly away toward the line of corpses, slumping to her knees at her friend's body. Dorothy followed to comfort and share their grief.

"She cannot have suffered, she must have taken the full blast," said Dorothy softly.

"Oh God, why didn't she just wait for me?" cried Jean. "We could still be together."

"Somehow she knew," said Dorothy.

"I don't know what you mean," Jean said.

"She was never afraid of what was happening around her," continued Dorothy. "She brought those canteens of tea during that air raid, not caring. Coming to the ward while the bombs were falling would never bother her."

"But that was Mary," Jean stated, wiping her eyes. "What could she know?"

"She talked on the boat coming here about being afraid of waiting, as if she knew this was going to happen," said Dorothy.

"She never said anything to me. How could she know she was going to die?" questioned Jean.

"Mary accepted it, I suppose. Maybe that's why she showed no fear," explained Dorothy slowly and thoughtfully. "She's at rest now…Her waiting is over."

Jean burst into tears and hugged Dorothy.

"Sister Wainwright," called Nurse Williams. "Quickly, it's Doctor Sparrow."

"Jenny, take care of Jean, would you, please?" asked Dorothy as she followed Nurse Williams toward the tented quarters of Doctor Sparrow.

Stretcher-bearers were just carrying Doctor Sparrow from his tent as Dorothy and Nurse Williams arrived.

"No, not Doctor Sparrow too," cried Dorothy. "He's not dead, is he?"

"No, I'm not dead," said Doctor Sparrow from his horizontal position. "Just scratched, that's all, Sister."

"It's a little more than a scratch, I'm afraid," said Sister Jones, emerging from the doctor's tent. "Shrapnel hit his tent and the doctor, Sister Wainwright. He has some nasty injuries to his arms and body."

"Scratches, Sister, mere scratches," repeated Doctor Sparrow.

"It looks like you'll be taking some much needed rest, Doctor," said Dorothy, smiling.

"No more charade either, Sister," replied Doctor Sparrow with a wink.

"No more charade?" questioned Sister Jones, looking at Dorothy.

"I haven't a clue what he's talking about." Dorothy smiled again.

"There's an ambulance waiting at the end of the tents," said Nurse Williams to the stretcher-bearers.

"We'll get you off to the evacuation hospital, Doctor. They'll take care of you there," confirmed Sister Jones.

"Nice to have met you, Sister Dorothy Wainwright," replied Doctor Sparrow from his departing stretcher, "and thank you for everything."

"You take care of yourself, Doctor. You've done your bit," said Dorothy, smiling at the doctor and giving his hand a comforting squeeze as the bearers carried him past.

"Hmm, Sister Dorothy Wainwright?" assumed Sister Jones, looking at Dorothy.

"Come along. We have patients to care for and a field hospital to rebuild," answered Dorothy, shrugging her shoulders at Sister Jones and following Doctor Sparrow's stretcher.

Dorothy spent the next day hard at work erecting a replacement field hospital in a prepared trench with sandbagged walls, for extra protection, before resuming her care for the casualties that began arriving at the new receiving ward.

She monitored Jean's somber and fragile mood, wearily performing her duties, occasionally breaking down and weeping over the loss of Mary, while she herself fought to subdue her emotion, hiding them behind her work, behind a charade as Doctor Sparrow had done.

Dorothy watched as the defence perimeter came ever closer, concentrating the Allied infantry, guns, and tanks into closer proximity to the beachhead and the small vital port of Anzio. German Panzer Tanks and field artillery fired relentlessly, asserting their superior advantage.

The field hospital was stretched to overflow as the battle amongst the fields and outer villages raged, stretching the Allied defences to their breakable limit.

"The situation doesn't look to good for us at the moment, Sister," said Nurse Williams.

"Be patient, have faith, Nurse," replied Dorothy as they changed a soldier's dressing together.

"That's the spirit, Sister. We're not done yet," added the soldier.

"Well, you're perky for someone who's lying in bed wounded," remarked Dorothy.

"Aye, we all are, Sister. We might have our backs against the wall at the moment, but we'll see this job done, you just see if we don't," answered the soldier.

"Who's we?" asked Nurse Williams.

"The lads, all of us out there, Nurse," replied the soldier.

"Oh, of course," said Nurse Williams.

"Gerry nearly broke through yesterday. He came close to splitting us in two, and that would have made things very difficult for us. But it's given us more determination, Sister," enthused the soldier. "We want to see Rome, Sister, and Gerry isn't going to stop us."

"That's encouraging news," Dorothy commented. "Many more of these daily bombardments and there won't be much left of anyone to go to Rome, us or Gerry."

"Perhaps we should get this man patched up and send him back out there." Nurse Williams smiled. "He could lead the way for us."

"Aye, give me a day or two for these scratches to heal. I've not come all this way for nothing, Nurse," replied the soldier. "Ah, steady, Sister, that's a bit tight."

"Oh, sorry," said Dorothy. "I think the only way you will get to see Rome, Soldier, is to come back after all this is over."

"Do you think so, Sister?" questioned the soldier.

"Unfortunately, yes," replied Dorothy. "It will be some time before you are up and walking again, but I admire your spirit. If all our boys have your determination, perhaps we will see Rome."

The wail of the air raid siren broke their conversation.

"Here we go again," said Nurse Williams.

Once more the bombs began falling on the shrinking beachhead. Allied anti-aircraft artillery opened fire; field guns and tanks commenced shelling the enemy's advanced positions as the relentless barrage continued through the day and into the night.

The chilly nights and rain-soaked days of winter months were now replaced with the warmth of early spring. Trees along the Albano Road blossomed, and crocus bloomed amongst the craters of the grassland. Afternoons in the receiving ward were hot and sweaty as the sun beat down upon the brown canvas tent.

Dorothy preferred the coolness of her grey Queen Alexandra dress and white apron and disposed of her khaki trouser uniform. She observed the growing distance of the defence line to the proximity of the field hospital as the new spirit of the Allies drove Gerry farther inland. Air raids had become less frequent, and a new, assertive mood was present in the receiving ward.

Senior Sister Robinson brought news of their boys regaining ground at the factory along the Albano Road and at Cisterna farther to the east of Anzio. Reports of the Allies breaking through at Monte Cassino and the possibility of support spurred the new offensive forward.

On the morning of May 30, roars and shrieks and cries echoed from the field hospital as an ambulance stopped outside the receiving ward, and the happy, smiling young driver announced that Gerry was gone.

Fatigued sighs of relief, warm hugs of comradeship, and smiles of accomplishment passed among the doctors, nurses, and patients as they reflected on their hard-earned victory. Dorothy was drawn into the jubilation and thanked each of her staff for their hard work and dedication as her feeling of relief gave way to tiredness and fatigue.

"It's over. They've gone," said Jean as she greeted Dorothy.

"Yes, thankfully," replied Dorothy. "They've gone."

"I wish Mary were here." Jean sighed. "It's not the same without her."

"No, I know. Some things will never be the same," said Dorothy. "I wish she were here too. How are you? You look tired Jean."

"I've not been able to sleep since she died. I keep thinking it's my fault," answered Jean.

"You can't blame yourself, Jean. Any of us here could have been killed at any time," replied Dorothy, comforting her friend. "Go and lie down. Try and get some sleep. I'll come and see how you are when I get finished here."

Dorothy watched Jean as she walked wearily out of the receiving ward.

"I sometimes wondered if we were going to make it," said Nurse Williams.

"Go and get some rest, Nurse. You've hardly slept for the last two days," replied Dorothy. "I can manage here until Sister Jones comes to take over."

"I'm fine, thank you, Sister. We still have work to do," commented Nurse Williams.

"I'm going to recommend you are promoted to Sister, Nurse Williams," said Dorothy. "You have performed admirably throughout this whole operation; we wouldn't have managed without you. Thank you, Sister Williams. Now will you go and get some rest?"

"Thank you, Sister Wainwright. It's much appreciated, ma'am. I'll just check the patients first," said Nurse Williams, smiling gratefully, "then I'll retire, promise."

The advance from the Anzio beachhead quickly followed the retreating Germans. Dorothy and Jean were to join up with the Allied troops forging north from Cassino along Highway Six, while the Americans took Albano Road and Highway Seven, direct to Rome.

Dust from the churning wheels of the military convoy blew across the grassland toward the Alban Hills as Dorothy's field ambulance filed out of Anzio, through Nettuno, and took its turn to cross the railway line before passing through Cisterna. The battle-scarred grassland gave little indication to the months of destruction inflicted upon the German stronghold of the little Italian village, nor at the Allied beachhead of Anzio, left to rebuild their future from the rubble that was once homes.

Dorothy stared out of the ambulance window, lost in her thoughts. The flat grassland gave way to the undulations of the Alban Hills. Distant villages nestled on the hillside among the olive groves and vineyards showed no sign of conflict or Gerry as the procession of dust-lifting exhaust belching, engine-grunting vehicles filed into Valmontone on Highway Six and united with the Allies advancing from Cassino.

Local inhabitants, reluctant and weary of the frequent grey blue German convoys, lined the roadside covering their mouth and nose from the grime and dirt as they waved and cheered the brown green vehicles of the Allies, a greeting and welcome from which the advancing liberators drew encouragement and determination.

The united Allied convoy dropped down the lush Alban slopes, through the Cypress and fir trees, and back onto the coastal plain that surrounded Rome. The grand spectacle of liberation reception had already been conducted as Dorothy, in her field ambulance, passed unobserved along the shaded Via Labicana and into the afternoon shadow of the Colosseum before heading to their rendezvous point and the prospect of a good night's sleep.

Jean had slept, propped in the corner against the ambulance door, leaning on the window most of their journey from Anzio, while Dorothy watched the passing scenery and chatted with their driver.

"Do you fancy a stroll before you retire, Dorothy?" asked Jean. "We're not far from the river."

"I just want to sleep," replied Dorothy. "You should get some rest too."

"I'm not tired now," answered Jean.

"Then you should be careful. We may have liberated Rome, but it does not mean there are no Germans here," said Dorothy.

"Of course, you're right. Perhaps I should just get some rest," said Jean.

"Maybe tomorrow we can see some sights, when we know what will happen," concluded Dorothy.

The following morning Dorothy was engaged in preparations for supporting the advance north and pursuing Gerry's retreat. Her interest in sightseeing waned at the thought of being enthusiastic for something she had looked forward to doing with her absent friend. She made excuses to Jean while encouraging her to go with other off-duty nurses before returning to the quiet sanctuary of her bed.

Startled pigeons flapped from their high, sunlit balconies, their fluttering silhouettes disappearing across the pale sky as waking engines of the Allied convoy roared into life, billowing black exhaust smoke into the shadows of the still morning air. One by one the canvas-covered trucks, tanks, jeeps, field ambulance, and motorcycles filed over the Tiber heading north along Highways Two and Three, away from Rome and in pursuit of the retreating Germans.

Reconnaissance aircraft reported the enemies retreating defence positions, to which the Allies responded by directing assault forces to flush Gerry out of hiding and continue to drive him northward. The process was slow and arduous, sometimes taking days to dislodge a few German guns strategically placed to protect their retreat and stall the Allies' advance.

Forging through the Apennine Mountains in the high July sun, Dorothy observed the picturesque villages perched on the cool hilltops, like vultures watching their weary victim as the Allie convoy crawled through the heat of the valleys. The green shades of orange, lemon, and olive groves, vineyards, tall Cypress, silver fir, and birch trees surrounding the villages added to the lethargic beauty that distracted from the war machine carrying her slowly northward.

It was mid-July as Dorothy and her ambulance crew followed the Allied convoy, descending from the mountains toward the plain of Florence.

FLORENCE, ITALY

1944

The high afternoon sun beat down on the octagonal dome of the Duomo dominating the terracotta roofs of distant Florence. The crawling Allied convoy slowed to a halt on the southern slopes of the Apennine Mountains, dust lifting into the still air drifted through the field ambulance open window as Dorothy wiped her dry lips on the back of her hand and reached for the water canteen.

Plumes of smoke rose above the ancient Tuscan city, black against the green shimmering backdrop of the northern range of Apennine Mountains as one by one Gerry blew the bridges spanning the Arno River.

"It looks like this is going to be as far as we get for a while," said the ambulance driver.

"How do you know?" enquired Jean.

"That smoke you see, it looks like Gerry is blowing the bridges.

Which, I would guess, means this is going to be their defence position," continued the driver. "Without bridges, that makes it difficult for us to cross the river and buys them time to dig in."

"What will we do?" asked Dorothy.

"Fight it out, I guess. Try and find a way across the river," said the driver thoughtfully.

"You mean like Anzio?" said Jean.

"Yeah, something like that," replied the driver.

"But that's Florence," stated Dorothy. "All those art treasures, the cathedral, the architecture, David, the Statue of David."

"Well, if I was him, I wouldn't be hanging around," said the driver. "Things like that don't count for much when you have a job to do."

"A job to do!" remarked Dorothy. "Surely they won't blow Florence to pieces just because it's the war and we have a job to do."

"Do you think Gerry thought about that while he was bombing London, ma'am?" commented the driver.

"No, I guess not," replied Dorothy dejectedly. "Not when you put it like that."

The convoy remained parked along the winding mountain road. Soldiers, drivers, nurses sheltered from the sun in the vehicle shadows, smoking, sleeping, quietly chatting, waiting for reconnaissance reports and the order to descend into Florence.

Dorothy sat alone in the hot cab of the ambulance, wiping her neck and forehead with a cool cloth dampened from the water canteen. Her mused thoughts were not of anything particular, more absorption and reflection of the mood surrounding the quiet convoy as she relaxed in her seat and looked toward Florence. Unconsciously, she rested her arm through the open window onto the burning metal of the ambulance door. She jumped and withdrew her arm back into the cab, placing the cool cloth against the red welt forming on the soft skin of her forearm.

"Oh … you stupid girl," she said aloud as she pressed the damp cloth hard against the sharp, stinging sensation.

"Come again?" asked the driver as he opened the opposite door and climbed into the ambulance.

"Nothing. I just put my arm on the door and burnt myself.

It's nothing," replied Dorothy, sitting upright, paying attention to the sudden activity and the growl of engines starting all along the stationary convoy.

The Allied Army descended to the floodplain and dispersed among the olive groves and Cypress trees surrounding Florence. The setting sun bathed the makeshift campsites in a red shimmering haze as the heat of the day died away and darkness fell on the travel-weary allied forces.

It was dark when the worn tent of the field hospital was once more ready for patients. Dorothy was tired and still had her own tent to erect before she could sleep. The night was still and quiet, broken only by the occasional distant gunfire of reconnaissance patrols searching Florence for enemy snipers.

The still morning air carried the sound of allied assault forces bombarding the northern banks of the Arno River, searching for a weak defence and crossing point. Only the Ponte Vecchio was spared destruction and remained spanning the river. It was heavily mined, booby trapped, and defended by Gerry.

Defence strongholds were established within Florence, as German sniper positions were cleared and allied forces began occupying the city. Dorothy was sent orders to move the field hospital and occupy a small abandoned convent on the edge of Florence, from where they were able to serve the main allied assaults that were directed east and west along the river, away from the old Tuscan city.

"This will be much nicer than that worn-out field tent," commented Nurse Goodwin, looking round the large dormitory.

"At least we haven't had to build it before we can use it," Jean stated as she prepared a bed that had been left in the room. "We have to be thankful for that."

"And we will have a dry room to sleep in ourselves," added Sister Williams.

"I hope we stay here for a while," said Jean with a sigh. "The last few weeks chasing Germans across Italy has worn me out."

"That depends on Gerry and how soon we get across the river," replied Sister Williams.

"Well, there was no river at Anzio, and look how long it took there," answered Jean. "And besides, it's so hot. It's the heat that's wearing me out, not the putting up and taking down of that field tent."

"How are we doing? Are we ready to take patients?" enquired Dorothy as she entered the dormitory.

"Ten minutes, ma'am," replied Sister Williams.

"There are patients arriving in the courtyard now," said Dorothy, turning and departing from the room. "I'll have them sent right in."

"Yes, ma'am," answered Sister Williams. "Quickly, get those three beds ready. I'll put the patients over here when they arrive," continued Sister Williams to Jean and Nurse Goodwin.

Steadily throughout the day the old, disused convent was transformed into a hospital. The kitchen was cleaned and the aroma of an evening meal wafted through the narrow corridors. Nuns' quarters were occupied by nurses, two large dormitories were converted into a receiving and a casualty ward, and the largest of the anti-rooms became the theatre. The small chapel remained dusty and undisturbed.

Dorothy sat behind a desk in what she assumed was Mother Superior's office, by the main entrance.

"Has that supply truck arrived yet?" Dorothy called to Sister Williams as she passed the open door of the office.

"Not yet, ma'am," replied Sister Williams, stopping and standing in the office doorway.

"How are we for supplies, Sister?" asked Dorothy. "I know things are stretched until that truck gets here."

"If we don't have anymore cases arrive we should be able to manage for a day or two," replied Sister Williams. "It's mainly penicillin we're short of, ma'am."

"Yes, I believe it's the Neapolitan currency on the black market. The sooner we get ships landing supplies to other places than Naples, the better we shall be, Sister," commented Dorothy with a sigh. "Do your best... and let me know if the situation changes or that supply truck arrives."

"Yes, ma'am," said Sister Williams, turning to depart down the narrow corridor.

"That food smells rather nice, don't you think?" asked Dorothy, relaxing back in her chair.

"Yes, ma'am, it's making me quite hungry. It's been a long time since I last smelt food being cooked," replied Sister Williams, hesitating to see if Dorothy was going to continue the conversation.

"Well, we have established a hospital, Sister Williams," stated Dorothy. "It's nice to be in a building again rather than the field tent."

"Yes, ma'am. It's been a long journey. I was in the hospital in Naples before joining you in Anzio. Though I quite liked the field tent, ma'am, in a strange way they're cosy and easy to work in," replied Sister Williams.

"Come now, Sister Williams, it was downright dangerous. I remember meeting you prostrate on the floor between two beds during an air raid." Dorothy chuckled.

"Yes, ma'am, happy times, weren't they?" Sister Williams smiled.

"Let's go and see if that food is ready to eat. It's been a long day and I'm hungry," said Dorothy, smiling back and getting up from her chair. "It feels more like a hospital now, don't you think, and an acceptable alternative for the convent. I'm sure the nuns won't mind us being here for a while. They do quite some nursing of the sick themselves, and look there's still a crucifix on my wall to remind us where we are."

Military manoeuvres continued to probe along the Arno River for a crossing point with only a small number of casualties being admitted to the hospital. The supply truck duly arrived, though the penicillin replenishment was insufficient for the requirements of the hospital, and Dorothy sent urgent requests for more. Additional nurses and doctors steadily arrived as the field support transport caught up with the stalled frontline units, and the daily hospital routine became quite settled in comparison to the previous months since landing on Italian soil.

It was early morning, and Dorothy had just arrived on-duty when a green canvas-covered truck pulled into the hospital courtyard. It was accompanied by two officers in a staff car and an armed motorbike and sidecar escort.

Dorothy came out of her office to meet the officers as they rushed into the hospital entrance.

"Can I help?" enquired Dorothy.

"Yes, thank you, ma'am," replied one of the officers as he politely led Dorothy back into her office by her elbow.

The second officer entered and closed the door behind him.

"What's going on?" said Dorothy sharply, removing her elbow from the officer's hold.

"Sorry, excuse me, ma'am. We have a slight situation," began the first officer. "We had a rendezvous last night with the local partisan movement, and Gerry interrupted us, injuring the captain."

"Where is he?" asked Dorothy.

"He's in the truck," said the second officer.

"Well, bring him in. We can't attend to him out there," replied Dorothy.

"It's not that simple, ma'am. He'll need a room, separate from our regular soldiers," continued the first officer.

"That is quite normal for a captain. We have a room already prepared," commented Dorothy.

"He's not our captain, ma'am. It's the partisan captain," informed the officer.

"Oh, I see," said Dorothy thoughtfully. "We shall have to find somewhere for him then."

"We had no choice. We couldn't get him back across the river, his injuries are too bad," said the first officer.

"As soon as he's able, we'll get him back to his outfit," added the second officer. "In the meantime, he'll be your responsibility. Just let us know as soon as he's well enough to travel."

"Our little secret, you mean?" said Dorothy.

"If you like," said the first officer, looking directly at Dorothy.

"Does he speak English?" asked Dorothy.

"Some, I believe," said the second officer.

"You mean you don't know?" replied Dorothy.

"We're only delivering the patient, ma'am," confirmed the first officer.

"Give me a moment, Lieutenant, while I think," said Dorothy. "Perhaps I could put him in the chapel. It's not being used. Yes, take him to the chapel. You can sneak him in the front door, and then my staff will have access through the side door from inside the hospital, that way no one will suspect anything. Pull your truck up to the chapel door. I'll get help from inside."

"Yes, ma'am," said the first officer, turning and following the second officer out of the office.

Dorothy went to the casualty ward to look for Sister Williams, where she also found Nurse Goodwin.

"Sister Williams, would you find Nurse Lawrence and come quickly to the chapel. Use the side entrance from the end corridor and be discreet," said Dorothy quietly. "Jenny, come with me."

"Gosh, what's happening?" whispered Nurse Goodwin, walking quickly half a stride behind Sister Wainwright.

"You'll see in a moment. Follow me," said Dorothy.

The side door to the chapel was not locked and opened freely. Inside rays of sunlight streaming through the stained glass window above lighted the altar. A second round window above the main chapel entrance cut through the dim shadow of the nave to cast an oval light on the floor of the main aisle. The chapel was still and quiet. Dorothy's and Jenny's footsteps across the stone slabs of the floor echoed loudly as they made their way to the main doorway. The door was not locked. Dorothy cracked opened the heavy door until a bright sliver of light cut through, blinding her vision to the outside.

The first officer pushed open the door, causing Dorothy to fall back against Nurse Goodwin while he stood holding the door wide open.

"Quick, bring him in," said the second officer.

Two soldiers from the motorcycle escort lifted the canvas flap covering the rear of the truck and lowered the tail flap. Two more soldiers emerged from the truck, jumping to the floor, their boots crunching loudly on the stone flags of the chapel entrance. They pulled a stretcher from the rear of the truck, and before the trailing end had chance to fall, the two motorcycle soldiers took hold of the handles and quickly marched the partisan captain into the chapel. The first officer firmly closed the door behind them.

Only the sound of heavy breathing broke the silence of the

chapel as the four soldiers holding the stretcher stood recovering from their burst of exertion, waiting for instructions.

"Put him on the altar," instructed the first officer to the four stretcher-bearers.

Sister Williams and Nurse Lawrence entered through the side door of the chapel. The partisan captain was laid onto the stone altar, and the four stretcher-bearers retreated to the main entrance.

"Do whatever it takes to get him well enough to be returned," said the first officer firmly. "Let us know as soon as he can be moved. He is an important man for us to have back where he belongs, and you must keep his presence here quiet, ma'am. The fewer people who know about him, the better. It would be complicated for him to return if his being here was discovered by Gerry."

A burst of light flooded the chapel as the officers and their escort departed through the main door before Dorothy had time to ask further questions.

"What was all that about? Who's this?" enquired Sister Williams, looking at the figure motionless on the altar.

"I'm not really sure," replied Dorothy, looking slightly bemused by the whole event. "Jean, would you fetch some bedding?"

"Yes, ma'am," replied Nurse Lawrence.

"And be discrete," whispered Dorothy loudly.

"Our patient has severe shrapnel wounds. He has injuries all over, Sister," said Sister Williams, observing the captain, "and he's not conscious. He must have lost a lot of blood already."

"Jenny, help Sister William attend our patient," Dorothy answered, assessing what should be done next. "Get whatever supplies you need while I see if I can find somewhere more suitable to put the captain. Until I know exactly what we are doing here, this doesn't go beyond the four of us."

"No, ma'am," replied Sister Williams and Nurse Goodwin in unison.

Dorothy opened a door to the side of the altar. Inside were cupboards and ceremonial regalia.

This should do for the time being, thought Dorothy, returning to the altar.

Nurse Goodwin had gone for medical supplies, leaving Dorothy and Sister Williams alone with their secret patient.

"Can I ask who he is, ma'am?" enquired Sister William, carefully pulling at the captain's clothing in order to further assess his injuries.

"Apparently, from the vague information I have been given, he is a captain in the Italian partisan movement."

"But he's dressed in civilian clothes, apart from his shirt," replied Sister William, "which looks to be Italian Army issue. He could be anyone, ma'am."

"Well, I have to take the word of the officers who brought him here, Sister. What else can I do?" questioned Dorothy. "I can't go asking too many questions either if we're to keep his presence here quiet."

"These partisans, aren't they deserters?" asked Sister Williams.

"Revolutionists, I think," answered Dorothy.

"He has a rather bad injury near his throat; he's lucky it hasn't severed the carotid vein," said Sister Williams, holding open the captain's shirt collar, exposing a nasty gash to his neck.

Nurse Lawrence returned with the bedding.

"Jean, get one of the orderlies to put a field bed in the corridor. Make some excuse to him and then bring it in here, please. Oh, and bring some water...and get Jenny to hurry along too," said Dorothy thinking aloud. "We'll lose this patient if we don't do something soon."

"He's going to need penicillin too, Sister," added Sister Williams.

"Yes, I was afraid of that. His wounds have been left far too long," replied Dorothy.

"That will mean taking from our already short supply," stated Nurse Lawrence.

"But we have no alternative, Jean; get the things I've asked for, please. I will get the penicillin. Hopefully questions will not be asked if I take it." Dorothy sighed. "Sister Williams, as soon as Nurse Goodwin returns, attend to the patient's injuries and you will have to do something for that neck wound."

"It really needs a doctor to look at it, Sister," replied Sister Williams.

"We cannot risk a doctor knowing about this!" exclaimed Dorothy. "Nurse Goodwin will have to put her theatre experience to good use and put some stitches in it. We have no choice!"

The conversation fell silent. Dorothy followed Nurse Lawrence through the side door of the chapel back into the hospital and stood watching the door to the supply store from the end of the corridor for a short while, hoping no one was inside. She readied herself for what she was about to do and walked purposefully toward the supply room.

Dorothy began to feel tension building in her limbs as she neared the doorway. A sick hollowing in her stomach stopped her as she entered the empty room and leaned against the door as it closed behind her. Quickly she crossed the room and opened the cupboard containing the penicillin, taking a jar from the shelf. The lid clattered to the work surface as she nervously fumbled opening the dark brown bottle. Her heart beat heavily, confusing her counting the tablets into a dispensing container before returning the jar back to the cupboard. Dorothy put the small container of stolen penicillin in the pocket of her grey uniform dress. She felt sick and was trembling nervously.

"God, what am I doing?" she said to herself.

Sister Williams and Nurse Goodwin were bent over attending to the partisan captain as Dorothy returned through the side door of the chapel. Their concentration distracted their awareness of her presence, and she stood watching them work while thinking, trying to grasp a perspective of what was happening.

Suddenly the side door to the chapel burst open, and Nurse Lawrence clattered through with the field bed. "Can someone give me a hand, please?" she said in a loud, hoarse whisper.

Dorothy helped Jean assemble the bed and placed it by the altar. Sister Williams and Nurse Goodwin finished attending the captain, and together they all lifted him onto the field bed and carried him into the small side room Dorothy had prepared. The captain lay unconscious, a plasma bottle hanging from a cupboard door attached to his arm.

"Thank you, Jenny, that was very courageous of you to tend that wound. You did very well. I'm sure the captain will think so too when he has recovered," said Dorothy, standing back, feeling a little relaxed now that the situation was more under control.

"I have had to do stitching for the doctors after they have finished surgery, but I have never before had to assess what should be done," replied Nurse Goodwin. "I hope I have done the right thing. Sister Williams helped me a lot, really."

"It was well done, both of you," said Dorothy. "Now we shall have to keep an eye on the captain, and let's hope he soon regains consciousness. Sister Williams and I can do that and hopefully not attract attention. I can call on you, Jean, as needed. Jenny, you return to theatre so you're not missed. If any complications arise, I'll send for you, and remember... not a word to anyone."

"No, ma'am," replied Nurse Goodwin, quietly leaving the chapel.

"Sister Williams, you stay and watch the captain for a while. Here, take this, and let's hope I don't have to take any more," said Dorothy, handing over the penicillin and feeling guilty. "Come on, Jean. We had better get back before we are missed too."

Dorothy took her turn watching over the captain. It was early in the afternoon of the following day that Dorothy watched the captain's stirring movements as he regained consciousness. His eyes blinked open and closed. Dorothy crouched over her patient, observing his tanned face. Again his eyelids fluttered and slowly opened. Dorothy found herself staring into warm brown eyes. Awareness and a questioning expression began to appear on the captain's face as he looked back at Dorothy's smiling face. His dry lips parted, emitting a soft, incomprehensible croak. Dorothy reached for the glass of water and offered it to the captain's lips. He sipped slowly, allowing the cool liquid to soothe his dry throat. The captain coughed as he tried to swallow and screwed his eyes tightly shut against the rough, gravel pain.

"Slowly, you'll be sore for a day or two," said Dorothy softly. "Your neck has been badly injured."

The captain opened his eyes and looked questioningly at Dorothy. He croaked once more and gritted his teeth as he tried to swallow against the coarse roughness of his injured throat. Dorothy offered some more water. The captain allowed the water to run down his tongue and lubricate his dry throat. He relaxed back into his pillow, not trying to speak, looking at Dorothy, observing his surroundings.

"You're quite safe. You are in an allied military hospital." Dorothy smiled.

The captain smiled back.

"Well, I presume you speak sufficient English to at least understand me, even if you cannot reply," said Dorothy warmly.

The captain smiled back.

"You do understand me?" questioned Dorothy.

The captain lay and smiled at Dorothy before closing his eyes.

"Now you're confusing me," said Dorothy, feeling flustered. She allowed the captain to sleep, attended his dressings, tidied his bed, and went to tell Sister Williams the news.

Dorothy returned later that evening taking soup she had obtained from the kitchen. The captain lay awake, staring at the fading light entering the small window at the end of his bed. He gave Dorothy a warm smile as she entered, his eyes following her movements round the room.

"I've brought you some soup. I hope you can drink it without too much difficulty," said Dorothy.

The captain gave a warm smile as he watched Dorothy squat down at the side of his bed.

"Would you like to try some?" enquired Dorothy.

The captain gave a warm grin and slowly nodded.

"So, you do understand what I'm saying?" Dorothy sighed.

Tilting his head to one side, the captain smiled, slowly shrugged a shoulder, and lifted his closed hand, showing a small gap between his extended index finger and thumb.

"A little, you understand a little?" repeated Dorothy questioningly.

She received the captain's confirming smile and slight nod of his head.

"Try and drink some soup. It will give you some nourishment until you are able to eat," began Dorothy, offering a spoon of soup to the captain's lips. "You're very lucky. You have shrapnel lacerations all across your torso, the main one being your neck, which has just missed your jugular and larynx and the reason for your discomfort. If it had hit you either way from where it has, you would probably not be here."

The captain turned his head away from another offering of soup, closing his eyes as he swallowed.

"Sorry, too busy talking and not paying attention," said Dorothy apologetically.

Turning his head back toward Dorothy, the captain smiled and slowly gestured for more soup, continuing to drink until the bowl was empty.

"You will have to spend most of the night on your own, I'm afraid. Sister Williams will pop by around midnight to check you are all right, and I will come again in the morning. You have water here in this jug," concluded Dorothy before checking the captain's dressings and tidying his bed.

The captain gave a warm smile in appreciation and watched as Dorothy left the room.

"Good night," said Dorothy, closing the door.

Dorothy and Sister Williams continued their vigilant observations of their secret partisan patient, alternating their visits, varying the timing of each in order not to draw attention to his presence.

It was late on the fourth day since the captain's arrival when Dorothy entered the chapel. It was dark as she carefully made her way to the small hideaway at the side of the altar, carrying warm soup for the captain. She opened the door and stepped into the dark, shadowed room. The captain was lying in his bed and propped up on his pillows. Dorothy turned and closed the door.

"Good evening," said the soft, gravely voice slowly.

"Oh, you're talking," said Dorothy, startled and almost spilling the captain's soup. "You must be feeling better."

"Thank you ... yes," replied the captain slowly.

"Well, your wounds are healing quite nicely also. I suppose I shall have to see about returning you to wherever it is you came from," said Dorothy. "Though I think it would be better if you stayed a little longer."

"Mi scusi?" croaked the captain.

"Sorry, just thinking aloud," replied Dorothy, offering the captain his soup and sitting on the small chair that had been placed by the bed. "Here, drink some soup. I think you should at least be able to eat before I think about letting you go."

"Thank you," said the captain, taking the bowl.

"Finish your soup first, and then I will look at your neck wound," continued Dorothy, distracted by the captain's progress and thinking more about what she should do next than the fact she could now talk with her patient.

The captain quietly drank his soup, occasionally glancing and smiling at Dorothy as she talked.

"Sorry, listen to me chatting away," said Dorothy, noticing the captain had finished his soup. "How much of what I say do you understand?"

"A little," answered the captain.

"I think more than a little if the truth is known, Captain," replied Dorothy.

The captain smiled warmly, his eyes staring through the dark shadows at Dorothy.

"Tell me, what's your name?" asked Dorothy.

"Antonio," croaked the captain.

"Just Antonio?" questioned Dorothy.

"Antonio … Gi …" began the captain, stopping to clear his sore throat. "Antonio … Giuseppe … Liumbardo."

"How much do you understand, Antonio? I have been here talking to you for three or four days now. I'm curious to what you have understood," asked Dorothy.

"A little … not all," replied Antonio with his warm smile.

"Well, Antonio, you seem to be an important man," said Dorothy.

"I am … who say so?" questioned Antonio.

"The men who brought you here," replied Dorothy. "They want you back as soon as you're able to travel."

"What is your name?" Antonio softly asked.

"Oh...Dorothy...no one has asked me like that. I mean, no patient has...my name's Dorothy," said Dorothy awkwardly and with a sigh.

"Dorothy," echoed Antonio slowly. "You are...beautiful woman, Dorothy."

"Thank you," said Dorothy, her face flushing in the darkness. "Well, I think I will leave your dressing until the morning, when I can see more clearly."

Dorothy stood and picked up the soup bowl from the captain's bed.

"Get a good night's sleep, Captain. I'll return in the morning and assess if you're ready to be returned," Dorothy said, flustered and heading toward the door.

"Thank you, Dorothy. Good night," said the captain before he began coughing.

"You should stop talking so much...Good night, Antonio," said Dorothy.

Dorothy quickly left the room and closed the door behind her, pausing to stand for a few moments to regain her composure. Her heart was racing, and she still felt the warm glow on her cheeks.

"Oh gosh." Dorothy sighed as she left the chapel.

"Are you all right, Dorothy?" said Sister Williams, catching Sister Wainwright as she was about to enter her office. "You look a little flushed."

"Come in and close the door," replied Dorothy.

Sister Williams followed Dorothy into her office.

"He can talk!" exclaimed Dorothy, turning to face Sister Williams.

"Sorry, who can?" questioned Sister Williams.

"Our captain. He started talking this evening when I went to check on him," said Dorothy, sitting in her chair.

"Whatever he said has certainly flushed your face, Dorothy," replied Sister Williams.

"I thought all his smiles were just politeness, a communication because he couldn't talk," said Dorothy excitedly. "He's so charming, he told me what a beautiful woman I was...am. I didn't know what to say."

"So what did you say?" questioned Sister Williams.

"I don't remember. I left the room. I said something about returning in the morning and that he shouldn't talk so much," answered Dorothy.

"He shouldn't talk so much!" repeated Sister Williams.

"Oh gosh, he said good night or something and started coughing. Then he called me Dorothy, and I said he shouldn't talk so much." Dorothy sighed.

"Would you like me to go and attend him in the morning?" asked Sister Williams.

"No!" answered Dorothy immediately. "I just haven't been spoken to like that before, it's lovely. I'm sure he could see me flush, even in the dark."

"Fraternizing with patients is not permitted, ma'am," smiled Sister Williams.

"Antonio is not a patient," replied Dorothy.

"We don't know who Antonio is, ma'am," said Sister Williams. trying to bring some reality to the situation.

"Of course, you're right, Sister Williams. He just caught me unaware, Sister, that's all," replied Dorothy thoughtfully.

"He is quite a dish though." Sister Williams smiled.

"We shall go together in the morning. We need to assess how much longer he should stay here now that he is recovering so well," said Dorothy. "The two officers seemed to think it important that he is returned as soon as possible."

"As you wish, ma'am," replied Sister Williams. "I'll be here at six."

Early morning light crept through the small window of the captain's hideaway as Sister Williams entered, followed by Dorothy.

"Good morning, Captain," greeted Sister Williams. "I understand your voice has returned."

"Ah...good morning, ladies," replied the captain croakily, sitting up to welcome his visitors.

"We need to give you a thorough examination this morning, Captain," said Dorothy. "So if we begin with that, we can bring something for you to eat later."

"Antonio, please...I am not Captain," pleaded Antonio.

"Captain, Antonio...whoever you are, please, we have a job to do," replied Dorothy. "We need to see if you are well enough to travel. Your injuries look to be healing well enough, and if you can eat something later it would seem our job is done."

"Where are you from, Captain?" asked Sister Williams while reapplying his neck bandage.

"A small village in the hills…north of Florence," replied the captain.

"Why have we been told you are a captain if now you say you are not?" asked Dorothy.

"I am partisan. I fight for you British and the liberation of Italy," said the captain.

"An important captain of the partisan?" suggested Dorothy.

"Per favore…no. I am leader for small village, not a captain," answered Antonio. "I have information about the German movements, that is all."

"How do you get this information?" enquired Sister Williams.

"Our village, it is occupied by the Germans. Our mayor, he does what is best for the village. He pleases them, and in return the village can go about its business," said the captain.

"But that doesn't tell us how you get information about the German movements," prompted Dorothy.

"Moment, please," replied Antonio. "Our mayor, the Germans, they occupy his office. He works every day in the office and he listens to all. He tells me, I tell you, capisco?"

"That must be dangerous for your village," said Sister Williams.

"Si, for my village and my father," said the captain.

"The mayor, he's your father?" asked Dorothy.

"Si, that is why I must return," said Antonio.

"Well, you're certainly like your father, Captain Antonio. You have been here listening to…all…since you've been here," commented Sister Williams. "Let's hope you are who you say you are when the officers return."

"Nurse Goodwin has made an excellent job with her stitches," said Dorothy. "If he can eat something, I think we should call the officers to come and collect the captain, what do you think?"

"I'll go to the kitchen and bring something before things get too busy," replied Sister Williams, departing from the room. "You'll be all right alone with the captain, Sister?"

"Yes, thank you," answered Dorothy.

Dorothy quietly busied herself tidying the room and Antonio's bed, not knowing quite what to do or say.

"Mi scusi, Sister," began Antonio softly as Dorothy neatly folded his bed covers. "For last night, I sorry. I am wrong."

"That's quite all right, Captain. It's forgotten," said Dorothy.

"No, I make you uncomfortable, is not what I want," continued Antonio slowly. "You are kind to me and I thank you."

"I am doing my job," replied Dorothy, sitting on the chair and looking at Antonio. "That's all."

"Si, and I am big fool," said Antonio.

Dorothy smiled.

"What will you do when you return? Must you hide?" asked Dorothy, not taking her eyes from Antonio's sun-tanned face, trying to guide the conversation. "The Germans, they occupy your village."

"It is not safe for me in my village. I must live in the mountains," replied Antonio. "When the Germans see me, I am dead."

"But your father...how do you—"

"Shh..." Antonio interrupted. "What you not know is good."

"Your life is difficult," said Dorothy softly.

"I trust no one," answered Antonio. "This way I stay alive."

"You must trust someone," replied Dorothy. "What about your father?"

"For my father and my family, is better this way," said Antonio, his eyes staring back at Dorothy.

"You have a family?" asked Dorothy as Antonio's reply focused her attention.

"My father, my mother, my brother, two sisters...and one mule," replied Antonio with a smile.

"You can trust the mule." Dorothy smiled, relaxing.

"I can trust the mule," said Antonio, his laugh cutting short as it tore at his throat.

"Oh, I'm sorry." Dorothy gasped, feeling his discomfort.

The door to the captain's hideaway opened.

"Well, what's going on here?" commented Sister Williams.

"I'm just stimulating the blood flow to his oesophagus, Sister, in preparation for the food you have brought," Dorothy quickly replied, still smiling.

"Let's hope your attention is successful, ma'am." Sister Williams smiled, offering Antonio a plate of food. "I have managed to bring the captain some toast."

The captain ate slowly, taking small bites of his warm toast, chewing well to soften each mouthful before swallowing. His grimaced face relaxed as he became accustomed to chewing and swallowing. He handed back the empty plate to Sister Williams, who had watched every mouthful.

"Would you like some water, Captain?" asked Sister Williams.

Antonio nodded, still chewing.

"It would seem that our captain is sufficiently recovered to travel," said Dorothy, thinking aloud her observation. "I will arrange for the officers to collect him this evening, after he has had a good meal to send him on his way."

The day passed quickly as a rush of new casualties arrived at the hospital and patients sufficiently recovered were prepared for onward transportation later that afternoon. Dorothy called the officers, informing them the captain would be ready for collection that evening, and arranged for his departure. The officers arrived early and left with the captain during the afternoon's commotion that provided distraction while transferring the captain but allowed no time for ceremonial farewells. Sister Williams and Nurse Lawrence helped dispatch the captain as the two officers offered thanks, detaining Dorothy in her office.

Dorothy sat shuffling paperwork; the morning sun illuminated a narrow window image against the adjacent wall while shining on the large wooden crucifix that dominated the office. Sister Williams knocked at the door and entered.

"I've come to return this, ma'am," said Sister Williams, offering Dorothy the small dispensing container used to keep the penicillin for the captain. "There is still some left to be returned to the store, unless you would like me to do it."

"Gosh, I had forgotten about that, Sister," said Dorothy, looking at the container. "It wasn't all used then?"

"No, I think you were allowing for an influx of partisan captains for the amount of tablets you put in the container, ma'am," replied Sister Williams.

"I was so nervous, Sister. I regularly use the medicine store without thinking, but to do that was so worrying, I couldn't think straight. Leave it with me and I will return them. They will be needed," explained Dorothy, looking thoughtfully as she took the small, round container. "I was just thinking about the past few days as you came in, how we can easily be distracted from things going on around us. The captain took away some of the daily routine, don't you think?"

"It did have a sense of excitement to add to the day," said Sister Williams.

"Though I was surprised how quickly the officers came and took the captain. I hope they get him back safely." Dorothy sighed.

"He was quite handsome, ma'am. I can understand your distraction," said Sister Williams.

"Yes, I thought so too." Dorothy smiled. "Now it's over and he's gone."

The progress of war made no allowance for personal adjustment, and military offensives, in search of a crossing over the Arno River, brought a flurry of casualties into the hospital. Beds became full, and the less injured were accommodated on the ward floor as frontline activities intensified in an effort to cross the river before winter arrived. Dorothy's memory of the partisan captain was lost among the daily chores of hospital routine.

Occasional quiet periods during night duties allowed Dorothy time to reflect. She missed Mary and longed for the times they'd enjoyed together, the comfort and support they shared during stressful times. She reflected on the news Jenny had brought, of the loss of her family, her father, mother, her young brother, Christopher, her eyes flooding with tears that she would not allow to fall. Thoughts of Doctor Sparrow, thankful for his charade that she used to help her cope with the daily carnage she witnessed. She smiled when she remembered Barry, his slim figure buried in his oversized khaki uniform and their promise to meet after the war. She thought of her tired body, fatigued, longing for rest.

Autumn sunsets coloured the sky as news of a breakthrough east of Florence filtered through to the hospital. Orders for frontline medical support were received, and hospital activities increased to meet the required preparations.

Dorothy stood in the hospital courtyard watching the last of the supplies being loaded as the field ambulances prepared to depart and join the allies' advancing convoy. Jean walked slowly toward Dorothy, tears streaming down her sunburnt cheeks.

"I wish you were coming," sobbed Jean as she embraced Dorothy.

"Come on, you'll be fine," said Dorothy, returning Jean's embrace. "We have come a long way together."

"I thought we would go all the way. This isn't how I imagined it to be," replied Jean, holding onto her friend.

"What will be will be, remember? We shall be together in our thoughts and our prayers, three of us, always," Dorothy spoke softly into Jean's ear as she squeezed her tightly.

"I'll miss you," whispered Jean, kissing Dorothy gently on her cheek. "I'll look for you when this is over."

"I'll miss you too," said Dorothy, letting go as Jean turned and headed for the field ambulance.

Dorothy felt a sense of loss as she stood and waved at the vehicles filing out of the courtyard. She had become accustomed to the spontaneity of the front line, where her actions responded to the demand of the moment, where she felt she belonged, where she had little time to dwell on the events that had happened. Managing the support field hospital as a senior sister would be something new.

"I know how you feel, ma'am," said Sister Williams, coming to stand beside Dorothy.

"Do you?" questioned Dorothy.

The pace of the converted hospital slowed. Emergency cases from frontline action stopped; the busy thoroughfare of vehicles and patients coming and going reduced as the Allies pushed Gerry farther north. Daily routine began to resemble life at Maltland as

Dorothy conducted her morning inspections, and the sense of war seemed a long way away.

Dorothy spent her time managing the logistics of receiving treated wounded, administering interim attention, and forwarding those able to travel onward to Naples and home, caring only for those less fortunate and who where too ill to continue their journey.

Autumn rain began to wash the hospital windows and pattern the many puddles that covered the empty courtyard. Northerly winds blew a winter chill into the corridors. Patients arriving from the front brought tales of strong resistance from the Germans well entrenched along their Gothic Line defensive positions in the northern range of the Apennine Mountains. Deteriorating weather conditions were hampering Allied offensives and the transportation of necessary supplies. Winter brought a stall to military action, as snow made access through the mountains slow and difficult.

The hospital activities became quiet; it was almost empty of injury-related casualties and began receiving sick and fatigued patients. Dorothy thought of Jean out in the cold winter conditions of the mountains and prayed for her safety.

"It must be awful out there," said Dorothy, staring at the crucifix hanging on her office wall.

"Some of the patients are completely exhausted when they arrive," added Sister Williams. "We have received a few cases with frostbitten hands and feet already, ma'am."

"Yes, I've seen them," replied Dorothy. "Let's hope the weather does not worsen for those still out there. I remember Anzio being cold, but there wasn't snow to contend with."

"It's only December, ma'am. It's a long time until spring and nicer weather," said Sister Williams.

"One year," mumbled Dorothy.

"Pardon?" enquired Sister Williams.

"Oh, nothing," Dorothy sighed sombrely. "I was just thinking how long I have been here. I was on a ship just coming out this time last year. I knew nothing of what to expect, what the war would be really like."

"I remember you saying so, ma'am," answered Sister Williams.

"In a way, sitting here, it all seems a long time ago, and yet I remember it as if it were yesterday," said Dorothy. "Now it's as if none of the fighting has happened and the war is something far away that we talk about."

"Not exactly, ma'am. We have all these poor men to care for," replied Sister Williams.

"Yes, Sister, it is exactly that. A year ago I was caring for men just like these. The fortunate ones, returning from hostile and barbaric frontline action to a hospital just like this one. Only this time I've been there," said Dorothy. "I've seen the wasted lives, the fallen heroes, the men who give everything...I've seen it, cared for them. I've shared their loss, and it's horrible and wasteful. And now...none of it seems real. It's something that happens and is gone...that scars you for the rest of your life...and for what? Nursing is about caring for the sick, the needy...this is like being in a butcher's yard."

"We are at war, Dorothy," said Sister Williams. "This is what happens in war."

"I'm tired, Sister Williams, with too much time to think. Perhaps a good night's sleep will do me good." Dorothy sighed.

THE APENNINE MOUNTAINS, ITALY

1945

The approach of spring stimulated Allied offensive activities far away on the Adriatic Coast, along the supply routes through the Futa Pass, and high in the Apennine Mountains north of Florence.

Dorothy took advantage of the fine Italian weather to wander the narrow Florentine streets with their grand military-style buildings and Renaissance architecture. Passing along Piazza de' Pitti, Dorothy picked her way through the rubble of the destroyed buildings that surrounded the approach to the Ponte Vecchio and compared it to Pulteney Bridge that spanned the River Avon in her hometown of Bath. The defensive mines put down by Gerry that had caused much of the destruction had been cleared, allowing access to the bridge. Crossing over, Dorothy continued to Piazza della Signoria with its Torre d'Arnolfo standing tall at the entrance to the square. Dorothy was thankful that the pounding field guns and artillery had spared much of the city and admired the splendour of pietra forte buildings that surrounded her, their windows shuttered against the anticipated hostilities. Dark shadows encroached across the stone flags and cobbles of the square as the sun hovered above the overhanging rooftops.

It was dusk as Dorothy walked quickly down the narrow street returning to the converted convent hospital. She approached the courtyard gates when suddenly an outstretched arm pulled her into a darkened doorway. A hand came round and gagged her mouth. Panic ripped through her body as the figure held her close, bringing her into the darkness.

"You are Dorothy?" enquired the strongly accented man holding her firmly, his voice soft and calm.

Dorothy sensed the calmness in the voice and felt a little relieved that she should be known by her abductor. She gave a small nod of her head but remained tense in the man's firm grasp.

"I am friend," said the man, preventing Dorothy's movement. "Antonio, he send me."

Dorothy relaxed a little more as she heard the name Antonio.

"Please, I let go," spoke the abductor a little softer, slowly loosening his hold and releasing his hand from Dorothy's mouth.

"Thank you." Dorothy gasped nervously, taking a deep breath, moving away from the man holding her, turning to face him. "What do you want, who are you?"

"My name is Luca. Antonio, he ask you to come," said Luca.

"Come … come where? What does he want?" Dorothy thoughtfully replied.

"Please, my English is not good … slow," said Luca.

Dorothy sighed, relieving her tension.

"What does Antonio want?" asked Dorothy slowly.

"Come to village, is very bad," said Luca, his English heavily accented and broken. "Bring medicine."

"What has happened?" enquired Dorothy alarmingly, staring back at Luca.

"Germans, they shoot many people," answered Luca. "Antonio, he say you can help. We no have doctor."

"Oh God, how can I help? I can't just leave here." Dorothy sighed, thinking of the injured villagers, of Antonio and what might have happened. "When did this happen?"

"Mi scusi?" replied Luca.

"How long ago did this happen?" said Dorothy slowly, trying to speak simply.

"I wait you four days," replied Luca.

"Four days, one day to get here maybe, that's nearly a week ago," Dorothy thought aloud.

"Scusi?" repeated Luca, looking a little bewildered.

"Nothing," said Dorothy, slightly panicked, trying to assess what had happened, how she could help, what she should do.

"You can come?" enquired Luca anxiously, trying to progress the situation.

"Wait here," replied Dorothy, slowly patting her outstretched palms toward the floor before turning to leave the doorway.

"You come back?" questioned Luca, taking holding of Dorothy's arm, preventing her leaving.

"Yes, I'll come back," replied Dorothy, her thoughts confused. She turned and headed toward the courtyard gates of the allied military hospital.

It was some time before Dorothy returned to the doorway along the dark, narrow street and panicked when she found it was empty. She looked up and down the road, a small black covered truck pulled up at the curb, its door swung open.

"Get in," said Luca, leaning over from the driver's seat, a warm smile lighting his bronzed face.

Dorothy threw a brown medical field bag into Luca's lap and put a second one on her knee as she sat down in the truck's worn passenger seat. Luca looked at Dorothy and grinned as he handed back the canvas bag and drove the truck slowly along the narrow road.

"Thank you, grazie," said Luca, nodding his head, a large grin on his face as he peered into the darkness ahead.

Luca drove steadily north into the night, leaving Florence behind, climbing into the foothills of the Apennine Mountains and toward the German's defensive Gothic Line. Dorothy sat quietly, watching out of the windscreen, questioning what she was doing. Sister Williams had tried to make her see sense and stay at the hospital, but Dorothy was determined and convinced Sister Williams that she would be back in three days. The winding road guided the truck higher into the mountains as distant snow-capped peaks became visible, adding light to the dark night. Several times Luca stopped the truck, turned off its engine, and stood on the roadside listening and looking through binoculars at the distant slopes. The old truck rounded a bend, and a small village perched on the edge of the mountainside became visible. Dorothy had not seen it during the climb along the twisting road.

"My village," said Luca, his first words since leaving Florence.

Luca parked the truck in a small alcove tight against the mountainside, blocking Dorothy's door.

"Wait here," commanded Luca politely as he climbed from the truck, taking a machine gun from behind his seat. He headed toward the village, hugging the rugged vertical wall, disappearing quickly into the shadows as if being swallowed by the mountain.

Dorothy sat in the silence. The chill of the rock, inches from her, penetrated the thin steel door of the stationary truck. A gentle wind whispered in the eerie silence as it blew along the mountainside. Dorothy breathed her hot breath against the cold windscreen of the truck, becoming a little nervous as the glass misted over and reduced further her limited view of the dark and empty road ahead. Time passed. Dorothy convinced herself she was doing the right thing, that these people needed her help, and that it was nothing to do with Antonio.

Luca emerged from the mountain shadow, followed by a taller man also carrying a machine gun. The two men climbed into the truck, the taller man squashing in next to Dorothy and pushing her against the cold steel door.

"Buongiorno, Dorothy," said the taller man. "Mi chiamo Alfonso."

"Hello." Dorothy smiled at the mention of her name, not understanding the rest of the taller man's greeting.

"Prego." Alfonso smiled, his machine gun pointing across Dorothy and out the side window.

Luca started the truck's engine and headed toward the village. He drove carefully through the narrow streets, avoiding rubble from the damaged homes and buildings still strewed across the road. Passing round the small, ornate fountain on the paved square in front of the church, Luca brought the truck to rest.

A dim light from inside the church spilled out into the morning chill and onto the road as a plain wooden door opened in front of the truck. Dorothy followed Luca and Alfonso inside. Wounded villagers lay on the floor and among the pews, while others sat nursing, grieving.

"This is our priest, Father Luigi," introduced Luca as a robed figure stepped forward.

"Buongiorno, thank you for coming," said Father Luigi.

"Where is Antonio?" asked Dorothy, anxiously looking round the church.

"Is no here," replied Luca. "He in the mountain."

"Oh gosh, where do I begin?" Dorothy sighed, looking at the injured people, thinking what to do next.

"Mi scusi?" replied Luca.

"Per favore, per favore," said the young girl, taking Dorothy's hand and leading her to a woman lying by the main aisle.

Dorothy squatted by the woman and removed her blood-stained shawl.

"Have you antiseptic?" enquired Dorothy hopefully, looking up at the surrounding faces.

"Antisettico, si, antisettico," replied Father Luigi, gesturing for someone to fetch the antiseptic.

Dorothy returned her attention to the injured woman, taking the antiseptic as it was thrust in front of her and passed one by one, wound by wound amongst the injured congregation. Daylight flooded through the elaborate windows, washing the nave and sleeping patients with colour while Dorothy listened to the gentle murmur of the huddled villagers as she sat exhausted on the end of a pew.

"You are tired," said Farther Luigi, offering Dorothy a glass of water. "We give thanks for you coming."

"Thank you," replied Dorothy, taking the water. "You are welcome."

"You must come and rest," suggested Father Luigi.

"I must return to my hospital, Father," answered Dorothy anxiously as she thought of being missed and the consequence of leaving her duties.

"You must wait," said Father Luigi calmly. "First take some rest."

"What do you mean I must wait?" exclaimed Dorothy, agitated by Father Luigi's comment.

"It is not safe during daylight," replied Father Luigi softly. "The mountains are full of the enemy, we must be careful."

"Yes, of course." Dorothy sighed, realising the gravity of her situation. "But as soon as possible," she added instructively.

"Of course." Father Luigi smiled. "As soon as Luca returns."

"Where's Antonio?" enquired Dorothy looking up the priest.

"Is no longer safe for him to remain in our village," answered Father Luigi. "Now he must hide in the mountains."

"What do you mean... now?" asked Dorothy.

"When he was at your hospital, the Germans, they ask where is Mayor Liumbardo—"

"Mayor Liumbardo?" Dorothy gasped enquiringly, interrupting Father Luigi. "Antonio is the Mayor?"

"Si," replied Father Luigi, surprised by Dorothy's response. "Before him his father and his grandfather. Why do you ask?"

"He never said... I don't understand..." Dorothy said slowly, thoughtfully. "Why am I told he is a partisan captain?"

"Because is true," answered Father Luigi. "Is why he must hide. Is why the Germans destroy our village."

"That's why he had to be returned so urgently," realised Dorothy. "Gerry would certainly ask why the mayor was not in his office."

"Mi scusi?" enquired Father Luigi. "I am lost."

"It is all right, Father, you have explained enough." Dorothy smiled. "When did the Germans leave?"

"Two weeks ago they pack everything, burning what they did not want. One morning they ask where is Antonio. We cannot say so they shoot ten of our village... here, in front of our church. Then they were gone. The next day their guns destroy many of our homes," explained Father Luigi. "Now we fear the fascist Brigate Nere, the Black Brigades, will find our village."

"Your lives are full of danger," said Dorothy. "Life must be very hard."

"We pray that this war will soon end." Father Luigi smiled. "Come, I will show you where you can rest."

It was dusk as Father Luigi woke Dorothy from her sleep and returned her to the village church where Luca and Alfonso were waiting. She glanced at the bloodstained paving slabs in front of the fountain as she entered the church. A chill ran down her spine as she thought of the danger that surrounded this beautiful, isolated village and its people.

"Buongiorno," greeted Luca, his grin returning as Dorothy approached.

"I have prepared some food," said Father Luigi. "For your journey."

"Thank you, Father. First let me attend to these people," replied Dorothy, passing amongst the injured and wounded scattered round the church.

"Come," said Luca, finding Dorothy crouched over a pregnant young woman, attending her injuries. "We must go, it is time."

"One moment," replied Dorothy. "These people need care."

"It can be dangerous, we must go," answered Luca.

"I can't just leave them, Luca," stressed Dorothy. "Just a few more minutes."

Dorothy attended the last remaining injuries before giving future medical instruction to Father Luigi, bidding him farewell and accompanying Luca to the waiting truck. Alfonso and his machine gun already occupied the worn passenger seat. Dorothy leaned against him, pushing him to the middle, up against Luca as she claimed her half of the seat.

Luca drove off into the night, his ravaged village steadily disappearing into the darkness. Dorothy sat quietly, her attention drawn to the two men when, occasionally, they exchanged a few emphasized words. The truck stopped and Luca turned off the engine. The two men got out, listening, looking, passing the binoculars to and fro, leaving Dorothy alone with her thoughts.

Ahead lay the trauma and brutality to which she had temporarily surrendered her life; behind she had experienced the communal compassion of lives inflicted by a war, forced on all of their lives. Her heart went out to the broken and maimed soldiers who had followed their orders and to the wounded villagers suffering the pain of military intrusion, each bearing their scars.

A vision of Mary's dust-covered body lying amongst the debris of the burning field hospital materialised in the darkness through the truck's windscreen.

Alarmed and panicked, Dorothy jumped out of the truck and leant against its bonnet breathing heavily, startling Luca and Alfonso.

"Mama mia," said Luca, coming over to assist Dorothy.

"I'm all right...I'm all right." Dorothy sighed, calming herself.

"Come, we must go," informed Luca reassuringly. "I take you back."

"It's all right, Luca. I just wanted some air," lied Dorothy.

"Si," said Luca slowly, helping Dorothy back into the truck. "Now we go."

Luca stopped the truck in the narrow street away from the courtyard gates of the Allied Hospital. It was still early morning. Dorothy prepared herself to leave and looked across the small dark cab of the truck at her two partisan escorts. Nothing had been spoken between them for the duration of the journey.

"Ciao, grazie," said Alfonso, smiling, nodding his head slowly.

"Bye," smiled Dorothy in return. "Where—"

"Antonio, he say thank you," interrupted Luca in his accented broken English, his broad grin spreading across his shadowed face.

"Where is Antonio?" asked Dorothy, her eyes fixed on Luca's.

"He say one day you meet him," replied Luca, his eyes reflecting warmth and sincerity. "He like to meet Dorothy one more time."

"I would like that too, tell him," replied Dorothy.

"Si, prego...I must go," said Luca, nodding his head. "Ciao, Dorothy."

"Bye," replied Dorothy, climbing down from the worn passenger seat and standing back against the convent wall watching the truck blend into the darkness. She sighed and cautiously made her way to the hospital's courtyard entrance.

"Attention," said Dorothy as she approached the sleeping sentry.

The soldier jumped, flummoxed at Dorothy's presence, and grappled with his machine gun.

"Would you like some tea?" asked Dorothy, further confusing the young soldier.

"Err, yes, ma'am … please, thank you, ma'am," replied the puzzled sentry.

Dorothy turned and passed through the gates into the courtyard, a sigh blowing through her parted lips and puffed cheeks, relieving her anxiety of returning to the hospital as she headed toward the entrance and the safety of her office.

"Dorothy, oh, thank God you're back!" shrieked Sister Williams, expressing her relief as Dorothy entered her office. "I've been so worried."

"Have I been missed?" questioned Dorothy fretfully as she approached and embraced Sister Williams.

"Just one difficult moment that I was able to overcome." Sister Williams sighed. "You look exhausted, ma'am."

"No more than usual, Sister," said Dorothy, relieved that her absence had not been discovered. "If you don't mind, I'll retire to my bed and enlighten you later with my escapade when I relieve your duty, Sister."

"Yes, ma'am. I'm pleased you made it back safely," replied Sister Williams.

"Oh … and would you send that sleepy young sentry a cup of tea, please, Sister? He has earned one tonight," concluded Dorothy as she left her office.

SPRING, ITALY

1945

The Allies' frontline offensives had pushed far to the north along the western Adriatic Coast, stretching the supply lines through the Apennine Mountains, while the turmoil of German retreat from the mountains north of Florence was slow and torturous for the towns and villages they vacated, deploying Fascist Black Brigades to cover the retreating Germans and confront the active partisans fighting to liberate Italy.

April sun reflected brightly off the busy hospital courtyard as Dorothy watched from her office window the arrival of transit casualties. Those still requiring attention were transferred to the wards, while others from the hospital had recovered sufficiently climbed into the waiting trucks for their homeward journey.

Dorothy thought of Jean, somewhere in the mountains, tired and drained, attending butchered soldiers arriving at the receiving ward direct from the battlegrounds of the front line.

Weary of squinting at the activities through the low spring sunlight, Dorothy returned to her desk and paperwork.

"A priest is here requesting to speak with you, ma'am," said Sister Williams, knocking and entering the office.

"A priest, you say?" enquired Dorothy responsively, looking up from her paperwork.

"Yes, ma'am," answered Sister Williams. "He asked specifically for you."

"Oh, very well. Send him in," replied Dorothy, sitting patiently at her desk as Sister Williams went to bring her visitor.

"Father Luigi, ma'am," said Sister Williams, showing the priest into the office.

"Father Luigi, welcome. What can I do for you?" Dorothy gasped, trying to cover her surprise and knowing the priest.

"Buongiorno, Sister." Father Luigi smiled.

"Thank you, Sister. I'll deal with Father Luigi," said Dorothy. "Would you close the door, please?"

"Yes, ma'am," replied Sister Williams, leaving the office, closing the door behind her.

"I sorry, I must come," said Father Luigi apologetically.

"Please, sit down, Father. What can I do for you?" asked Dorothy, looking concerned and regaining some of her composure.

"Thank you. Is good to see you," replied Father Luigi, sitting on a chair placed in the corner between the window and the crucifix hanging on the wall.

"It is good to see you again." Dorothy smiled, curious at Father Luigi's visit. "But why are you here?"

"I bring bad news, Sister. Fascist soldiers, they find our village. There has been much bloodshed," began Father Luigi. "Many people have been killed and injured."

"I'm sorry," said Dorothy sympathetically. "When did this happen?"

"Three days now," replied Father Luigi. "It has been difficult to come. La Guardia soldiers are everywhere."

"Where's Antonio? He's your mayor, he should be helping," Dorothy asked curiously.

"Antonio, he is good mayor. Now is not possible he come to

our village," jabbered Father Luigi, losing his calmness. "He talk with German officers and all is well in the village when we cooperate. Now is different."

"I don't understand," questioned Dorothy. "What is different, what German officers... please, slowly."

"Before the war Italy is very... how shall I say... divided," began Father Luigi slowly. "Fascist government controlled our people, spies... secret police, they are everywhere. It was difficult to resist. Our lives are full of danger. The Germans come; they impose curfews and take our young boys. Antonio, they want send him to work."

"What do you mean, work? What happened?" enquired Dorothy curiously.

"Many of our people are sent to work camps, building for the Germans. Antonio, weeks he is locked up. One day he returns to his office in the municipio. He tells us to cooperate and all will be well," continued Father Luigi.

"But you said before Antonio is a partisan captain," queried Dorothy.

"Si, is true. The Germans, they not know this, he is mayor and cooperates, all is well," said Father Luigi. "Now is different, now Brigate Nere soldiers look for him."

"And now they attack your village," concluded Dorothy.

"Si, is why I come," replied Father Luigi. "For your help."

"Father Luigi, I sympathise with your situation." Dorothy sighed. "But I have my responsibility here at the hospital."

"I would not come if it is not needed," replied Father Luigi. "There are many injured who need help."

"There are many soldiers here who also need help, Father," said Dorothy.

"Si, I understand and thank you for your kindness," said Father Luigi. "I would not come only for the injured, but Maria is with child."

"Oh God," replied Dorothy, slumping back in her chair. "Maria... she is the young woman I saw in your church?"

"Si," said Father Luigi.

"I checked her baby as best I could. Everything seemed to be all right," stated Dorothy, trying to remember.

"It is possible the baby is hurt," added Father Luigi calmly. "She is in great pain."

"Father, I understand your concern. What am I to do? I am a nurse," stressed Dorothy. "She needs a doctor, Father."

Father Luigi sat quietly.

"Yes, I know you have no doctor," continued Dorothy thoughtfully. "What about the next village?"

"He was our doctor," replied Father Luigi, touching his forehead and each shoulder in turn as he spoke.

"How long has she been sick?" asked Dorothy anxiously.

"More than one week now," answered Father Luigi.

"She is only two months pregnant," remembered Dorothy, thinking aloud.

"Three months...I think," added Father Luigi, shrugging his shoulders.

Dorothy paused a few moments for thought.

"How did you get here?" asked Dorothy curiously now that she had overcome the initial surprise of Father Luigi's visit.

"Luca." Father Luigi smiled, sensing success. "You will come?" he continued.

"I must give it some thought," replied Dorothy.

"We must leave after dark," Father Luigi said.

"I must give it some thought, Father," repeated Dorothy, her mind racing. "If I come...Luca will know where to find me."

"Si, grazie," said Father Luigi, standing up to leave. "Thank you, Dorothy."

"*If* I come," emphasised Dorothy, reminding Father Luigi.

Father Luigi turned and faced the crucifix hanging on Dorothy's wall. He made the sign of the cross and mumbled a few words.

"I go now," said Father Luigi, turning back to face Dorothy.

"Come, let me take you to the door," said Dorothy, walking round her desk.

Dorothy argued with Sister Williams, trying to convince her that going to help Maria and the wounded partisan fighters would be just the same as her last visit. Sister Williams stressed she would not cover for Dorothy if her absence was detected, hoping it would stop her from going.

"I was only missing two nights," stated Dorothy. "Not as long as we thought. This time will be the same, I'll be gone a day at the most."

"Last time you were lucky. Maybe it won't go so well if you go again," said Sister Williams.

"I have to go. Who else is there?" sympathised Dorothy.

"Your responsibilities are here, Dorothy," stressed Sister Williams.

"The paperwork, you mean. You think I should remain here doing paperwork when someone is out there suffering and all it would take is a day's cover," argued Dorothy. "It's no loss to the army or the hospital; it will manage without me for a day or two."

"There are rules and we should follow them—"

"And sometimes we should not," interrupted Dorothy recklessly. "Oh, I don't mean we should go breaking rules . I'm not breaking any rules. I'll just be absent for a day."

"Absence Without Leave is a serious breach of rules," replied Sister Williams, trying to make Dorothy's reconsider her intention.

"Do you think I haven't thought about that?" Dorothy sighed. "I don't want you to get yourself into trouble. If it cannot be avoided, I'll have to face the consequence, but I can't not go and help."

The two nurses looked at each other, pausing their fraught discussion.

"I'll do what I can," said Sister Williams reluctantly. "You are obviously determined to go through with this, but after tomorrow you're on your own. I can't go beyond that, it was hard enough last time."

"Thank you, Sister, you're an angel," replied Dorothy, embracing Sister Williams. "I'll be back after midnight tomorrow. Let's hope that young sleepy sentry is on duty again."

"Just be careful, Dorothy," said Sister Williams, sitting back onto the edge of Dorothy's desk, feeling dejected.

Dorothy gathered medical supplies together in a field bag, rushing to leave the hospital before dusk and the complications of exiting closed gates. She walked steadily along the narrow street to the doorway where she expected to find Luca. It was empty. Dorothy continued down the road, wondering what was wrong, why Luca was not there. She turned the corner at the end of the road and crossed over to the square surrounded by small shops scattered among three- and four-story buildings and homes. Fascist posters and propaganda slogans torn and daubed adorned the walls of the buildings and billboards. Dorothy ambled amongst the dwindling residences going about their business, wondering what she should do before returning to the narrow street by the hospital and the doorway where she first acquainted Luca. She waited. Anxiously Dorothy walked back to the corner, impatient that Luca had still not arrived. Turning to return to the doorway, she saw Luca's small covered truck coming along the narrow street and waved.

Luca stopped the truck alongside Dorothy. Father Luigi opened the door.

"Buongiorno," said Father Luigi as Dorothy climbed in beside him. "Dorothy, you must take care. The streets are dangerous. Florence has many spies."

"Where have you been?" Dorothy sighed, relieved at their arrival and only half listening to Father Luigi. "I have been waiting. It's well after dark."

"Mi scusi," said Luca, looking apologetically.

"We must get fuel…for the truck," explained Father Luigi.

"I thought something had happened," replied Dorothy.

"I say we go after dark…now is after dark." Father Luigi shrugged.

"We go now," said Luca, his smile returning to his bronzed face as he drove off.

"Oh gosh…sorry, I'm not used to your complicated lives and spies," said Dorothy, leaning back against the seat, relaxing against the steel door of the truck, and clutching the canvas field bag on her lap. "I thought something had happened. I got confused."

"Dorothy, please slowly, my English is not good," said Father Luigi.

Luca drove steadily through the mountains, making his precautionary observation stops and arriving safely at the village church.

Dorothy stood for a moment and looked toward the ornamental fountain, thoughtful, trying to imagine the execution of ten villagers and what to expect when she entered the church.

"Come, Dorothy, it is safer inside," persuaded Father Luigi.

Dorothy entered the church, observing the new partisan casualties amongst the attentive villagers. Three bodies lay before the altar covered with sheets and blankets. Maria slept on a makeshift bed, constructed to provide her comfort and lift her off the cold stone slab floor.

"Please, this way," said Father Luigi. "Gloria, she is very sick."

"Gloria...there are women here?" startled Dorothy questioningly.

"E' andata padre," said Alfonso sadly, standing close by Father Luigi, hearing his instruction. "Bungiorno, Dorothy."

Father Luigi stopped and looked toward the altar, making the sign of the cross in the air in front of him.

"I am sorry, she has passed on," said Father Luigi softly, repentantly, not registering Dorothy's comment. "Come we should attend—"

"Father, why are there women here?" interrupted Dorothy.

"They choose to fight, they are partisan." Father Luigi sighed, leading Dorothy down the row of pews. "And is their revolution."

"Oh gosh," said Dorothy, standing in front of an attractive young woman, her long black hair spilling over the dried blood-stained sling supporting her arm. "Father, pass me the field bag."

It was several hours before Father Luigi interrupted Dorothy in her work.

"Dorothy, Maria, she is waking," said Father Luigi.

"Let me finish here and I will come," replied Dorothy.

Dorothy finished applying a field dressing to the partisan fighter's wounded thigh and made her way to Maria's bedside.

"Buongiorno." Dorothy smiled, crouching beside Maria. "How are you?"

"Buongiorno," whispered Maria, returning Dorothy's smile and looking up at Father Luigi for support with Dorothy's question.

"Come ti senti? Dove senti dolore?" said Father Luigi.

Father Luigi continued to translate while Dorothy attended Maria's rib injury and diagnosed the symptoms causing her pain and distress for her unborn child.

"I think the baby is all right, Father," said Dorothy, standing upright from conducting her crouched examination of Maria.

"Si, grazie." Father Luigi sighed. "Is good news."

"She has some swelling below her rib that is tender and causing the pain," continued Dorothy. "I can only think to try penicillin, but I don't have penicillin with me, Father."

"Penicillin," repeated Father Luigi from what he grasped of Dorothy's long explanation.

"Yes, penicillin. Without a doctor I cannot think what more we can do," stated Dorothy.

"One moment," said Father Luigi, turning away, calling, "Luca...Alfonso!"

The three men huddled together mumbling.

"Is possible to get penicillin but will take time," said Father Luigi, returning to Dorothy.

"There isn't much time," replied Dorothy.

"Perhaps one day...we must go to Pistoia," informed Father Luigi. "Florence would be difficult."

"But I must return to the hospital," urged Dorothy.

"Luca will take Carla and go for penicillin," explained Father Luigi. "When they return, we can take you to Florence."

"That could be days," Dorothy said, alarmed.

"They go now...in the evening they will return," said Father Luigi reassuringly. "When they are gone you can rest...you are tired. Is not possible you return to Florence before the evening."

Dorothy sighed, reluctantly accepting Father Luigi's explanation.

"Carla...come...you are needed," called Father Luigi across the nave.

A pretty, buxom woman rose from the pews on the opposite side of the church, picked up a machine gun, and left with Luca.

Dorothy lay resting in Father Luigi's small and tidy home at the side of the church. She remained curious at sending Carla with

Luca and could not let go of thinking of the partisan women, fighting to liberate their country alongside their male counterparts.

Afternoon warmth drifted through the shuttered window of the tiny, dim, and shadowed room. Christopher lay on the crisp white bed, his head wrapped with bandage; Sister Williams stood by the bedside holding a plasma bottle high in the air, attached to Christopher's arm. Dorothy's father sat at the bedside reading a newspaper in his surgical gown; her mother, dressed as a partisan fighter, carrying a machine gun, stood at the end of the bed; her words, shaped by the slow-motion movement of her mouth, were drowned by the noise of a Stuka dive-bomber descending to its target.

Dorothy sat bolt upright, screaming on the bed, hot, breathing heavily, tiny beads of perspiration on her forehead. She reached for the jug of water at the side of the bed and poured shakily into the adjacent glass. Placing the jug down in the spilt water, she gulped the refreshing liquid hastily from the glass and sat trembling on the side of the bed.

Regaining her poise, Dorothy returned to the church to relieve the anxiety of her vivid dream and distract her thoughts, she monitored Maria's progress and attended other injured partisan casualties.

Dusk had turned to darkness and there was no sign of Luca and his voluptuous comrade-in-arms.

"How much longer will they be?" said Dorothy, sitting beside Father Luigi, facing the chancel and the elaborately covered alter.

"Soon," replied Father Luigi, his fingers playing with the small crucifix he wore round his neck. "We must wait."

Dorothy watched the lone candle burning on the altar, slowly shrinking to its wide silver support base.

"Father, surely they should be back by now," asked Dorothy, standing irritably.

"Patience, Sister," said Father Luigi. "Patience, they must be careful."

"I must be going or there will be no time to return." Dorothy sighed, remembering Sister Williams's words of caution.

Father Luigi remained seated on the pew looking at the altar, softly whispering Latin prayers.

Dorothy wandered among the pews and whitewashed nave of the church rechecking wounds and dressings of the recovering partisan soldiers.

Alfonso entered through the side door of the church and made his way to Father Luigi. They talked quietly together as Dorothy approached.

"What has happened?" enquired Dorothy enthusiastically.

"Alfonso asks if I have heard something," replied Father Luigi. "He knows nothing."

Dorothy sat back down on the pew behind Father Luigi and returned her gaze to the remains of the single altar candle before drifting into sleep.

Morning sunlight flooded through the stained windows, filling the church with colour as Dorothy stirred from her sleep, instantly getting to her feet, looking frantically around for Father Luigi and interrupting his conversation with Alfonso.

"Where's Luca, have they returned?" enquired Dorothy fretfully.

"Si, they rest," replied Father Luigi.

"Why didn't you wake me, how long have they been back?" asked Dorothy, annoyed at being left to sleep.

"There is no time, Sister," said Father Luigi calmly. "Is sunrise when Luca return."

"Sorry," said Dorothy. "I am anxious to return to the hospital."

"I understand, Sister." Father Luigi smiled. "This evening you shall return. Come, let us see Maria. Alfonso has the penicillin."

Dorothy administered the penicillin to Maria before once more attending the wounded and rejoining Father Luigi and Alfonso. They enjoyed a small breakfast together of bread and salami brought in by one of the villagers.

The day passed slowly. Dorothy became restless and impatient as the sun passed steadily across the cloudless sky. Mountain shadows began to creep back into the silent valleys, and the tall church tower cast darkness over the ornate fountain in the deserted village square.

Luca and Alfonso entered the church accompanied by two younger men. The more handsome of the two men went directly over to Maria, crouching at the side of her makeshift bed, taking her hand in his. Alfonso and the other young partisan passed among their wounded comrades, assisting and preparing those who had recovered sufficiently to return to their less-vulnerable mountain hideaway.

Luca came to greet Dorothy.

"Buongiorno," said Luca.

"Buongiorno," answered Dorothy with a relieved smile.

"Parla Italiano," replied Luca, his broad smile showing his smooth white teeth.

Dorothy looked blankly at Luca.

"He ask if you speak Italian," said Father Luigi as he approached.

"Antonio, he say thank you...one more time." Luca smiled.

"Where is Antonio? Why does he not come?" asked Dorothy.

"Here is not safe for him," replied Luca slowly.

"Spies are everywhere, watching," added Father Luigi. "We must all be careful; they watch everyone."

"When can we go?" asked Dorothy anxiously.

"Un momento, we go," said Luca, putting his machine gun down on the pew behind Dorothy and going over to Alfonso.

Calls and commands passed round nave as the recovered partisan fighters began leaving the church, led by their young comrade. The handsome visitor left Maria's bedside, threw his machine gun over his shoulder, and approached Dorothy. He took hold of her hand.

"Grazie...grazie," said the young man before following through the side door of the church.

"You're welcome" Dorothy said quietly and smiled, watching him leave the church, still feeling the touch of his hand on hers.

"Two minutes and we go," said Luca, picking up his machine gun, distracting Dorothy.

"Yes, I'm ready." Dorothy startled, returning to the moment.

Machine gun fire began to echo from the mountain. Alfonso and Luca rushed to the side door and disappeared into the darkness.

"Get down, Dorothy. Fascists. Hide in the pews," said Father Luigi as he went and knelt before the altar.

Dorothy squatted among the rows of seats leaning against a cool stone pillar. Her heart raced as she listened to the bursts of machine guns and single cracks of rifle fire as it reverberated round the church. She thought of Maria lying alone in her makeshift bed and went to sit and comfort her. Pauses between the gunfire were filled with silence and the gentle murmur of Father Luigi praying, still knelt before the altar.

The side door to the church burst open, and Alfonso entered carrying, dragging a wounded partisan colleague. Alfonso laid him on a pew, called to Father Luigi, and rushed out of the open door.

Dorothy rushed to the partisan fighter, whose leg she had attended only hours previous; his newly gained stomach wound was bleeding profusely. Dorothy watched her hands turning red as she tried to stem the flow of blood. She had no dressings. The soldier lay panting, whispering.

"It's all right...it's all right," said Dorothy calmly.

The partisan gently exhaled, and his body went limp as he lost his fight to survive.

"God rest him," whispered Dorothy as she slumped onto the pew beside the lifeless soldier and stared at her blood-covered hands resting on her lap.

The sound of gunfire had been silent for some time. Father Luigi left his prayer and came to sit with Dorothy.

"Is over," said Father Luigi reassuringly.

"Is it?" questioned Dorothy. "Do you really think it's over?"

"Come...clean your hands," continued Father Luigi, missing the meaning of Dorothy's reply. "Luca will soon return. Perhaps is possible you go back to your hospital."

The morning sun began lifting the shadows from the mountain valleys. Dorothy sat quietly at the end of Maria's bed.

"Dorothy, you must come. Today is Sunday," began Father Luigi. "The village will come to prayer. Is better they not see you. What they not know they cannot speak of."

"Where is Luca?" replied Dorothy.

"Soon he will come," said Father Luigi. "Now you must come to my home."

"I must get back, Father. I will be in serious trouble," informed Dorothy. "Why hasn't Luca returned?"

"When is safe, he will come," said Father Luigi. "Please help Maria to my house. The village must know nothing of this."

Dorothy looked at the clean, empty pew where the partisan fighter had lost his final battle.

"Where's the dead soldier, Father?" queried Dorothy.

"I put him behind the altar while you sleep," smiled Father Luigi. "No one will know."

Dorothy smiled at the thought of Father Luigi praying over the soldier's body to his unknowing congregation as she helped Maria to Father Luigi's house, followed by three remaining partisan soldiers who were still too ill to return to the mountain hideaway.

It was late in the afternoon when Father Luigi brought Dorothy back to the church. Luca and Alfonso sat eating bread, cheese, and olives laid out on the pew between the two men. They shared a silver goblet of red wine.

"You must eat, Dorothy. Is a long journey," said Father Luigi, offering Dorothy a similar plate of supper.

"Thank you, Father," replied Dorothy, sitting across the aisle opposite her two engrossed escorts.

"Vino?" asked Alfonso, offering over the silver goblet.

"No, thank you." Dorothy smiled, nibbling at her bread, pondering the two men's recent fraught activity and their ferocious appetites.

Father Luigi lit a candle as the church slipped into darkness.

"Is time," said Luca, looking at Dorothy, smiling and picking up his black machine gun.

Alfonso smiled and winked as he made his way out of the church to check that all was safe for their departure.

"Thank you for your kindness, Dorothy. We will not forget," said Father Luigi warmly.

"Good-bye, Father. Take care of Maria. It will be a few days before she is well," replied Dorothy.

"Si, grazie." Father Luigi smiled. "Arrivederci."

Luca drove cautiously through the mountains, stopping frequently to check the safety of their route until they reached the lower foothills. Dorothy sensed the more relaxed mood of her escorts and questioned the previous night's fighting, searching for the reason of their delayed return.

The slow bilingual conversation helped pass the time of their journey, and soon they were passing through the outskirts of Florence toward the Allied Military Field Hospital.

Luca stopped the small black truck along the narrow street, away from the hospital's courtyard gates. The street was empty. The sentry was missing from his post, and Dorothy sensed the large wooden gates were open.

"Something's wrong," said Dorothy, suddenly anxious. "Please wait."

"Si," said Luca as Dorothy climbed from the truck and made her way slowly along the high convent wall toward the arched entrance.

The hospital stood deserted through the wide-open courtyard gates. Dorothy felt her stomach knotting as she returned worriedly to Luca waiting in the truck.

"They have gone," alarmed Dorothy, climbing back beside Alfonso. "The hospital is empty."

"No," said Luca. "You mistake."

"Mi scusi?" questioned Alfonso.

Luca explained to Alfonso before accompanying Dorothy back to the empty hospital. They entered the hallway of the main entrance and walked cautiously into Dorothy's office. Its contents remained the same, only the desk was clear of files and paperwork. The large crucifix cast a broad dark shadow across the wall, and Dorothy felt an eerie, silent atmosphere.

"They go," confirmed Luca.

"One moment." Dorothy gasped, rushing from her office into the casualty ward.

"Oh God." Dorothy sighed, standing in the large, empty ward before returning slowly to Luca and the darkness of the main entrance hall.

"They have gone, Luca," said Dorothy. "What am I to do now?"

"Mi scusi?" replied Luca.

"What must I do? They have gone," repeated Dorothy, running her fingers through her hair, standing silent, thinking.

"Come, we go," said Luca suddenly.

"Go where?" enquired Dorothy.

"My village," replied Luca.

"I don't belong in your village, Luca," said Dorothy, staring through the darkness. "I belong here."

"Mi scusi?" said Luca.

"It's not possible," replied Dorothy, frustrated with Luca's limited English.

"Where you go?" questioned Luca.

"I don't know," answered Dorothy slowly, thoughtfully.

"Come…I go," said Luca. "Is not possible I stay here."

"One moment," said Dorothy. "I must get my belongings. Please, one moment."

"Si, un momento." Luca smiled.

Cautiously Dorothy made her way through the dark, empty hospital and entered her room. The bed was stripped of blankets, and her open cupboard doors revealed bare wooden shelves. She searched through the draws for her belongings, desperate for something of her uniform other than the grey nursing frock she was wearing. The draws were empty. Going quickly to the open bedroom door, she pushed it closed; her scarlet and grey lanyard swung from the single coat hook on the back of the door.

Dorothy put the lanyard in her pocket and leaned against the wall, looking toward the ceiling, thinking of the difficult position in which she had placed herself before making her way back to Luca and Alfonso waiting in the small black truck parked in the shadows of the empty courtyard.

She was Absent Without Leave and had deserted her position.

THE PARTISANS, ITALY

1945

"Luca...Alfonso, buongiorno...Dorothy!" exclaimed Father Luigi.

"Buongiorno, Father Luigi," greeted Dorothy as she followed her two partisan escorts into the church.

"Why are you here? What has happened?" questioned Father Luigi, alarmingly.

"The hospital has closed, Father," said Dorothy as a simple explanation. "It has moved."

"You must find it, Dorothy," replied Father Luigi. "You must go back; here is no good place for you."

"It is difficult now for me to return, Father," informed Dorothy, slow and dejected, sitting on a pew across from the doorway. "I don't know where to find the hospital, and now I am afraid. I am in very much trouble if I return."

"There is no place here for you, Dorothy," said Father Luigi sympathetically but anxious at Dorothy's return. "It would be danger for the village and for you to remain. I must talk with Antonio."

"Yes, Antonio," repeated Dorothy confidently. "He will think of something, Father."

"One moment. Luca, Alfonso," called Father Luigi, excusing himself and going off to talk with the village's partisan fighters.

Dorothy remained seated on the wooden bench at the side of the church and stared thoughtfully through the open door, remembering Sister Williams's precautions and her reluctance to help, trying to persuade Dorothy not to go back to the mountains and the partisans. She thought of her position as a deserter and what she should do.

"Dorothy," interrupted Father Luigi, closing the church door, "Luca, he will go to Antonio. For now we must wait."

"Yes, Father," said Dorothy, partly listening to Father Luigi's explanation while maintaining her focus and attention on her confused thoughts.

"Please, you wait here. I must arrange food. I was not expecting guests," said Father Luigi. "You can sit with Maria."

"Thank you, Father," replied Dorothy, observing Maria sitting on the opposite side of the church.

Luca had already departed for his discussion with Antonio about Dorothy's presence at the church, Father Luigi left on his mission to arrange lunch for his visitors, and Dorothy joined Maria in an unexpected reunion while Alfonso sat alone cleaning his machine gun.

It was almost noon when Father Luigi retuned to the church, followed soon after by an elderly woman delivering lunch. She chattered endlessly while laying out the food and busying herself around the church, stopping, nodding her head and pausing her chatter to smile approvingly in front of Dorothy before shuffling to her exit.

Dorothy collected bread and cheese, two ripe red tomatoes, and a portion of large black olives for herself and Maria. Father Luigi joined Alfonso and sat eating by the food laid out on the wooden bench seat between them.

The church was quiet following the midday feast. Dorothy

stood admiring the elaborate needlework of the embroidered cloth covering the altar while Maria dozed, supported by a cushion in the corner of her pew. Alfonso resumed his attention to his machine gun, and Father Luigi gathered the dishes and remains of the lunch, placing them on the elderly woman's tray ready for her collection.

A black-uniformed soldier silently entered the side entrance of the church and began speaking loud and commandingly.

"Alfonso!" called Father Luigi, startled and fearful, recognising the Fascist uniform.

Alfonso stood, simultaneously turning to face the intruder and lifting his machine gun.

The soldier calmly raised his arm, and two pistol shots rang through the church. Alfonso fell to the floor, spatters of crimson staining the grey stone slabs.

Dorothy ducked, hoping she had not been noticed as the church fell silent, not wanting to be the next corpse that lay behind the elaborately decorated altar.

A rhythmic click of boot heels began striding slowly along the stone aisle of the nave accompanied by a rich, unwavering voice that echoed round the church, steadily approaching the chancel.

Dorothy trembled as she squatted behind the altar trying to control her heavy, trembling breath, thinking it could be heard by the closing Fascist soldier.

The footsteps stopped at the chancel steps and left the articulate voice resounding round the high walls of the chancel. Father Luigi's calm, quiet voice filled a short pause in the intruder's dialog.

Dorothy heard the sound of leather on the steps as the black-uniformed Fascist made his way closer to the altar.

Maria shrieked nervously, afraid, trying to distract the soldier from his intended direction.

One, two, three … four cracks of gunfire resonated, followed by the sound of Maria's body slumping to the floor.

Dorothy fell to her knees, gritting her teeth and covering her mouth with her hand as her stomach wrenched and vomit seeped between her fingers.

Father Luigi spoke angrily into the calm void.

Another single pistol shot pierced the silence, and a third body collected on the grey stone slabs.

"Antonio," gasped Father Luigi.

The sound of footsteps flooded into the church as Luca and Carla, and the young handsome partisan fighter entered through the open doorway.

Dorothy emerged nervously from behind the altar and observed the bodies strewn round the grey stone floor.

The young partisan soldier franticly made his way to Maria, dropping to his knees, clutching her in a desperate embrace. Slowly he lowered Maria's body to the ground and walked purposefully to the black uniformed murderer lying on the chancel steps. Standing over the Fascist soldier the young partisan angrily fired his machine gun into the dead body.

"Dorothy, come," called Luca, squatting at the side of Alfonso. "Alfonso, he lives."

Dorothy glanced at the frightening intruder's blood-covered body as she cautiously passed the revenged young man standing over his prey, quietly sobbing.

She crouched beside Luca and attended Alfonso's injuries.

"He'll survive," said Dorothy, looking at Luca. "His arm is just a flesh wound; his torn flesh here will need some attention where the bullet has passed through his side, but he should live."

"He will live?" questioned Luca, not understanding all of Dorothy's diagnosis.

"Yes," said Dorothy with a weary smile. "He will live."

Dorothy began to stand up from Alfonso's prostrate position and felt a hand take her elbow, helping her rise to her feet. She met Antonio's attentive gaze.

"You are a remarkable woman, Dorothy," said Antonio softly.

"Thank you for coming when you did," said Dorothy, looking at Antonio.

"It was fortunate," answered Antonio with a sigh. "For Maria... for her we were too late."

"You weren't to know," replied Dorothy mournfully.

"Luca told me why you are here," said Antonio, trying to move away from the terrible event Dorothy had just experienced. "You can see why we must be careful. Here is not the place for you, Dorothy."

"Where can I go?" asked Dorothy. "I will be in serious trouble if I go back…if I knew where to find the hospital."

"It is too dangerous for the people here," replied Antonio. "The Fascists would destroy our village if you were discovered."

"At least until Alfonso is well," bargained Dorothy desperately. "Allow me to nurse him and stay until he has recovered while I think about what I should do."

"Alfonso can not remain here. He must return with me to the mountains," said Antonio.

"There…I can go with you…into the mountains," answered Dorothy.

"It is no place for a woman." Antonio sighed.

"Is she not a woman?" asked Dorothy, turning her head toward Carla. "Do you think we nurses do not follow our fighting men, go where they go? Just because I don't carry a machine gun does not make me weak, Antonio."

"Very well…while you care for Alfonso," Antonio spoke slowly, smiling. "While we think what is to become of you, Dorothy."

Antonio gave orders for the young partisan to help Father Luigi take care for Maria's body and dispose of the Fascist's corpse and black uniform. Dorothy once more bid Father Luigi farewell and climbed into the back of Luca's small black truck where she could comfort Alfonso during the journey. Carla sat in the tiny cab, lodged between Luca and Antonio.

The expedition by truck was quite short, and Luca soon drove into a secluded mountain thicket overlooking the village. Antonio helped Alfonso and began climbing through the steep mountain woodland while Luca camouflaged the truck. Carla passed Dorothy the small bag of provisions as she collected the machine guns from the truck. She smiled as she handed Dorothy Alfonso's clean black gun before heading through the inclined trees. Luca collected his own weapon from Carla as she passed and indicated to Dorothy that she should follow Carla.

Dorothy found trekking through steep woodland cumbersome

in her grey nurse's frock and thought her rough khaki trousers would be better suited. She was warm and perspiring, her breath heavy as the ground levelled and they began to traverse the wooded mountain. Following close behind Carla, they came to a small grassed clearing in front of a dark recess in the steep rock that climbed before them and prevented any further progress.

Antonio laid Alfonso carefully on the ground; his wound had begun to bleed during his exertion up the mountain. Dorothy knelt beside Alfonso, putting his machine gun to one side, and attended his makeshift dressing.

"How much farther? I need water," said Dorothy, looking up at her new partisan comrades. "I must clean this wound."

"One moment, we are here," said Antonio, vanishing into the mountain.

Dorothy got up, amazed at Antonio's disappearance and went to look at his point of departure. Approaching the rock face, an angled protrusion that cut back into the dark recess became visible, and a tall, narrow crack opened up into the mountain.

Antonio emerged from the opening carrying a bottle of water.

"This is amazing. You would never know it existed," said Dorothy, astonished at her discovery. "How did you find it?"

"I would come here when I was a boy," replied Antonio. "Here…your water."

Dorothy took the water and returned to Alfonso's bleeding injury.

"I am sorry you have become left by your hospital," said Antonio softly, crouching down beside Dorothy, watching her work.

"It has happened," replied Dorothy. "How was I to know?"

"But so quick," commented Antonio, enquiringly. "You never knew the hospital was to move?"

"I was part of the frontline support. We would move regularly to keep up with offensive action. The hospital had become a long way from the front line. They must have decided to move somewhere closer," said Dorothy with a sigh. "If I had known, I would not be here."

"The hospital has been there a long time? Why would it just move?" asked Antonio.

"There are new offensives now that the weather has improved, you know this, you talk with our intelligence people," answered Dorothy. "The supply lines have been stretched, and the hospital was never on the supply route. I should have realised it would happen."

"Perhaps I could enquire where the hospital is now," suggested Antonio.

"And go back to a court martial," replied Dorothy thoughtfully. "I'm a deserter, Antonio. I left my position when I should have known better."

"I could speak for you…explain," said Antonio sympathetically.

"It would be no use. I made the decision to leave. Now I must face the consequence," answered Dorothy.

"Come, it is getting dark. We must get Alfonso inside; it gets cold out here at night. We can decide what is best for you later," concluded Antonio.

"Why didn't you tell me you were the mayor?" questioned Dorothy.

"Now is not the time, Dorothy," replied Antonio, looking thoughtfully at Dorothy. "We must move Alfonso."

Dorothy picked up the machine gun and followed Antonio, helping Alfonso down the narrow passage into the mountain. A flickering glow was visible as the ground began to descend deeper into the rock.

"Careful, the ground gets quite steep until we get inside," echoed Antonio's voice.

The passage opened into a large chamber, and the ground became more level as they made their way toward Luca and Carla, who were busy lighting a small fire. The flames' flickering light illuminated the cave, and monstrous shadows slid around the high walls, mimicking Antonio putting Alfonso on a bed of blankets.

Dorothy observed the munitions boxes stacked on the opposite side of the cave, a circle of blanket beds surrounding the central fire and mounds of filled backpacks piled against the cave wall. She put Alfonso's machine gun carefully against the wall and made her way toward the growing fire, feeling its warmth replacing the chill that seeped from the cold rock. Sitting on a brown ruffle of blankets, Dorothy succumbed to the heat from the fire and soon fell asleep.

"I have to go," said Antonio, gently waking Dorothy. "Carla knows what must be done here. Take care of Alfonso. I'll be back in a day or two."

"Where are you going?" asked Dorothy, drowsily.

"Go to sleep. I'll return soon." repeated Antonio.

Dorothy watched Antonio leaving; other giant shadows, cast by the fire's embers, passed around the cave wall.

The clatter of movement at the munitions boxes drew Dorothy's attention, and she sleepily propped herself up on one elbow, peering into the dimness at the boxes being carried out of the secret hideaway. The cave fell quiet, and Dorothy lay back on her blankets. Still tired from her sleepless journey to and from the field hospital, she slipped back into sleep.

Daylight entered the cave high above the spent fire. Dorothy lay looking up at the shaft of sunshine reflecting round the dark rock walls, allowing her eyes to become accustomed to the muted light. She sat up on her blanket bed and looked around the cave; realising she was alone. Getting to her feet, Dorothy made her way outside. The blinding sun stopped her exit, and she shielded her eyes with her hand. Carla sat with Alfonso eating bread and salami, leaning against the mountain, enjoying the warmth of the sun and the shade of the trees.

"Buongiorno," greeted Alfonso and Carla simultaneously.

"Where is everyone?" questioned Dorothy, making her way out of the cave.

Carla looked at Dorothy and pointed to the bread and salami laid on a small coloured cloth covering the ground.

"No, where are Antonio and Luca?" asked Dorothy, trying to remember what had happened earlier that morning.

"Antonio, Luca." Carla smiled, nodding her head and indicating the opposite mountain.

"Thank you," replied Dorothy, not understanding the full

meaning of Carla's gesture but looked toward the distant mountain, assuming that was where Antonio and Luca where.

Dorothy gazed at the scenic mountain view through the cover of trees before collecting bread and salami and joining her two comrades sitting against the side of the mountain to eat her breakfast.

The day passed slowly. Dorothy attended Alfonso's wounds, watched the mountain view, and took a short afternoon nap. Carla disappeared before midday, returning late in the afternoon with more provisions and indicated to Dorothy they should collect wood together if they were going to be warm during the night.

The next day followed a similar pattern. Dorothy became concerned that Alfonso's waist wound was not healing, his torn tissue becoming enflamed and swollen. Carla brought Dorothy a change of clothes more suited to a young Italian civilian woman and enjoyed a few light-hearted moments as Dorothy changed from her grey military nurse's uniform. Luca and Antonio did not return.

It was now three days since Alfonso sustained his injury. Dorothy was anxious that the wound was becoming infected and needed proper treatment. She talked deliberately with Carla, trying to determine when Antonio would return and that Alfonso needed penicillin to stem the spread of infection to his wound.

"Si, penicillina," said Carla, grasping a word from Dorothy's patient dialogue.

"Yes, penicillin," Dorothy responded to Carla and pointed to Alfonso's injury. "How can we get penicillin?"

The excited progress was short-lived, as Carla looked at Dorothy with a vacant expression.

"You ... penicillin," said Dorothy, pointing at Carla and then toward the opposite mountain, hoping it would mean more to Carla than Carla's similar indication had meant to Dorothy two days earlier.

"Ah ... si ... capisco." Carla smiled, patting her chest. "Vuoi che procuri io la penicellina."

"Yes, si," replied Dorothy, smiling, hoping she had understood correctly and was saying the right thing.

"Un momento," said Carla, going to talk to Alfonso.

Carla disappeared into the mountain and returned a few

moments later. She had changed from a fighting partisan soldier in her brown shirt and pants into a beautiful young Italian woman in a blue-patterned frock, buttoned down the front. Her black wavy hair tumbled round her open collar, accentuating her ample breasts, straining the frock's buttons. She carried her machine gun and a small backpack.

"Mama mia." Alfonso smiled, resting against the mountain.

"Per favore," said Carla, smiling at Alfonso and indicating to Dorothy that she should follow.

Dorothy got to her feet and began to follow Carla, returning down the mountainside, stopping at Luca's camouflaged truck.

"Si puoi guidare?" questioned Carla, pointing first at Dorothy, then at Luca's truck and extending her arms and acting as to be holding a steering wheel.

"You want me to drive?" asked Dorothy, patting her chest and imitating Carla's steering wheel gesture, wondering why Luca's truck was still there.

"Dobbiamo andare a Pistoia," said Carla, putting her machine gun and backpack on the floor of the truck and commencing to remove the camouflage.

"I haven't driven anything since my training." Dorothy panicked, helping remove the camouflage while realising Carla had not understood and was progressing regardless of Dorothy's driving ability.

Carla reached inside the truck and handed Dorothy a workman's jacket, indicating for her to put it on. She then offered out an old flat cloth cap.

"You want me to wear that?" Dorothy sighed.

Carla insisted, helping Dorothy to hide her hair inside the cap before cajoling her into the truck and behind the steering wheel. Carla closed the door and stood back looking at Dorothy, smiling.

"Si prego," said Carla, pleased with her achievement, walking to the passenger door and climbing in beside Dorothy. "Ora andiamo a Pistoia."

Dorothy followed Carla's instructions driving nervously, carefully along the mountain roads, slowly gaining confidence with each passing mile. By the time she reached Pistoia, she drove like the Italian peasant driver she portrayed.

Carla guided her through the narrow streets, indicating to stop at the side of the road as they entered a busy square. Together they sat quietly, looking ahead through the truck's windscreen, allowing time for their arrival and presence to pass and to gain their composure. The church on the far opposite side of their parked truck dominated the long, narrow square. Benches spaced round the inner pedestrian area faced inward to the trees, providing shade from the warm, bright sunlight. Tall stone and whitewashed buildings lined the square's perimeter as people busied themselves in and out of the bakers and grocers stores, shading and chatting on the square's parameter benches.

Carla gave a big sigh and rummaged through the small backpack, retrieving a red lipstick that she proceeded to apply to her full, dry lips. She placed the machine gun lying at her feet under the seat and prepared to leave the truck.

"Aspetta qui, Sarò andato per un po'…capisc?" stressed Carla, proceeding to get out of the truck. "Aspetta qui!"

"Yes…si," said Dorothy, smiling nervously, not understanding Carla and unconsciously gripping the smooth black steering wheel while observing the activities of the people in the square through the truck's windscreen.

Dorothy watched Carla proceed along the line of buildings, stopping at a small hardware store and pausing to look back at Dorothy in Luca's parked truck. Turning her attention toward the store Carla ran her fingers through her black wavy hair and stepped through the shop doorway.

The truck's steering wheel became wet and slippery as Dorothy watched Carla enter the store. She removed her hands from the wheel, nervously wiping the perspiration along the thin frock material covering her thighs. Dorothy glanced at the floor and the small brown envelope that must have fallen from Carla's backpack. Retrieving the envelope, Dorothy glanced at the Lira it contained and looked back toward the shop doorway.

Dorothy thought for a moment then removed the cloth cap and workman's jacket, took a precautionary, nervous look round the square, and climbed from the truck, clutching the brown paper envelope. She walked quickly to the hardware shop and entered.

Carla stood close to a balding, portly man, her hand resting on his shoulder, their cheeks almost touching.

Dorothy's sudden entrance startled the preoccupied couple, and Carla stepped back from the chubby, untidy shopkeeper, shocked by Dorothy's appearance.

"Mi scusi," said Dorothy, thinking quickly, hoping she had said the right words as she handed Carla the envelope, realising it did not contain the payment required for the penicillin.

"Grazie," scowled Carla, politely taking the offered envelope.

"Ah...Questa volta avete portato con voi qualcuno di speciale," said the portly storekeeper, turning his attention to greeting Dorothy. "Buongiorno."

"No, No...paghero' io per la penicellina," exclaimed Carla sternly.

"Buongiorno," replied Dorothy anxiously, looking worryingly at the leeching storekeeper, using up her Italian vocabulary.

"Guarda, io ho i soldi," stressed Carla earnestly, stepping across the storekeeper's vision, standing in front of Dorothy and holding up the brown paper envelope to distract his attention.

"Non è un problema, il solito pagamento è accettabile," said the storekeeper, a wide, approving grin appearing on his face as he fixed his eyes on Dorothy and brushed Carla to one side.

Dorothy's feet became rooted to the floor as the fat storekeeper stepped closer and fear strangled her senses. She thought of running, of what was happening, of Alfonso and the quest for penicillin. She smelt the stale odour of the man's closeness but remained paralysed, listening and watching Carla and the slick storekeeper, wishing she knew what was being spoken, knowing that she was the topic of their discussion.

"Per favore...La ragazza non è parte del pagamento," pleaded Carla, taking hold of Dorothy's hand. "Sono il pagamento."

"Il pagamento è aumentato." The storekeeper smiled dryly, sliding his arm across Dorothy's shoulders and guiding her to his lair behind the counter.

A terrifying calm swept over Dorothy, and the storekeeper's

words became slow and muffled as he moved her forward. Gliding toward the opening door behind the shop's counter, she turned her head, smiling, observing Carla's mouthed soundless words and fearful expression. Dorothy felt Carla's outstretched hand grip her departing fingers as she passed through the closing door.

Inside the untidy and jumbled room Dorothy stood transfixed, watching the portly figure taking a brown jar from a wall cupboard above piles of boxes, holding it in front of her and placing it on the desk beside her. She heard nothing as the fat storekeeper stood before her, loosening his pants. His face became red, his expression angry as he stepped forward and forced her over the desk, lifting her thin, fragile frock.

Dorothy looked at the jar of penicillin before her and shrieked silently into the cluttered room, grasping, gripping the edge of the desk, gasping for air as a piercing pain ripped between her thighs.

Slowly Dorothy became conscious of hands helping her to her feet. She focused on Carla's tearful face as she pulled her frock, covering her blood-smeared thighs.

The fat storekeeper spoke energetically as he pushed his shirt back into his waistband.

Carla angrily returned the resentment to the storekeeper and spoke softly, caringly as she helped Dorothy to her feet.

Dorothy rested on the edge of the sacrificial desk, nauseated, her legs uncontrollably trembling. She consciously grasped the jar of penicillin from the desk, smothering it in her frock as she crouched forward, holding her stomach and shuffled slowly out of the lair.

Angrily, the displeased storekeeper ranted across his shop as Carla assisted Dorothy through the door, out onto the street, and steadily made their way toward the parked truck, helping her climb onto the passenger seat.

Dorothy sat bent, leaning forward, her arms crossing her numb abdomen, and Carla dispensed with the cautious workman-like disguise, hastily scrambling behind the steering wheel and fleeing quickly through the streets of Pistoia.

Luca's truck pulled into the safety of the mountain thicket, and Carla jumped from behind the steering wheel, grabbed her machine gun and small backpack, and rushed round the front of the truck to help Dorothy.

"You will need this." Dorothy smiled wearily, handing Carla the jar of penicillin. "For Alfonso."

"Dove l'hai preso," Carla gasped, an astonished look of realisation spreading across her face as she suddenly remembered the purpose of the journey.

Carla helped Dorothy climb through the trees to the mountain hideaway where Antonio, Luca, and several new partisan fighters greeted their return.

"Can I have some water please?" said Dorothy loudly, to no one in particular as she stopped at the edge of the gathered group of males sitting and lying on the small grass mound outside their hideaway.

"The climb is tiring, Dorothy. Go slowly, you would not need so much to drink," said Antonio, smiling at his comment. "Qualcuno dia l'acqua a Dorothy."

"Thank you," said Dorothy, half smiling at Luca as he offered a bottle of water.

Dorothy turned and made her way among the trees and bushes, searching for a secluded thicket where she could wash her soiled body. It was dusk when she returned, avoiding eye contact as she passed through the chatting, laughing men, going directly to the cave and slumping remorsefully onto her blanket bed. She lay watching the flicker of flame illuminating the subdued darkness, turning her face to the shadow and lying silently, avoiding contact with the other partisan occupants as they began entering their hideaway for the night. Dorothy woke startled, propping herself on her elbows, looking round at the sleeping figures before settling back on her blankets and looking up at the soft fire glow in the cave roof.

"My joking was wrong," said Antonio softly, sitting at Dorothy's side. "I am sorry. I did not know what has happened... Now I don't know what I should say."

Dorothy lay quiet, looking high into the emptiness above her.

"This war brings many heartaches... killing... sadness... How can we continue our lives?" whispered Antonio thoughtfully, staring at Dorothy's shadowed face. "How do we face our future? How can we begin to be happy again…forget? Alfonso, he would kill this man. He is angry for you. You have given so much to our village…now this. This is not how we live. Our village was different; you would have liked it here…before all this fighting."

Antonio paused and looked at Dorothy. Gently, affectionately he brushed her hair back from off her tired face, knelt forward, and softly kissed her forehead.

"Try and rest," said Antonio.

✛ ✛ ✛ ✛ ✛

Dorothy stood outside the cave entrance, amongst the waking partisans, and enjoyed the warm morning sunshine, looking through the trees at the view across the valley. She was concerned at the tenderness and presence of blood still seeping from her inside and asked Antonio if he would explain to Carla to accompany her to Father Luigi's so she could wash more thoroughly, as it had been several days since she had been able to clean herself properly.

Antonio was not too pleased at Dorothy's request and tried to explain the danger of going to the village before conceding to her demand.

Dorothy made her way down the mountain and offered light conversation in her greeting with Father Luigi before requesting somewhere to wash. Upon return, she noticed the priest's caring and sympathetic mood as he bid her farewell, realising Carla had informed him of the payment she had made for Alfonso's penicillin.

The climb back up the mountain left Dorothy tired, and she returned to the sanctuary of her blankets inside the hideaway.

The cave was in darkness as Dorothy lay tossing and turning on her ruffled bed. Her inside was sore and tender; her mind raced, her breath short and panting, calling Mary…Mary! She heard the cannon fire and the air raid siren, picturing line upon line of wounded soldiers streaming from the field hospital, vividly dreaming of the fat storekeeper standing before her. She woke sharply from the torment, sighed heavily, and swallowed hard the saliva filling her mouth.

Dorothy lay calming herself, conscious of the pain in her stomach.

Carla sat quietly, comforting Dorothy, holding her hand, smoothing her brow with a damp red neckerchief.

"Do we have some penicillin left?" asked Dorothy, smiling at Carla and squeezing her hand.

"Penacillina?" questioned Carla.

"Si, penacillina," repeated Dorothy, realising she was going to need medication if she was going to stop the deterioration and infection of her internal injuries.

"Un momento," said Carla, getting to her feet and going to find Alfonso.

Dorothy remained on her blankets, her condition becoming more uncomfortable as her temperature began rising throughout the day.

For two more days Carla stayed by Dorothy's side, offering water, providing the penicillin and attending her needs.

"I'm hungry," said Dorothy softly, looking at Carla, squeezing her hand and waking her from her drowsiness.

"Scusi," said Carla, startled by Dorothy's movement and focusing her attention.

Dorothy gestured her desire for something to eat, and Carla left her alone in the silence of the cave as she went to fetch food for her patient.

The pain in Dorothy's stomach was gone; she felt only a slight tenderness as she sat jadedly on her blankets.

Getting to her feet, Dorothy wearily made her way to the daylight flooding through the cave's entrance. She joined Carla in the bright sunshine and sat leaning against the warm mountain rock to enjoy her crisp-crusted bread and juicy red tomatoes that had been prepared.

Together Dorothy and Carla quietly enjoyed absorbing the radiating heat of the sun, the gentle breeze blowing through the trees as it passed along the side of the mountain and carried on down the valley.

The war was a long way away. The quiet of the mountain, the warm sunshine on her body, Dorothy closed her eyes enjoying the peace and calm, the occasional draft of the wind as it caressed the softness of her skin.

Time slowly slipped by as a distant chime of bells drifting in the breeze began to multiply along the valley. Dorothy and Carla stirred from their lethargic relaxation, drawn to the sound of the church bells ringing through the mountains; they stared through the trees, listening to the bells echoing loudly along the rugged peaks, lifting from the valley, rejoicing in their announcement of the end of war.

BEMUSED

"Good gracious," interrupted the doctor slowly, leaning back in his chair, bemused by Dorothy's story. "Mister Harry, I'd like you to stop there please. I have patients to see. However, I would like to know more about Dorothy. How would you like to continue this conversation this evening over dinner?"

"Yeah, sure," replied Harry, instantly falling hungry. "Thank you."

The doctor provided Harry with arrangements for the evening and summoned a nurse to take him to visit Dorothy.

"Seven o'clock," confirmed the doctor as Harry was leaving his office.

"Yeah, sure, thank you," replied Harry and followed the nurse down the corridor.

Harry sat at Dorothy's bedside holding her hand. She was sleeping and still looked quite pale in comparison to her familiar, lively, weathered complexion he was used to seeing. She was propped up, her head resting deep into the crisp white pillows, her face peaceful. Harry admired the strength Dorothy possessed to confront her life's challenges and continually give of herself, despite the torment that persistently raged within. He sat quietly for some time, looking at her, thankful that she was able to rest and recover, properly cared for.

"Perhaps you should come back later, when she's awake," whispered the nurse over Harry's shoulder.

"Yeah, no problem," replied Harry, standing up to face the nurse. "Would you tell her I've been and I'll come back tomorrow?"

Harry wandered the streets for the remainder of the day, going nowhere in particular. He window-shopped and wanted to buy something for Doris for his next visit but only felt angered by his poor lack of finance. He cursed his situation and determined to change and be able to get both himself and Doris off the street. Daylight was fading as Harry headed back toward the railway station and the Gents. He decided to look a little more respectable for his evening with the doctor, and the Gents Wash and Brush-up was the only place available to him.

Hmm, what a coincident, Italian, thought Harry, his stomach turning and mouth watering as he sat at the restaurant table opposite the doctor.

"So, tell me, Mr. Harry, what prevented Dorothy from returning to England?" asked the doctor as he noticed Harry had finished his rather large serving of ravioli.

THE END OF WAR, ITALY

1945

Rejoicing villagers gathering at their church made way as Luca drove the small black truck into the square. Dorothy watched as Carla climbed down and immersed herself joyfully into the celebrating and happy throng of friends. Alfonso appeared, standing beside the truck's door, stretching out his arms, welcoming Dorothy. She hesitated before climbing down and was smothered by Alfonso's hugs.

"Grazie, grazie," said Alfonso, wrapping his arms round Dorothy, lifting her feet from the floor and twirling her round. "La Guerra...è finita."

Luca came round the front of his truck, rescuing Dorothy from Alfonso's excitement and embraced her warmly before Alfonso grasped them all into a celebratory hug.

Dorothy became dizzy and sat on the wall of the fountain as

Alfonso released his grip, and the two men were swallowed by a group of cheery partisan comrades entering the square to join the impromptu celebration.

Tables were being erected by the fountain, wine and bread, cheese and olives and pasta dishes were placed on the white cloths spread over the makeshift tables. A band of mature musicians gathered on a wooden platform placed in front of the church. Young children played in the fountain's water and chased through the gathered inhabitants. Elderly men and women greeted and chatted and comforted each other in the warm afternoon sun while the mature women of the village busied themselves with the celebration's preparations. A small group of young partisan men and women collected in the centre of the square.

A warm smile lighted Dorothy's face as she looked round, observing the gathered friends and families basking in the spontaneous relief that the ringing bells had brought. She too was pleased to hear the war was over, but she couldn't help notice the absence of men from the happy gathering. In that moment she felt lost, isolated, alone among the villagers. She looked to the ground and let here eyes close, wondering where she belonged, what she should do, where she could go.

"Now we must count the cost," said Father Luigi, standing before Dorothy.

"Sorry," replied Dorothy, surprised by Father Luigi's comment, opening her eyes and looking up at the priest.

"Now it is over. Tomorrow we must return to our lives," said Father Luigi, taking hold of Dorothy's hand affectionately. "First we should rejoice."

"Yes, now it is over." Dorothy smiled.

"Come, first let us eat something together. We should enjoy this day," suggested Father Luigi, keeping hold of Dorothy's hand and leading her toward the long, inviting food table. "Tomorrow we have a new beginning."

Dorothy joined Father Luigi, indulging in the celebration food before he surprisingly paraded her round the square and introduced her to members of the community, finally arriving at a small table occupied by Luca and Antonio.

"This is our mayor, Mr. Liumbardo, and his brother, Luca, who I believe you know." Father Luigi smiled. "Gentlemen, Sister Dorothy."

"Oh, you're brothers," said Dorothy, looking at Antonio a little surprised.

"Yes, Luca is my young brother," replied Antonio, smiling at Dorothy. "I had him watch over you when you came to our village."

"Buongiorno, Luca," greeted Dorothy, pleased to see his happy, grinning face while her mind quickly retraced the events of the past few weeks, looking thoughtfully at Antonio. "Where is the mule, Antonio?"

"It is somewhere." Antonio smiled.

"Boungiorno, Dorothy," said Luca, pulling her a chair from under the table.

"Did you also arrange for Father Luigi to visit me at the hospital?" enquired Dorothy, focusing on Antonio, confused, feeling some deeper motive lay behind her presence in the village.

"No...I was not here. Please sit down," explained Antonio, politely gesturing to Dorothy. "My village was desperate after the Germans fired on our homes and shot our friends and families."

"Yes, I remember," replied Dorothy, sitting at the table next to Luca.

"I asked Luca to visit you for help. Antonio told me about you, and we had no one to turn to," interrupted Father Luigi, claiming a close-by chair and sitting down at the table.

"They shot your family?" enquired Dorothy, sympathetically looking at Antonio while accepting Father Luigi's explanation to relieve some of her curious suspicion.

"My father," replied Antonio.

"I'm sorry," said Dorothy caringly.

"Perhaps it was to bring me back to the village." Antonio sighed. "They shot my father...my friends. If I returned they would shoot me...and I could not avenge their murders."

"We are sorry also...for what has happened bringing you here," stressed Father Luigi. "We did not want for you to be left here."

"What will you do...now the war has finished?" asked Antonio.

"I don't know." Dorothy sighed; flashes of war images, disasters, and events that had brought her to the village passed through her confused mind. The feeling of being lost, knowing her home and family where gone welled up inside to bring a lump in her throat and tears to her eyes. "There isn't much left for me now. My family in England have also been killed."

"I'm sorry, I didn't know," said Antonio, sitting forward on his chair, alarmed.

"Where will you go?" asked Father Luigi with concern.

"You can stay here. We will find somewhere for you...while you decide," offered Antonio calmly, reassuringly, his eyes now fixed on Dorothy.

"You are welcome, Dorothy...You have many friends here," said Father Luigi.

"Thank you, you are most kind...but I must think," replied Dorothy. "It's all so quick, and now I must think where I belong."

"You are welcome at my house, Dorothy. The war may be over here in Italy, but it is not over for some," offered Antonio warmly before grinning. "I can have Luca watch over you ... while you think."

Dorothy let her attention wander to the music and the people starting to dance.

Everything previous to this day had been simple; she had followed orders and gone where she had been sent. There had been nothing to decide, nothing to think about, no hesitancy, just do her work as she had been instructed. Now she was confused, alone. Now she had to think for herself and the situation she now found herself in. How was she going to survive and face her future?

"There will be a service in the morning...for thanks, now the war is over," said Father Luigi, bringing Dorothy's attention back to the table. "We would like you to come, Dorothy."

"Yes, thank you, Father," replied Dorothy.

"Si, scusi, now I must see my people." Father Luigi smiled, leaving the table.

Long shadows began to stretch across the square as dusk crept inch by inch toward darkness. The band played slowly as Dorothy watched the remaining aged dancers shuffling round the square.

"Would you like to dance?" asked Antonio.

"No, I'm fine, thank you," replied Dorothy nervously, her heart suddenly beating strongly in response to Antonio's attention and request, her mind torn between her attraction and her doubt about his conduct.

"Come, one dance ... to forget the past and welcome the future," said Antonio, getting from his chair, taking Dorothy's hand, and leading her from the table.

Antonio put his arm round Dorothy and guided her slowly to the music's rhythm. Dorothy relaxed from her initial, anxious response and allowed herself to drift away with the music and motion of the dance and Antonio's charisma. She thought of the one dance she had shared with her father, of his firm and masculine presence and confident posture, his gentle touch and warm smile as she glided round the ballroom, secure and loved.

The music ended. Dorothy and Antonio stopped dancing, looking into each other's eyes, and for a split moment remained holding hands, Antonio's arm round Dorothy's waist, Dorothy's arm across Antonio's broad shoulders. Dorothy panicked and stepped back from Antonio.

"Thank you ... that was lovely," said Dorothy, unsure of what had happened.

"Come, I will show you to my house and you can rest," responded Antonio, smiling warmly. "It has been a long day."

Leaving the band to put away their instruments, Dorothy left the square and walked through the narrow village streets with Antonio and Luca, climbing cobbled steps that rose steeply between high, adjacent houses before opening onto a broader road that ran downhill toward the edge of the mountain village. It was dark as Antonio pushed open a heavy wrought iron gate at the side of a large detached villa.

Antonio opened the solid wooden door leading into a grand entrance hall; he passed across its wide mosaic floor and indicated for Dorothy to follow up the stone and railed stairway. Luca bid them goodnight and disappeared through a doorway at the bottom of the stairs. Dorothy climbed the turning steps as they contoured round the edge of the impressive hallway, observing the paintings adorning the high walls.

Walking along a windowed landing, Antonio opened the end door that faced back along the marble floor.

"You will be comfortable in here, it was my sister's room," said Antonio.

"She is dead?" exclaimed Dorothy, standing at the doorway.

"No...she has married and lives in another village," replied Antonio, closing the curtains and offering Dorothy a lighted candle.

"Thank you," smiled Dorothy. "Good night."

Antonio closed the door behind him as he left Dorothy holding the candle high above her head, looking round her new bedroom. She placed the candle on a dresser between the elaborate curtains that hung from the high ceiling, resting delicately on the polished wood floor. Dorothy sat on the edge of the large, soft bed, kicked of her shoes, and fell back onto the lush covered mattress.

Muted sunlight filtered through the curtains, and a dry pool of candle wax remained in the base of the brass holder sitting on the dresser. Dorothy stirred and made her way to the window, sleepily drawing back the curtain. Rugged, tree-covered mountains gave way to green rolling hills; distant village rooftops reflected the morning sun, surrounded by silhouettes of Cypress and fir trees. Below, a small, ornate garden blossomed in the spring warmth.

"Oh gosh, how lovely!" exclaimed Dorothy, wiping her sleepy eyes, remaining at the window.

Her thoughts turned to Antonio, reflecting on his behaviour: his denial of being a partisan captain, his misleading of who was mayor, and discovering Luca to be his brother. She knew little more about him than during her discussions while hiding and caring for him at the hospital. Yet the two British officers seemed to know who he was, or at least how important it was to have him returned. Here Father Luigi had hidden nothing, only praising his actions to protect the village and its people from the Germans, who seemed only to want to shoot him.

"Perhaps I'm imagining too much." Dorothy sighed, making her way downstairs to try and find someone.

Dorothy called out as she reached the bottom of the stairs, looking inquisitively through the door Luca had disappeared through the night before. It was a spacious sitting room with a grand fireplace and fine antique furniture. It was empty, and Dorothy closed the door, calling again into the echoing hallway. Luca opened a large door on the opposite side of the entrance hall.

"Buongiorno." Luca smiled, beckoning for Dorothy to follow him into the room.

Inside was a large stone-floored kitchen filled with a coffee aroma, a plain wooden table dominating the centre of the room, surrounded by heavy wooden chairs. Antonio sat at the table, eating and gulping coffee with each mouthful of bread and salami.

"Buongiorno, Dorothy, you have slept well?" greeted Antonio.

"Thank you, yes," replied Dorothy.

"Please ... help yourself to bread. Would you like coffee?" asked Antonio generously. "We have some time before Father Luigi's service."

"Where is everyone?" asked Dorothy, sitting at the table, breaking off a portion of bread from the crusty loaf.

"We are here," replied Antonio, curiously observing Dorothy and looking wide-eyed at Luca.

"What about the rest of your family?" enquired Dorothy. "Where are they?"

"Oh, Mama, she is getting ready for church. You will meet her soon. She is old. Things take her time now, but she will not ask for help," answered Antonio. "Muriel is somewhere fighting. The last I knew she was north in Milano."

"She is a partisan?" asked Dorothy.

"She is very passionate about her country. I fear for the Fascist who would stand against her," replied Antonio. "Perhaps soon she will return. The war is over between the Germans, but we still have to rid our country of Fascist dictators."

"Looking from the bedroom window it is hard to imagine the conflict. The view, it is so lovely," said Dorothy. "How long have you lived here?"

"This has always been our family's home," said Antonio.

"It is very nice, Antonio," remarked Dorothy.

"Grazie, scusi," said Antonio, turning to talk with Luca.

Dorothy listened to the rapid conversation between the two brothers, observing the calm, motionless posture of Antonio in comparison to the articulate gestures of Luca. The conversation stopped, and Luca left the kitchen. Antonio sat and poured another coffee before turning his gaze toward Dorothy.

"Why did you not tell me you are the mayor of the village?" asked Dorothy, looking back at Antonio.

"Please, is not important, now you know," said Antonio. "My village is important, not who I am."

"It is important to me, Antonio," replied Dorothy. "So is the reason that I am here. You brought me here."

"The village needed help," said Antonio. "Father Luigi sent Luca only to ask if you would come."

"But Father Luigi...you sent him?" queried Dorothy. "You asked Father Luigi to visit me."

"Si." Antonio sighed in admission. "I send Father Luigi."

"There was no reason for me to come a second time. You used Maria," stated Dorothy. "You knew the hospital would move...that I would be left."

"How can I know such a thing?" argued Antonio. "It happened."

"You have contacts; you talk with our intelligence people...That is why it was important for you to be returned, because you provide their information," reasoned Dorothy. "You knew they would be moving the hospital, and so you sent for me. Why?"

"Because I—"

The kitchen door opened, and a rounded elderly lady dressed in black entered.

"Ah, Mama," said Antonio.

Dorothy was introduced to Antonio's mother, followed by a short exchange of greetings and pleasantries, interpreted by Antonio before he excused himself to dress for church. Dorothy returned to her room and sat at the dresser brushing her hair. She cursed his mother's untimely entrance, wondering what Antonio was about to tell her. Her mind was confused by the emotional desire and cautious acceptance of Antonio's explanations and her cold feeling of isolation and belonging. Dorothy tidied her appearance, smoothing out her grey nurse's frock and loosening her collar before returning to the kitchen to join Antonio's family and departing for Father Luigi's service of thanks.

The fireball of sunlight descended slowly to the distant, rolling hills of Tuscan landscape, and Dorothy savoured the peaceful moment among the blossom of the villa's mountain garden. Antonio joined her, together observing the tranquil view.

"I apologize for this morning," said Antonio quietly. "You are right...I brought you here. I thought there was time."

"Time, Antonio, time..." Dorothy sighed. "Look what has happened."

"I new the hospital was to move, and I wanted to see you. To talk with you," explained Antonio, "and I became trapped in the mountains. I'm sorry for what has happened, but it has not changed how I feel."

"How you feel," repeated Dorothy.

"I am in love with you, Dorothy," said Antonio. "From the first moment in that hidden room...I tried to say something even then, but I only caused you embarrassment and made a fool of myself."

"I wasn't embarrassed, Antonio," replied Dorothy affectionately, her heart softening to Antonio's words. "You surprised me. I wasn't expecting you to say something like that."

"I had to let you know how I felt...before the hospital left and you were gone," continued Antonio, "so I sent Father Luigi."

Dorothy closed her eyes, comforted by Antonio's admission, elated by his warm proclamation, confused with what she should do.

"And now..." whispered Dorothy.

"Now it is for you to decide, as it was meant to be if I had spoken with you before...before this happened. You asked for time to think what you must do. Now you know how I feel, that I love you. What more can I say?" Antonio sighed. "I will respect your answer. I would have done that before, but I had to let you know before you decide."

"What about being mayor?" asked Dorothy. "Do I become a mule?"

"It is nothing. You have not lived in Italy these past years," said Antonio. "Every day you must be careful what you say and to whom. What you do not know you cannot repeat...that is all."

Dorothy took Antonio's hand.

"Thank you. I will let you know what I decide." Dorothy smiled warmly.

Returning to her room, Dorothy took her time pondering her dilemma. She wandered the village and strolled mountain pathways, visited Father Luigi, discussing the village history and Italian lifestyle and customs. She practiced her Italian talking with Carla, bonding their friendship as their communication and understanding became clearer. Antonio provided money for Dorothy to buy clothes and together with Carla went off in Luca's truck shopping.

The journey to Pistoia was steady and bumpy, and Dorothy watched Carla as she wrestled the steering wheel left and right, concentrating on the twisting, turning mountain road. She observed the style and casual fit of Carla's simple one-piece dress with flowing skirt and open blouse neckline, her curls of thick black hair cascading over her shoulders and sleeveless outfit. Summer was fast approaching, and perhaps it would be wise to find something similar for the hot weather to come.

Arriving in Pistoia, Carla parked the truck and led Dorothy to a small costume shop, giving instructions to the assistant who presented a collection of dresses comparable to Carla's. Antonio's money provided for three costumes with change for shoes and handbag, purchased from another specialised shop.

Carla had persuaded Dorothy to wear the shoes and one of the outfits before taking her to a crowded coffee bar, sitting her in the window to show off her friend in her new clothes.

"Now you are Italiano." Carla smiled, drinking her strong black coffee, enjoying the simple pleasure of shopping with her friend without the conflict of war that had installed a previous cautious tone to their lives and conduct.

Dorothy's face shone with the thrill of her new dress, looking down at her shoes and smiling at Carla. They chatted elatedly over their coffee, laughing loudly as Dorothy used the wrong words of her new language. The pitch of conversation lowered as Dorothy divulged Antonio's pronouncement and made known her torment of what she should do.

"You would do well by Antonio, he is a good man…and he is mayor." Carla smiled.

Leaving the coffee shop, Dorothy strolled the narrow streets, guided by Carla, their arms looped together as they chatted and giggled while walking back to Luca's truck. Dorothy tensed, recognising the imposing church that dominated the square they had just entered. Her stomach knotted and churned, her body flushed with the rush of blood as her heart thumped against her chest, and she nervously glanced along the row of buildings to the small hardware shop. Carla noticed the hesitancy in Dorothy's stride, the pause in her conversation as they crossed the road and passed under the shade of the trees, then quickening her pace to make a hasty exit and disappear along the shaded street that returned them to Luca's waiting truck.

Climbing into the passenger side of the black vehicle, Dorothy sighed with relief and slumped into the worn seat, spilling her shopping bags onto the floor. She calmed her breath, looking ahead out of the windscreen as Carla got behind the steering wheel.

"It is all right, Dorothy," said Carla calmly.

"What if I had seen him? I felt so sick," replied Dorothy, trying to dispel her thought and remain composed.

"The pig is dead," Carla informed Dorothy, reassuringly, turning to sympathise with her friend.

"Dead? What do you mean? How do you know?" Dorothy questioned.

"He met with an accident…apparently." Carla sighed.

"When?" asked Dorothy. "How do you know all this?"

"Let's just say I know." Carla smiled, starting the engine of the old truck.

Dorothy removed one of her dresses from the shopping bag and held it up to admire and examine it, using it as a distraction from Carla's comments while the truck weaved its way out of Pistoia. Climbing the mountain road, Carla's comments returned, and Dorothy contemplated what kind of accident the gross hardware storekeeper could have met with and remained quiet, watching the scenery and darkening shadows, leaving Carla to concentrate as they journeyed home in the fading light.

Several days passed, during which Dorothy visited the village church and sat among the pews staring at the altar, her thoughts turning over what she had learned from talking with Father Luigi and Carla, recalling her comment about doing well by Antonio and offering a prayer as she remembered Maria. She recalled the cold-blooded murder of her death and envisioned a similar accident had befallen the obnoxious storekeeper.

Dorothy returned to Antonio's villa, dawdling through the narrow streets, returning greetings from passing villagers as she climbed the steep cobbled steps, reflecting on the tranquil pace of life, the resilience of its people that absorbed the atrocities of German retaliation, murder, and Fascist slaughter. She thought of the dividing conflict between the people and their struggle to rid the country of Fascist oppression and the contrasting peace and isolation of the village and mountains. Dorothy dejectedly acknowledged the absence and loss of her home and family in Bath as she pushed open the hefty wrought iron gate of the villa's courtyard and made her way to the large family kitchen.

"Ah, Dorothy," greeted Antonio. "Tomorrow I have business in Florence, perhaps you would like to accompany me?"

"That would be lovely, Antonio." Dorothy smiled.

"We should take Carla, and together you can enjoy the sights of Florence and take coffee in Piazza d. Repubblica while I do business and join you for lunch," suggested Antonio.

"That would be nice," replied Dorothy, a little dejected at not having Antonio to herself for the day.

"Fine…then that is what we shall do," concluded Antonio, pleased with his arrangement. "We must leave early if I am to be there on time."

"What business do you have to conduct?" asked Dorothy, hoping to pry a little into Antonio's commercial affaires.

"It is just a meeting to discuss preparations for moving some paintings," replied Antonio casually. "The war has finished, and Florence's art treasures are scattered far and wide. Now they must be returned to their rightful place."

"You have some dealings with the restoration of Florence's

paintings?" asked Dorothy, surprised by Antonio's answer to her prying question.

"Just a small involvement." Antonio smiled. "Art and antiques are the family business, Dorothy, you have not noticed?"

"I thought it was just an interest, that the wine and vineyards were your business," replied Dorothy.

"Unfortunately the vineyards are not large enough to be commercial in wine production, Dorothy," informed Antonio. "That remains my hobby but an enjoyable one. Oh, Dorothy, would you wear the blue dress tomorrow, please? I like that one."

"We shall have to see," said Dorothy teasingly.

Dorothy sat between Antonio and Carla in her new blue dress as Luca's truck descended the Apennine Mountains and approached the floodplains of the Arno River, en route to Florence. The descent had been much quicker without the frequent precautionary observation stops she had previously made with Luca. Sunlight lifted from behind the mountain backdrop into the morning sky and bathed the distant Duomo that dominated the outlying Renaissance city. Antonio stopped the truck at the Piazza della Liberta to allow Dorothy and Carla to alight.

"We'll meet at the Savoy in Piazza d. Repubblica, just after noon," said Antonio, preparing to rejoin the steady flow of traffic passing round the large island. "We can have lunch there."

Crossing the road toward the narrow Vias that lead to the awe-inspiring centre of the ancient city, Dorothy watched Antonio and Luca's small black truck disappearing into the flow of vehicles. Meandering along the shaded footpaths, the dome of Cattedrale di Santa Maria del Fiore became visible as the avenue converged toward Piazza del Duomo. Entering the square, Dorothy stopped and marvelled at the magnificence of the green, white, and pink marble façade of the church's exterior walls. Carla took Dorothy inside the cathedral where she was amazed by the vast expanse and rather spartan interior in comparison to the external radiance. Newly built walls still protected the frescoes that adorned the church's more recognised structure behind, while the splendour of Brunelleschi's dome captivated her view and stressed her neck.

Passing from the dim interior of the church and out into the sunlight of the piazza, Dorothy shielded her eyes as she searched for a café to relax and take some much needed refreshment. She chatted endlessly with Carla over coffee before taking to the streets to wonder once more at the impressive spectacle of the Renaissance architecture. She observed the removal and opening of dark-shuttered windows, the progressive elimination of Fascist propaganda posters, and the relaxed mood of the city. Dorothy persuaded Carla to just walk to the Ponte Vecchio before returning to meet with Antonio, as her last visit had been rushed, unable to take her time and absorb the ambiance of the bridge and the flow of the Arno River passing beneath.

Dorothy sat at the restaurant table waiting with Carla for Antonio to arrive; it was approaching one and there was no sign of his appearance.

"So sorry I am late," apologised Antonio, sitting at the table, unfastening the buttons of his black double-breasted jacket. "The meeting lasted longer than I anticipated. So, how was your morning? Florence is a beautiful city, Dorothy."

"It is lovely," answered Dorothy, unsure if Antonio was making a statement or asking her a question.

"Do you like my tie?" asked Antonio, lifting his blue-and-black diagonally striped tie and wafting it in the direction of Dorothy and Carla. "I chose it to go with your dress, Dorothy."

"So that was the reason I was to wear the blue one," said Dorothy, smiling. "Thank you ... and your tie is nice too."

"What shall we drink, Chianti?" suggested Antonio.

A smart, mature waiter duly arrived, taking their order, and the threesome ate and drank and chatted throughout the course of their lunch, finishing relaxed and satisfied and the lone table remaining occupied in the restaurant.

"I think it just remains for me to settle the bill and we should make our way home," announced Antonio. "That was a splendid occasion, very enjoyable."

Dorothy watched for the mountain village as they climbed the winding road, not seeing it until it suddenly appeared rounding a bend, like her first encounter. Antonio parked the truck in the square, said farewell to Carla, and with Dorothy walked casually back toward his villa.

"Thank you, Antonio. I have enjoyed today," said Dorothy thoughtfully. "If it's all right with you, I think I would like to remain here in the village. I find it very comforting here."

LIFE IN ITALY

Dorothy began her day at her bedroom window observing the misty Tuscan landscape warming to the morning sunlight. She was pleased with her decision to build a life in the mountain community and was happy to accept Antonio's request for her to operate the village clinic until arrangements to replace their unfortunate doctor could be made, stressing that she was a nurse and had little ability to diagnose or treat sickness.

Accompanying Antonio, she made her way to the small civic building, located in the village square opposite the church. Antonio showed her to the ground floor room previously used by the doctor to conduct his surgery. It was spacious with a central desk and three chairs, one for the doctor situated between the desk and the tall window that overlooked the square, two for the attending patients to provide comfort while they divulged their ailments. A filing cabinet and tall wooden bureau stood against the wall behind the patients' chairs, and a row of five additional chairs lined the corridor wall outside the office door.

"I'll send someone to help clean and tidy while you find your way around," said Antonio before departing to his plush first-floor office. "The Germans are such pigs. I'll place a letter on the village notice board and ask Father Luigi to also announce the commencement of your clinic at mass on Sunday."

"Thank you," replied Dorothy, sitting in the doctor's chair.

Dorothy looked at the weight scales standing against the wall and small corner washbasin to the right of her desk. Opening a drawer at her desk presented the remains of German paperwork, while the bottom drawer contained a sheathed dagger with the swastika emblazoned on the end of its handle. She gathered the paperwork and piled it on the desktop, ready for disposal, and closed the drawer on the forgotten weapon. More abandoned papers remained in the filing cabinet along with the villagers' medical records. Inspection of the tall glass and cupboard bureau uncovered a minute supply of dressings and medicines, while a small enamel dish contained scalpel, tweezers, and a magnifying glass. Dorothy made a list of what additions she would likely need.

Activity through the civic building increased with the morning; loud and rapid conversations ensued along the corridor, while slower and quieter greetings of welcome were offered through the clinic's open door. The approach of noon brought a lull in the commotion, and Antonio returned, requesting Dorothy's company for lunch, eating at a plain café along a narrow street adjacent to the square popular with the working fraternity for the quality of its food. The afternoon was free, and Dorothy arranged for Carla to accompany her to Pistoia the following day in order for her to purchase the additional and necessary medical supplies.

The opening of Dorothy's surgery passed with patients' curious attendance gaining with confidence clinic by clinic. Days became routine, attending lunch with Antonio on the three alternate mornings of her clinic while passing other days assisting Father Luigi in the church, helping Luca with supervision of the family vineyards and olive groves, and spending time with Carla, learning Italian while they talked, walking the mountains or sitting by the village fountain.

Frequently Antonio would ask for Dorothy's company while

performing civic duties or on trips to Florence when pursuing his business interests, all through the hot summer months their relationship blossoming and ripening like the fruit on the vines.

"How are the grapes?" asked Antonio, gulping his morning coffee. "Are they ready for harvest?"

"Another week or two and they will be ready," replied Luca, sitting across the breakfast table.

"The grape harvest is a big occasion, Dorothy," said Antonio. "Especially the festa dell'uva that follows."

"I'm looking forward to it. Luca has been telling me," answered Dorothy.

"Tomorrow I must visit Florence. I would like you come, Dorothy," said Antonio. "I'm sure Luca can spare you for the day."

"That would be nice, thank you," replied Dorothy. "You don't mind, Luca?"

"We must only wait for the sun to complete its work. Enjoy your day," said Luca. "But be ready for hard work when you return."

"I'll take the truck, Luca. I have a piece of furniture to move," added Antonio.

Antonio drove steadily into Florence, proceeding through the maze of back streets, arriving at an old, dilapidated building nestled among a row of similar structures.

"Wait here one moment while I collect my prize," said Antonio, leaving the truck and disappearing into the ramshackle building.

Dorothy waited in the quiet, shaded street. The rear of the truck creaked as the tailgate was lowered, and several men lifted a beautiful polished and ornately carved table onto the flat bed. Sheets and blankets covered and protected the table as it was secured in place. The tailgate was closed and Antonio climbed back into the truck.

"This is a part of Florence I have no interest in wanting to return," said Dorothy. "It's rather seedy, don't you think?"

"You find antiques in the strangest of places, Dorothy. It is my job to know where to find them if I am to make a living," replied Antonio, driving out of the back streets and across the city, stopping outside an equally sleazy looking antique shop. "Please excuse me one more time while I reluctantly part with the merchandise."

Striding into the dingy shop Antonio talked with a tall, well dressed, blond-haired man, watched by Dorothy while three rogues offloaded the precious table. Peering through the shop window, Dorothy saw Antonio receiving a long envelope from the tall blond patron who quickly and slightly bowed his head while standing upright, as if to attention and all in one movement as he stretched out his arm and handed over the slim package.

A *strange ritual,* thought Dorothy as Antonio emerged from the store, pushing the envelope into the inside pocket of his jacket.

"Now we shall go for lunch," said Antonio, climbing into Luca's truck, a slight trace of satisfaction appearing in his smile and composure.

"I would have thought something as fine and intricate as that would have been sold at auction," commented Dorothy.

"Not all buyers like to be known or seen at auctions, Dorothy, and besides, there is far more money in trading direct with a client if you have the right contacts and goods they are interested in purchasing." Antonio smiled. "Now, where would you like to eat?"

Sitting at a window table overlooking the Piazza d. Repubblica, Dorothy enjoyed her lunch in the plush comfort of the Savoy Restaurant and the attentive, caring company of Antonio.

"I am pleased you decided to stay." Antonio smiled. "I have enjoyed you being here these past months."

"I have enjoyed being here," replied Dorothy, looking admiringly at Antonio.

"People in the village have commented too," added Antonio.

"Oh, commented on what?" asked Dorothy, curiously.

"You, how happy you look," replied Antonio, affectionately reaching across the table to hold Dorothy's hand.

"I am happy, thanks to you … understanding, caring." Dorothy smiled.

"Good, I want you to be happy … always," said Antonio, returning Dorothy's smile. "If you're not sure of something, please tell me."

"Sometimes I worry about my being here … in the village," confessed Dorothy.

"Why, where else would you go?" Antonio asked, alarmed.

"I don't want to go anywhere. I sometimes worry that I have

no identity here. What if someone should come and check?" Dorothy queried.

"Don't worry Who would come to check? Besides, your Italian is very good, no one would know," assured Antonio, reassuringly and gently squeezing Dorothy's hand.

"I have no papers, Antonio, no proof of who I am, English or Italian," stressed Dorothy.

"Perhaps I can do something about that." Antonio smiled. "First I must talk with Father Luigi."

Dorothy returned Antonio's smile and gripped his hand.

"Ah, tomorrow they begin to take down the walls that protect the two large frescoes in the Duomo," stated Antonio, suddenly remembering.

"It would be exciting to see the return of some of Florence's treasures taking place," replied Dorothy. "Perhaps with your work you could arrange something?"

"I can try." Antonio smiled.

Departing for home, Dorothy observed the work of clearing the war's destruction inflicted upon ancient Florence, and again while making a brief return visit while accompanying Luca on a shopping trip for provisions for the approaching harvest, she witnessed the gradual transformation of steady rebuild and removal of enforced German occupation defences. Extensive progress on replacing the bridges that spanned the Arno River caused traffic confusion, scattering packs of modern scooters to narrow side streets as the river was dammed and dredged while recovering the stones of the original structures. Slowly, brick by brick, treasure by treasure, Florence recaptured its former splendour and displayed its new youthful society.

The toil and bustle of grape harvest was soon dominating Dorothy's spare time, assisting Luca while continuing with her morning clinics. The village was busy with people and tractors and carts loaded with lush ruby red grapes, their aroma filling the air from the squashed pulp of fallen fruit scattered along the route from vineyard to vat. Antonio was noted for his absence during the early part of harvesting the fruit of his pleasured pastime, returning late one evening, joining Dorothy and Luca at the kitchen table after their long and busy day.

"How is the harvest?" asked Antonio eagerly, excitedly throwing his jacket over the back of the heavy chair as he entered the kitchen and looked warmly at Dorothy.

"It goes well, Antonio," answered Luca. "The harvest looks very good this year."

"We must wait until the fruit has fermented and the wine... the wine is ready, Luca," romanced Antonio. "Then we shall know at the festa dell'uva and we can all enjoy the fruits of our labour."

"Where have you been, Antonio, you have been missed?" asked Dorothy, greeting Antonio with a short embrace and kiss of his cheek, a look of concern on her face.

"Just delayed with a meeting, that is all. Now we can finish with the harvest and begin the real work of fermenting," said Antonio, shrugging aside Dorothy's concern.

Luca excused himself from the kitchen, and Antonio sat beside Dorothy at the large table.

"I have talked with Father Luigi," said Antonio, turning and directing his full attention toward Dorothy.

"Oh, so soon... and such a long meeting," replied Dorothy sarcastically before enquiring, "What did Father Luigi have to say?"

"I want you to marry me, Dorothy," spoke Antonio, softly, carefully, ignoring Dorothy's concerned remarks.

"Antonio!" gasped Dorothy, surprised and flustered. "You're proposing?"

"I want you to marry me and live here... together with me," whispered Antonio, passionately. "Yes, I'm proposing. Will you marry me, Dorothy?"

"You have surprised me, Antonio... again," replied Dorothy, her heart beating quickly, her face flushing.

"Father Luigi will give us a license. You will have identity," added Antonio.

"Antonio, please... let me think." Dorothy gasped. "You don't do this just for my identity."

"I'm not asking for you to have a piece of paper. Perhaps it was wrong of me to bring you here, the way I did... and how it has turned out," admitted Antonio, "but I love you, Dorothy, and want you to be able to remain here so we can live together."

"It didn't take much for me to come, Antonio, don't you realize?" Dorothy smiled, looking affectionately at her partisan captain. "There was magic for both of us in that little secret room. I didn't get to say good-bye when you left the field hospital, and I thought I would never see you again. When Luca came for help at your village, it was a chance to see you."

"You never told me?" queried Antonio.

"I thought you knew how I felt," replied Dorothy reassuringly.

"Will you marry me, Dorothy?" repeated Antonio, quietly, anxiously.

"Yes...of course I'll marry you," answered Dorothy, elatedly leaning forward, kissing Antonio firmly on his lips.

"I will make an announcement at the festa dell'uva," said Antonio excitedly, "and we can marry in the spring. I'll talk with Father Luigi about the arrangements."

"Spring sounds very nice for a wedding," agreed Dorothy breathlessly. "I must tell Carla."

Wine fermentation and preparations for the annual festa dell'uva continued; the village buzzed with excitement and anticipation. People smiled warmly, greeting Dorothy with a sense of knowing and support that almost negated an announcement from Antonio. September arrived, and Antonio placed a jug of deep red wine onto the kitchen table. He set out four large wine glasses and proceeded to steadily wipe clean each glass before placing one in front of each of the three observers.

"I guess this is the moment," said Dorothy hesitantly.

"It is the same every year, Dorothy," answered Antonio's mother. "The sampling of the wine, it is our seal of approval. Antonio already knows if it is good or not, he has drunk sufficiently already."

"Mama, it is customary," stated Luca. "Of course we do it every year. It is the measure of our work."

Without speaking, Antonio poured wine into each of the glasses and took his place at the table. He lifted his glass and swirled the red liquid round the goblet before placing it to his nose and breathed slowly, inhaling the bouquet. Dorothy lifted her glass and also swirled her wine.

"Momento, Dorothy…first Antonio," said Antonio's mother, looking on in expectation.

Tipping the glass, Antonio sucked the nectar into his mouth and carefully chewed the wine before swallowing.

"Beautiful," declared Antonio.

Luca and his mother picked up their glasses of wine and followed the same ritual process. Dorothy did likewise, adding her endorsement to the warm approval of success offered toward Antonio.

The bright sun refracted through the goblet of wine, casting a red shadow on the long white tablecloth. Music ensued from the aging performers Dorothy had previously witnessed in the village square when the end of war had been declared. Villagers and visitors gathered to dance and reacquaint, catch up on local news and gossip, eat and savor the delights of the annual festa dell'uva. Dorothy watched from her seat at the host's table, the motion of the dancing, the bustle of people amongst the tables, and the flow of wine in the afternoon frolic. She spied Alfonso chatting, drinking with his friends, wondering if he was the accident the portly storekeeper had met with. She danced with Luca and sat with Carla and discussed children's bumps and bruises with parents who attended her clinics. Dorothy felt as though she belonged, standing beside Father Luigi while Antonio made his intended announcement of marriage to a knowing and approving audience.

Dorothy danced with Antonio before the gathered villagers, returning to the head table and taking her place among the family she was soon to become a part. She talked endlessly with Miriam, Antonio's sister, whose bedroom she occupied and had journeyed from the southerly range of Apennine Mountains and across Florence to attend the village festa dell'uva and meet her future sister-in-law. Miriam told of family tales and sisterly comments regarding her brother Antonio, accepting Dorothy enthusiastically before her departure while looking forward excitedly to her next visit in the spring.

Winter was cold and wet. A doctor had been found to resume

the responsibility of the surgery, retaining Dorothy to assist the doctor and maintain her clinics between his weekly visits. Antonio made several rushed and urgent business trips, each time remaining absent for several days, leaving Dorothy to care for the well-being and deteriorating health of his mother.

Grey peaks began to appear around the mountain village as snowcaps melted and trickled toward the Arno River. Dorothy returned from shopping in Pistoia with her friend and pending bridesmaid, Carla, giggling excitedly as they entered through the villa's large front door, making their way into the warmth of the kitchen. A petite woman in black-laced boots and military-style pants and shirt occupied a chair at the table. She stopped talking with Antonio's mother as Dorothy and Carla entered, standing slowly, her eyes fixed on Dorothy.

"Muriel, it's good to see you. When did you return?" greeted Carla, stepping forward, embracing her old friend with hugs and kissed cheeks. "Dorothy, this is Muriel, Antonio's sister."

"Boungiorno," said Dorothy, unsure of how to respond.

"Boungiorno." Muriel smiled, looking closely at Dorothy, her small frame edging closer as she spoke. "So, you are the woman who steals the heart of my brother!"

"I wouldn't put it quite like that," replied Dorothy hesitantly.

"But you have captured his heart," said Muriel.

"I choose to think he surrendered," answered Dorothy, uncertain of Muriel's intention.

"Do you love him … as I love him?" asked Muriel, running her long, thin fingers through her mass of black hair, sweeping it back from her dark and weathered face, her slight curved and feminine structure now standing dominantly and firmly before Dorothy. "Do you care fore him?"

"Not as you love him, no," said Dorothy. "But as a woman who loves a man she is to marry, that is how I love him."

Muriel reached out and clasped Dorothy across her shoulders, pulling her forward as she stretched upwards and firmly kissed Dorothy on each cheek.

"Bravo, now we can be friends," said Muriel, softening her

poise, putting her arm round Dorothy's waist and hugging her in a manly, comrade-like fashion.

"Bravo, bravo," repeated Antonio's mother as the tense mood drained from the kitchen, and the women chatted excitedly over Muriel's homecoming and Dorothy's approaching wedding.

✦ ✦ ✦ ✦ ✦

Father Luigi arranged flowers on the altar and wore his best robes. A growing congregation began to gather for the Sunday Mass, to be followed by the uniting of Dorothy and Antonio in holy matrimony. Dorothy sat on Muriel's bed, her eyes flooded. She thought of her parents and the occasion that was about to commence, hoping they were watching and would be proud of their daughter. Then walking at the side of Luca through the village, her simple, tight, and full-length gown brilliant white in the reflection of the warm sunlight, she arrived at the church.

Sideways glances from the congregation sneaked preview glimpses as Dorothy passed down the central aisle, her heart beating excitedly, nervously. Ahead was Antonio, standing, waiting, his tall frame draped in a fine black suit that enhanced his masculine figure. Father Luigi smiled as Dorothy joined Antonio, and he beckoned them to step forward and join him at the altar.

Images of Dorothy's previous war-torn visits to the church mingled with Father Luigi's words as he united her to Antonio. She looked affectionately at her soon-to-be husband and smiled lovingly. A short pause in Father Luigi's progression followed his question of reason for Dorothy and Antonio not being joined together in wedlock. Dorothy steadily turned and looked. Muriel smiled and blew her an approving kiss.

"I now pronounce you husband and wife," said Father Luigi.

The village square filled with the rejoicing congregation, and the bells tolled the joyful news, echoing across the high, sunlit peaks of the Apennine Mountains. Dorothy danced enthusiastically among the friends and family she had come to love and respect, letting the memories of past and vivid torments fade gradually into the shadows of her mind as she built her new life.

Dorothy witnessed the resurgence of Florence as it slowly and steadily returned to its past and previous splendor, the mountain village as it recovered from the military assault that destroyed and damaged homes and property, and the growth and success of Antonio with his flourishing art and antiques business. She basked in the communal spirit and harmony of the mountain village and its people, their steady pace of life and social structure, their toil and daily commitment to their family and village neighbour. Dorothy knew where her life now belonged.

The funeral of Antonio's mother cast a quiet, sombre mood on Antonio and the family. Once more the church was focal to the event of respect and prayer, and its pews were filled with family, friends, and the local community. The death and loss of Antonio's mother triggered a brief period of anxiety and unease as buried memories of the loss of Dorothy's own parents surfaced in her thoughts. Slowly, gradually, Dorothy became central to Antonio and his brother, Luca, combining their actions and consulted with on family affairs, growing close to Muriel and accepted sister to Miriam.

Marriage to Antonio, with his association and respect within the art and antiques business, provided social recognition for Dorothy as she visited art galleries and museums, was invited to special functions and occasions within the Florentine calendar. Her presence at civic functions within the mountain village community was accepted and frequently requested, and her nursing clinic was always attended and respected.

It was almost midday as Dorothy sat waiting behind her desk in the clinic; her last morning patient had gone, and she anticipated the arrival of Antonio to take her for their usual luncheon arrangement. She accepted Antonio's cavalier attitude and self-assured lifestyle but knew he was always respectful of his commitments and duties to those around him, whom he loved and cherished, and she decided to go up the flight of stairs to his office and see what was detaining him.

Antonio's door was closed. Dorothy knocked sharply and entered without waiting, eager for her lunch. The conversation in the room stopped abruptly.

"Oh, scusi, I didn't realize you had someone with you," apologised Dorothy, looking at Antonio and the man sitting in front of the office's large oak desk.

"That's quite all right. Please, come in," stammered Antonio, surprised by Dorothy's entrance. "We were just talking."

"I came for our lunch arrangement, but I can see you're busy. Please excuse me," said Dorothy, remaining beside the office door, looking at Antonio's guest.

"I'm sorry. I didn't realize it was so late. Perhaps we should cancel lunch today. My guest's business is important," replied Antonio, looking a little apprehensive, wondering what he should do next. "I do apologize, Herr Hepnar, my wife, Dorothy."

"Pleased to meet you," said Herr Hepnar, getting from his chair, standing erect and bowing his head slightly to the accompaniment of softly clicked heels.

"Yes, very well," said Dorothy, dazed by Antonio's decision to forgo lunch and Herr Hepnar's responsive manner to her introduction. "I'll see you at home this evening. Excuse me, Herr Hepnar."

Dorothy left the strained atmosphere of Antonio's office and closed the large, polished door. She paused thoughtfully for a moment before descending the stairway, listening to the raised and agitated voices of the two men as they resumed their conversation. Missing lunch, Dorothy sat on the fountain wall pondering over Antonio's restlessness and Herr Hepnar's manner. She thought of Antonio's guest, his tall posture and bowing of his head, trying to recall who he reminded her of, suddenly remembering the seedy antique shop in Florence. His hair was more grey than blond, but that had been quite some years ago now.

Returning home, Antonio poured himself a glass of wine and sat at the kitchen table.

"You look troubled, Antonio," said Luca, cutting himself cheese and bread to accompany his wine.

"It has been a busy day." Antonio sighed, glancing and smiling thoughtfully at Dorothy.

"Relax...enjoy the wine," continued Luca. "You work too hard."

"Someone must," responded Antonio, agitatedly taking a large gulp of his wine.

"I do my share," replied Luca sharply, leaving the kitchen.

"Herr Hepnar, was he the man in Florence all those years ago?" asked Dorothy calmly, not wanting to aggravate Antonio.

"Florence, you saw him in Florence?" queried Antonio.

"I only ask if he was the man in that seedy antique shop where you sold that rather nice table, remember?" answered Dorothy.

"Oh, yes, that was him. He was much younger then," replied Antonio anxiously. "He has been a good client over the years."

"I was surprised to see him in your office. You don't normally mix your business affairs with civic responsibilities," stated Dorothy.

"No, he was in Florence. He would like me to go with him and look at some pieces he is interested in purchasing," informed Antonio, "for my opinion."

"Go...go where?" asked Dorothy.

"Just for a few days...to Austria, just for a few days," repeated Antonio, "tomorrow."

"Tomorrow, so soon?" queried Dorothy, slightly alarmed.

"Yes, I have arranged to meet him in Florence and we can travel by train," informed Antonio.

"I had better prepare you some clothes. What time will you leave?" asked Dorothy, standing to leave the kitchen table.

"Early. I will get Muriel to drive me," replied Antonio.

The morning light barely penetrated the bedroom as Dorothy stirred from her sleep. She observed Antonio dressing in the dimness.

"What time is it?" asked Dorothy.

"Go to sleep," replied Antonio, kissing Dorothy tenderly on her forehead. "I'll be back in a day or two."

"Mm, you've said that before," murmured Dorothy, remembering Antonio's departure from the mountain cave with his partisan comrades.

Sunlight shone brightly into the still, quiet bedroom as Dorothy looked out over the view of rolling Tuscan hills. She made her way to the kitchen and poured herself a large coffee, relaxing at the table, pondering what she should do, cutting salami and a large piece of bread from the crusty loaf. The kitchen door flew open, and Luca and Muriel burst through.

"You're here," stated Luca restlessly.

"Steady. What is all the rush?" said Dorothy, trying to calm the haste out of the moment, sitting upright on her heavy kitchen chair.

"Antonio has been arrested!" blurted Muriel excitedly.

"Oh my God! Where, how do you know?" stammered Dorothy.

"Muriel saw it at the railway station." Luca sighed. "He was with a German, someone he was mixed up with during the war."

"He was here yesterday," said Dorothy fearfully. "Herr Hepnar, a German, he was here yesterday."

"He was here," remarked Muriel angrily.

"Yes, he was in Antonio's office. Who is he?" asked Dorothy fretfully.

"He was the German commandant posted here when they occupied our village," said Luca wrathfully. "If I had seen him there would have been no need for his arrest."

"Antonio's been selling him antiques all these years," realized Dorothy loudly.

"That's not true!" raged Muriel, not wanting to hear of the treachery of her beloved brother.

"Oh no, he can't have been. How do you know?" asked Luca.

"I saw him many years ago and again yesterday." Dorothy sighed dejectedly. "How was I to know who he was?"

"What can we do?" asked Muriel. "They will come here…looking."

"This will disgrace our family, our village," gasped Luca agitatedly. "He has ruined us."

"We must do something," stressed Muriel. "We can't just let this happen."

"There is nothing we can do. They have been caught together. Perhaps the police have been watching them for years, just waiting for this moment," suggested Luca, sitting down at the kitchen table. "Muriel, take Dorothy, get away from here. They will come here soon, and there is no reason for you to be involved in Antonio's corruption."

"Where can we go, Luca? This is our home," cried out Muriel.

Dorothy remained silent, her forgotten memories bursting to the surface, her feeling of isolation returning to nervously shake her body. Her thoughts were filled with the memories of recent years, the friends she had gained, the clinic she ran, her marriage, suddenly shrouded with uncertainty and loss.

"I will stay and try to salvage what I can from this situation, but I fear they will take our home." Luca sighed.

"I will stay here with you Luca," whispered Dorothy dejectedly. "This is my home too. I have nowhere else."

"Muriel can get you home to England, Dorothy. She has contacts who can smuggle you into the country. You must go with her, you cannot remain here," suggested Luca. "You are surely to be arrested."

"I am married to Antonio, he is my husband, whatever he may have done," stated Dorothy. "This is my home, Luca."

"That is why you should go. His crimes are serious, Dorothy," said Luca. "If what you say is true, Antonio has sold many of our country's treasures and that will not be received well by anyone. The whole country will be against him."

"I have friends in Milano. We can go there, and I can arrange to get you to England, Dorothy. Luca is right. We must go," persuaded Muriel, interrupting.

"Take this, it will be easy for travelling," said Luca, convincing Dorothy to follow Muriel and collect what few clothes and possessions she could pack into the rucksack he provided her.

Dorothy felt numb, cocooned, her motions effortless and involuntary as Luca's and Muriel's words mingled with distant cries of smoky battlefield and joyous merriment of villagers at the festa dell'uva. She gazed at Muriel packing clothes into the worn rucksack and looked through the window at the hills and trees disappearing in the haze. Sadly she collected her nurse's scarlet and grey lanyard from the drawer in her fine antique dresser and pushed it into a pocket on the bulging bag, her hands trembling as she pulled a light overcoat from her wardrobe and returned to the kitchen.

"I'll get word to you when I know what is happening. Here, take this; you will need it," commented Luca, reassuringly pushing a wallet into Dorothy's coat pocket. "Wait here while I bring the truck and I will drive you to the station at Pistoia before we are too late."

Slowly the village square and ornate fountain slid into the distance as Dorothy looked through the rear window of Luca's truck, watching her life disappear.

RETURN TO ENGLAND

1966

Under the cover of nightfall, the small fishing boat bobbed and rocked on the dark, choppy water as it forged its way closer to the English shoreline. Dorothy stood alongside the captain watching the coastal lights rise and sink beneath the swell of the tide carrying them forward, remembering her last horrific landing at the Italian port of Anzio. This time there would be no volley of rockets to announce her intended arrival; their boat mingled among the armada of fishing boats merging on the green beacon that guided them to the harbour, but still her heart beat anxiously.

The rucksack fell against Dorothy's leg as the rock of the boat displaced it from its resting position in the corner of the wooden wheelhouse. Dorothy bent and secured her possessions, firmly jamming the sack back into the corner, returning her gaze to the boats converging on the approaching harbour entrance.

Her training for the landing had been quick and simple; disembark quickly when the boat comes alongside the quay and walk away.

Dorothy reflected on the simplicity of her task as the dark and calmness of the sea crossing gave way to lights and commotion, and the fishing vessel motored past the flashing harbour light. The boat slowed its pace in the smooth, calmer water, manoeuvring to a quieter section of quayside where Dorothy would not be so noticeable climbing ashore.

Bumping gently against the jetty, two fishermen held the boat securely against the wall as Dorothy clambered over the side and onto the busy quayside. Her rucksack landed at her feet, thrown up from the boat as it pushed away and motored out across the black inky water of the dock.

Dorothy grabbed her belongings and walked quickly along the quayside, keeping to the shadows, heading for the array of harbour buildings and searching for an exit. Her heart sank as she nervously glanced over at the fishing boat disappearing into the darkness of the sea beyond the port's green flashing beacon. Hurriedly passing along the busy wharf way, the noise of winches and trucks and the activity of unloading the night's catch from the fleet of fishing boats distracted any attention toward Dorothy as she passed unobserved out of the port and into the sleepy silence of the English fishing town.

Walking through the deserted streets, Dorothy remembered the grand Victorian architecture of the large formal buildings, the row of quaint shop doorways and windows lighting the pavement either side of the road, the English pub standing majestically on the street corner, its decorative name sign swinging steadily in the early morning breeze.

A car passed along the street, causing Dorothy to nervously tense. Her homecoming was not what she had anticipated, and she was uncomfortable with being seen so openly on the quiet street. She thought confusedly about what she should do, afraid of being caught. Spring morning light had begun to appear in the sky; soon people would be out on the street and the shops would be opening their doors. Dorothy decided not to stay in the fishing port and made her way to the railway station, thinking it would be better to be in a larger city where she would not be so noticeable. Where she could hide until she felt more comfortable with her smuggled entry and lack of identity.

Dorothy sat in the station waiting room twiddling her train ticket between her fingers. The tension and fear of being caught at the fishing port subsided and gave way to thinking of Antonio and how he had betrayed her, how he had betrayed his village and his friends and family, how her life had been suddenly turned upside-down. Almost without warning or thought she was here sitting on an English railway station. Dorothy had dreamed many times over the past years of one day returning to England, but it had always remained a dream. Looking at her ticket, she read the word "London," and her eyes suddenly filled with tears.

She felt a cold loneliness wash over her and thought back to the rejoicing in the village square at the end of the war, remembering her feeling of isolation among the villagers, wondering where she belonged and what she should do. Now the wheel had turned and once more she felt the loneliness. Dorothy's stomach churned with fear and hunger, knowing she had only herself this time. She felt for the wallet in her coat pocket, drawing on the security and comfort of the money it contained, deciding she would relieve her hunger with a sandwich before her train arrived.

Clutching her rucksack and holding her breakfast sandwich, Dorothy observed the diesel railcar purr its way along the side of her platform. She boarded the train and found a seat in the long open compartment. It was not the England she remembered leaving, and a quiet life in the remote mountain village and Renaissance Florence had done little to prepare Dorothy for the England that confronted her.

Sitting apart from other travellers, Dorothy watched the fields and stations pass and the train compartment fill with other passengers, engulfing her in their presence. Her thoughts were filled with reflection and observation, comparing stable, unchanged countryside and villages that reflected the England she remembered with new, unfamiliar fashion and attitude that distracted her from her plight.

The diesel train pulled slowly into London's Liverpool Street Station. Disembarking the train, Dorothy was swept along the platform amid the scurrying passengers forging their way to the station's main entrance before dispersing in all directions. Dumped by the parting, hurrying crowd, Dorothy sat on a platform seat, flustered by the endless flow of station traffic.

She tried deciding what she should do; her concentration was muddled, flitting between her torn and sudden departure from Italy and the lonely fear of being back in England. She was relieved at not being discovered at the fishing port and comfortable with the lack of attention she attracted during the train journey. Now Dorothy became more nervous about her presence and remaining on the platform but was bewildered with where she should go. She determined she would first find somewhere to stay temporarily.

Emerging from the station, Dorothy was struck by the sight of the busy London street. The road was congested with cars and trucks and busses, crowded pedestrians spilled across the pavements as they filed out of the station and made their way, blending amongst the throng. Gone was the black and dated motorcar chugging its way sedately amongst the traffic; gone was the high sandbag walls protecting air raid shelter entrances; gone was the dowdy grey and brown of dress and fashion, flat cap and daring hat, and the smatter of military uniform peppering the busy pavements.

Amazed, Dorothy stood and gawped. Change and colour flashed from all direction, confusing her faded memory. Bright, littered billboards spread word of new attractions; motorised boxes of varying size and shades of tint conveyed along the tarmac strip; reflective glass and glossy towers rose among the bastion architecture; and women bared their white legs.

A passing pedestrian hurrying from the station, bumping apologetically and knocking her rucksack from her shoulder, startled her, and the rumble of fallen bombs and flashes of cannon fire mingled with the spectacle before her. Dorothy gasped; bewildered and panicked, she stepped back against the safety of the station wall. Her hands momentarily trembled as she tightly gripped the strap of her rucksack, and the noise of the street triggered the confusion of the war-torn memories she had tried hard to put to rest.

Regaining her composure, Dorothy put her rucksack securely on her back and ventured onto the congested pavement. She made her way aimlessly and cautiously along the streets, frequently stopping to window shop or observe a street trader promoting his goods on a busy corner. A window displaying property caught her attention, remaining several minutes to read the pricey content of the notices before dejectedly moving on. The aroma of coffee wafting from the door of a café drew Dorothy inside.

Enjoying the café's quiet atmosphere and hot coffee, Dorothy relaxed at a window table watching the busy London street, reflecting on her time in the mountain village where the only change she witnessed was the rebuild and repair of shell-blasted homes. Excited or rushed activity had been limited to preparation for occasion and harvesting the wine, and the restoration and modern development of Florence was peripheral to its Renaissance heart, where painstaking time and precision had been lavished upon its treasures.

Dorothy distracted herself away from her saddening thoughts, remembering her task at hand and asking the waitress if she knew of somewhere she could stay.

"You had best get the paper, love, there's lots of places in there. Careful mind, cos some of them want tearing down. You're not from round here?" replied the waitress, enquiringly.

"No. How do you know?" ask Dorothy guardedly.

"Well, you want some place to stay for one, but there ain't many folk round here with a tan like yours this time of year," concluded the waitress.

"Oh, thank you," replied Dorothy. "Where can I get a paper?"

"There's an agent up the road, next to the butcher's," informed the waitress.

Dorothy wriggled into the straps of her rucksack and followed the waitress's directions for a paper. Standing on the pavement outside the newsagent's shop, she slowly turned the pages, part reading articles and looking at pictures as she went, until reaching the property page. Reading down the columns, Dorothy discarded the adverts requesting references and those with a long-term rental commitment, stopping at "Flat To Rent" and a telephone number.

The advert looked to be uncomplicated thought Dorothy in her precarious position and searched the street for a telephone box. Her conversation was brief and without complication, though the rental seemed too high for her limited finances, and Dorothy declined to progress further with her enquiry. Returning to the paper, she scanned the column for a further possibility and dialled the number of an available room.

The room was still vacant and at a much lower price than the previous flat, which encouraged Dorothy with her enquiry and asked if she could view the room. She panicked when asked to give her name and for a few moments struggled with what to reply, finally deciding that after all she was English and gave her name as Wainwright, Miss Wainwright.

Relieved at finding somewhere to stay, Dorothy followed the instructions to guide her to the room's address, arriving midafternoon as arranged.

Litter collected in the curbs of the road and strewed the pavements. The row of four-story townhouses predated the recent war and reflected the scares and grime of times past. Dorothy stood outside number fifty-seven, looking at the broken window and open door. She stepped forward and peered inside, squinting to see down the dark, narrow hallway. A male voice from an upper landing welcomed her and called her up the stairway to the second floor. Dorothy reluctantly ventured forward and climbed the creaky, bare wooden steps.

"It's the room at the back, just down the landing," said the male voice, pointing into the dimness of the corridor.

Without looking at her host, Dorothy passed down the corridor and pushed open the room door. A damp, musty smell caught her breath and filled her nostrils. Daylight broke through the unwashed window and rested on a grubby, sunken mattress. A wardrobe stood to the side of the bed on bare floorboards, its door hanging on one hinge. Dorothy looked back at the window and its transparent, dirty grey, yellow-coloured curtain.

"Do you want it?" enquired the male voice still standing on the landing at the top of the stairway.

"I have another room to visit before I decide," replied Dorothy, thinking quickly and returning down the corridor.

"As you wish," said the male voice. "It won't be available for long, so make your mind up."

"I'll let you know," said Dorothy as she passed the male voice, her rucksack's weight assisting her hasty descent of the creaky stairs and departure from the building.

Bursting through the front doorway, Dorothy walked briskly along the pavement toward the main road, gradually slowing her pace as she distanced herself from the grimy building. With the realisation of evening approaching, the prospect of finding some-where to sleep began to play on her mind. She opened her paper and scoured the adverts, desperately searching for somewhere to stay the night. Her eyes fixed on a small box of text offering bed and breakfast, and she rushed urgently along the road searching for another public phone box.

The prominent red and glass structure was in use as Dorothy approached, and she stood impatiently looking at the occupant silently mouthing words into the large black handpiece. Dorothy watched eagerly as the phone was placed back on its cradle and the door swung open. She pushed into the tight square receptacle and wrestled her paper to the text-boxed number she needed to call. Her large rucksack pressed against the glass and steel door preventing it from completely closing as she dialled the number. Dorothy struggled to hear for sound of traffic on the busy street flooding through the open doorway while a soft, patient voice repeated guidance to the address, and Dorothy sighed with relief as she replaced the heavy black handset.

"Have you come far?" enquired the mature landlady as she showed Dorothy to the room.

"Not really," replied Dorothy cautiously, trying not to get involved in a difficult conversation.

"You look like you've been abroad. Here's your room," contin-ued the landlady, smiling as she opened the door.

"This is fine, lovely," said Dorothy, avoiding the landlady's comment while observing the inviting bedroom. "The bed looks very comfortable."

"How many nights did you say?" enquired the tubby landlady.

"One, perhaps two," replied Dorothy thoughtfully.

"Breakfast is from seven to nine and you have to vacate by ten," the landlady informed. "Unless you stay two nights, that is. Cash is in advance, please … if you don't mind."

Dorothy thought quickly and paid for two nights, deciding she did not want to rush and have to contemplate accommodation she had just experienced. Paying the landlady, Dorothy closed the door, placed her rucksack against the side of the wardrobe, and sat dolefully on the bed. She counted the remains of her English pound notes, concluding she would need to change some of the Italian Lire Luca had provided before trying to estimate how long her money would last. She looked through her crumpled paper for further possibilities of accommodation before tiring and climbing into bed.

Tossing and turning, Dorothy struggled to relax; her body and her eyes were tired but her mind raced worryingly over her money and what she should do. She thought of Luca, caringly trying to help protect her and the rushed decision to send her back to England, questioning what more he knew of Antonio's arrest that he had not explained. She woke startled by the image of her parents' home exploding in the bomb blast and sat breathing heavily on the edge of the bed, listening to the silence of her bedroom.

Dorothy lay back on her pillow, staring at the shadows, remembering her parents and life when she was young and at home—her loving, caring father and how he would sit and talk and guide her with her problems and how she wanted his wisdom there, now, to help her. Dorothy thought of her life and her struggle, how confident she was with her decision to be a nurse and go to war, wondering how she had become so lost and at such a time in her life. She thought, like she often had over the years, of going home but was afraid of what she would find and lose the cherished image of the home and family she remembered.

"Is everything all right, love?" enquired the landlady, serving Dorothy a plate of toast. "Only I heard you shouting in the night."

"Yes, fine, thank you, just a bad dream, I expect," replied Dorothy, sitting at the table in anticipation of her breakfast, not wanting to divulge too much detail into the anxieties of her sleep.

"My Bert had bad dreams, more like nightmares, they were. He was never the same when he came home from the war," informed the landlady.

"Where is he now?" asked Dorothy, taking a drink of the strong English tea the landlady had poured.

"He's died now, that's why I do bed and breakfast," said the landlady, pausing to think of her husband. "We never had much, and you have to make ends meet."

"Oh, I'm sorry," offered Dorothy apologetically. "How did he cope … with the dreams?"

"I don't think he did. He never said much about what went on, but I could tell from what he shouted it wasn't much good, a bit like you where shouting last night," said the landlady slowly, thoughtfully. "No, he just got on with it. He seemed fine most of the time, but every now and then he'd have a bad spell, something would start him off."

"I'm sorry," repeated Dorothy, eating her toast, recognising the symptoms of the landlady's explanation.

"There's no need to be sorry. He's resting now. What brings you to London?" enquired the landlady, smiling.

"I've come to look for work," answered Dorothy, simultaneously realising a solution to her dilemma.

"Well, I can't help you with that," replied the landlady. "Sorry."

Thanking the landlady and leaving the table, Dorothy returned enthusiastically to her room, encouraged by her recognition that finding work would help her position. She retrieved a pen and paper from her rucksack and together, with her ragged newspaper, set about looking for somewhere to live and the possibilities of finding work.

The day became long and fruitless. Vacant rooms at the time of her enquiry had become occupied during the time preceding her arrival to view. A flat for female-only occupancy, shared with rowdy students, was rejected, as were other flats of similar squalor to her first experience. It was late as, wearily, Dorothy thought of returning to her room at the bed and breakfast lodging, stopping to purchase fish and chips and realising breakfast had been her last meal. She walked slowly along the pavement enjoying the battered fish and portion of salted chips, stopping to look at the displays in the shop windows. Arriving at the landlady's house, Dorothy excused herself and retired to her room, explaining only that she was tired and that she hoped tomorrow would be a better day.

Early at the breakfast table Dorothy discussed her experience of the previous day with the landlady, explaining how difficult it had been to determine the true content of what lay behind the advertisements before once more venturing out onto the street and pursuing her quest. The bright early morning sunshine turned to afternoon rain, and Dorothy's activity was reduced to looking through her newspaper of possibilities while drinking coffee in a corner café. Close by was her link of communication, periodically dashing to the glass and steel phone box only to return dejectedly moments later when another enquiry was lost or deemed unsuitable. Dorothy returned early to her bed and breakfast accommodation and paid the landlady for two more nights.

The following morning continued with more of the previous day's rain, and it was almost lunch before Dorothy ventured outside to purchase a newspaper. Rain had begun to penetrate her light Italian overcoat as she returned to the guesthouse. Her limited choice of replacement clothes and scarce selection of underwear determined the requirement for Dorothy to attend her laundry, and she ventured out to the launderette, taking her latest edition of newspaper with her. She sat quietly identifying and marking possible rooms and their contact numbers between attending her laundry. The washing process was slow and timely, and Dorothy became conscious of the costs steadily eating into her limited funds as she put the coins into the push-and-pull slide that automatically started the washing machine.

Her room at the guesthouse was comfortable and quite adequate, Dorothy thought, and worryingly decided not to spend more time looking for a room or flat but try to find a job instead, turning eagerly to the jobs section of her paper, hoping that would result in more success. She thought carefully about what she could do that would not attract too much interest or raise difficult questions regarding her past, anxiously thinking about what she could say as she looked at the list of jobs. Her washing machine stopped. Dorothy fumbled with the door, pulling and tugging, trying to open it.

"You have to wait a bit before it will open," said a large lady, sitting and smoking on the opposite side of the launderette, watching Dorothy struggle.

"Thank you." Dorothy smiled, feeling a little silly.

Dorothy opened the door of the washing machine and gathered up her clean clothes. She looked for a vacant dryer, but all were operating. Placing her wet clothes in a pile on the row of wooden benches, she sat down with a sigh and waited for a machine to stop, watching the colour of clothes inside the dryer drum in front of her rotate, round and round. Her thoughts drifted from the monotony of the rotation to the realisation of where she was, wondering where it had gone wrong. She thought of Mary and her carefree attitude and longed for the sharing support their friendship had enjoyed. A drying machine stopped, and Dorothy began gathering her clothes.

"I'm waiting for that one," said the large lady, stubbing out her cigarette on the laundry floor. "Yours is the next one."

"Yes, sorry," replied Dorothy, sitting back down on the wooden bench and hiding her frustration behind her newspaper.

Slowly Dorothy's mood changed as she read the advertisement for a shop assistant in a local chemist. She put down her dog-eared paper and smiled triumphantly at the large lady sitting by her rotating dryer, lighting another cigarette. Feeling this was her salvation, Dorothy eagerly completed her laundry and departed for a phone booth to telephone the chemist. Securing an appointment for an interview, she returned with poise to her bed and breakfast accommodation, discussing with the landlady her intention and requesting her room for three more nights.

The pavement outside the chemist was busy and provided distraction from Dorothy's repetitive, caged-tiger-like passing of the window as she tried to observe the inside of the shop. Nervously she rehearsed her story and prayed she would be successful as the time of her interview approached.

Entering the shop, Dorothy noticed the calm and quiet atmosphere, the hospital-like orderliness, and the polite reception. She gave her name and waited for the chemist to receive her. Her hands perspired as she waited quietly, observing the shelves and arrangement of medications on display and felt her heart begin to thump as she heard the shop assistant call her name, announcing that the chemist would see her.

The chemist's friendly greeting was followed by polite explanation of the job's requirement and questions of experience, ability, and commitment. Dorothy cautiously provided answers that followed her rehearsed story, hopeful that it would be accepted without complication. She was relieved to hear the chemist offer her the job and ask when she could commence the position.

"Would Monday be suitable?" replied Dorothy.

"Fine, Monday would be fine," confirmed the chemist. "Thank you for coming."

"Thank you," said Dorothy smiling, excitedly leaving the small, cluttered office.

"Would you bring your P45 with you on Monday morning please?" added the chemist as Dorothy was departing. "It saves time at the tax office."

Dorothy continued out of the shop, her stomach knotting, her confidence drained, her future dashed. The chemist's request for her P45 repeated in her head, and her legs trembled as she walked resignedly along the row of shops. Street after street, road after road passed aimlessly by. Dorothy wrestled with her thoughts and her sadness, trying to resolve her traumatic predicament, annoyed with Luca, angry at Antonio, afraid of the lost, lonely feeling that was difficult to control. The afternoon turned to early evening darkness, and Dorothy trudged wearily homeward, avoiding her talkative landlady, going directly to her room.

A light knock on her bedroom door woke Dorothy.

"It's Saturday, Dorothy. I have to go to the shops," called the landlady. "You have to come now if you want breakfast."

Dorothy suddenly felt hungry and rolled out of bed. She pulled on her clothes and went downstairs. The smell of toast cooking intensified her hunger as she entered the kitchen.

"Everything all right?" enquired the landlady, pouring Dorothy a cup of tea.

"Yes, fine, thank you," smiled Dorothy, stirring milk into her tea. "Just tired."

"How did your interview go?" asked the landlady, placing a plate of hot toast in front of Dorothy. "I didn't hear you come in last night."

"They wanted someone younger," replied Dorothy, spreading butter across her piece of toast.

"Happens all the time these days," said the landlady, sitting down with her cup of tea to join Dorothy. "I don't think they know what they want. The world's gone mad if you ask me. All this pop music and smoking ashes, the young ones aren't interested in work. Things are too easy for them; they should give the jobs to someone who wants to work."

"Aren't you going to the shops?" Dorothy reminded the landlady, trying to avoid another long session of chatter.

"Yes, that's why I got you to come down," replied the landlady. "I know you have nowhere to go, and it's all right if you want to stay in your room while I'm shopping. You can't do much on a Saturday."

"Thank you, that's kind of you," answered Dorothy.

Finishing her breakfast, she returned to her room and lay dejectedly on her bed, listening to the silence of the house, trying to find a ray of hope. Two more weeks of despair followed, and Dorothy lay nervously counting the remains of her riches. She had lost weight worrying, not eating, and relying on the landlady's provision of breakfast in an effort to conserve her money. One more night remained before she must commit to further use of her room. Anxiously she calculated how many nights she could afford at the bed and breakfast, avoiding the reality of her conclusion and choosing to go for a walk.

Dorothy dressed, pulling on a pair of trousers and fastening her waistband. She looked at the loose fit round her stomach, lifting and lowering the trousers as they slid easily up and down her waist. She reached into her rucksack pulling out her grey and scarlet lanyard. Sitting on the bed she clutched the coloured cord between her hands and held it to her breast. Tears flooded into her eyes as war-torn memories and happy thoughts of Jean and Mary mingled and flashed through her mind. The tears dripped from her cheeks as she unravelled the lanyard and threaded it through the loops of her loose waistband. Pulling it tight, she tied a knot and adjusted the comfort of the trousers before putting on her light overcoat and leaving her room.

The morning was overcast and the clouds matched the grey of Dorothy's lanyard supporting her trousers as she walked aimlessly through the streets.

Standing before an Underground station, Dorothy decided she would go to central London, see some of the sights, and take her thoughts away from the taxing quandary that raged inside her mind. Standing at the ticket counter, she discussed the cheapest option and purchased a day-trip ticket that allowed her freedom to roam the central Underground stations and return before the end of the day.

She stepped onto the escalator and descended the short ride to the platform before boarding the rocky tube train and alighting into the sunshine and the Embankment. The open expanse of the River Thames and its green-brown water lifted Dorothy's spirit as she inhaled deeply, looking up to the sunlight and letting her worries fall away with her parting breath. She leaned over the Embankment wall and watched the river flowing by, feeling the warmth of the sun seep through her overcoat, remembering her first time on the Ponte Vecchio watching the Arno River wind its way through the shadows of the grand Renaissance buildings lining its banks.

Dorothy also remembered her daily journey to work, observing the endless flow of water cascading over the weir as the River Avon flowed steadily under Pulteney Bridge and she passed hurriedly across the top on her way to the hospital.

Walking along the bank of the river, the Houses of Parliament and Big Ben became visible through the trees, and Dorothy let the memory fade, looking up at the large clock face, waiting for it to chime before making her way along Whitehall. She looked into the cul-de-sac of Downing Street, toward number ten, passing it by, attracted to the tall cenotaph column isolated in the centre of the road by the steady flow of traffic. She crossed over the road and stood quietly looking at the stone monument.

Traffic roared by either side, unnoticed, unheard. Dorothy knelt on the steps and bowed her head. She had prayed many times in the Apennine Mountain church for her friends and her family, for the brave men she had cared for and lost. Here she felt different; here was where they all belonged; here she was at home where she belonged and she bathed in the reunion of her presence. Dorothy stayed, letting her memories flow until her eyes dried and she had said all her prayers.

Solemnly Dorothy left the isolation of the cenotaph, lifting her mood as she mingled with the crowds of people feeding the flocks of pigeons fluttering and scurrying round Trafalgar Square. She purchased food for the birds then shrieked and laughed as the pigeons packed round her feet, scavenging for the scattered seeds, landing on her arms, trying to raid the bag of grain she held in her hand. Throwing her last fist of seeds, Dorothy was confused with where to go next, and she casually walked the streets, arriving at Leicester Square.

The journey and walking had given Dorothy an appetite, and she searched for somewhere to eat, deciding on a small corner café where she could watch the busy activity of the square. She was enjoying her time, allowing herself to be distracted from the torment bubbling just below the surface. Her sandwich had not satisfied her hunger, and she ordered a slice of chocolate cake to go with her unfinished coffee, conscious of the money she was spending.

Satisfyingly nourished, Dorothy made her way slowly through Leicester Square, looking at the billboards advertising the attractions and the street vendors promoting their souvenirs of London. Carried along by the flow of people, she looked through the windows at laughing faces eating, drinking, and motionless mannequins dressed in mini skirts and trendy new fashion. The pavement was becoming packed, and Dorothy concentrated on passing through the overcrowding, following behind pedestrians mauling between the motionless traffic and red London busses circling below the flashing, moving neon signs fastened high above on the sides of buildings.

In the centre of the busy traffic circle stood Eros, permanently drawing his bow. Crowds of people gathered on the island, sitting on the steps round the base of the famous black statue.

Dorothy stopped and stood, pushing back against the movement of the horde, remembering her promise to a young, skinny soldier while looking at the statue between the movement of red busses as they passed slowly round Piccadilly Circus.

"I'm sorry, Barry," whispered Dorothy.

She crossed over the road and climbed Eros's steps, avoiding people posing for their picture and groups of rowdy students, stopping on the top ring of stone and turning to look out at the mass of faces staring upward at the winged archer. Dorothy stood looking at the faces, slowly circling round the statue, acting out her promise, trying to see a young, khaki-clad soldier through the blurred vision of her teary eyes. Dejected she sat down on the smooth step, her hands trembling as a strong sensation of loss swamped her heart.

Surrounded by groups of noisy people busy with their activity, Dorothy felt isolated, alone among the crowd. Sitting watching the busy traffic, her mixed emotions overlapping, she remembered her time at Inveraray, smiling at the image of Mary pushing her forward, encouraging her to talk with Barry, young and polite, buried in his oversized uniform. Angry and confused by Antonio, annoyed at not realising his secrecy and disappearances hid a criminal association that wrecked the life and happiness she had found in the mountains surrounding Florence. Sorrow, as the images of war and the mutilated bodies of the field hospital flashed before her, and lonely, for the loss of her friend and her family, her father, her mother, Christopher.

Darkness fell over Eros as evening turned to nighttime and the neon signs bathed the circus with their colour. Dorothy's stomach rumbled, and her hunger drew her from her thoughts, realising the time, recognising the darkness she wearily made her way back toward Leicester Square, looking for somewhere she could eat.

Dorothy sat nibbling at her sandwich, staring blindly out of the window, sipping her lukewarm coffee and wondering what she should do. How could she escape her trouble, what must she do to find a new life, where could she go? She sat looking at her day ticket for the Underground, gnawing at the remains of her sandwich. Slowly she stood up from the table, threw her ticket on the empty sandwich plate, and walked dejectedly out of the café.

The throng of people crowding the pavement began to dwindle as they found their ways home. Traffic along the road became infrequent. Dorothy walked steadily along the rows of shops. She observed the doorways littered with blankets and curled-up bodies sleeping under sheets of cardboard and layers of newspaper. Huddled together smoking, drinking. Alone, crouching, squatting back against the shop door, away from the cool night air.

Dorothy's pace quickened as she became nervous of her location and hastily made her way, away from the shops and their nighttime tenants, searching the solitude of the quieter streets. She drew on her experience in the field hospital, pushing herself as drowsiness crept slowly into her sleep-laden eyes. A bench on the corner of the park invited her to sit and rest. Her eyes heavy, her head nodding, she dozed. A cold shiver woke her and she left the bench, walking briskly to regain some warmth.

Daylight crept into the cloudless sky, and Dorothy found herself sitting on a bench on the Embankment, close by the Underground station from which she had arrived. She let the morning sun soak through her fastened overcoat and warm her chilled body. She was quiet and relaxed. She listened to the early morning chatter of birds, the occasional buzz of traffic passing along the road. Her torment rested as she enjoyed the early dawning of a new day.

Leaving the calm of the riverside, Dorothy walked along the Embankment toward the Underground Station. She was torn between returning to her room at her bed and breakfast lodgings or choosing an unknown future and wander the streets of London. Both her choices contained uncertainty. She reflected on her struggle to find somewhere to stay and the cost draining her limited funding, the realisation of not having legal recognition for gaining employment. Decidedly, Dorothy continued past the tube station and headed for a café and a hot cup of coffee to quench her morning thirst.

It was afternoon when Dorothy returned to the steps of Eros. Climbing the broad steps, she resumed her place on the top circle and leaned against the statue. The bustle of Piccadilly Circus surrounded her as she joined the young students and hippies sprawled lethargically, colourful in their strange costumes and dominating excessive space round the love island's steps.

Dorothy felt calm, almost numb by comparison to her recent days. She had let go of the struggle that tormented her, directing her concern only for the day and what it may bring. She found herself content to sit by the statue and reflect on her life, smiling inwardly at cheerful thoughts while her eyes flooded at more difficult memories, and apprehension crept steadily into her mind as the afternoon sun began to sink behind the high neon signs and darkness loomed.

"Are you all right, miss?" asked a voice, drawing Dorothy's attention away from her thoughts.

"Fine, thank you," Dorothy replied, looking up at the young student standing beside her.

"Only you have been sitting there for some time," continued the student.

"Thank you, I'm fine," repeated Dorothy.

"I saw you here yesterday. You look upset," the student persisted.

"Really, I'm fine, thank you." Dorothy sighed, looking thoughtfully at the student's concerned and enquiring expression.

"Do you mind if I sit down?" asked the student, politely.

"If you must." Dorothy smiled, amused by the young man's perseverance.

"I come here quite regularly," the student informed Dorothy. "I like to sit and watch."

"Watch?" enquired Dorothy. "Watch what, people?"

"Yeah, people, the traffic—" replied the student.

"Like me, you mean?"

"No, really, you look upset about something," said the student with concern. "I thought maybe talking would help."

"Why would you want to help?" enquired Dorothy.

"No reason," replied the student. "Just sometimes talking with a stranger helps."

Dorothy accepted the company of the young student, and she remained sitting below Eros, quietly talking together as the night sky fell around them.

"Do you have a name?" asked Dorothy inquisitively.

"Harry," replied the student, quickly getting to his feet and bowing before Dorothy. "Harry Brown, at your service, ma'am."

Dorothy laughed then smiled and quietly thought.

"You all right, ma'am?" asked Harry, slowly sitting back on the stone step.

"How old are you, Harry?" enquired Dorothy.

"Twenty, ma'am, sorry, twenty," repeated Harry as he noticed the calm, thoughtful expression on Dorothy's face.

"Some years ago I promised to meet someone here in Piccadilly Circus. He was twenty years old too," explained Dorothy. "That was more than twenty years ago now."

"I guess he didn't show?" concluded Harry.

"I don't know. I've only just got here," said Dorothy quietly, remorsefully.

"I'm sorry," whispered Harry, not knowing what else to say at that point.

"His name was Barry, almost like yours," said Dorothy, smiling. "Funny how things like that happen, don't you think?"

"Do you know what happened to him?" asked Harry thoughtfully.

"Something wonderful I hope," answered Dorothy.

"Would you like to drink something?" suggested Harry. "A cup of tea, coffee?"

"That would be nice," replied Dorothy, smiling at Harry's suggestion.

Dorothy accompanied Harry down the crowded steps and across the busy road to a large, bustling café where they enjoyed hot coffee, a sandwich, and continued chatting until the café began to close around them.

"I think we should be leaving," said Dorothy.

"Where are you staying?" asked Harry as they left the darkening café.

"I'm not sure," replied Dorothy.

"Sorry?" quizzed Harry.

"I don't really have anywhere to stay," confessed Dorothy. "I let my room go."

"You can stay with me … if you like," offered Harry.

"I don't think I should," replied Dorothy. "I couldn't put you to all that trouble."

"It's no trouble." Harry grinned. "I'm in the same situation as you … nowhere to stay. At least it would be company; the nights can get pretty long."

"Really? And I thought you where offering some warm castle." Dorothy smiled.

"Sorry about that, I thought you realised." Harry laughed.

Leading the way, Harry guided Dorothy through the dark, quietening streets toward Charring Cross Railway Station, continually looking either side of the street they passed along, eventually crossing the road and rushing into a vacant shop doorway. Harry suggested for Dorothy to remain in the shelter of the narrow doorway while he went for some bedding, disappearing beneath the arches of the station. Moments later Dorothy observed Harry returning with cardboard and sheets of newspaper, and she remembered the cluttered doorways of the previous night.

"Here, put this inside your coat … front and back," said Harry, handing Dorothy sheets of newspaper and laying out a strip of cardboard across the doorway floor. "You can push some down your trouser legs if you like."

Sitting on the cardboard carpet, Harry waited for Dorothy to join him before wrapping the remaining sheet of cardboard round their bodies.

"It's better if we sit closer together," suggested Harry. "We'll keep warmer."

"Why are you doing all this?" asked Dorothy suddenly.

"Sorry?" retorted Harry.

"Why are you helping me like this?" Dorothy questioned curiously.

"Why not? You'd only be cold and on your own," replied Harry simply.

"That's not the answer. You didn't know I had nowhere to go," suggested Dorothy, "not when you first met me you didn't."

"I felt sorry for you," sighed Harry.

"When, now...before at Piccadilly?" asked Dorothy.

"I saw you yesterday. You cried a lot...and were there hours...sitting. I was surprised when I saw you again today. You still looked unhappy then," explained Harry.

"So you felt sorry for me," stated Dorothy.

"You remind me of my mum," said Harry sheepishly.

"Your mother, why your mother?" replied Dorothy, taken by surprise.

"She was unhappy most of the time, her life wasn't so good," continued Harry. "She cried a lot too."

"Why, what was wrong?" asked Dorothy quietly, sympathetically.

"My dad...he beat her a lot. He'd come home drunk and..." Harry sighed.

"Where is she now?" enquired Dorothy.

"She died," said Harry

"I'm sorry," said Dorothy caringly.

"It's okay. At least her beating stopped," added Harry.

"So how long have you lived here?" asked Dorothy, changing the subject.

Time flowed by as together Dorothy and Harry chatted endlessly through the night, pausing only to watch an old drunken vagabond stagger toward the arches of the railway station and observe two more homeless youths settle down in an opposite doorway.

"Oh you're an artist!" exclaimed Dorothy.

"Yeah, sort of." Harry shrugged. "My mother used to encourage me when I was younger, and I've had my work exhibited, though my dad, he wasn't keen on me spending time painting. He thought I should do some proper work."

"So what happened?" enquired Dorothy.

"I started at university, that's when I had some pieces exhibited," explained Harry. "But when mum died, Dad made it difficult for me, and then...then he began taking his anger out on me."

"So you left home?" stated Dorothy conclusively.

"Yeah, sort of," said Harry.

"And university?" quizzed Dorothy.

"I finished my year off then got a job to keep my dad happy," replied Harry, "and now I'm here."

"Well, if I told you I was in Florence and ... "

Dawn was breaking; Harry yawned and rested his head back against Dorothy's as she nodded, steadily falling asleep, tired and relaxed from the endless chatter, warm, huddled together under the cardboard cover.

STREETS OF LONDON

1966

The railway station was crowded with commuters rushing, scurrying in all direction, forming flow paths that weaved through the mass of bodies heading for platforms or exiting the station. Dorothy waited for Harry while he stood queuing for hot morning drinks, standing by a small buffet stall. Handing over a mug of coffee, Harry tried to clarify that he only lived with the homeless rather than among them, explaining that it was best to only use the station during the busy commuter times when he would not be so noticeable and associated with the vagabonds and druggies who regularly frequented the hallway and littered the entrance. He encouraged Dorothy to do likewise, using the station only for emergencies and personal hygiene, thus reducing the risk of recognition and the loss of use of the facility.

Finishing their coffee and wandering through the station into the sunlight, Dorothy was unsure of what they were doing or where they were going.

"Come on, I'll show you the village round the side of the station and you can walk under the arches...see how the homeless live," suggested Harry.

"Do you think I should?" replied Dorothy apprehensively.

"You need to know something about them," encouraged Harry, "and anyway, if they see you with me, maybe they'll recognise you if you find yourself here alone."

Passing out of the station's side entrance, they walked downhill to a dead end in the roadway. Weathered, unshaven, old-looking men, overdressed in shabby, torn, and miss-fitting clothes gathered in groups, standing, sitting, fallen, lying along the pavement adjacent to a small park and in the roadway that led to the archways passing under the railway station.

Dorothy tensed nervously as she approached, quickening her step, isolating herself ahead of Harry and nervously waiting for him to catch up. The smell of alcohol and stale urine caught her breath as, together, they entered the arched tunnel and walked steadily through. Emerging once more into the sunshine and fresh air, Dorothy breathed deeply and relaxed.

"That wasn't so bad, was it?" suggested Harry.

"If you say not," replied Dorothy, dazed by the experience.

"They're the harmless ones," said Harry.

"Harmless," quoted Dorothy.

"Yeah, relatively. They're usually too drunk to be of any threat, and they're not too interested in what's happening elsewhere. Leave them alone and they're not interested in you." Harry smiled reassuringly. "But they talk and argue a lot, which leads to some bizarre fighting."

"So who are the harmful ones?" asked Dorothy.

"They're the weird ones you passed through in the station," stated Harry. "They're usually druggies as well. A bit younger, and you never know what they may do, so I always keep away."

Dorothy listened while Harry chatted and they wandered the streets, emerging on the Embankment, spending time to watch the Thames flow by. She suddenly realised her torment had gone and she was relaxed, unworried. She tried to grasp where her anxiety had gone when she had nothing and nowhere to go, letting her thoughts melt away as she listened to the music, joining a group of people sitting on the grass watching a young, colourfully dressed wanderer play his guitar.

Slowly the day drifted by. Dorothy slept on a park seat, tired from her sleepless nights of walking the streets and chatting with her new companion. She woke as the musician packed away his instrument and headed off along the pathway.

"Gosh, I'm hungry," said Dorothy.

Harry suggested a small café where they could buy a cheep meal and fill up on the large portions they served, as he was also hungry.

It was early evening when they finished their filling meal, heading back toward the railway station to find somewhere to sleep.

"Why do you come here to sleep, with all these…all these people?" asked Dorothy curiously. "Why not on the main road? It seems less trouble."

"It's quiet, safer," explained Harry. "There's only the ones who sleep down here that come here. Yeah, you can sleep on the main road, but the police move them on. Sometimes there's trouble and they cop for it."

"Don't the police come down here?" enquired Dorothy apprehensively.

"Yeah, when there's trouble. Then they clear everyone away and you have to stay clear for a day or two," replied Harry.

"Look, we could use the same door as last night," said Dorothy, pointing eagerly.

"Home sweet home, eh." Harry smiled.

Dorothy let Harry go and find bedding for the night, resisting another breathtaking experience of the homeless village, especially a nighttime one. He returned with a fresh set of mattresses and blankets, laying them out in the doorway before settling down for another night.

Woken by the wind, Dorothy watched the quiet street, leaning forward to see the movement of the village as an occasional vagrant wandered. Rain splattered onto the pavement outside the doorway. Each raindrop spread and merged until the foot-path washed with water and flowed into the curbside, streaming toward the grated drain. She pulled her legs away from the water encroaching into the doorway. Her mind wandered to the grass-land battlefields of Anzio, and the soldiers camped among bunkers and foxholes, sheltering from the winter rain, their dugouts slowly filling with water.

Harry woke Dorothy from her sleep, explaining he must attend the Dole Office and collect his financial handout if he wanted to survive the week ahead. Stopping for mugs of coffee at the rail-way buffet stand, Harry explained the Dole system to Dorothy, surprised to learn of her predicament regarding reference of iden-tity and her lack of possibility to draw Dole Money. Arriving at the crowded Employment Office, Harry joined the queue while Dorothy mooched around on a corner farther along the road and waited for his return. She observed the flow of people coming and going, old, young, walking, cycling, alone, and dower faced, together mumbling their conversation, the encouraged greetings and bantered comment that passed from Bill to Bob. Dorothy toyed with the wallet in her overcoat pocket, reflecting on the value of its contents.

"Are you all right?" said Harry, arriving at the corner.

"Oh, yes...just thinking," startled Dorothy, turning to face Harry.

The day passed uneventfully, and Dorothy was restless as she tried to settle down on the shop doorway floor. Her mind chewed at the money in her wallet, and she wondered what she would do when it had all gone.

"Can we sleep somewhere else tonight?" said Dorothy.

"It's late to find somewhere now," replied Harry. "What's wrong?"

"Nothing...I just can't get comfortable," answered Dorothy awkwardly.

"It's like that sometimes," grunted Harry, curling up. "Just be patient."

Dorothy floated round the field hospital, looking down on the maimed soldiers lying in their cots; she argued agitatedly with

Sister Williams, vigorously waving her empty wallet in her face. Suddenly the face changed, becoming the portly Italian store-keeper, perspiring, grinning.

"It's all right...it's all right," whispered Harry, trying to calm his new friend. "It's just a dream."

Dorothy sat up and leaned back against the shop door. Her hands trembled and her brow was clammy with perspiration.

"I need to go for a walk," said Dorothy, getting up from the floor, leaving her night's accommodation, heading back along the quiet street toward the main road.

Harry quickly followed, walking silently beside Dorothy until she rested and sat motionless on the steps in Trafalgar Square, looking at the fountain; its endless spray rhythmically dancing on the water's surface before merging in the rippled depth.

"Do you want to talk?" asked Harry softly.

Dorothy remained silent, not responding to Harry's question, but inwardly thankful for his patience and his presence. Quietly she began to explain a little of the reason for her disturbed sleep. Commencing slowly, pausing and closing her eyes, reliving the moment of her elucidation, Dorothy stopped and watched the con-tinuous motion of the fountain. Inch by inch the morning light spread across the square and glistened on the water's surface.

"Come on, we can walk down to the Embankment, watch the river a while," whispered Harry, sensing Dorothy's lift of mood, suggesting a change of place and environment would dispel the remains of her anguish.

The Embankment was still quiet, and Harry requested Dorothy to sit on a bench while he sketched. He reached into his pocket and took out a tobacco tin full of coloured pastel chalks. Clearing some paving slabs of loose stone, he knelt down and began to sketch a circle and outlines of rock formations. Dorothy watched as a large, bright moon materialised above strange tinted stone that reflected the moon's silver glow. Moving over, Harry created a strange orange parched and deserted landscape that confused Dorothy, tilting her head to grasp the perspective of the picture. A dead tree appeared to have two decaying trunks, its branches reaching from one to the other, or was it two trees that shared the same branches?

"I don't understand this one," said Dorothy.

"Moment... it's not finished yet," replied Harry.

Harry placed a fireball of sunlight to the right of the right-hand tree, and wisps of flame that scorched, on opposite sides, the two dark trunks, distorting the representation of the heat radiating from only one direction.

"I still don't know what you're doing," confessed Dorothy, drawn by Harry's puzzling talent.

"All will be revealed." Harry smiled.

Round the picture, from top to bottom and across the centre line of the two burning trees, Harry drew a large arc that he transformed into a mirror. Instantly Dorothy recognised the reflection of one burning tree against the other.

"Very good!" Dorothy applauded.

Harry took off his coat and laid it open between the two pictures, throwing a few coins onto its centre lining before joining Dorothy on the bench.

"Thank you." Harry smiled.

"What inspired that?" asked Dorothy.

"The Americans launched another satellite the other day," replied Harry. "They'll soon have men up there, maybe even someone on the moon one day."

"No, the desert and the mirror," corrected Dorothy.

"I just like doing that sort of thing," said Harry. "It makes you think."

"Well, it confused me until you put the mirror there," admitted Dorothy.

Harry watched as strolling tourists now populating the Embankment began to drop coins onto his jacket, answering their questions, appreciating their praising comments.

"And don't worry about money... we'll get by," assured Harry, leaning against Dorothy and whispering into her ear.

The early morning sunshine continued throughout the day, and Dorothy and Harry remained on the Embankment, allowing the formation of copper and silver to continue spreading over the lining of Harry's coat. Deliberately, Harry started another picture, pausing to chat with Dorothy, allowing onlookers and passers-by time to dwell in anticipation of watching Harry at work before making their contribution to his growing reward. The afternoon became hot, and together they retired to the shade of the park to count Harry's earnings.

The evening was spent strolling the streets window-shopping; returning to their preferred sleeping zone, quite late, they hoped a doorway remained vacant for their use. Taking a shortcut through the archway tunnel, Harry collected cardboard and newspaper to save returning after finding a doorway accommodation for the night. Emerging from the darkness of the archway, they passed a vagrant lying on the pavement, his face bloodied. Dorothy stopped and crouched down, looking for the source of blood.

"Dorothy, come on. We need to find somewhere to sleep," said Harry, surprised by Dorothy's sudden attention to the prostrate figure.

"Just a minute, the man's hurt," replied Dorothy, cautiously checking for any alarming signs.

"Come on, they're always falling over and injuring themselves," stated Harry.

"One minute. I'll just check there's nothing serious," replied Dorothy, rolling the man over, pulling him up to a seating position, and propping him against the adjacent lamppost, coughing on the man's alcoholic breath and turning her head away as he exhaled and grunted in her face.

Harry stood and watched, amazed at Dorothy's ability to manoeuvre the weight and fluid mobility of the drunkard. He was uneasy, unsure of her impulsive involvement, and was reluctant to help or become involved and departed quickly along the road the moment Dorothy had completed her Samaritan gesture.

"I can't believe you did that," said Harry, hurrying along, looking keenly for a vacant doorway.

"I'm a nurse, Harry," replied Dorothy, following closely behind Harry's eager strides.

"But he's just a tramp," stated Harry, "and a dirty one at that."

"I've seen worse than him, believe me," informed Dorothy.

"Oh, I believe you after some of the things you've been telling me," replied Harry, slowing to a stop. "It's no use, we're too late tonight. The doors are all taken. We'll have to find somewhere else."

"Let's go to the park. It's a fine night and not as cold as last night," suggested Dorothy.

"It's risky in the park. The police don't like you there, and you sometimes get the druggies in there," replied Harry.

"Can't we just see?" suggested Dorothy.

"Okay, it's as good a place as any, seeing as we've lost out on a doorway," stated Harry.

"Thank you." Dorothy smiled, heading off toward the park.

The night passed without incident. Dorothy woke early, pushing off her layer of brown cardboard box and waking Harry, persuading him to return to the archway so she could check on the previous night's injured vagrant. Harry first wanted a coffee and something to eat, as he was hungry. He submitted to Dorothy's argument to first let her check on the injured tramp before finding a relaxing café and enjoying a slow hot coffee and toast.

Days began to mingle, flowing similarly one after the other. Dorothy gradually became more involved, customising herself to the aroma and habits as she attended to the self-inflicted injuries of the vagabonds.

It was late in the morning, the station rush wash almost over as Dorothy and Harry quietly finished their coffees and a sausage rolls at the buffet bar. Dorothy had completed her inspection of the injured vagabonds and stood looking at Harry.

"I thought you said you went regularly to Piccadilly Circus," said Dorothy. "To watch."

"I do," replied Harry.

"Well, you haven't been since you met me there," reminded Dorothy.

"We've been busy," said Harry thoughtfully.

"Shall we go?" asked Dorothy, enthusiastically.

"What now?" quizzed Harry, taken by surprise.

"We can sit and watch," suggested Dorothy, smiling. "Unless you have other plans?"

"Yeah, okay," answered Harry, bemused. "If you want."

Leaving the railway station, they walked steadily by Trafalgar Square, stopping to watch the early bird tourists stand among the pigeons, throwing their seed, and the football supporters gathered on the steps eating and drinking.

Together Dorothy and Harry continued into Leicester Square. Met by larger crowds of soccer fans, they observed their boisterous antics as they mingled among other pedestrians walking round the square, while still more supporters occupied the small enclosure of park to lie on the grass and drink.

Slowly moving along toward Piccadilly, they found the Circus swamped with a mass of rowdy football fans. Eros was draped with coloured flags and banners displaying slogans and names of heroes who could kick a ball, while supporters chanted and sang, their blazoned shirts duplicating their national team colour.

Dorothy and Harry leaned against the wall by a street trader's booth promoting World Cup memorabilia and souvenirs.

"Well, I didn't expect this," said Dorothy.

"No. It seems strange standing here," Harry commented. "Usually it's best to be on the Circus watching everything go by. However, it is quite a spectacle."

"Don't you watch football, Harry?" asked Dorothy.

"Not really," replied Harry, watching the antics being conducted beneath Eros.

Dorothy tired of watching the growing hoard of boyish males coarsely chanting in choral voice while continually lubricating their strained larynx with still more drink.

"Can we go somewhere less rowdy?" suggested Dorothy.

"I think that might be difficult with all this going on," answered Harry, "but we can try."

Dorothy quietly wandered the streets, keeping close to the shop walls and windows, insular to other pedestrians and their activities. Harry followed, distracted by the groups of football fans, stopping and standing to one side to let pass the animated clan dominating the footpath and roadside.

The morning's enthusiasm petered out; their intended pleasure altered by the invasion of their shrine and the afternoon found Dorothy and Harry heading back toward the railway station and the vagrants' village. Harry claimed an early doorway, squatting back against the door, staring blindly across the road. Dorothy offered to go and find bedding while making a quick tour of inspection on the welfare of the homeless tramps.

Returning to the shop's doorway, Dorothy passed in the sheets of cardboard mattress. Harry spread them over the floor of the shop's entrance, back by the door, and the two friends sat calmly chatting to pass the time. The sound of police sirens could be heard as a series of squad cars scampered past the end of the quiet side street. A short time passed before a skirmish of activity charged along the main road, flags and scarves high above waving arms. Harry leaned forward to see as a gang of coloured football shirts charged past the road end, shouting, jeering.

"That's why we don't sleep in main road doorways," said Harry.

The noise returned at the top of the side street as the uncontrolled mob raced past in the opposite direction, their banners lowered, followed by a second, an imposing and alternative coloured foe, chasing the first. A splinter group peeled away from the first section of frantic supporters and charged down the quiet side street. Harry pushed Dorothy into the corner of the doorway and squatted behind a held-up cardboard mattress, hoping it would disguise their presence. Harry remained poised, crouching, ready for action.

"Don't come out. Stay in the doorway whatever happens," ordered Harry.

The coloured horde ran down the road chanting and yelling, kicking cans. The sound of glass breaking on the road as a bottle, thrown back toward the main road, startled Dorothy and she cowered down behind Harry. The pack of football supporters flashed past the doorway. Harry tensed, his eyes flicking back and forth as he watched the crowd for any sign of direction toward his shelter. A resonant roar of chanting, taunts, and scattered debris could be heard as the hooligans passed through the arched tunnel and bewildered vagrants. Silence gradually returned to the side street as choral echoes faded into the twilight of the evening.

"You all right?" enquired Harry, caringly, noticing Dorothy's quivering body still huddled in the corner of the doorway.

"I've been in many battles, Harry," replied Dorothy, leaning back against the door and letting her tension slip away, "but you always knew the intent and rules of engagement. That was different... or maybe it was all a long time ago and my memory is fading."

The night passed quietly, and Dorothy nodded, her head bowing as she fell to sleep.

"Come on you, lazy lump," jibed Dorothy, shaking Harry's shoulder, waking him from his slumber.

"What... what do you want?" replied Harry, slowly opening his eyes, crawling from under the stiff brown cover.

"I've been to look at the mess those idiots caused last night," Dorothy began.

"Yeah, what about it?" Harry yawned, almost disinterested.

"They knocked a few things over and broke a couple of bottles, but you know the man with the white beard and wild hair?" asked Dorothy.

"The one that always wears that long black coat?" confirmed Harry.

"Yes, him—"

"No, don't know him," said Harry, sarcastically interrupting.

"Harry, I'm trying to tell you something," replied Dorothy. "Listen."

"Okay, what about him?" Harry smiled before glaring at Dorothy.

"Joe, I think he said his name was or maybe Jones, it was difficult to understand him he was so drunk," mumbled Dorothy.

"You were going to tell me something," reminded Harry, losing interest.

"Sorry, he got pushed over or fell during all the commotion last night and has a nasty bump on his head," said Dorothy.

"Is that it?" asked Harry.

"Well, he's different to all the others. I feel sorry for him somehow," replied Dorothy. "He's always on his own."

"Come on, let's go for a drink," suggested Harry. "They'll be fighting one another before the day's out, and Mr. Joe Jones or whatever his name is will be just fine, you see."

Harry led the way to the railway station and dug into his pockets for the remains of his money.

"I'll get these," said Dorothy. "This is the last of my money, and I want to share it with you."

"There's no need," answered Harry, looking at Dorothy. "Keep it, you might need it."

"But you buy everything. Every week you spend all yours," continued Dorothy. "I want to buy you a drink. When it's gone, it's gone, and I'll feel better if I've spent it with you."

"Thank you, but you don't have to." Harry smiled.

"I want to. What would you like?" asked Dorothy.

The summer months passed by, and Harry continued to care for Dorothy, spending his government handouts on essential food and coffee into the cooler period of autumn. The vagabonds of the homeless village had become less mobile, spending more time round the warmth of an ever-burning fire contained in an old oil drum. The railway arch became littered with cardboard beds and an occasional blanket while a beaten old supermarket trolley, stacked with pieces of scavenged wood, stood by the burning fire. Dorothy became affectionately known as Doris amongst her vagrant patients, and the onset of cooler weather and heavy rain played its part, dampening the mood and spirit of the weary villagers, controlling their numbers and wandering activities, effecting Joe's gradually deteriorating condition.

MEANWHILE

"I think not sleeping the nights she cared for Joe and getting caught in the rain drained her strength, Doctor," concluded Harry. "That's why I brought her to the hospital."

The doctor sat quietly, sipping his red wine for some time after Harry had completed his account of Dorothy and how she had arrived at the hospital.

"Mister Harry—" began the doctor.

"My name is Brown, sir, Harry Brown," interrupted Harry, wanting to correct the doctor before the situation became difficult to explain or embarrassing.

"Oh," remarked the doctor, pausing to register the name change. "Mister Brown."

"You can call me Harry if you prefer," Harry quickly replied, not wanting his surname to be used.

"Very well, Harry." The doctor smiled, trying to deliver his comment. "I am fascinated by your story. Dorothy is a remarkable woman."

"Yes, sir," said Harry, very respectful of the doctor's interest and generosity.

"I would like to do some research into Dorothy's past, if you don't mind," continued the doctor, deep in thought. "I am very intrigued by what you have told me, and I want to see if there's anything I can do to help her. You understand?"

"No, sir, I appreciate your helping her," Harry answered, wondering what the doctor wanted to investigate.

"So Harry, what about yourself, can I give you a lift somewhere?" asked the doctor.

Harry declined the ride, not wanting to inconvenience the doctor, and walked the streets back to the cardboard village by the railway arches. The evening's conversation had left Dorothy's experiences fresh in his mind, along with a full stomach and niggling question of what the doctor might reveal with his investigation. Harry stood by the blazing fire in the old oil drum, oblivious to the brawling drunks farther back in the archways. His thoughts were reliving the short time he had gotten to know Doris and her amazing story. A feeling of loneliness passed over him as he prepared for a second night without Doris and realised he missed her. Having a long wait until the next afternoon before his visit with Doris and his appointment with the doctor, he trudged up the side street looking for a vacant doorway.

The morning was cold with bright sunshine reflecting from windows down into the shop doorways. The traffic and pedestrians were already busy in the day's activities. Harry was still sleeping in his cardboard and newspaper bed, his head buried inside Joe's black city coat. He had no reason to rush from his burrow or peep out at the disapproving faces passing by. His thoughts tormented him to get up and look for the way out from the street life he now wanted to leave behind. Consciously he decided to wait until after his visit to Doris. He lay still, letting the sun warm him while the cold tiled floor of the doorway penetrated through his cardboard mattress and kept him shivering. Finally the urge to urinate determined his departure for the railway station Gents and the commencement of his day.

Now knowing the way to the hospital ward in which Doris was

recovering, Harry decided to go straight there without asking the reception nurse. He found the double swing doors at the end of the corridor, peered in through the window panel, and was just beginning to push open one of the doors.

"Stop!" boomed a voice from along the corridor he had just travelled. "Where do you think you are going?"

Harry turned to see a stout nurse in blue uniform marching toward him, her eyes burning into him as if he were some form of parasite.

"I've just come to see my friend," answered Harry as the ward matron stood menacingly in front of him. "She's—."

Harry was cut short and returned to the reception to wait for visiting time before being allowed to see Doris. He sat on his usual seat on the end of the front row and closed his eyes in order that he would not have to look at the faces staring back at him. An hour slowly passed, and the reception began to fill with people waiting for visitor's hour when they would be released, in mass, into the hospital. Harry stood and gave his seat to an elderly lady who stood awkwardly, resting on her walking stick.

"Thank you, young man. Your legs are much younger than mine," quipped the old dear as she sat on Harry's warm seat.

Harry smiled and looked up at the clock above the reception window.

"Only ten more minutes," whispered Harry.

"Sorry, what did you say, young man?" enquired the Old Lady.

"Ten more minutes." Harry smiled.

Harry walked briskly along the corridor to Dorothy's ward, bursting through the double doors, through which he had previously been prevented from passing. He looked steadily along the rows of beds trying to see Dorothy and failed. Anxiously he walked back to the nurse's office just outside the swing doors.

"I'm looking for Dorothy Wainwright. I brought her in the other day," enquired Harry, knocking politely on the office door.

"She's in the room just to the left as you go through the doors," replied the nurse sitting behind the desk. "Oh, would you mind giving her this letter? I was supposed to put it in her room earlier."

"Yeah, sure, no problem," said Harry.

"Thank you." The nurse smiled.

Dorothy lay wearily in her bed; her loss of weight and bout of pneumonia had sapped her strength, leaving her weak and frail. She smiled as she saw Harry enter the room.

"How are you?" Harry smiled, greeting Dorothy with soft kiss on her cheek.

"I've not been awake long really. How long have I been here?" asked Dorothy.

This is the third day," Harry informed Dorothy, taking her hand. "I came yesterday, did the nurse tell you?"

"I don't remember. I've slept most of the time. I think I was on the main ward yesterday," said Dorothy, looking round the room. "They must have moved me here during the night. How are you, still sleeping in doorways?"

"Yes, I'm fine. Don't worry about me." Harry chuckled. "I think the doctor must have had you moved in here. He's been very good."

"Which doctor? I don't remember seeing a doctor," questioned Dorothy.

"It doesn't matter, so long as you're being looked after," said Harry cautiously.

"Would you pass me a drink of water, please? I'm quite thirsty," requested Dorothy, sitting up in her bed and resting back against the pillows.

"Sure. Oh, the nurse asked me to give you this too," said Harry, passing Dorothy the letter before concentrating on pouring her drink.

Dorothy took the faded envelope and marvelled at the addresses, slowly removing the contents.

"Where did you get this?" asked Dorothy, her voice trembling, her heart racing.

The nurse in the office, why?" replied Harry, holding out the glass of water he had just poured.

Dorothy was not looking; she was engrossed in the letter, tears streaming down her face. Harry picked up the envelope from the bed and looked at the names on its cover.

"Where has it come from?" cried Dorothy, fretfully, handing Harry the letter. "Where did you get it?"

"From the nurse, like I said…" answered Harry, going quiet as he read the letter.

Dearest Father, Mother, Christopher,

I hope my letter finds you all well and hopefully reaches you before Christmas.

I will not begin to tell you where I am, as I know it will be censored from my letter, but I want you to know that I am thinking of you all, especially as this will be my first Christmas away from home. I do hope the New Year brings an end to this war and we can all be together again.

I have some news and also want to share something with you so that you will always know.

Recently I have begun working with a woman who has become angry and bitter through the consequence of this war. Her husband has returned home with only one leg and her only son is presumed missing, leaving her worried and not knowing his fate. I am sure that because of this she has become short and sometimes quite hostile to those around her, when I know she longs for the happy times she shared with her husband and family before this war was inflicted upon her (I should say all of us actually, don't you think?).

Deep down inside I have seen she is a caring, loving woman trying to cope with her life. I have forgiven her for her attitude toward me and feel that in time we could be friends.

I want to share this with you because wherever this war takes me and whatever happens to me, I want you to always know that I love you, that I have chosen to be here and will one day return home safe and well.

Your loving daughter,
Dorothy

PS: I will send cards for Christmas and one for Christopher's birthday at my next opportunity.

"I'd better fetch the nurse," said Harry, confused, disbelieving as he put down the letter.

Harry turned to leave the room as the door opened and the helpful doctor entered.

"Hello, sir." Harry smiled. "This is the doctor I was telling you about."

"Hello, Dorothy, I'm Doctor Wainwright... Christopher Wainwright. Welcome home."

FROM THE AUTHOR

When I first conceived the idea to write *Dog Dirt Doris*, I had already thought of becoming a writer some years previous but could not find a niche in which to express myself. However, the event that determined I should write a book, the details of which I will not begin to disgust you with, happened quite accidentally while out walking one autumn Sunday afternoon. After a long, thoughtful period, putting a plot and storyline together with my idea, I began to write.

I quickly realised that I should research some of the places and events that began to unfold within the story, recognising that I was tripping myself up with some of the events I had concocted.

Inveraray and HMS Quebec were discovered as a result of my research, for which I am truly thankful. Located in a beautiful setting on the shore of Loch Fyne, Inveraray is a Scottish Heritage Town and has not changed since the 1700s when it was first built. Unfortunately, the same cannot be said for HMS Quebec. All that is left of the Amphibious Landing Training Centre and dockyard are the cinema and slipways that can be found on the Argyle Caravan and Camp Site, the same site on which the centre once occupied.

Bath was chosen as Dorothy's home city for its close Roman association and similarity to Italy and Florence, to help the storyline and establish some respectability to Dorothy's background. Coincidentally, I also learned of the naval wartime association with the city that became a bonus to my selection.

From discussion with an old and experienced war veteran acquaintance, I learned and determined Anzio, Italy, would be the best place to introduce Dorothy into the war, and together with my research plotted the events that led her to Florence. Please allow me to apologise here for liberties taken in order to weave my story, but I have tried to retain the correct sequence of events and maintain respect for the organisations referred to within the content of the book, as I am sure there may well be some readers more knowledgeable than myself.

My research period took me to almost all of the places mentioned in the story in order that I could gain some idea and feel for their ambience. Without exception, allowing for a little rebuild and modernisation, the places still retain most, if not all, of their wartime and historic appearance. Perhaps you may want to follow the route depicted within the story from London's Embankment past Parliament Square and on to Piccadilly Circus and enjoy an afternoon among the sights that now exude a modern image but still retain, in essence, the flavour of the book. However, the Apennine Mountain village and fishing port through which Dorothy returns to England are fictitious.

My characters and Doris, or Dorothy, whichever you prefer, materialised from of my thoughts; their manifestation on the pages are purposefully and mostly vaguely described to allow you, the reader, to build you own image of their appearance, with one exception, pieced together from life's experience and observations that reflect situations we can all recognise. How we approach them may differ. I believe we all have the opportunity to control our destinies and manage our lives, appreciating that some have a harder road than others, but it is how we approach and respond to the experiences that are presented to us that make us the person we are.

The one exception to my characters is Joe, whom you encounter in the first paragraph and again later in the book; he is, or maybe now was, a real person. I met Joe many years ago in Dirty Dicks, a London pub, and had the privilege of buying him a drink in order to prevent him from being evicted by the unpleasant landlord or manager at that time, though how he justified his decision to throw Joe out of an establishment that boasted its reputation for not being cleaned for scores of years baffles me. However, I learned that Joe was unfortunate to suddenly lose all his family in a traffic accident, from which he lost his direction in life and gravitated to the London streets. His background, from what I understood, as he was quite drunk, was banking and his cricket boots were magnificent. He unwrapped the newspaper and showed me them. He also, apologetically, for having no money and in appreciation for his drink, gave me a grimy black walnut from his pocket. I remember Joe, not only for the unfortunate, lost, and unsavoury character that he had become, but because he is the only person to have given me almost everything he owned.

As for being a writer, an author, who knows? I will have to wait and see the concluding interest in this book before that can be determined. But in getting me to this point, I would like to thank The Queen Alexandra's Royal Army Nursing Corps in allowing me the use of their museum and library to gain respected facts and detail. My appreciation goes to Mr. James (Jim) Jepson, R.M.N. General Secretary and Treasurer of the Combined Operations Association, for his divulgence of knowledge regarding the Number 1 Combined Training Centre. To Linda King and Jax Nunnerly, in no particular order: Jax for her femininity and tears reading and rereading each line and her assistance with the Italian translation, and Linda for her contribution in tidying up continuity and adding credibility to plot and relationship association. Without their much valued support and encouragement, the book may still be in my head. In appreciation for their efforts, I have requested them and allowed them, for it's a bit like throwing myself to the wolves, to contribute some words about me. Last and by no means least, my thanks go to the Anzio Beachhead Museum for their prized contribution of explicit fact and detail.

If you should pass by Anzio, be sure to visit the war cemeteries and pay respect to the men and women who "did their bit" to change the course of history and make our world and lives what they are today.

I hope you have enjoyed reading this story and it has provided you something to reflect upon, as I have.

A second book? I am sure somewhere I have another adventure of life's experience turning over in my head, but we shall have to wait and see.

and when he told me that he was writing a book, I just smiled and said I would like to read it.

Well, there came the surprise, the Howard I had not met. When the first chapter arrived in my inbox, as an avid reader of life novels, I must admit that I did not expect very much. I could not have been farther from the truth. The Howard that wrote the book was warm, sensitive, and extremely literate (all of the things I had least expected).

Over the time that I have been reading *DDD* (as it became known), I have seen a new person and have thoroughly enjoyed not only every page but getting to know the "other" Howard. If you take the time to read what I can only describe as a sensitive walk through the life of a lovely lady, with its highs and heart-wrenching lows, then you will have a glimpse of the real Howard, the one that he hides away for fear of people sensing his sensitivity.

I thank the day that I met him. I know that wherever he is in the world (and he is currently thousands of miles away in the desert), I have found a friend for life who will have me climbing walls with his pedantic need for everything to be correct in his working life, laughing at his humour, missing him sitting in the chair in my office discussing his writing, and begging for the first chapter of his next book.

About the author by Linda King

I first heard about Howard through school friends, about the same year that Doris arrived back in London. At that time he was known in the area for his swimming achievements both locally and for the county and regional teams. Truth be told, as I hadn't met him at that time, I'd thought that because of all the fuss that surrounded the name, he must be one arrogant teenager!

It was two years later when our paths crossed for the first time, through a mutual friend, and my assumption could not have been more wrong.

For the next few years, Howard, a group of about a dozen others, and myself became firm friends, and I remember that time as being an extraordinary time of *fun*. I was privileged to grow through my teenage years in such fine company.

Over the years, as usually happens, work, relationships, and life changed, and we all seemed to go our separate ways. But I'm happy to say Howard's and my own path have continued to cross, even though his career has taken him all over the world for considerable lengths of time. The friendship has endured, standing the test of time, and I like to think that with his friendship I've grown older (certainly), wiser (maybe), but thankfully not grown up. *Fun* is still around, whether it's trying to keep him out of the children's ball pool at Ikea or sharing a Chinese meal (his favourite) with an endless range of topical conversation.

Some are surprised that he started to write at this time in his life, but one thing I've learnt over the years is to always expect the unexpected with Howard. Roll on the next surprise.